Romances by Katharine Ashe

CAPTURED BY A ROGUE LORD
SWEPT AWAY BY A KISS

Captured by a Rogue Lord

Katharine Ashe

AVON

An Imprint of HarperCollinsPublishers

This is a work of fiction. Names, characters, places, and incidents are products of the author's imagination or are used fictitiously and are not to be construed as real. Any resemblance to actual events, locales, organizations, or persons, living or dead, is entirely coincidental.

AVON BOOKS
An Imprint of HarperCollins*Publishers*
10 East 53rd Street
New York, New York 10022-5299

Copyright © 2011 by Katharine Brophy Dubois
ISBN 978-0-06-196564-7
www.avonromance.com

First Avon Books mass market printing: April 2011

Avon Trademark Reg. U.S. Pat. Off. and in Other Countries, Marca Registrada, Hecho en U.S.A.
HarperCollins® is a registered trademark of HarperCollins Publishers.

Printed in the U.S.A.

10 9 8 7 6 5 4 3 2 1

To my son, with whom I built my first pirate ship.
And to Cynthia, wise and compassionate.
Thank you.

CAPTURED
BY A
ROGUE
LORD

Chapter 1

Many were the men whose cities he saw and whose minds he learned, and many the woes he suffered in his heart upon the sea, seeking to win his own life.

—HOMER, *ODYSSEY*

"Gorblimey, Cap'n Redstone. Cut off his head already."

With his long, leather-clad legs braced upon the pitch-sealed deck, Alexander "Redstone" Savege stared down at the cowering form, his broad brimmed hat casting a shadow over the figure. The whelp's skinny arms encircled his head, his pallor grayish from a dredge in frigid coastal waters. He wasn't more than fourteen if he were a day. Far too young to be living such a wretched life.

Alex rubbed his callused palm across his face, sucking in briny air laced with the scent of oncoming rain, his gray eyes shadowed. He gripped the hilt of his cutlass, a thick, inelegant weapon, long as his arm and meant for only one purpose—the same as the ten iron guns and pair of agile pivots jutting from the *Cavalier*'s sleek sides, all at rest now but easily primed for battle.

Violence, the hell's ransom of a pirate. Once mother's milk to Alex, now a curse.

He cast a glance at his helmsman, a hulking, chestnut-skinned beast sporting a missing earlobe and a leering smile. Big Mattie was always eager to see blood spilt. The faces of the five dozen sailors clustered around showed the same gleeful anticipation.

Alex withheld a sigh. He'd brought this on himself. The lot of them knew, after all, the swift ease with which their master's blade could fly.

"Pop his cork right off, Cap'n," cackled a sexagenarian with cheeks of uncured leather. "Or slice his nose and ears."

"Stick 'im in the ribs, just like you did to that Frenchie wi' the twenty-gun barque we sunk in 'thirteen," an ebony sailor chimed in.

Alex repressed a grimace, his hand tightening around the sword handle. He fixed the grommet with a hard glare.

"Are you ready to die for your crime, Billy?" he grumbled in his deepest, scratchiest voice, the sort that never saw the inside of a St. James's gentlemen's club or a beautiful lady's Mayfair bedchamber. The sort that his mother, sister, and most of his acquaintances would be shocked to know he could affect.

The Seventh Earl of Savege never cussed, rarely swore, and only in the direst circumstances raised his voice above an urbane murmur. Handy with his fives, expert with saber, épée, and pistol alike, he never employed any of them, to the eternal vexation of not a few cuckolded husbands. He preferred perfumed boudoirs to malodorous boxing cages, and the elegant peace and quiet of a fine gaming establishment to the dust and discomfort of a carriage race.

But each time Alex stepped aboard the *Cavalier*, he left the Earl of Savege behind.

"Blast and damn, Bill, are you trying to fob off a

whisker?" He glowered. Several of his crew members echoed his discontent with mumbles.

"I didn't cackle, Cap'n. I swears it," the youth mewled. "You can't kill me for not telling them nothing, can you?"

Alex took a long breath, steadying the blood pounding through his veins, fueled by a dangerous cocktail of anger, frustration, and pure cerebral fatigue.

"I can kill you for soiling my ears with that sound," he grunted. "What's that coming from your throat, a plea or a girl's whimper?" He tapped his sword tip to the boy's bony rear and nudged. "Stand up and let me hear if you can speak like a man instead."

The lad climbed to his feet.

"On my mother's grave, Cap'n, I didn't tell any of them smugglers about our covey. I didn't."

"Your mother is still alive, Billy, and happy you've nothing to do with her any longer, I'll merit." Alex sheathed his sword.

The whelp's eyes went wide. "Then you ain't going to kill me after all?"

"Not today, but you'll scrub the decks for a fortnight," Alex growled. "And caulk that crack on the gun deck at the bowsprit. Caulk the whole damn deck, for that matter. The rest of you get back to work."

Nothing stirred atop but the fluttering banner, gold rapier upon black undulating in the fresh breeze.

"Now!" Alex bellowed.

Billy jumped, and the crew scattered like grapeshot. Alex moved toward the stair to belowdecks. Big Mattie lingered.

"You ain't gonna even strap him to the capstan for a day, Cap'n?" he prodded. "But he gave up our covey to those curs at the tavern in the village. Got to make an example of him. What do you want, for the rest of these lilies"—he gestured around the ship"—to go spouting their mouths off?"

"Stubble it, Mattie, or I'll stubble it for you," Alex warned without breaking stride, hand still upon the metal at his hip. He forbore grinding his straight, white teeth, the only bright spot on his polish-blackened face except the whites of his eyes.

"Big Mattie has a point, Captain," his quartermaster said quietly, falling in beside him, matching him stride for stride. Jinan stood a mere inch shy of Alex's considerable height, of similar build though somewhat leaner in the chest, like his Egyptian ancestors.

Alex met Jin's steady blue gaze, the intelligence glinting in it reminding him as always why he left his ship in this man's hands for most of the year.

"Big Mattie has an unhealthy thirst for blood, like his master," he muttered, swinging down the steep steps to the gun deck, leaving the gray of the spring day behind. "We don't need to worry about the smugglers. They'll keep to their own if we keep to ours." From habit his gaze scanned the cannons before he ducked beneath the beams.

They entered the day chamber, appointed in Aubusson carpets, with brocaded upholstery sheathed in walnut, cherrywood furniture, and a crystal carafe cradling French brandy on the sideboard. A silver and onyx writing set graced the desktop in the adjacent office, and ivory bookends supported leather-bound volumes of Greek verse. Along with the bedchamber opposite, and the finest linens, it looked like the private rooms of a lord of the realm. Unbeknownst to all aboard except Alex and his quartermaster, they were.

Jin closed the door and affixed the shutters of the windows letting onto the deck. He folded his arms.

"Thirst for blood, my arse. Mattie might gripe, but your mercy stands you in good stead with the men, as always. Even when they're itching to be ashore."

"Lilies, the lot of them, just like he said." Alex waved a dismissive hand. "They ought to be ashamed to be weary of the sea after a mere seven weeks abroad."

"They're not weary, merely looking forward to a lick at the grog we took off that Barbadian trader." Jin shook his head. "You're right about the smugglers, of course. But, Alex, the hull won't clean itself. We've got to careen the ship."

"Which you should have done before the last cruise."

"I couldn't heave to for that. Not after the *Etoile* challenged us off Calais."

"And left you twiddling the sweeps when the wind died and she failed to show for the fight. Jin, I did not give you permission to go after that blasted privateer. We are at peace with France now, or hadn't you noticed? Even if we weren't, that is not our purpose."

"The men think it is, at least since you put French merchantmen off limits after the treaty last November."

"You sound as though you agree with them." Alex moved into his washroom, pulled off his sash strung with dagger and pistol along with his leather waistcoat, and hung them upon a hook. His sweat-stained linen shirt came next. "Have you finally become greedy for pirate's gold after all these years, my friend?" He drew on a fresh garment.

Jin scowled, marring the aristocratic lines of a face that mingled the blood of English nobles and eastern princes.

"Don't insult me. But after our run-in with that American frigate last week and the quick repairs, the crew deserves a break." He paused. "And so do you."

"Have a yen to take the summer cruise without me?

Are you hoping to storm the Channel and win a fat French prize despite my prohibition?" Alex chose a dark, simply tailored coat from his compact wardrobe and took up a wrinkled cravat. Tubbs would have his head for donning such a rag. But he didn't answer to his valet, or to anyone else.

"Of course not," Jin replied. "If you say we mayn't take merchantmen any longer, we will not. The men got accustomed to it after three successful years, though."

"The war did not last long enough for some."

"Long enough for you to take out a half-dozen French men-of-war," Jin murmured.

Alex ignored his friend's look of measured admiration and wound the linen about his neck. It smelled of salted fish, but that was a good sight better than plenty of the other aromas on the *Cavalier* at the end of the seven-week cruise. Jin was right. Both ship and crew needed a break before the next trip out. And, according to the note Billy brought back from his trip ashore last night, he had business at home.

He wrapped the cravat about his jaw, stretching it over his nose and tucking it fast at the base of his skull. With the black face paint and a concealing hat, the disguise had not failed him in eight years. It still astounded him, despite the *Cavalier*'s repeated visits to the north Devon coast of late, that no one among the *bon ton* had connected the notorious buccaneer Redstone with the seventh Earl of Savege. With a vast, prosperous estate stretching across miles of remote Devonshire coastline, the earl was far too busy in London whoring and gambling away his fortune to set foot at home often.

Alex took some pride in Redstone's mysterious identity. His brother, Aaron, positively delighted in it. Blast him.

"Last autumn the men grew richer than bilge rats should," Jin commented.

Alex dropped a nondescript hat atop his head and tugged it low over his brow.

"Then they should be content this season with an occasional English yacht. In the meantime, allow them ashore, north as usual. But for God's sake tell them to behave and stay clear of those blasted smugglers. I don't want them getting mixed up with that bunch of miscreants, or being mistaken for them."

"The locals know the boys well enough by now." Jin frowned. "But Billy didn't like the looks of the *Osprey*'s crew, and he brought back news." He shook his head, bracing his stance against a sudden sway of the ship. The far-reaching eddies of Bristol Channel were friendly enough in gentle weather, but rain beckoned. Alex could feel it in his blood like he felt sunset, moonrise, and the ebb of the tides.

"What have they done?"

"Seems they roughed up a girl."

His gaze snapped up. "Roughed up?"

"Aye." Jin nodded. "A group of them."

"What girl?"

"A dairy maid. Did it right under her brothers' noses. In a barn."

"They took a girl from a barn and no one challenged them?"

"*In* a barn—"

"No." He lifted his hand. "I understand. The farm sits upon the shore, doesn't it?" Weeks ago he'd come upon the smuggling brig out of a fog and had a good look at it. Well armed and deep in the draft, the *Osprey* was an impressive vessel. Even if she sat too far off shore for the cannon shot to reach land, sailors' muskets, cutlasses, and pikes could readily best a farmer's pitchforks and axes. The girl's brothers could not have saved her virtue, much like his own brother could not save their younger sister years earlier.

Alex headed toward the door. "Why did you wait until now to tell me this?"

"You always say you don't wish to know the business of English smugglers. Let them go their own way. But this is a nasty one. Captain goes by the name of Dunkirk."

"I don't care about the *Osprey* or her captain. Only—"

"The pleasure boats of spoilt English nobles. I know."

Alex set an even gaze upon his friend.

"If you object to the *Cavalier*'s purpose, you are free to find other employment. I have made that perfectly clear many times, and you must have enough gold stored in London banks by now to buy yourself a fleet. You owe me nothing."

Jin returned his steady stare. "I will decide when my debt to you is repaid. And you need me, now more than ever."

Alex refused to bite at that bait. He reached for the door handle.

"What about Poole, then?"

Alex paused, a hot finger of anger pressing at the base of his throat once more. But it did not spread to fill his chest as it had for so many years. Now it merely lapped at his senses, taunting him with what might have been. Revenge was sweetest served hot, and eight years had in truth cooled his thirst for blood. Now the sole reason he pursued his present course sat in solitude at Savege Park, awaiting his return.

"I will concern myself with Lord Poole when and if he ever finds us." He could wait to confront the man who, barely knowing it, had twice turned his life inside out.

"By which you mean never," Jin said casually as Alex opened the door. "He's been making very friendly with the Admiralty, if rumors can be believed. Perhaps you should spend some time sitting in your seat in Lords. Then you can ask him to his face what he intends to do about Redstone."

Alex lifted a single brow. "When you hold a peerage yourself one day, Jin, remind me not to give you foolish, unsolicited advice, will you?"

His quartermaster laughed. "See you in June?"

"I will send word. Until then, keep them out of trouble. I don't want to hear any stories of the crew getting up to rigs in the villages. My ship deserves it, if not its master."

"Aye aye, sir. I will take good care of her. And you take care of those other ladies you're abandoning this one for."

Alex grinned, his chest loosening. He left the cabin and climbed onto the main deck. Fore and aft the schooner stretched sleek and sparkling, in top order. A 135-ton, twelve-gun beauty, she was one of the fastest ships in the Atlantic. In the eight years since he'd purchased her gleaming new at St. Eustatius, then four years later sailed north into the English Channel, no one had come close to finding her. Only two ships—the American *Wasp* and the free-agent *Blackhawk*—had outrun her.

Alex had no worries that the Earl of Poole's hunters would track him down. The *Cavalier* lived much like its master, present one day, gone the next. The devil himself threw up his hands at the farcical journey into mingled heaven and hell Alex took every spring and summer for weeks upon end.

He loved the sea, its breadth and depth, scent and texture. He needn't be a blasted pirate to partake of it.

But as much as he envisioned a different sort of enjoyment of the ocean, he could not give up Redstone. Not yet.

Propped at the helm, Big Mattie threw him a surly farewell, all bluster. Below, a skiff bobbed upon the green water, sailors from prow to stern with oars in hand. Alex climbed down the rope ladder and took his place in the stern. Finally he turned his gaze to the land.

The *Cavalier* had come in sight of his property the previous night, but he hadn't allowed himself to look. Now he took his fill of the coastline's narrow strips of gold sand and jutting gray rock painted with verdant moss, jewellike beneath the sky's shuttered gaze. Beyond the coast, protected from the wind by the hill's crest, sharp, sloping fields of emerald green dotted with sheep or striped with early crops gave way to pine and elm woods and winding streams, fragrant with fresh water.

The sight met his senses like the beckoning arms of a woman, shapely, beautiful, full of promise. It was always this way. While at sea, he wished to be nowhere else. When heading toward home, he wanted nothing but his land. It was the tragic irony of his life that he spent the lion's share of every year in his Mayfair mansion.

It hadn't always been thus. Not until that night when Lambert Poole looked him dead in the bloodshot eye and assured him that they were alike as two brothers.

The skiff pulled south a league and came ashore along a modest dock Alex had built four years earlier for the purpose. In the shadow of a low cliff, overhung with stripped trees and striated rocks, a cavelike indentation provided the ideal place to shift identities. A half-mile walk inland brought him to a cottage at which his valet stored fresh linens and a change of clothing. The day still hung gray but without fog. If they'd seen the *Cavalier* from the house, Tubbs would be at the cottage waiting for him.

Alex climbed from the boat and waved off the sailors. He started up the path away from shore with nothing but a pistol and a dirk tucked in his boot, legs swiftly steadying to land. The transition never bothered him. Seven weeks at sea did not suffice to dim the sensation of walking upon solid earth. More than enough time had elapsed, however, to make him eager for his first stop when he returned to London. La Dolcetta awaited. When Alex's valet met him at the cottage door, his placid face a study in grimness, the voluptuous opera singer's boudoir seemed all the more appealing.

"What's happened, Tubbs?" Alex pulled off his hat and cravat, moving to the washstand. He accepted the soap from his manservant and scrubbed at the blacking upon his face.

"Welcome home, my lord. Your brother awaits you at the Park."

"So Billy said. You will not tell me what this is about, I suspect." Alex wiped his jaw and cheeks clean and glanced aside at his servant. Tubbs's expression remained shuttered. "No, of course not. So let us make this quick and be off."

Tubbs helped Alex dress in fresh garments suitable for his country consequence and they left the cottage. Alex's head groom already awaited them in an unmarked carriage.

"Fine to see you so soon again, my lord." Pomley tugged his cap. "Didn't know when you'd be back this time."

"It was a short cruise." Alex climbed into the seat beside the wiry old fellow and took the ribbons. Years earlier Pomley had purchased the rig and team for this use, an unremarkable carriage and unremarkable horses. Alex knew perfectly well it did not fool anyone upon his lands. Pomley and Tubbs were the only men who assisted him with his biyearly masquerade, but everyone else knew precisely who Lord Savage became each spring and summer while away from home. Not one person, from scullery maid to tenant farmer to villager, ever said a single word about it.

Occasionally, when Alex allowed himself to ponder that miracle, it awed him.

"A paying one, as always?" Pomley said with familiar ease.

Alex snapped the reins. "Relatively."

"The orphans won't go hungry this year." The groom's toothy smile broadened.

"The orphans wouldn't have gone hungry even if we had picked up only saltwater," Alex mumbled. They all thought Redstone's prize money funded the foundling hospital in Exmoor, as well as the home for sailors and soldiers' widows in Bideford. For the past four years it had. But Alex had more than enough funds to maintain those institutions for decades even without the *Cavalier's* help.

"More satisfying this way," Pomley continued. "A right Robin Hood do-gooder, you are, sir."

Alex stifled a cringe and glanced at Tubbs sitting behind. The valet's face was stony. Alex chuckled and whipped up the team.

Two miles along the twisting, scrubby road his house came into view. Atop an outcropping close to the coast, Savage Park arose in solitary, hulking splendor. Seat of the earldom for centuries, its construction was a mish-mash of styles and purposes, built of local limestone around a medieval keep. Dotted with moss upon the leeward side, stripped by wind and rain of artifice on the windward, its gray stone walls, turrets, and terraces marked the hillcrest as though declaring to enemies, be warned, and friends be ever welcome.

Alex inhaled deeply, anticipating the fresh scent of polished wood, the smooth comfort of dry bed linens, the quiet stillness of his study.

A boy sitting atop a hillock caught sight of the carriage, leapt up and went streaking toward the house. Alex pulled to the stable gate, threw the reins to Pomley, and jumped from the box. Fifty feet took him to the front door. Why bother with further pretense when everyone now knew of his arrival?

The door opened and guilt stirred in his belly. As always.

The butler, a long line of liveried footmen and maids, and the housekeeper met him as he entered.

"It's fine to have you home, my lord." His housekeeper bobbed a curtsy, rustling starched cambric. Alex smiled at the woman who had kept his house without aid of a mistress for eight years since his father died and his mother settled in London.

"Thank you, Mrs. Tubbs. It's good to be home." He removed his long duster and hat, and his gaze traveled up the broad staircase. Leaning against the top rail, his brother cracked a mild smile.

"All hail the conquering hero." Aaron Savege's voice came lightly down into the hall, smooth yet considerably thinner than Alex's.

Everything about his twin was like that. Alex's hair and eyes were dark to Aaron's British fairness. His tall, broad frame contrasted with the slighter, slender form that lent his sibling the appearance of the churchman he ought to have been.

Alex scoffed and started up the stairs. He reached the landing and extended his hand. His brother released a vise grip upon the banister to greet him, clutching the handle of his cane with his other hand.

"Billy made it back to the ship with my note, I assume? He's a wily one. No wonder you keep him on despite his youth." Aaron turned awkwardly on the landing and in jolting steps moved toward the drawing room door.

"He carried news of all sorts," Alex replied.

Aaron cast him a glance, light brown eyes aware. "He told you about the farmer's girl?"

"And the sailors from the *Osprey*. Which family?"

"Your tenants remain unmolested. The news traveled here quickly, but I don't know the people. It was south, beyond Carlyle's land."

"Then why the urgent missive calling me to shore, little brother?"

"If you were not ready to return yet, what were you doing skulking about the Devonshire coast?"

"The hull needs scraping. I might as well come ashore here than anywhere else."

"Ah, good. You must have taken a prize or two, then." Aaron smiled. "Who this time?"

"Two dingies worth nothing—"

"I doubt that."

"—and Effington's sloop. Tidy little boat, full of silver plate, port wine, and champagne. The crew was in alt. They're probably drinking to my lord Effington's health right now."

"And the silver will go to the orphans, no doubt. Effington? The fellow who took up with that actress after you gave the woman her *congé*. Didn't you say that he beat—"

"Yes." Alex closed the door and strode across the chamber to the sideboard. Aaron lumbered to a chair by the hearth.

"What is the pressing business you mentioned in your note that could not have waited another fortnight or two?" Alex poured a finger of brandy and swirled it in the cut crystal glass. "Has Kitty gotten into a scrape?"

"No, of course not. Last I heard from Mother, she and our sister were enjoying the season in town from the comfort of your house, as always. Gambling, also as always, but not to excess."

"Then what? Trouble with tenants? I cannot imagine anything you and Haycock together aren't able to manage without me."

"You know that's not true, Alex. He is a splendid steward. Matchless. But no one knows this estate like you do. And the people practically worship you."

"Silly fools," Alex mumbled, moving toward the window.

"You've no one to blame for it but yourself." Aaron's voice hinted at pride. "But it's not the tenants. Carlyle came over here the other day to offer his daughter's hand."

Alex turned from the sight of sloping green lawn and lifted a brow.

"To *me*?"

"Certainly not to me," his brother replied without a flicker of his even gaze. "Surprised your reputation for game and women still fails to deter hopeful parents? But, you see, you have wealth, title, and good looks to boot."

Alex ignored him. "Carlyle? Isn't his daughter firmly upon the shelf by now?"

"You know that?"

"A wise man attends to his neighbors' business, upon both sea and land."

"Forgive my impertinence." Aaron smiled, the expression lightening his habitually sober face. Alex's breath came easier for the first time since he entered the house. He grinned.

"You are forgiven." He swept a magnanimous hand through the air. "Continue."

"You have the right of it. Miss Carlyle is indeed rather long in the tooth."

"And he hopes to foist her off upon me simply because our lands march?"

"No. She isn't the daughter he offered, though she is still unmarried, I've no idea why."

"A younger sister then. Or—" He placed a palm upon his chest. "—do not say it—*elder*?"

"Because you are so discriminating when it comes to the age of a beautiful woman, of course," Aaron murmured.

"Younger, then. So the chit is beautiful?"

"Yes. Quite."

"Splendid. I shouldn't wish my countess to be an antidote."

"Will you take Carlyle's proposition to heart, then?" His brother tone's was abruptly serious.

"Why not? I might as well set up my nursery and assure the dynasty with some pretty little thing now as later." Alex's blood ran to still, unease slipping through his veins.

"What of Redstone?" his twin said slowly. "You cannot very well continue disappearing every spring and summer for weeks upon end with a wife at home."

Alex turned back to the window, wishing he stood at the rear of the house where through the glass panes the expanse of sea could be seen stretching far beyond the craggy shoreline, blue, deep, alluring.

"I have been thinking, Aaron," he ventured.

"Thinking of what, Alex?" His brother's tone revealed nothing now, damn his training for the Church.

"After the summer cruise this year I might put to shore once and for all."

Silence met him. Slowly he pivoted about upon the heel of Hoby's finest. Aaron's face was like stone.

Alex's throat tightened. "What would you think of that?" he asked with supreme nonchalance.

"You would sell the *Cavalier*? To Jinan, presumably."

"She is already his ship for most of the year."

"She is your ship, Alex, and Jin knows that better than anyone. He only remains with you because—"

"She is our ship, Aaron. Yours and mine, no matter who captains it." A dull ache settled in his chest. He struggled not to allow his gaze to slip to his brother's useless leg. "Why don't you come along on the summer cruise? It will be our last run. We'll pick off that rogue Abernathy's yacht, as planned, and a few others I will ferret out in town this month. Maybe an old French merchantier for a finale."

"A French ship? You would not dare."

"Oh, wouldn't I?" Alex squared his shoulders. "The infamous Redstone fears neither man nor government. If they want me, let them come." He waggled his brows.

His brother's face relaxed and Alex's heart began beating again. He could not stand this, the tangled guilt, anger, and hopelessness, the searing regret that would not fade even after three years. He missed his lands and longed to linger at the Park, to walk the hills with his steward and drink a pint at the tavern with tenant farmers he'd known since he was a boy, when he was freshly returned from the West Indies with stories to tell that they listened to kindly.

But blast if his hands weren't already itching to grip the ribbons and fly to London. Remaining in his twin's company was simply too difficult.

At thirteen, Alex had learned to withstand the rigors

of life upon the sea, and at twenty-three he'd chosen that life for part of each year. He could scud through a storm at ten knots, face off against a ship with twice his weight in guns, stare a musket down the barrel without flinching, and hold a blade to another man's throat with no hesitation. But when it came to what he had done to his brother, he would rather flee than face the daily reminder.

"You cannot leave the *Cavalier* behind, Alex," Aaron said quietly. "She is your true love."

Alex slanted his twin a mock-derisive look. "You think it's time I shift my affections to a human?"

"Can you?"

"Not in this lifetime, brother," Alex grunted.

Aaron dropped his gaze to his hands lying upon his lap, palms up. "You imagine me foolish to speak of love."

"Indeed I do. But I always have." Alex smiled. He must smile, ever making light of the dreams his brother had left behind when they carried him off the battle-field a broken man.

"How will you respond to Lord Carlyle?"

"Does he expect me to pay a call?"

"No. They have gone to town for her come-out."

Alex nodded. Here, fate was handing him a concrete reason to leave the country.

"What is the chit's name?"

"Charity Lucas. She is Carlyle's eldest stepdaughter."

"Lucas? Sounds familiar."

"Her brother is a baronet, young fellow, deep in the pockets. Perhaps you've seen him playing at the club. He and Carlyle are offering a mint for her dowry."

"Ah, a bride rich in both beauty and gold. For what more could I wish?"

"What more, indeed?"

An end to the charade his life had become. A wife could provide sufficient justification. A lady whose father's estate abutted his suited the purpose ideally. She would eschew town, wishing to be close to her family, and Alex would indulge her by keeping to the country more often than not. And if by chance this girl did not suit him, he might take this opportunity to find another. He knew few ladies of unblemished reputation amongst the *beau monde*, but his mother and sister would willingly oblige in that matter if he asked.

"Will you to town immediately?"

"To make the fair maid's acquaintance and determine if we shall suit? Why not? I'll have to start scouting out our next prizes anyway." He moved toward the door. "Consider it, Aaron. One final lark before we farthel the sails for retirement. Like old times."

His brother regarded him steadily across the chamber, gentle resignation in his eyes. Alex turned about and left his twin behind.

Chapter 2

When I was a little boy, or so my mother told me,
That if I did not kiss the girls my lips would
*   soon grow moldy.*

—"HAUL AWAY JOE"

At the edge of the dance floor, Miss Serena Carlyle scanned the crush of London's most exalted denizens and wished she were looking upon a fairy ball.

Throughout the double-tiered ballroom, swags of red tulle twisted about faux Corinthian columns and marble amphorae stuffed with crimson roses. The air hung thick with the cloying scents of the overblown flowers, lamp oil, and beeswax candles. Ladies in wilted gowns with spirals of hair sticking to their brows, and gentlemen whose high-starched collars drooped from heat, crowded the chamber. A weary orchestra, tucked into a corner, complained in four-four time.

On the other hand, if Serena were at a fairy ball, she might see branches of willows old as the stars gesturing to one another in the nighttime breeze, as though waltzing in place. Creatures as ephemeral as the mist would glide about in garments of gossamer dew and moonlight, caressing each other's alabaster cheeks like lovers as nightingales and crickets filled the glade with song.

Additionally, if her present entertainment were a fairy ball, she would not be clad in the silliest, dullest yellow gown in England, with at least three too many flounces, and wrist-length sleeves that emphasized her square shoulders and thin arms. Nor would her long hair be plastered to the sides of her head in unbecoming, ironed ringlets held in place with pins. Rather, her gown would be woven of tissue-thin silk of spring green, so diaphanous it would float about her as she danced, which naturally she would do barefooted. The twinklings of fireflies would play in the lighter strands in her loose-flowing hair, making it shimmer like gold in the dark.

Finally, instead of haughty pinks and snuff-taking dandies passing her by as though she did not exist, a dashing knight from an otherworldly realm clad in white armor would canter toward her upon a splendid charger. She would smile a gentle welcome and, in a sprinkling of silver mist, he would extend his hand. For her.

A dancer bumped Serena's shoulder, jostling her back to reality.

She smothered a sigh. Only foolish girls envisioned fairy balls, and she had long since passed girlhood. This very day, her twenty-fifth birthday, she had finally become entrenched in placid maturity, thus fulfilling her Christian name and her father's fondest wishes at once.

She swiped a bead of sweat from her upper lip, glancing aside at her stepmother. Ensconced in conversation with their hostess, eyes half lidded as she scanned the chamber assessingly, Davina did not notice.

"I am sorry Mama and Papa forgot your birthday."

Serena's stepsister Charity's voice was nearly inaudible above the chatter and mediocre music.

"Pish tosh," Serena replied. "At my advanced age, I don't give a fig for birthday celebrations, Chare. You mustn't worry your pretty head about that."

"You deserve a celebration. You are the best person I know, Serena."

"Thank you, darling." Serena added a silent prayer of thanks to her mother as well. As of today, the first Lady Carlyle's dowry rested in an account at the bank with her daughter's name upon it. Someday, Serena would use the tidy sum to purchase a cottage in a quiet corner of Devonshire and finally escape Davina's dominion. But until then she must see Charity well settled. Then fifteen-year-old Diantha. Then, of course, little Faith. Serena had spent eight precious years of her young womanhood without a mother, and the remainder with a stepmother worthy of fairy tales. She refused to leave her sisters to the second Lady Carlyle's careless custody.

Charity's gentian gaze darted about the ballroom. "Do you think he will come?" Her light voice trembled.

Serena schooled her tone to evenness. "Of course he will. He sent Papa word only this morning."

"Will he be horrid?"

"Certainly not. He is an earl."

The girl's cheeks paled. "They say he is a rogue."

Heart clenching for her stepsister's innocence, Serena squeezed Charity's elbow and offered brightly, "They also say he is most handsome."

"And most licentious."

"Licentious implies the superlative, darling."

Her sister's eyes widened, guinea lashes fanning upon porcelain cheeks.

Serena could not withhold a small grin. "You needn't add 'most.' "

"Is he, then?"

Most certainly licentious.

"Yes, apparently he is quite handsome. A true paragon." Serena allowed her smile full rein, as usual trapping her thoughts behind her lips. Rumor accounted the Earl of Savege a man of exceptional appearance: a fine aristocratic countenance, soulful gray eyes, an enviable physique that he clad in garments purchased from the most exclusive tailors, boot makers, and haberdashers. Everyone agreed that he personified the words elegant and handsome. Virile, scandalous, and, of course, licentious were the other words most commonly used to describe him. One gossip columnist had particularly noted his "devilishly alluring smile."

Serena had no reason to doubt such reports. Despite the fact that for two and a half decades she had lived fewer than four miles of craggy coastline from Savege Park, she had never once met the reprobate peer, not before or after he took possession of the estate six years earlier upon his father's demise, returning from a lengthy repairing lease in the West Indies to do so.

But distance did not prohibit gossip, and she had heard plenty during her come-out season. Since then, from the remote solitude of Glenhaven Hall she had read the newspapers with avid interest. Who knew when it might come in handy to know about her father's closest neighbor?

Now, apparently. And most unfortunately.

"Oh." Charity's perfect rosebud lips quivered, the lower one especially. It gave her the appearance of a kitten, sweet and vulnerable. Those qualities went deeper than the skin. A less suitable bride for the rakish Lord Savege could not be found in London or the country. Davina's stepmother must be insane. Or rather, insanely self-interested.

She glanced aside once more at the woman who would eagerly sacrifice her firstborn daughter upon the altar of social advancement. Lady Carlyle's pale blue eyes caught Serena's interested gaze and flickered with annoyance. Her narrow face, framed by a fashionable array of silvery-gold curls topped with an elegantly feathered bandeau, pinched into mild disapproval. Her lips barely moved, but Serena could discern the perpetual downward tilt. At one time, Davina had been as beautiful as her daughter, but a lifetime of nastiness had marred her looks, undoubtedly.

Serena's gaze skittered away.

"I am persuaded Lord Savege will make an inestimable husband, Chare," she said, patting Charity's hand. "Marriage always settles gentlemen down."

"Does it?"

"Oh, yes. Depend upon it." And perhaps a scaly dragon would arise from a crack in the floorboards and swallow Davina whole. If Charity were lucky, Lord Savege would keep his mistresses in town rather than at the Park. If she were blessed with a miracle, he simply would never come home. He did so rarely now, after all.

"Oh, then," Charity's fingers trembled and her gaze softened, "if you say it is so, it must be. You always know what is best for me. I am so fortunate to be your sister, Serena."

"Good heavens, darling. Do not weep. Your nose will turn pink and your mother will scold."

Charity blinked away tears. Serena wrapped an arm about her soft waist.

"You are so lovely, Chare, even weeping you take the breath. He will be smitten with you upon the spot."

Charity's fingers within Serena's spasmed.

"Smitten? Oh, no. Not truly? I could not wish for that." Her translucent brow creased.

Serena pet her stepsister's limp hand. "It is not such an unpleasant thing to have the admiration of one's husband, I understand." Or of any man. Serena's cheeks grew warm as she pushed memory back into the recesses of her well-disciplined, placid, highly adult mind.

"But if he admires me he—he— Mama says he will wish to—" Charity broke off with a flurry of lashes.

"I daresay he will," Serena mumbled, chewing upon her lower lip. One thing appeared certain, the Earl of Savege appreciated beautiful women. And many of them. "Davina says it is simply to be borne." Or longed for, if one were a plain, foolishly dressed spinster without hope of ever marrying and experiencing it. Again. "But I daresay you won't mind it in the least, and in any case it will go quickly." Far too quickly.

Charity's cheeks bloomed with spots of distress. "I will do my best to be a dutiful wife and not disappoint Mama."

"I know you will, darling." Serena's heart tightened. If she could wrest her sister from this unsuitable match, she would do all in her power. But Davina had decreed, and as always Serena's father acquiesced. Even now, before the bride and groom made each other's acquaintance, her father's solicitor busied himself preparing the contract. If Lord Savege liked what he saw tonight—and what man would not want a beautiful, biddable, well-bred and wealthy daughter of a baronet and stepdaughter of a baron?—the wedding would go forth as Lady Carlyle desired and Serena feared.

She could do nothing to halt it. She must, instead, turn her attention to matters that she might truly affect.

Her gaze surveyed the ballroom again, not for the unknown Earl of Savege but another elusive gentleman. She spotted him and sucked in a quick breath of excitement.

The Marquess of Doreé stood near a window, alone by all appearances. His warm complexion, black hair, and the foreign cast of his features lent him an exotic air, despite his fashionable coat and elegantly knotted cravat. He was handsome by any measure, certainly, but Serena could not be distracted by that. She needed answers from him.

His gaze shifted to hers. Awareness of her fixed attention flashed in his black eyes. Serena's palms went cold. She slipped her arm from Charity's waist and hid her hands in her skirts, dropping her gaze.

Good heavens, how would she ever summon the courage to interview him? But she must ask him why he had been in Devonshire weeks earlier, the day the smugglers came ashore and wreaked havoc upon the village in which Serena and her little sister, Viola, had spent the idle hours of their childhood cavorting about.

Before smugglers abducted Viola.

Lord Doreé did not belong upon their little coast. His estate was clear across England, and the only person he might possibly be visiting, Lord Savege, had not been in residence at the time, as usual. Serena forced herself to glance at the marquess again. His attention remained upon her. Her mouth went dry and her stomach knotted.

She needed a plan, but the stuffiness of the ballroom made thought difficult. A breath of fresh air would subdue her fidgets. After a short interval collecting herself, she would screw up the courage to approach him.

"Stepmother?" She touched Davina upon the arm.

Lady Carlyle turned a cool look upon her. "Slump

your shoulders, Serena. You are a veritable Amazon beside your sister. It sullies her surroundings."

Charity's eyes widened and her lips parted as though to protest. But Davina cast a sharp glance and the girl's cherubic face fell. So it always went.

Serena took a steadying breath. "Stepmother, I have the need to visit the ladies' retiring room."

"Do not be long about it. The earl will arrive soon and you must be at your sister's side supporting her for the introduction."

Serena curtsied, darted Charity a sympathetic smile, and moved toward the corridor, a quick glance assuring the marquess's post by the far window. What on earth did her stepmother expect Charity to do once she married, drag her along on the honeymoon?

Serena nearly giggled aloud. But there could be no levity concerning this. Like a princess cursed by a wicked witch, Charity was simply doomed.

Ball guests meandered through the corridor that ran toward the rear of the Berkeley Square town house. The place was commodious enough but something of a rabbit warren. A cluster of young ladies lingered just beyond a closed door. Serena went toward it. She opened the door a crack and cool darkness assailed her. An empty chamber or closet, probably. Even better than the ladies' retiring room.

She slipped inside, shut the door quietly, and leaned back against it. Her quick breaths lost themselves in the blackened emptiness, suggesting a space larger than a closet. Perhaps it was a sewing parlor, the sort Davina had converted the housekeeper's sitting chamber into, relegating that longtime servant to Glenhaven's upper story with the maids and footmen.

Serena fiddled with the doorknob. The key rested in the keyhole. With a flick of her wrist she could lock it and steal a few minutes to prepare for confronting the Marquess of Doreé. Her skin already felt cooler, the inky black wrapping around her like a bath in fresh springwater on a sultry summer day.

She turned the key.

"By all means, lock us in," a deep voice came from a few yards away, low like a lion's rumbling purr. "Privacy is much to be preferred in such circumstances."

Serena gasped, her fingers jerked, and the key fell with a soft clink upon wood.

"Good heavens, sir," she managed, dropping into a crouch and casting her palms about the floor, "you startled me."

"My apologies, madam." A soft creak of furniture suggested the disembodied voice stood up. Serena's hands searched faster.

"Oh, thank you! But no apology is necessary," she said with much greater calm than her racing heart recommended. "It was my mistake for entering this chamber. I was looking for the ladies' retiring room, you see, to catch my breath after dancing," she prevaricated.

Footsteps sounded upon the floor, heavy and even. One, two, three— Closer.

Aha! Small, metal, key-shaped.

Brass in hand, Serena leapt up. A tearing sound accompanied her haste. No matter. Hems could be mended. Reputations could not, and for the sake of her sisters she must hold onto hers, however unworthily.

She made to swing around to the door, and he was upon her. His large frame loomed in dim silhouette inches away, limned by the faintest hint of light penetrating draperies on the chamber's opposite end. Serena struggled to make out his features, but the dark was too complete.

"Allow me to assist you." His hand curved around

her elbow, big and strong. She gasped again, the heat of his touch sudden. With one simple movement that left her breathless, he stroked up her arm until his fingers curled around hers. He encompassed them then plucked away the key.

Her hand hung suspended between them. Music and conversation came muffled from the other side of the door, but Serena heard only her heart's raucous beating.

She blinked into the darkness and lowered her arm. Good heavens, where had her wits gone?

"Sir, I am well able to—"

"If you were well able to, you would not have dropped it in the first place," he said with smooth assurance. A shiver of awareness at the raw maleness hovering so close raced up Serena's back. He reached around her, his knuckles brushing her hip as he leaned forward. She sucked in breath and her senses flooded with the mingled scents of lavender, leather, and sweet tobacco. She adored the scent of fresh tobacco. She snuck another quick inhale.

He fit the key into the hole with an audible chink.

"There it is, my dear. Simply turn it and you are freed." His words came above her brow. He must be a head taller than her, and contrary to his suggestion, he had her thoroughly trapped. Serena's heart tripped into a gallop.

"Sir, in order to unlock the door and open it with ease," she said as evenly as she could, which was regrettably not very evenly at all, "I must ask you to back away."

He closed the distance between them to a mere sliver of increasingly heated air. Serena's heels met the door, then the small of her back met his hand. He spread his palm upon her.

"Ask me, then." He bent his head, his breath stirring wisps of hair fallen from her ridiculous coiffure.

"*Sir*," she rasped.

"My lord," he corrected, his touch like a branding iron upon the outward curve of her back. Hot. *Quite hot*.

"My lord, unhand me." She should scream. He intended to ravish her, in a sewing parlor within earshot of at least a dozen people and three hundred more close by.

"She interrupts a man deep in thought," he murmured, apparently to himself, "disturbs his ruminations, then speaks as though she is master of the place. Interesting." He seemed to draw in breath upon the final word. "Mm, cinnamon. More interesting yet."

"I—I was baking earlier." A birthday tart, her one indulgence to celebrate the day, made by her own hands under the disapproving glare of Davina's London chef.

"Have I a cook in my arms, then?"

He must be quizzing.

"You are very peculiar, my lord. I daresay you should not have anyone at all in your arms at a gathering like this. Least of all me."

He laughed, and Serena imagined she could feel the reverberation of air between them.

"Come now, my beauty," he murmured, "you do not wish to resist."

"But I do wish to. And you do not know that I am a beauty. I might be a thorough antidote." Her voice cracked, drowning her speeding heart in sheer mortification.

"The light from the corridor shone upon your face when the door opened."

"Only briefly."

His fingertip stroked along her brow and cheek. Tiny frissons of sensation scampered across her skin.

A quick breath escaped her. No one had touched her intimately in seven years, and never like this. Robert had done a great deal of grabbing and clutching. This was . . . *much nicer*. Soft, and yet deliberate.

"Too briefly for you to assess my appearance," she added upon another quaver.

"Ah, but I am a man of quick discernment."

"Sir, you must unhand me."

He ran his fingers along the back of her neck. The texture of his skin was surprisingly rough, sending more quivers of unholy delight along her spine and into other startling places. Then, without warning, his hand slipped down her waist and over the arc of her behind.

Serena gulped in air. But she could not summon the will to lift her arms and push at his chest. Her palms seemed glued to the door panel, his hold upon her derrière heavy, warm, and achingly pleasurable. Her shallow breaths echoed loud in her ears.

He closed the space between them to nothing.

Confusion subsumed her.

Seven years was the sort of interval that allowed memory to fade. Be that as it may, Serena knew she had never before experienced the sensations that filled her body now. If she had, she would have actively brought them to mind every day since. Everywhere she was soft he was hard against her, the firm expanse of his chest, his hips, and rocklike thighs all pressed to her flesh. Hard and absolutely delicious.

Belatedly she jerked her head back and knocked it upon the door. "Ouch!"

"Punishment for your reticence."

How on earth could a *voice* smile?

"I assure you," she said hurriedly, "I am a veritable pie face." She ordered herself to scream, or at the very least to shout. He inhaled deeply again, his chest expanding against hers, and she felt it as though he drew breath from her lungs.

"Perhaps. But your body is beautiful, and— Ah, yes, here we are," he murmured just behind her ear. "Vanilla. Enchanting."

"Good heavens." His hands holding her so firmly against him heated Serena's blood like whiskey. "You are a rake, aren't you?"

"Sticks and stones." Slowly, ever so slowly, he caressed her buttock. Serena struggled for air.

"Everyone knows rakes are horrid. I agree."

"Your tone does not suit your words, my dear. Nor do your breaths."

"My breaths?"

"You are breathing swiftly."

"Probably because you are holding me so tightly that I cannot draw in air."

"Paltry excuse." His amused tone acted upon her primed senses like a spark to kindling. He was not quizzing her, instead he seemed to be inviting her to enjoy this scandalous moment. No man ever cared about her enjoyment. Not even her beloved father. Her stepbrother Tracy tried, but never quite succeeded.

"I shall scream."

"If you intended to, you would have already," he said with great good sense.

"You know this from experience, no doubt."

He chuckled again, and his laughter cascaded through her, wonderful and intoxicating. Robert had never laughed when he held her tight. He had never laughed at all. This man's ready amusement felt marvelous. Her blood seemed to flow with warm honey.

He tilted up her chin with his fingertips as though hoping to get a clearer view of her face.

"I have no need to force myself upon unwilling women, my dear."

She did not doubt that, bathing her senses in his musky scent, his arms holding her with leashed strength.

"There is a first time for everything," she whispered.

"I daresay, but it will not be this time," he murmured. "Now be a pet and remain still so I can kiss you." His breath feathered over her cheek and lips, scented with wine. Despite the dark, Serena closed her eyes, her nerves singing with perverse anticipation.

He paused.

"Or perhaps I will not kiss you after all."

She swallowed lumpily. Her chance at escape beckoned. But a man's hand was already spread upon her behind. In for a penny . . .

"Why not?" she uttered breathlessly.

A beat of silence.

Another.

Finally, "Why not, indeed?" and his lips brushed hers.

It did not seem like the kiss of a ravisher, and Serena could not remain still as he required. The moment their lips touched, she wished more than anything to move her mouth against his, her hands to seek his waist.

She plastered her palms against the door, attempting a modicum of resistance. But there her willpower ended. He seemed to taste her, gently at first then with greater pressure. She responded with tentative gestures. She could not remember exactly how it should be done, though she hadn't truly known seven years ago either.

He showed her, caressing briefly, lightly, drawing away for an instant then returning. She imitated his touch as best she could, and lovely shivers cascaded down her throat and, surprisingly, in her belly. As though taking cue from her tacit consent, his broad hand spread at the base of her skull and he drew her into him.

Serena sighed. She could not prevent it. His lips were warm, firm, and wonderfully clever, teasing first her lower lip then her upper, then both at once. Simmering heat like lit coals crackled in her core. The sensation was distantly familiar.

Desire.

But beneath this stranger's touch, she barely remembered that other time when she had felt this heady pull deep within. He lapped at her lips with tender caresses, pleasing her into further dumb submission. She couldn't care. For years she had longed for a man to kiss her again. Now a man of extraordinary skill was doing so. It seemed a dream, another one of her fantasies she had long since put away in favor of sensible realism.

His thumb caressed her jaw languidly, tilting her chin up to fit her mouth more fully to his. She released another tiny sigh. He dipped the tip of his tongue between her lips, warmth flooded into her, and Serena awoke from her mystical sleep of sham respectability into the glorious, sparkling realm of her thoroughly tarnished virtue.

She gripped his sleeves, opening her mouth to the intoxicating sweep of his tongue along the inside of her lower lip. He delved deeper and her knees went to jelly, currents of delicious heat washing up into her breasts, prickling their peaks. In a far back chamber of her mind she insisted that she could not allow this perfect mingling of tongues within her mouth, then within his as she followed into the damp heat of his maleness. She should not allow this stranger to move his hands over her body, his mouth over her most tender flesh.

But it felt *so good*.

His arms encased in fine wool were thick with muscle. She struggled not to release them, *not* to wrap her hands about his neck to clamp him to her more tightly. Then he pressed her into the door panel and she ceased struggling with herself and simply moaned in soft, pure pleasure. If she were not experiencing it, she might never believe that to be trapped between a door and a man's body was to be in heaven. Especially when that man's mouth trailed away from hers to commence an exploration of the tender place behind her ear, then her throat, curling sublime feverishness all through her.

She sighed yet again, this time a whimpering sort of sound. Her hands climbed to his wonderfully broad shoulders then to the sides of his neck. He was taut with sinew, his thick, rather long hair sliding through her fingers like silk. His lips trailed a line of fire to the depression at the base of her throat, sending rivulets of pleasure low, and she shifted her hips against him.

He lifted his head.

Serena protested, only a tiny sound of displeasure. But he heard it.

This time when his mouth came down upon hers he left gentle exploration far behind. He seized her completely, forcing her lips wide and his tongue inside her. She stroked it, astounded at her temerity and her body's reaction. Heat ground within her, vital and shockingly pure. She pressed onto her tiptoes to flatten herself against him, to feel him even more fully. He groaned, a grunt of pleasure and frustration at once, and his hand swept down her throat between them to cover her bodice.

Serena hiccuped in surprise. Then in sheer pleasure.

His fingers curved around her breast. He held her like that for a moment, as though testing her size and shape. Then his thumb passed across her nipple slowly.

She melted, her bones liquefying, pleasure rocking through her at the soft caress so at odds with the urgent demand of his mouth. Through gown and corset, the blunt nail of his thumb dragged over the tight peak. She shuddered, he caressed again, and she moaned, the music and voices emanating from the other side of the door like some distant dream rather than the fantasy she was living now. She was in the arms of a rake, allowing him to fondle and kiss her, and she didn't care one whit about propriety. *She*—obedient, sensible, firmly upon the shelf and certain to remain there until her demise—wanted this stranger's embrace in the dark to go on forever.

Naturally, it could not. Serena knew from experience that such an embrace if continued at any length could lead to a great deal more than kissing. Once before she had escaped the practical consequences of that sort of encounter, safe except for her sorely abused heart. She could not wager upon meeting with such fortune a second time.

Of more immediate concern, someone might happen upon them.

But she could not shove him away, nor even release him. Her fingers and palms reveled in his texture, firm muscle, soft hair, and all she wanted of his hand upon her breast was that he would do it to the other one as well. She hadn't experienced anything so wondrously wicked in seven years, and, oddly, this encounter was already a great deal more satisfying. She would not have this opportunity again. She must make it last.

The door handle jiggled against her hip. She jerked in alarm, but he did not cease kissing her. With an effort worthy of Hercules, she dragged her lips away, dropped her hands, and turned her face aside.

Their quick breaths mingled in the blackness, his face a shadow above hers. Serena's heart thudded fast and hard. Or perhaps that was his heart?

Good heavens, she was beyond foolish. How could she have allowed her passions to run away with her again like this? Hadn't she learned the lesson of that folly well enough? He would expect more of her now. If he demanded, she might very well give in. Willingly. She was thoroughly trapped, veritably hoist by her own wretched petard. A greater widgeon did not exist.

She *could* not regret it.

He made a sound in his throat, at once thoughtful and pleased, and his arms about her loosened. Indignation, disappointment, and relief bubbled together inside her. But he did not back away. Serena willed her riotous heart to calm.

"I daresay I should go," she said unsteadily.

"I daresay you should." His voice was oddly rough. *Beautiful.*

"You will not tell anyone?"

"I beg your pardon?"

"No, of course you won't." Her knees actually shook. "I suspect you needn't share such a measly conquest with anyone. It would do you no credit either way."

"Either way?"

"For the good or the ill. No one would be impressed if you claimed to have kissed an unknown, unseen woman in the dark. No one would fault you for it either, I suspect."

He remained silent a moment. Then he bent to her temple and whispered in the smoothest, silkiest masculine tones Serena had ever heard, "What passes in the dark, madam, remains in the dark."

Her hands itched to grab him again. Her lips ached to press against his.

"Unhand me, my lord. Please."

He did, although it seemed reluctantly, his strong, warm hands slipping from her waist slowly. Foolish, contrary woman that she was, she trembled at their removal.

"Now step away," she managed, "and turn about while I leave."

"Afraid of the light?"

"Yes."

"But I have already seen your face."

"Not well, probably."

"Well enough. And I know your voice now." The amused tone returned to his, suggesting he knew a great deal more about her as well. She turned the knob, pulled the door open a crack, and slipped through it.

"Serena? Where on earth have you been?"

Her stepbrother's clear address brought her up short. She drew the painted panel shut with an audible click and gripped the knob behind her, praying the gentleman on the other side of it would not choose to depart the chamber also.

Tracy came toward her along the corridor.

"Mother is looking for you. She says Savege will arrive any minute and she wishes you present to encourage Charity. She sent me to search you out."

Serena touched her tender lips. Would they look now as sensitive as they felt? Good heavens, she hadn't even thought of her appearance, only of escaping. Escaping the best quarter hour she had spent in years. Perhaps her entire life.

Tracy furrowed his brow.

"Are you unwell, Ser?" Bright blue eyes the color of his sister's studied Serena's face. He was an elegantly slender man with hair like Charity's too, silvery gold, short and curly, lending him a classical aesthetic that suited his consequence as a wealthy baronet. "Your color is high."

"I am somewhat overheated from dancing."

"Dancing?" His eyes widened.

"Yes, Tracy. I do know how to dance. We used to dance quite often, if you recall."

"It is only that I haven't seen you dance in an age." His brow furrowed. "But if you aren't accustomed to it, perhaps you ought to sit down for a bit." He reached for the knob.

"No," she blurted out. "I am perfectly well, and Charity will be missing me. I only went to the ladies' retiring room and got caught up with conversation there."

He regarded her oddly then glanced again at the door.

"All right," he finally said, and offered his arm. "Let's go, then, and help Charity catch her earl." He winked, Serena released a tight breath, and they went to the ballroom.

"Millicent Gaffney tells me she spotted Savege," Davina hissed as soon as Serena stood beside her and Charity, her hand still tucked in her stepbrother's elbow. "He will look for us immediately, no doubt. You are a disloyal girl to stay away from your sister so long when she needs you."

Charity did look pale. Serena released a silent sigh. She drew her hand from Tracy and slipped it into her sister's, then glanced over the assembly once more. If he did not go straight from the darkened chamber to his carriage, somewhere among the guests would soon be a man who kissed like a fairy-tale hero and for a few scandalous moments made her feel like a princess.

Would she recognize him? He was quite tall, but

there were plenty of tall gentlemen about tonight. She couldn't very well wander around sniffing male guests and running her fingers through their hair.

If she were a regular sort of young lady, he might in the course of the evening ask her to dance. But she was not a regular sort, and the only gentlemen who ever asked her to dance always seemed to be short, balding, and dull as dishwater. God's gifts to her of an unfashionable face and figure, advanced age, and a stepmother who chose thoroughly unsuitable gowns for her guaranteed Serena's unpopularity with gentlemen.

Alas, the mysterious author of her amorous interlude must remain a mystery.

It was for the best. Still, Serena took comfort in the knowledge that now that she controlled her own fortune, she could purchase more suitable gowns.

Her father approached. As square-shouldered and thin-boned as she, with dirty-hay-colored hair like hers, he gave off an air of quiet complaisance, an attitude Serena had learned to mimic after he married Davina. For survival. Davina had not liked her daydreaming.

"I have just seen Lord Savege," he said with a kind look at his stepdaughter. "He is speaking with Wilberforce. Seems they have some Barbadian acquaintances in common. He will come over in a moment."

Charity's cold fingers tightened around Serena's. "Will he, Papa?" she whispered.

"Well he didn't come here for the lemonade," Tracy said under his breath. Serena flashed him a speaking look. He bent to her ear. "I've heard at least a half-dozen people tonight mention their astonishment over his attendance at a ball, Ser. He'd be at one of his clubs if it weren't for this, mark my words."

"Yes," she murmured for his hearing only. "That is what concerns me. Tracy, why is he interested in Charity? He must have dozens of mamas offering their daughters."

Her brother shrugged. "A fellow's got to get leg-shackled sometime or another. Might as well be a neighbor as not." He glanced at Charity. "Chare is as pretty as can stare, and rich. And since Grandfather was an earl, she's got good breeding too."

Serena worried her lip between her teeth. "Do you think he imagines—"

But she got no further. A gentleman stepped through the crowd toward them, and her breath failed.

He was, in point of fact, devastatingly handsome, but in a decidedly rakish manner. A strong jaw aligned with high cheekbones and a noble nose provided a perfect template for eyes the color of thunderclouds, and quite soulful—as reported—and a devilishly alluring mouth indeed. His hair, rich dark brown, wavy and carelessly long, curled upon his collar, a thick lock of it swept into a moon shape upon his brow, with the point dangling to his eyes. A tight-fitting coat of midnight superfine with large gold buttons, snowy white linen, and buff trousers flattered his broad shoulders, narrow waist, and long legs with apparently little effort.

Serena had absolutely no doubt that the infamous Earl of Savege stood before them. The satisfied twist of Davina's mouth and her father's nod confirmed it.

Lord Savege bowed to Davina, then his gaze went to Charity.

"My lord," Serena's father said, "may I present to you my daughter, Miss Lucas?"

Charity's cheeks looked like sheets of frost. Lord Savege extended his palm. Serena untangled her sister's fingers from her own and thrust Charity's hand forward. The earl bowed over it.

"Miss Lucas, it is a pleasure to make your acquaintance." His voice was smooth, deep, deliciously masculine, and—to Serena's utter horror—perfectly familiar. She didn't need him whispering in her ear to recognize the seductive tone and cadence. She sucked in breath, and the faintest hint of lavender and fresh tobacco wafted into her nostrils.

Panic flooded her. But perhaps he would not recognize her. He had probably exaggerated when he claimed to have seen her face well. He had called her a beauty, after all. She could disguise her voice, or— or—

"Good evening, my lord," Charity peeped, and curtsied.

The earl released her hand and turned his smoky gaze upon Serena. The corner of his fine mouth turned up ever so slightly, his rich eyes danced, and with sickening dread Serena suspected that, in the dark intimacy of the locked chamber, he had not in fact exaggerated.

Chapter 3

A handsome man and tall, a stranger? Where
   did she find him?
She must have brought some storm-tossed fellow
   from his ship.

                      —HOMER, *ODYSSEY*

Miss Carlyle, I presume?" he asked with an elegant bow.

Oh, good heavens, this could not be worse. But she deserved it for behaving like a wanton. And for once again falling into fantasy. On the other hand, she might be mistaken. He might not actually recognize her.

She ducked her head and curtsied. If she avoided speech, given time he would no doubt forget her voice. He was a rake, for pity's sake. He must have heard the murmured sighs of hundreds of women.

He was still looking at her when she straightened. She bit her lip. His gaze went to the action, then shifted to her stepbrother.

"Tracy Lucas, my lord." He bowed and the earl returned the gesture.

"Your estate is near Basildon, as I understand it."

"Closer to Chelmsford," Tracy said. "Makes it deuced inconvenient to visit the family, except here in town, of course."

"It must be difficult to eschew the company of such lovely sisters for so many months upon end," Lord Savege said, looking again to Charity with a pleasant smile. The expression rendered him even more attractive. Serena's stomach twisted. "Or do you stay in London for more than the spring season?" he asked.

Charity emitted a soft yelp, then chirped, "Oh, no, my lord. This is my first visit to town."

Davina must have pinched her. The earl did not seem to note anything amiss.

"And you, Miss Carlyle? Are you also more fond of our remote strip of coast than London?"

A direct question. Everyone stared at her, awaiting a response. She could not avoid speech.

"I like them both," she uttered as though her throat were lined with lint.

A small crease appeared in the earl's cheek.

"Good God, Ser," Tracy chuckled, "you sound as though *you* could use a glass of lemonade."

"You must take your sister to the refreshment table, Tracy," Davina said, a flash of disapproval in her eyes.

Serena had never been so glad to accede to her stepmother's orders.

"What's wrong with you, Ser?" Tracy handed her a cup. "I've never seen you so overset as tonight, least not since Mama and my silly sisters came to live with you." He smiled, peering at her face again. "You don't seem yourself."

"I am perfectly well, thank you." She gulped the beverage. It did not suffice to moisten her throat or lips. Lips that her sister's husband-to-be had thoroughly kissed only moments ago.

She was a wretch. A knave. A strumpet. All those words she used to read in the stories of knights and wizards and hapless, virtuous, innocent females like

Charity. But the Earl of Savege was no better. Minutes before making the acquaintance of his future wife, he had accosted a woman in a darkened room and tried to have his way with her.

Abruptly, it dawned upon Serena that being a rake truly entailed complete disregard for others.

If he hurt Charity, she would kill him. She hadn't any idea how. But she would devise a method. Perhaps she would send a message to the local hero Redstone and inform him that Savege Park was a treasure trove of swag. She would have to discover the location of the *Cavalier's* covey in order to do so, the very reason she had not yet begged the pirate's help to apprehend the smugglers.

Who else could she turn to? Certainly not the absentee landlord her sister was about to marry, and her father had already made it clear he did not wish to interfere. Smugglers brought useful goods and money to the coast, Papa had said, surprising Serena with his disregard for the virtue of the milkmaid the sailors had abused, not to mention the purloined goods they took from the local village. She had argued that Glenhaven Hall could be their next target, but he turned the conversation aside.

She looked again for the Marquess of Doreé in the crowd.

"Who are you searching out, Ser?"

Serena's attention snapped back to her stepbrother.

"Oh," she caught sight of Lord Savege and Charity in the set forming, "I am appreciating what a fetching pair Charity and his lordship appear. Don't you agree?"

"I think he could eat her for breakfast and still have room for steak and kippers," he muttered.

The sensation of the earl's hungry mouth upon hers washed Serena's cheeks with flame.

"If you do not like the match," she managed to say, "Why haven't you said so to your mother?"

Tracy fiddled with the lip of his glass. "Mother will do as she pleases, without my approval. I cannot control her actions."

"I wish my father could."

"He has always been more interested in his books and studies of nature than his children, hasn't he?"

Serena nodded. But long ago it had been different. With vivid detail she remembered one day in particular. The sun had glowed in the August sky, the waves washing onto shore white with foam as her father dashed into the water, she and her younger sister Viola cinched under either arm, their mother laughing from the beach. They spent the entire day like that into evening, with only a picnic basket and each other for entertainment. It was more than enough.

That was the last truly happy memory Serena recalled having for years. A fortnight later, when the search for her sister's body upon the rocky shoals came to nothing—as only Serena predicted—and her mother lay in state in Glenhaven Hall's best drawing room, she wrapped her skinny arms about her father's waist and told him they still had each other. He did not return the embrace. And even then at the tender age of twelve she knew everything had changed.

She glanced across the ballroom. Her father stood silently behind his second wife, gazing at nothing in particular, not even his eldest stepdaughter on the dance floor with one of society's most notorious libertines. Tracy was correct about him, although it had taken her six years of her girlhood to discover that. Six years and Lord Robert Bailey.

The beleaguered orchestra drew the set to a close

and spectators applauded. Serena's belly tittered as the earl led Charity toward them.

"Miss Carlyle, your sister informs me that you are an exceptional dancer. May I beg the privilege?"

Serena now wished the floor would open and disgorge a dragon to consume *her*. Or perhaps Lord Savege. It was a toss-up.

"Oh, I could not—"

"Go ahead and have a dance, Ser," Tracy said. "You have the opportunity so rarely. Only, don't allow yourself to become overheated as earlier."

"But, I—" Serena halted her words. Charity's eyes shone with a silent plea. Clearly she wished to be extricated from Lord Savege's company.

For seven years, since Serena had given away her virtue to a cad and subsequently given up hope of a respectable marriage, her younger sisters' welfare had been her entire world. She could no more refuse Charity's entreaty than fly to China upon a puffy cloud.

She curtsied. "Thank you, my lord."

The earl passed Charity to Tracy and extended his arm for Serena. Every nerve straining in discomfort, she propped her hand upon his sleeve and he led her into the set.

"Are you not fond of dancing, Miss Carlyle?" he asked as they took their places in the lines.

"Oh, no. I like it very much." She peered at him closely. He seemed not to note her undisguised voice. Her shoulders relaxed a bit.

"Your brother suggested that you haven't the opportunity to dance often," he said without particular inflection. If he knew her identity as the woman in the parlor, surely he would be teasing her now. She had understood that aspect of his nature well enough.

"Has your family only recently arrived in town?"

"We have been in residence here more than a month already, my lord."

He cocked his raffishly tousled head. "And yet you dance infrequently?"

Beneath the warm blanket of his interested gaze, Serena's rational thoughts scattered. He had unsettled her in precisely this manner in the parlor, although with his words and touch. She supposed she had the advantage now. He could not very well murmur delicious phrases at her throat or caress her in inappropriate places here upon the dance floor.

More the pity.

Serena scolded herself silently and roundly.

"We have attended few entertainments in London, and we go on in generally the same manner in Devonshire."

"Your father hasn't the taste for amusement, then."

"My stepmother sees no purpose in balls if not in the service of my sister's marriage prospects. Thus our presence here this evening." She gestured toward him.

"Ah." He nodded thoughtfully.

The dance separated them. Serena had time to consider how disappointingly and thus reassuringly banal a rake's conversation could be—at least in public— before the pattern reunited them.

"And this has been the situation since your introduction into society?" he asked. "When might that have been?"

Despite herself, Serena's cheeks warmed anew. "Sir."

"Forgive me." His brow creased. "I am ungracious in inquiring."

Unaccountably, Serena's belly tickled with butter-flies. How lovely to have a man of such consequence concern himself over her sensibilities. Perhaps the gossips had gotten it wrong. The Earl of Savege seemed the most conventional gentleman, polite, mildly pleasant, and not at all threatening in the common run of social intercourse. If he behaved in this manner with real ladies, perhaps Charity would not suffer so much. Perhaps she might even enjoy being his wife.

With renewed peace of mind, Serena met the earl's gaze. Her stomach seized up again. His eyes glinted as though lit by sparks of lightning.

"And upon the infrequent occasions upon which you do attend entertainments, Miss Carlyle," he said as though continuing a thought, "do you typically seek out darkened, locked chambers in which to catch your breath?"

Serena's insides melted. She ought to be appalled, at the very least affronted. But the only emotions she could summon were gratification at the appreciative glint in his smoky eyes, and pleasure at the memory of *his* breaths coming so hard against hers.

The pattern divided them, but his gaze remained upon her as they parted then circled back. After two more similar intervals Serena finally gathered the courage to look at him again. An expression of intent study marked his handsome face.

"Miss Carlyle," he took her hand briefly as the dance required, "you have the most extraordinary eyes."

She choked upon air.

"Oh, no, they are really quite ordinary, except for being two different colors from one another."

"Not so different." His gaze shifted between them. "And not so ordinary. The left is nearly violet."

"It must be the light. My lord?"

"Hm?"

"You are staring."

"I am."

"It is improper."

"Then I beg your pardon."

"But not with any sincerity, it seems." She plunged in. "Your tone does not suit your words."

His mouth twitched up at one corner and his eyes warmed. Soulful, *indeed.*

"*Touché*, madam," he murmured.

Serena took a quick, hard breath of resolution. Now that they had both acknowledged the interlude in the parlor, they could put it behind them. The man she had kissed was in fact a rake, and therefore the embrace meant nothing to him. He would not speak of it to anyone, and she could simply forget it had occurred.

"Hypocrite." The word came forth softly from his mouth, his beautifully shaped mouth that had filled her with shivering delight and at which she was now staring quite fixedly.

She tore her gaze away, setting it upon her sister dancing not far off with their brother. Charity stumbled along in the pattern, Tracy scrabbling for her fingers as they slipped beyond reach. For all her beauty and delicacy, Charity was a dreadful dancer. No matter, she had a husband now, or nearly so. She needn't impress anyone with her light feet or graceful air.

Although, it was quite a shame she did not shine upon the dance floor. For all his reprehensible qualities, not the least of which was his propensity to tease, Lord Savege danced beautifully. Serena found her gaze drawn back to his broad shoulders, muscular legs, and perfectly erect carriage, and prayed he would not shame Charity too wretchedly in public once they were wed. Charity did not deserve that. She was far too kind.

The music stumbled to a halt. Lord Savege took Serena's hand and bowed over it, watching her again.

"You are pensive, madam." His lips hinted at another grin. "Are you so unaccustomed to dancing that our pairing has proved too much for you?"

He meant quite a bit more than he said. She tugged away from his hold and met his gaze squarely.

"I am only wondering what sort of husband you will be to my sister."

His expressive eyes sobered.

"None yet, madam. I have not yet agreed to your father's terms."

"But if you do, how will you go on?"

He regarded her silently for several moments.

"As I have never been married," he said, quite seriously it seemed, "I cannot say."

"I see."

"Perhaps you do, but I doubt it." His words were odd, but his mouth twitched up at one edge again. Serena could not resist its lure, just as she had not been able to resist his lead in the parlor. Her life under Davina's dominion required mature, responsible sobriety. But the spirit inside her yearned for days long past, for play and fantasy and even—wickedly—dalliance.

"You enjoy laughing at others, don't you, my lord?"

"Only when I suspect they will laugh along with me." His voice was warm again, and rather low, like in the dark.

Serena tingled. A handsome rake had kissed her and was now speaking to her like an equal of sorts. For what more could a lady wish to inspire confidence? Approaching the Marquess of Doreé suddenly seemed like the simplest task in the world.

She cast her gaze about but did not find him. She glanced at the earl and curtsied.

"Thank you for the dance, my lord. I must go now."

"May I return you to your mother?"

"Oh," Serena said, anxious to be off in pursuit of her

quarry and out from beneath the entrancing gaze of her sister's intended. "She is not my mother." With a quick smile, she moved toward the corridor.

She scoured the buildings, but Lord Doreé was nowhere to be found. Still, her spirits soared. Somehow she would track him down and make him come clean with her. By the time she encountered her father, Davina, and Charity in the drawing room, she nearly had a plan.

"Where have you been?" her stepmother snapped. "Charity tore her flounce and needed you to mend it."

"Oh, I am sorry, Chare. Did you manage it yourself?"

"Of course she did not. I was obliged to do it, you faithless girl."

Serena's gaze flew to her stepmother's. Normally the sight of Davina's disapproval made her stomach hollow and her palms damp. Now Serena's belly tweaked, but her hands tucked in her skirts remained dry.

She had done something she dreamt of doing for years. She kissed a man. Thoroughly. Additionally, she was now chasing down an elusive peer in an attempt to bring an end to the havoc smugglers wreaked upon her beleaguered countryside. She had allowed Davina to crush her dreams for so long it had become habit. But now she wanted them back.

"I am not faithless. I am as loyal to my sisters and brother as a hound." She drew a tremulous breath. "Papa, Charity is weary. She has met and danced with the earl, and he cannot very well ask her to dance again. May we go home now?"

"My dear?" He turned an anxious look upon Davina. She twisted her lips, but nodded. He offered his arm to Charity, the other to his wife. They walked away, Davina's shoulders rigid.

"Well done, Ser," Tracy murmured over her shoulder.

"Was it?" Her hands shook again.

He smiled, a gentle, caring look. Her father and Tracy might not be her gallant champions, but she was fortunate to claim the affection of two such fine gentlemen. Now, if Charity could find contentment marrying a scandalous rogue with smoky eyes alight with deviltry, Serena might learn to be happy again.

Chapter 4

*Be ashamed yourselves, and feel shame before
your neighbors who dwell round about, and fear
the wrath of the gods, lest it happen that they
turn against you in anger at evil deeds.*

—HOMER, *ODYSSEY*

Alex slid a card onto the table, shifting his gaze along
the faces of his opponents as he leaned back into
his chair. The elegant gaming club hung heavy with the
musky-sweet coupling of cheroot smoke and Parisian
perfumes. Lamps burned low behind yellowed glass,
casting the luxuriously appointed chambers in an aura
of somnolent ease.

But the atmosphere and Alex's casual pose held little
in common with most of the club's denizens. Anxiety
laced the hazy air, and fevered, frenetic determination
scored the visages of the men scattered about the tables.
The Marquess of McFee, the Duke of Yarmouth's portly,
middle-aged heir, was present tonight, and young-
bloods were losing fortunes.

With his jovial, avuncular air, McFee drew them in,
played carelessly for a few hands to boost the lads' confidence, then closed in for the kill. Alex had watched
him already for a fortnight. He had the man's measure

now, as well as the useful information that McFee planned to take out his yacht for a pleasure cruise at the end of the season.

The *Cavalier*'s next quarry would prove a windfall for the orphans and widows.

A young lord across the felt-covered table stacked his hand and slid the cards to the center, facedown.

"Too clever for me, McFee. I'm out," he said with dignified calm, then met Alex's gaze. Alex nodded. He had played against the Marquess of Doreé on several occasions. The man was good and scrupulously honest, no fool despite his youth. No doubt he had learned how to conduct himself prudently at an early age. Of necessity.

Doreé departed without fanfare.

"Guess they don't teach them how to win in Mother India, hm?" McFee grunted, garnering a few nervous smirks from the lads he was trouncing. He played his final card, the others cast theirs in hopelessly, and McFee scooped up the winnings.

Alex sighed with affected nonchalance and pushed his chair back.

"I am finished as well, gentlemen. Good evening." He bowed with mild indolence and moved toward the door. A footman met him with his hat and cane, ivory handled and iron-tipped, and Alex gave the chamber a final glance. He would not miss the place if he never returned.

Likewise, he would not regret giving up the house he kept on Stacey Street, empty since the previous week when, along with a string of emeralds and diamonds, he gave La Dolcetta her walking papers. The opera singer wept and pouted, and then, fist around the baubles, kissed him a final time and bid him adieu.

Alex had given his solicitor instructions to sell the house the following day. At one time, cutting a dash in that particular style amused him to no end, no matter who suffered for his indiscretions. But in the past few years he had grown weary of greedy courtesans and angry husbands. Now more than anything he wanted peace.

He stepped into the murk of the late spring night. It was comfortably past midnight already, but the day's warmth still clung to the pavement, mingling with the detritus of coal fire and a hint of rain visible around the gas lamps in halos. Wishing for fresh sea air and gray cliffs striated with green, he set his boots to the street. He had left his carriage at home. And as usual, he had plenty to ponder during his walk to Mayfair, and he needed the activity. Indolence chafed.

Halfway down the block, at the mouth of a narrow alley, a carriage stood motionless at the curb. As Alex passed, the coachman perched atop the box tipped his hat, but his gaze darted anxiously to the alley.

Curious.

The hairs on the back of Alex's neck prickled. As a lad mastering seacraft in the West Indies, he had learned that only foolish men ignored the curious.

A stifled gasp came from the shadowed alley. Then a woman's cry. Alex moved swiftly into the blackness, plucking the dirk from his boot top.

A pair of figures stood close in the gloom, a cloaked woman and a man. A quick exchange of voices came to Alex through the mist—a man's growl of warning, a woman's breathless rejoinder. He recognized both voices, slid the dirk back into its sheath and made his steps heard.

Lord Doreé's head swung around, followed by the lady's. The marquess held her fast, both wrists gripped in his left hand. Alex moved closer, and Doreé's black eyes registered recognition.

"Lord Savege," Miss Carlyle exclaimed, but not in relief. She sounded, of all things, irritated. Good Lord. If Doreé's face weren't crossed with keen suspicion, Alex would only imagine one thing.

The marquess released his captive and stepped back. "Are you acquainted with this lady, my lord?" he asked shortly.

So, he did not know her. Points to the fellow, though, for recognizing her as quality.

"She is a neighbor of mine in the country." He tapped his cane upon the pavement. "How do you do, madam?" He bowed.

"Not particularly well *now*," she said with a meaningful look. "What are you doing here?"

"Taking a stroll. I daresay I might ask the same of you."

"That is none of your business."

Doreé gave her a hard look. "But it is mine. Why did you follow me?"

She glanced at Alex with a clear expression of mingled panic and guilt. Then her face went blank.

"I—I have forgotten," she said.

A chuckle worked in Alex's throat. The woman was an atrocious liar, and apparently a great deal more troublesome than he'd imagined three nights earlier when she brashly questioned him about his intentions regarding her stepsister.

The marquess looked grim, but carefully aware, just as he did at the card table.

"I recommend that you not repeat it," Doreé said.

She flashed Alex another quick look, then back at Lord Doreé, but closed her mouth tight.

"My lord," Alex said, "allow me if you will to escort the lady to her carriage just up the street."

Doreé regarded him for a thoughtful moment, then

nodded and fixed his accoster with a serious expression.

"Forgive me for my hasty reaction, madam. Good evening." He bowed, then disappeared into the shimmering black of the alley.

She turned to Alex. "This is not at all what you must think." She stumbled over the words.

"I haven't an idea as to what you imagine I may think, Miss Carlyle," he replied. "Uncannily, I also haven't the least doubt that whatever brought you to this alley will not be the story you produce for me presently."

She took her lower lip between her teeth—a habit, apparently, and not unappealing—and buried her hands in her cloak. Her little chin crept up.

"I am not required to explain myself to you," she said, as though trying for a confident air. She nearly achieved it.

"You certainly are." Alex settled into a relaxed stance. "Lord Doreé was displeased with your ambush. Correct me if I am mistaken."

"You are absurd. I did not ambush him. I merely approached him from behind."

"With what intention?"

She stiffened and sealed her lips once more. Lovely lips, not in the usual rosebud or bowtie fashion but full and wide, made for much greater use than conversation. After three days their flavor still lingered upon his. He could not recall ever noticing the savor of a woman's lips before. Perhaps because no woman he had ever kissed tasted like cinnamon and vanilla. Like Christmas biscuits.

His steady, silent regard wore down her resistance.

"Well if you must know . . ." She took a visible breath, straining the fabric of her bodice over her breasts. Supple, beautifully shaped breasts quick to respond to a man's touch. "I—my intentions were—" She stuttered to a halt.

"Of an amorous nature?" he offered.

"No!" Her eyes shot wide. In the dark they appeared identical in color. Alex knew better. Unique eyes. But troublesome chit. Amusing, though.

He needed amusement in his life now. Or rather, distraction. He craved it.

"No?" he drawled.

"No, of course not."

"Of course not." He nodded in mock seriousness. She bit her lip again, her teeth straight and white. His tongue knew them to be beautifully smooth as well. "How did you know to find him here?"

"I heard that he frequented this club."

"You heard?"

She fidgeted with her cloak trim. "I overheard."

"Ah. Eavesdropping, Miss Carlyle?"

Clear reluctance to reply warred upon her expressive face with the desire to defend herself.

"My stepmother has a great many acquaintances," she finally said. "Some of them, I fear, are not as discreet as they ought to be in how they choose to gossip. The marquess is quite wealthy."

"I see."

She seemed to study his face. "You do not believe me."

"My dear, let us be frank, shall we? I haven't any reason not to disbelieve you, except your father's assurance to me not a sennight ago that his daughters are modest females." He ticked a brow upward. "It seems he may not know his eldest daughter particularly well, hm?"

"This is unendurable," she said in a tight voice.

"Yet perhaps well deserved."

"Well, that is certainly the pot calling the kettle black," she retorted, then pressed her lips together for a moment before bursting into speech again. "You kissed an unknown woman at a ball which you attended in order to meet your intended betrothed. Or have you forgotten?"

"I have not." Not remotely. It was the most enjoyment he'd had in the fortnight he'd been back in London, including his hours spent with the buxom La Dolcetta. "And may I remind you that you took part in the event as well. Rather enthusiastically." With those enchanting lips. He stepped closer.

She stumbled back, enlarging the space between them again.

"That is aside from my point. My wish to speak with Lord Doreé in private hardly qualifies me as the worst offender of morality currently standing in this alley. You kissed a complete stranger."

"I kissed a woman who likes being kissed."

"Your betrothed's sister."

"At the moment I was not aware of that detail. And I will note once more, madam, that she is not my betrothed yet."

"That hardly signifies. You will accept, of course. My stepsister is an incomparable, exceptionally well dowered, and the granddaughter of an earl. But she is an innocent and deserves an honorable groom." A martial glint lit her eyes now, protective like a mother goose over her goslings. "You should now behave with greater propriety, my lord."

"Hm." His gaze slid down her body, largely concealed by the dark. But he knew it with his hands better than his eyes, slender, again not precisely fashionable but curved in all the right places. "So you approve of the marriage? Two nights ago I took the strong impression that you were not particularly amenable to it."

"I was nonplussed to realize it was you. Understandably so."

He laughed. "I admire your honesty, my dear."

"Thank you." Her cheeks abruptly flamed and her eyes went wide. "But really you haven't the right to admire anything about me."

"Despite what you may have heard of my reputation, that was not a proposition. It was a compliment."

"Of course it was." She looked entirely prim, somewhat contrite, and remarkably adorable. Alex's cravat abruptly tightened.

"It strikes me now," he said slowly, "that you are not accustomed to kissing men in darkened parlors after all."

"I should say not."

"Yet you did not deny it the other night."

"Your insinuation did not dignify a response. You seem to forget, my lord, that not all ladies cavort about like doxies."

Her indignation seemed genuine now. But she kissed like a woman who had some experience at it. Yet there had been something else in the caress of her lips, something sweet and seeking he should have run from but that drew him in. Something that made it, in the end, difficult to release her in that shadowed chamber, as now it proved difficult to allow her to walk away toward her carriage.

"Why are you unmarried, Miss Carlyle?"

The pink upon her cheeks deepened, and her extraordinary eyes shuttered.

"That, sir, is also none of your business."

"I beg your pardon, then," he murmured, and took her elbow. "Allow me to escort you to your carriage, ma'am."

"Thank you, my lord, but I can—"

"Allow me," he said firmly.

She dug in her heels and glanced down the alleyway in the opposite direction.

Alex's eyes widened. "Do not tell me you intend to follow him?"

She turned a desperate gaze upon him, and Alex's collar cinched anew.

"He goes about so rarely in society, and I must speak with him. At the ball the other night I intended to, you know."

"Why didn't you?"

She threw him a speaking look.

Alex blinked. "You were to meet him in the parlor?" Something about the idea stuck in his compressed throat, perhaps the notion that he had been a substitute for a woman's desire for another man. A unique occurrence for sure.

"Of course not," she said with renewed indignation. "I intended to speak with him in the ballroom, in perfectly unexceptionable surroundings, but I lost my courage and went into the parlor to regain it, where *you* delayed me, of course, and he departed in the meantime."

He smiled, his chest loosening. "Then, my apologies, madam. It seems you regained your courage." He gestured about them.

"You truly are beyond absurd." She moved toward the alley's entrance, but a grin lifted her sweet lips as she turned away.

He caught up with her in two strides. "You must admit that your audacity in approaching a gentleman late at night in a dark alleyway is not in the usual run of things for respectable young ladies."

Her hands clenched. "I do agree. It is unusual for me too."

"I am all agog to know what inspired it."

She flashed him a thoroughly incomprehensible look that mingled a plea and indignant outrage.

"Tell me of the matter you wish to speak with him about," Alex prodded, "and perhaps I may be able to assist. I am well enough acquainted with the man."

She pivoted around to him.

"You don't care about the matter. I already know that. If you did, you would have done something about it." Her eyes shone with sudden hurt.

"My dear Miss Carlyle, I am afraid I haven't the foggiest notion of what you mean to accuse me." No notion, and a decided dislike of females with wounded, accusatory airs, especially when directed at him.

But he had never cared what respectable members of society thought of him. He never cared what anybody thought. Blast it, he'd been a damned pirate for eight years. Somehow, though, this woman's disapproval made his uncomfortably tight collar feel rather sticky.

He glowered.

"You have no right to look at me like that," Serena insisted. "Those wretched smugglers are plaguing the coast and all you do is sit in your clubs playing cards and your boudoirs doing heaven knows what when you should be taking action to stop their activities."

He folded his arms over his broad chest. He wore no overcoat, and the mist settled upon the dark fabric of his coat with a shine that made him look somewhat otherworldly. Serena tried to return his scowl, but the expression sat uncomfortably upon her face.

"In point of fact, they are not *my* boudoirs," he replied. "And I am, as you know, as contented in a parlor as anywhere else."

Good heavens, again with that kiss. More than a kiss. Embrace. Frenzy of caresses.

His eyes looked positively warm, his voice low. Serena's knees wobbled and her cheeks heated once more. She blessed the dark alley and the far distant streetlamp. Rakes were no doubt dab hands at causing ladies to become unsteady and uncomfortably over-heated. Lord Savege probably made this sort of comment in that tone of voice on a daily basis. Or, nightly, rather. He obviously wished to distract her.

His gaze raked her, lingering in places she had not known nerves could tingle from a mere glance, then slowly returned to hers. A lazy look came to his eyes now, relaxed and comfortable, no longer piqued. The transformation acted upon her like a tonic, turning the tingles into full-blown Chinese fireworks.

"You should do something about them," she stated as firmly as she could.

"The boudoirs or parlors?" The corner of his mouth tilted up. "I assure you, I am already doing my best upon both scores."

"The smugglers." She fisted her hands. "I realize that you consider taking your seat in Lords to be tantamount to heresy, but if you really do not wish to make the effort, you could at least instruct your secretary to pen a letter to the Board of Admiralty encouraging the commissioners to apprehend the villains. You do have one, don't you?"

"A heresy?"

"A secretary."

"Ah, yes. But he is engaged with other matters presently." The strangest light glinted in his smoky eyes, as though his thoughts ran to something else entirely than their conversation. "Miss Carlyle, I recommend that you leave the smugglers to themselves. The Marquess of Doreé, as well."

"But that is precisely the reason I wished to speak

with him. I saw him in Clovelly less than two months ago."

"How nice for you," he said with maddening disinterest.

"Well, yes, in the event that it made me believe that he must have something to do with those smugglers. His estate is in Kent, you know, miles and miles away. At the time, you were not in residence at Savage Park, so he could not have been visiting you, and of course my father does not often have guests. Why else would Lord Doreé have been in our district the very week the smugglers came ashore?"

He looked abruptly quite serious.

"Madam, a gentleman has many pursuits that take him far afield of his own lands. And a smuggling ship needn't have a titled patron to ensure its success. The Marquess of Doreé is above reproach. It seems to me that you have little but an overactive imagination to recommend you to the task of apprehending the smugglers."

Serena's heart throbbed against her ribs. Until that moment she hadn't realized she imagined him to be different. Different from *what* or *whom*, she did not wish to examine, not now that he had said words horridly like the sort Davina used to say, long ago when Serena still spoke her mind.

In their short acquaintance she had revealed more of her thoughts to the Earl of Savage than to anyone else in years. Perhaps because they shared a secret, he seemed like a confidant of sorts. A ridiculous notion.

Except that it did not *feel* ridiculous.

He grasped her hand. She flinched back, but he held it fast.

"Forgive me, Miss Carlyle. I fear I have spoken too candidly."

"I do not mind *candid*," she muttered, her gaze skittering away. This was simply too horrid. One moment he spoke severely, the next his touch made her joints feel all liquid again.

"I daresay you do not," he said in a peculiar voice. "Rather, perhaps I spoke too harshly. I beg your pardon. Again."

She tugged, and he released her.

"You needn't." She turned toward the alley's entrance. No one ever apologized to her except Charity, and then only for Davina's horrid behavior toward Serena. Perhaps her sister and the earl would make an excellent pair after all, continually begging pardon of one another, both for his offenses.

"Ah, the lady's smile returns. I am forgiven, it seems."

Her gaze shot up. Head ducked to study her face, his eyes shone with mild pleasure in the misted glow of the streetlamp.

"My lord," she said, halting near the carriage. "You are a great tease."

"And you, madam, have a considerably elastic sensibility."

"I suppose I should also take that as a compliment."

"You suppose correctly."

"Good heavens, two compliments in one evening. How pleasant." Rather, unprecedented. That made two for the calendar year, not including compliments from Charity, her innocent sister who had no idea that Serena now stood on a street corner with her betrothed. Nor that the lamplight served to highlight his shapely mouth that three nights ago had made her so breathless she could barely stand.

Serena shifted her gaze to his eyes. Her stomach knotted. He had caught her staring at his mouth again.

"I will be going now."

"I expect so." He folded his hands behind his back. A smile lurked upon his lips. John Coachman moved to jump from the box, but the earl gestured for him to stay, then opened the door and let down the step himself. Serena took his hand to climb in.

"Miss Carlyle, how is it that you are abroad alone like this so late at night? Won't you be missed at home?" He glanced at the coachman.

She paused upon the step. "John will not say a word. And after supper I told Charity I was ill and did not wish to be disturbed. If anyone asked, I knew she would give that story and do her utmost to ensure my rest." Guilt curdled in her stomach. "It is wretched of me to use her so. She is infinitely trusting. You are a fortunate man, my lord."

He regarded her for several moments. "I begin to see that."

"You will not tell anyone about this, will you?"

A slight crease appeared between his eyes. He shook his head, then passed her into the carriage and closed the door. The vehicle jolted from the curb. The sash covered the window, so Serena could not watch him as she rode off. But she had no business gazing after him anyway.

Chapter 5

*Now go to your chamber, and busy yourself with
your own tasks, the loom and the distaff, and bid
your handmaids be about their tasks; but speech
shall be men's care.*

—HOMER, *ODYSSEY*

Toward the end of her thirteenth year, shortly after
Viola's disappearance, Serena embroidered a small
sewing case with an image of a princess, a diadem set
atop her dark ringlets, surrounded by tiny purple flowers. Thereafter, this memento of her missing sister went
with her everywhere, including Yorkshire, where she
spent a month each summer in the company of her re-
cluse uncle and aunt, and now twice to London. In the
box, she stored not needles and thread, but her most
treasured objects.

Waking the morning after her encounter in the alley
with not one but two peers of the realm, with her head
aching and a sensation of regret heavy in her stomach,
she took the case from her dressing table drawer and
set it upon the bed.

Within it, Charity's first attempt at making lace sur-
mounted the modest pile, a mere scrap of a confec-
tion but perfect nonetheless. Next, Serena uncovered a

letter her father had penned to her before Viola's birth. It told Serena how he admired her quiet determination, discernable in her character already at age two. She would always be his special girl, he wrote, even if her new sibling turned out to be his heir. Beneath the yellowed foolscap, a braided length of her mother's hair slipped into Serena's palm. She tucked both back into the box.

At the bottom of the treasure chest she found the item she sought. The doll was no more than three inches tall, crudely concocted of yarn and bits of fabric by her six-year-old sister for her eighth birthday. The dark brown hair of embroidery silk fell a bit too long for a gentleman, but it was suitable for the knight Viola had been trying to fashion. A tiny sword of silver wire drooped from his floppy hand, a likewise sagging shield of felt upon his other arm. He boasted neither mouth nor nose, his button eyes covering most of the surface of his face.

Gray buttons, made of shell and richly luminescent.

Serena closed her eyes and prayed that it was not too horrible a sin to be so thoroughly attracted to one's sister's betrothed. Almost betrothed. Though really, she could not blame herself too harshly. Half the ladies in London must nurse a *tendre* for the Earl of Savege. Especially the ladies he had kissed, which would probably bring that number to more than half.

It was a good thing he had such a fine sense of the ridiculous. At least she could laugh with him about it. And at least he had promised not to tell her father or Davina of her escapade the previous night.

Her failed escapade.

She refused to be thwarted in her goal. The smugglers must be halted. Last month they took a dairymaid's virtue. Next time the villains might not stop until they had stolen the whole girl. Serena shivered. The next time it might be Diantha or Faith.

Just like Viola.

This time she would stop them.

She stowed the sewing case, dressed, and went to breakfast. Her father already sat at the table, tea and muffins forgotten in lieu of the journal.

"Good morning, Papa."

The baron lowered his journal as she sat down and fixed her with a sober regard. "Daughter, I have had a note from Lord Savege this morning."

Serena's wrist jerked and her toast leapt to the plate's edge.

"You have? Concerning what, I wonder?" Her foolishness. Her improprieties. Her thorough lack of delicacy upon each occasion he met her. His unwillingness to give his exalted name to the sister of such a depraved person.

Hope sparked in Serena's breast. Why hadn't she thought of that before? Charity might be saved from this *mésalliance* after all. She tucked the idea away for future consideration.

"He did not say," her father replied. "No doubt he wishes to speak with me directly concerning the terms of the marriage agreement."

"No doubt." She swallowed around the lump in her throat. "Papa, I wish to go home."

His brow furrowed. "But it is only the middle of the season."

"I am weary of London."

His eyes shadowed. "You are unaccustomed to town life. It is my fault for always keeping you in the country. I should have insisted to your stepmother that you be allowed to visit each year."

"I don't know why, when I am perfectly happy in

Devonshire and upon my summer visits to York. But you are kind, Papa."

"Then why your wish to depart? I know you cannot be jealous of the attention being paid your stepsister. You never have been."

"Of course not. Only, town does not suit me and I have business to attend to at Glenhaven."

"Business?"

Her foolish tongue. It had really been much easier when she employed it less frequently. Drat Lord Savege for loosening it, in a manner of speaking.

"Oh, this and that. Papa, may I go?"

He folded his hands upon the tabletop, an uncomfortable gesture. "Your sister depends upon you."

Serena had her defense prepared.

"Yes, I know. But Diantha and Faith do too. Since Diantha frightened off that last governess, she is positively plaguing Nurse, and sweet old Nurse simply mustn't be made to endure that alone. If I am home, I can distract Diantha. And in the meantime who knows what trouble she is getting up to?" She perked her eyebrows and twisted her lips a bit. Davina and her father, of course, had been off upon their wedding trip when Serena first met Lord Robert Bailey.

He screwed up his brow, lending his graying hair and wide mouth a weary air.

Serena loved her father, but she still sometimes wondered what had drawn Davina to him. Wealthy by her first husband's death, she might have married any number of gentlemen of title and means. She was intensely attentive to fashion and status. Yet she chose a reclusive baron more interested in natural philosophy than society, and seemed to be content with him.

"Papa?" Serena encouraged.

"How will Charity get along without you?"

"She might consider this practice in going along on her own, but in the warm, comfortable bosom of her family." She took a sip of coffee. "And here she has my stepmother and stepbrother to look after her."

Her father seemed to consider it.

"And since she and Lord Savege have already made each other's acquaintance," Serena added, "I'm sure that as soon as you and he conclude negotiations, Davina will be as happy to return home as to remain in town, anyway. I predict she will have the family decamp by June at latest."

"Do you think so?"

Serena's heart clenched. Usually she ignored the sensation, the disappointment lodged in her breast for her father—the man he had been when her mother was still alive, the hope she'd held as she grew older that he could find another wife to make him happy again, and his descent into this shadow since he found Davina.

"I suspect it. Can I go, Papa?"

"I will need to ask your stepmother if she approves of it."

"Approve of what?"

Davina stood in the doorway arrayed in aqua taffeta, a peacock feather jutting from her perfectly coiffed blond curls. She pinned Serena with a sharp stare.

"Where do you wish to go?"

"To Glenhaven Hall, Stepmother." She refused to ask permission. As of yesterday Davina no longer held any authority over her.

"You may not." She moved into the chamber. Gesturing to a footman, she sat and accepted a plate and cup.

Serena stood. "Charity will be fine without me. With you, Papa, and Tracy, she has all the support she requires."

Davina's lips slid into their perpetual purse. "We may expect a call from Lord Savege any time," she said, ignoring Serena's words.

"He sent a note this morning requesting an interview," her father said. "Regarding the terms of the marriage contract, no doubt."

"He was quite taken with Charity at the ball the other night," Davina said.

Serena's knotted stomach did an odd, exceedingly uncomfortable pirouette. "He was?"

"Oh, yes. Millicent Gaffney insists she has never seen Savege smile so much in all her life as he did that evening."

How Mrs. Gaffney could see the earl smile at all when he rarely went into polite society, Serena could not imagine.

"Perhaps he wishes to conclude negotiations swiftly." Davina's self-satisfied smile curled around her cheeks like a snake's split tongue. "Once a gentleman of his consequence makes a decision, he does not delay putting it into action. Ah . . ." Her eyes flared at the journal. "I see Lord Poole has plans to set the Admiralty upon that renegade Redstone finally."

Serena's pulse leapt and she moved to peer over her stepmother's shoulder.

"He does? Who is Lord Poole?"

Davina sniffed. "Proper ladies do not hover, Serena."

She backed up a step. "Papa, who is Lord Poole?" More importantly, could he ruin her plans?

The baron cast his wife an uncertain look. "The Earl of Poole. His estate is near Bath."

"Why does he wish to halt Redstone?"

"He claims to hold an old grudge toward him. Years ago Redstone took one of his ships off the coast of his plantation in Barbados."

"What was the cargo?"

"Sugar and molasses. But . . ." He paused, glancing at his wife still scanning *The Times*. His brow grew taut.

"But?" Serena prodded.

"Redstone besmirched Lord Poole's honor. At the time, Poole had not yet succeeded to the title. He was young, not above twenty-five, and caring for his father's business concerns in the West Indies. The old earl was infuriated by the loss of the ship and shamed his son publicly for it."

"He must have shamed him horridly for him to be so angry at Redstone eight years later."

"He stripped him of his allowance."

"Oh. Well, that must have been inconvenient. What happened to his son?"

"He borrowed a great deal, and played at the tables quite recklessly. I understand he barely scraped by until his father died and he inherited."

"And now he is about the king's business, encouraging the navy to rid the coast of that nefarious villain," Davina said with a self-satisfied smirk.

Clearly, Lord Poole's motive was revenge. This did not bode well for Serena's plans.

In the wee hours of the night after her unsettling encounters with two lords, she determined that if the Marquess of Doreé could not be interrogated, and her sister's fiancé refused to look into the smugglers' activities, she simply must approach Redstone. All the stories painted him as a hero, a lover of justice despite his illegal methods of obtaining it. He put his ship in the line of fire in the Channel during the war three years in a row, without any reward or hope of official recognition from the government. He only stole from the most disreputable, wealthiest English noblemen, and apparently donated the prize money to orphans and war widows. If she could discover a method of putting her case before him, he must agree to help her track down the smugglers and defeat them.

"Diantha wrote to me that the villagers saw the *Cavalier* off the coast just over a fortnight ago," she said.

Davina's peacock feather quivered.

"She did not write it to *me*. It is not true. She must merely be feeding your foolish proclivity for fantastical stories."

Serena chewed upon her lower lip. "John Coachman mentioned he had it in a note from Bess as well." John always told her all the gossip from the servants' quarters and the village. Year ago she had helped his wife, their housekeeper Bess, deliver their first son in a snowstorm. Serena glanced at her father, but his gaze was trained upon his wife. Like an anxious lapdog.

Davina stood. Her heavy perfume twisted into Serena's senses, as always muddling them. After seven years, her stepmother's appearance of cool, disinterested disdain never failed to discompose her.

"Only children and immodest girls find the despicable exploits of pirates of any interest." Davina's delicate nostrils flared like a rutting ram's.

Serena drew in a steadying breath. "And apparently the Earl of Poole." She turned to her father. "Papa, may I go home? I can send John back with the traveling carriage when I arrive."

He looked to his wife, his brow sliced into sections by three long horizontal lines.

"I am now in possession of my fortune, Papa," she added quietly. "If—If you do not allow me the use of the carriage, I will hire one and take myself home that way."

"Insolent girl," Davina hissed. "If you do, you will no longer have a home to return to."

"No." Her father's voice echoed unsteadily across the dining chamber.

Davina's glare snapped to him. "No?"

He addressed Serena. "My children will never be barred from my house. Yes, daughter, you may return to Glenhaven Hall at this time. I will accompany you."

"Thank you, Papa."

"But—"

"I will return the carriage to town," he said to his wife, "and when you and Charity are prepared to return home, dear, Tracy will bring you." He climbed stiffly to his feet. Serena's heart clenched anew for him. For years she had done everything she could to assure he would never be obliged to choose between her and his wife. But the stakes were too high now. Habits must change.

"If you wish it, Charles," Davina said, false sweetness dripping from her tongue now. "Naturally I will respect your decision. But it will seem odd to our friends to discover you have fled town so abruptly."

"They will believe I am a happy father. Charity is nearly settled upon Lord Savage," he said, sounding weary again, his shoulders slumped. "Since they all know we came to London to secure a husband for her, they cannot remark upon it."

"When will we leave, Papa?"

"As soon as I speak with Lord Savage. I intend to see him midday. Can you be ready by the time I return?"

"Of course." She rounded the table and reached up to kiss him upon the cheek. "Thank you."

"You are welcome, daughter." But his sad eyes did not convey the assurance of his words. Serena gave her stepmother wide berth leaving the chamber, as she had done in all matters for years.

* * *

Alex stood at the parlor window facing the green behind the house. The rain of the night before had washed away London's spring haze, and the sun shone clean and inviting. Weeks spent largely indoors after the fresh salt air of the spring cruise had him itching to be upon the coast again. But this swatch of nature tucked between buildings and streets must, for now, suffice.

He glanced once more at the letter in his hand, from his brother.

> *Sailors from the* Osprey *have come ashore again, to the north. The farmers, apparently, are thrown into a panic. Do you wish me to take action? Jinan asks the same. Naturally, we will await your orders. . . .*

His orders. As though his brother were merely one of his sailors or a servant, not a finer man than he himself could ever hope to be. Except for a minute and a half, his twin might be the lord his character deserved, while Alex might have lived a very different life. The life he had wished to live.

"Lord Carlyle," the butler intoned from the doorway.

"Thank you for inviting me to call, my lord," the baron said, crossing the chamber. Alex gestured for him to take a seat upon a sofa whose color he could not have recalled unless he were looking straight at it. After his father's death, he gave his mother and sister free rein to fix up the town house as they saw fit. At the time, he hadn't cared much for anything about any of his properties, only drinking, gambling, and bedding willing women.

The baron sat. About fifty, he was a spare man, thin

of both hair and frame, but intelligent enough in features and address.

"My pleasure," Alex murmured. "My solicitor is reviewing the terms of the contract you offered and will report to me upon it shortly."

Carlyle's pale brows rose. "I admit I anticipated discussing it today."

Alex went to the sideboard. "Brandy?"

"If you will." The baron sat.

Alex proffered a glass to him. He settled into the chair opposite Carlyle and allowed the aroma of the fruited wine to curl into his senses.

"I would like to speak with you about your daughters."

The baron peered at him behind the rim of his glass, then lowered it. A light smile creased his rather ordinary face, barely altering its hangdog look. His eldest daughter had clearly not inherited her animated eyes from him.

"They are a great comfort and joy to me, my lord. I hope you are as fortunate to be blessed with daughters."

"Thank you." He swiveled the crystal once more. "Have you only the two?"

"Four. One still in the schoolroom, the other the nursery."

Alex knew this. He knew a great deal more about Carlyle's family and estate, learned since Aaron first told him of the baron's proposal. What he did not know was how this mouse of a man had hidden an unmarried daughter with a clever tongue and an obvious thirst for adventure in the countryside for so many years.

"Your eldest?" He drew a sip of brandy across his tongue, savoring the rich, ripe flavor. "She is unmarried, I understand."

The baron's pleasant mien faltered.

"Some years ago my daughter decided not to marry."

"Did she? And you allowed it. How unusual."

Carlyle made an uncomfortable gesture with his hand. "You know how women will be, unpredictable and contrary."

"Is she typically contrary, then?"

"Oh, not at all. Serena is quite a good girl."

Not the woman Alex knew her to be. He set down his glass.

"My lord, let us speak plainly, if we may. As you say, I do in fact know women." He rested an even gaze upon the man. "Rather well."

Carlyle's brow creased. "I have heard something of that nature."

"I daresay you have," Alex murmured. "I wonder that nevertheless you have offered your daughter to me."

A gray pallor seeped into Carlyle's cheeks. "Charity is a fine girl, but quiet and attached to her mother. She wishes to remain close to Glenhaven Hall when she marries."

"Hardly sufficient reason to ally her to a man of my habits, especially when you have allowed your eldest daughter to live at home with you unmarried."

Carlyle stood. "My lord, Serena's case is a particular one."

Alex remained seated. "Is it?"

"It is. But more to the point, your tenants hold you in high esteem. They say you are a just and honorable master." He frowned. "A man's private affairs are his own. His public face must determine all other matters."

"Fairly stated." Alex climbed to his feet. "Thank you for clarifying that, Carlyle."

The baron's shoulders seemed to relax. He was withholding the full truth. It didn't matter to Alex. If he were to indeed ever have daughters, he wouldn't give one to a man with a reputation like his, no matter what his tenants claimed.

But he hadn't yet gotten what he wished from this interview.

"May I accompany you home, sir? I am overdue paying a call upon Lady Carlyle."

The baron bowed. "I would be delighted."

Carlyle had ridden horseback, so Alex called for his mount. The baron's town house sat neatly at the edge of a neat square. Without, it was unremarkably like its neighbors, brick and limestone. Within, it was appointed in the latest stare, from crystal chandelier festooned with multicolored glass to servants' formal livery. Seated in the parlor upon a chair upholstered in Egyptian silk, in a gown of red stripes with a trio of feathers jutting from her carefully arranged coiffure, Lady Carlyle appeared the picture of London style. She stood, her daughter beside her coming to her feet as well. Miss Lucas's pale cheeks flared with color.

"Dear Lord Savege," Lady Carlyle cooed, "what a lovely surprise. We wondered when we would see you next."

Alex bowed. "Good day, ladies." Aside from the two women, the chamber was empty. Disappointment stirred in his chest. He tried to shrug it off, but it clung.

He turned his most charming smile upon the girl. "I am glad to find you at home, Miss Lucas."

"My lord." She ducked another curtsy. Her hands clenched together, knuckles white. She was a taking little thing, pink and white and gold, appealingly rounded, with a demure air. A decade ago she might have appealed to him. Now her beauty inspired little but mild appreciation. She lacked *animation*.

"We are ever so glad to be at home to receive you,

my lord," Lady Carlyle said. "We are quite at our ease at this hour, but Lady Sefton expects us later. She is throwing a supper party and wishes my consultation upon the place markers. I would never claim it myself, of course, but there are those who say my taste rivals the Prince Regent's."

Alex nodded, the torpor of ennui threatening already.

"Before your visit to Lady Sefton, Miss Lucas, may I beg the honor of taking you and your sister up in my carriage for a circle through the park?"

The girl's eyes went round. Her rosebud lips seemed to quiver.

"Thank you, my lord," her mother replied. "My eldest daughter is not able to accept, but Charity may take along her maid for a chaperone instead of her sister."

The idea of Serena Carlyle in the mode of a chaperone stirred a frisson of humor in Alex.

"Is your sister otherwise engaged?" he asked, directing his words toward the girl.

"She is packing to go home today, my lord," she peeped.

Alex might have been astounded at the number of words the beauty uttered all at once if the keen prick of renewed disappointment did not distract him. Irritation followed. He shouldn't give a damn if the troublesome chit was returning to Devon.

"So soon? Is everything well with your younger siblings?" he asked.

"My stepdaughter is not fond of town, but keeps to the country whenever she may," Lady Carlyle said.

"Then you are all leaving?"

"My husband will convey her to Devon. We remain, of course, until the season's end." She waved it away.

"Charity, you may go change now. Do not keep Lord Savege waiting."

The girl dropped a quick curtsy, barely meeting Alex's gaze, and hurried from the chamber.

"My lady, I fear it momentarily deserted me that I came here upon my horse." A prickle of unease skidded across his shoulders. Nothing momentarily deserted him. "I shall take my leave now, but will return shortly with my carriage."

"Certainly, my lord." She saw him to the door. Alex mounted and set off for his house with the disconcerting suspicion sliding into his chest that matters had not just proceeded as he'd planned them. Or, rather, as he had vaguely hoped them to proceed. He hadn't actually had a plan. He had simply followed Carlyle home in order to catch a few words of chaperoned conversation with an unfashionable, troublesome spinster with a pair of mismatched, speaking eyes and alluringly animated lips.

The wealthy, libertine Earl of Savege, perpetually successful at the gaming tables as well as upon the sea as a pirate captain, had embarked upon a project—albeit a modest one: to see a woman—without a carefully crafted plan. Without any rational thought at all, it seemed. Without even acknowledging to himself beforehand how that was his intention.

Bemused, he reached home and called for his carriage.

He drove Miss Lucas about the park in the heaviest crush of the afternoon promenade. He greeted his friends—only those that suited a modest maiden's acquaintance; the others he nodded to at a distance. He conveyed the girl home and told her he enjoyed her company, although he wasn't certain if either of them uttered a word to the other the entire ride, winning a doe-eyed stare before he took his leave. Then he drove to his club, ordered a bottle of brandy, and began drinking.

At the end of the bottle and the evening, drawing away from the fragrant embrace of a stunning redhead, he was no closer to understanding his unprecedented preoccupation. In the foyer of her luxurious town house, he took up his hat and walking stick.

"You came all the way here only to give me a chaste kiss good night, Savege?" the fiery-haired widow purred from her parlor doorway. Her tissue thin gown slipped from her shoulder, revealing a sensual expanse of lily-white bosom, the rouged aureole peeking above the edge of her corset. "Are you certain you wish to leave so soon?"

No. Absolutely not.

"Regrettably, madam." He bowed and went out into the late spring night. Carriage wheels and horse hooves sounded at a distance, a Charley whistled at the opposite end of the block as he made his rounds, and the air hovered with midnight mist.

Perhaps, finally, the sea had gotten to him like it did to so many sailors. He had gone mad.

Or Miss Serena Carlyle had.

She must be returning to Devon in pursuit of the *Osprey*. Why else would she leave London so precipitously after her aborted attempt to speak with Doreé? But perhaps she had planned to return home in the midst of the season all along. He knew nothing of her, after all, only that her misguided determination to halt the smugglers had preyed upon his attention all day. And that he could not seem to wash the scent of her skin or the taste of her lips from his memory.

He wanted nothing to do with smugglers. Being neither ally nor enemy, they were not his concern. By damn, he would have peace and permanent rustication and a pretty little mouse of a wife who would give him an excuse to finally claim those, without suffering any guilt over having what his brother could never have because he wouldn't have it either. Happiness. But at least this farce of a double life would finally be over.

Brain still muzzled with brandy, Alex fell into bed in the certain conviction that he could not have chosen a better bride had he done so himself.

He awoke before dawn with a thick head and a hollow presentiment of doom echoing in the pit of his stomach. He rose, dressed, and called for coffee and his valet.

"Yes, my lord?"

"Order my traveling coach, Tubbs, and pack my personal effects." Alex pulled on his top boots. "We are going home."

Chapter 6

Not much longer shall he be absent from his
*   own native land,*
no, not though bonds of iron hold him.

—HOMER, ODYSSEY

Glenhaven Hall sat upon a rise a half mile inland from the coast, surrounded by thickets of ash, spruce, elm, and nut trees. Its roof of Welsh slate, broad windows, and modest turrets springing from pale Devonshire limestone walls gave it the look of a surprised old man with unkempt hair.

Serena adored it. Her happiest memories revolved around this place—tumbling down the steep hillside with Viola, John Coachman teaching her how to ride her pony, her mother weaving cornflowers through hers and Viola's hair while they picnicked beneath the oak just beyond the sprawling garden. She loved the half-mile walk to the craggy coast, and along the path to the village running past sheep fields and berry hedges. She loved the scent of the ocean always in her nostrils, violent summer storms and their brilliant aftermaths, long winter nights when the sea wind howled and stole into crevices so a person had to burrow beneath layers of goose-down blankets to find warmth.

Savege Park must be something like Glenhaven Hall.

Treading the curving path down from Glenhaven's rose garden toward the village, a basket of freshly cut buds hung upon one elbow and a ruined bonnet upon the other, Serena rued how fate had not dealt her stepsister a fair hand.

Charity feared storms, disliked the ocean, and shied from drama. She deserved a cozy cottage somewhere in the middle of England and a kind, gentle man—perhaps a mere Mister—entirely devoted to her comfort. Instead she was to be mistress of a splendid, centuries-old castle overlooking one of Devon's most spectacular cliffs, and married to a rake who had no qualms about kissing his betrothed's sister senseless, and while in the very same house as her, no less.

Reaching the village behind the vine-trellised parish church, Serena let herself through the churchyard gate and headed toward the milliner's shop.

"Good afternoon, Mrs. Hatchet." She entered, setting the basket of flowers atop a counter. "I brought you the Hall's first roses."

Glen Village's proudest gossip bustled from the rear room, a smile upon her cherubic face.

"Oh, Miss Carlyle, you do spoil me." The woman beamed, taking up the buds and hugging them to her ample chest. "I knew we'd see you soon as the blacksmith mentioned he saw milord's coach coming 'round when he was out at the Martin farm fixing that old nag's shoes again. For the third time this month, if I'm a day old. Oh, what pretty flowers these are. You shouldn't have, but you know how I love them."

"I have a bonnet in sore need of mending." Serena proffered the hat.

"Dear me, isn't it covered in dust?"

"I haven't worn it quite awhile, I suppose." At least four years, and she did not particularly care for it. But she needed an excuse to linger after delivering the roses. "Tell me the news since I have been away, Mrs. Hatchet. What has everyone in the village been talking about lately?"

"The vicar has taken it into his head that we should all be praying the Twenty-first psalm each Sunday, so he attaches it to the beginning of the service and refuses to begin until everyone is present and seated."

"Good heavens. How singular of him," Serena laughed.

"And that blacksmith has finally come around to asking Phoebe Martin to tie the knot. Probably why that nag needs so many new shoes."

"That is lovely news. Weddings are always happy occasions." Except between innocent maidens and rapacious earls. "I shall ask my father to supply a lamb for the celebration."

"Of course you will. If it weren't for you still residing at the Hall, we here in the village wouldn't see a jot of—" She caught her tongue. "Oh, but I shouldn't say such a thing, miss. I'll be begging your pardon." Her fingers fidgeted upon the bonnet ribbons.

"Don't think a thing about it, Mrs. Hatchet."

"You are a peach, miss. That's what I was telling those sailors the other day that stopped in for pretties for their girls back home."

"Sailors?" Serena's heart skipped. "In this shop?"

"Right nice young fellows they were too. One of them only a boy, but he knew the difference between grosgrain and chiffon. For his sweet mother, he said. They went off to the pub after that and Mr. Cobb said they were proper as priests and drank only as much as a farmer and no more."

"Good heavens, how astounding. They were not from the smuggling ship, were they?" Let them not be. Let them be—

"Not at all. Don't you know, the *Cavalier's* been seen nearby again. They were Captain Redstone's boys. Fine fellows, all of them, I'm not shy to say, miss. These two chose nice gifts, paid in coin like respectable folk, and went on their way with as pleasant a 'Good day to you' as any gentlemen I've met."

Nervous anticipation shivered through Serena. Redstone was close.

"Well this is wonderfully diverting, isn't it?" She smiled, hiding her excitement. "Are they still nearby, do you know? When did they come to the village?"

"Must have been a fortnight ago. More's the pity they haven't returned, such a nice boy that one. The other called him Billy." The milliner smiled in a motherly fashion then tut-tutted, studying the bonnet now with a careful eye. "Will you be wishing the brim cut? This one won't be saved, I'm afraid. And what color will you like for ribbons, miss? Blue and purple?" She glanced at Serena's eyes, one after the other.

"Oh, whatever you think best. Mrs. Hatchet, did the sailors mention whether they planned to remain in this neighborhood for long?"

"No, but I'll tell you I was so flabbergasted to have them in my shop at all, I didn't think to ask. Perhaps they mentioned something to Mr. Cobb."

Serena's glee fizzled. She couldn't very well walk into the pub unattended and interrogate the proprietor on the spot. Perhaps she could speak with him at church in the morning. It seemed ages away.

She thanked the milliner and made her way toward the church along the short stretch of the main street, mucky from the light rain that had fallen the previous day and left the sky sparkling now. The vicar's wife may well have heard a tidbit or two at the pub that Mrs. Hatchet hadn't gotten hold of yet. The vicar liked his ale as well as the next man. Sometimes Serena could smell it from the Carlyle pew in the first row.

At the rectory, the vicar's wife invited her in for tea. Serena demurred, claiming weariness from the journey, and asked after her husband.

"He went to the pub earlier, Miss Carlyle. But he likes to fix up the church for service before dinner. He may be there already."

Serena went around to the front of the church and inside, the heavy wooden door propped open, late afternoon sunlight spilling through the entrance. Within, wood gleamed, glass sparkled, and limestone shone with warm invitation. But she found no vicar. Still at his ale, no doubt.

Tomorrow after services it must be, then.

Sighing lightly, she wandered along the center aisle. As a child she had sat in that front pew inventing stories about tiny creatures—part mice, part elves—who lived in the mezzanine level she longed to explore. Later, when her imagination took a more mature turn, as the vicar's monotone wafted over her she envisioned the medieval church filled with ladies in sparkling diadems and knights with their gem-inlaid swords strapped to their sides, kneeling upon the bare stone floor and praying with the unshakable faith of folk of that era. Then, when the mass ended, they would feast.

Serena had imagined.

She had dreamt.

And when Lord Robert Bailey came home with Tracy during a holiday from university, she wove him into her fantasies, making of him something he was most definitely not. Since then she had been paying the consequences for that foolishness.

It was a great good thing she was no longer such a silly girl.

* * *

Alex stepped into the narthex of the little Romanesque church and came up short.

She stood in the midst of amber rays entering through the window above. The heavy stone divided the setting sun's blaze into narrow fingers, and yet the light seemed to seek her, attaching to her skin, tangling in her hair as though it wanted no other place to rest. With her face lifted, gaze upon some heavenly target, her profile was quite clearly visible, pure and clean from brow to chin. Her neck, unencumbered by the ruffled nonsense she'd worn before, stretched long and smooth to straight shoulders thrown back in an erect posture, her breasts tilted ever so slightly upward, the fall of her gown gentle over curved hips. A wide-brimmed straw hat dangled from her slender fingers, its ribbons tripping upon the floor.

Alex moved across the threshold and stumbled over his feet. The scuffle echoed through the nave.

Her gaze flew to him, her mouth opening in a surprised O that sent sudden heat into his groin.

"Lord Savage," she exclaimed, and turned fully about to face him. A nonplussed expression lit her eyes. "My sister is not here. She is in London. Why aren't you?"

He advanced into the church with greater care now.

"Thank you for that elegant welcome, madam. I feel quite at home already."

"Oh." She seemed to recall herself and curtsied. "Good day, sir." Her brow screwed up and she peered at him with unashamed perplexity. "I thought you still in town."

"I have business to attend to here." Business in the shape of a woman he could not seem to get out of his head. A woman who looked a great deal prettier with her long straight hair swept into a simple knot, and wearing an unadorned jewel-hued gown, despite its mud-stained hem. Quite pretty, in point of fact.

She cocked her head and the sunlight danced upon her hair and in her extraordinary eyes.

Perhaps, in fact, not merely quite pretty.

"I see," she said without any other indication that she did. "No doubt you have come over to speak with my father. He is with his steward about the estate."

Rather than lie, Alex bowed. "Your groom informed me of your whereabouts."

"Then you saw me enter the church?"

"Just so, ma'am. I hope I have not disturbed you at prayer."

"Oh, I am fairly certain you know you have not." She smiled, an impish curve of her generous lips that sent fingers of warmth again into a place that the barely clad widow three nights earlier had not roused in the least. Alex dragged his gaze back to her eyes. They smiled as well, but quietly, as though unaccustomed to sharing mirth with another.

"Have you finished here, then?" he said, his cravat rather snug, not to mention his breeches.

She nodded. He extended his arm. She did not take it.

"My lord." A crease of skepticism appeared between her winged brows. "Isn't this rather awkward?"

"I can safely say, madam, that I have never received that response from a lady to whom I have offered merely the use of my arm."

She half grinned. "There is a first time for—"

"Everything. Yes, you said that before. You were wrong upon that occasion, however."

She laughed, an unexpected full ripple of amusement, brief but thoroughly honest.

"Is this how it will be, then?" she asked, placing her hand lightly upon his arm. "You will tease me and I will pretend you have not offended me horridly? But I suppose that is the regular run of things for sisters and brothers, which we are to be soon enough." Her fingers tightened upon his sleeve for an instant and her gaze flickered to his then away again too rapidly.

Not so honest, then.

If this woman considered him in a brotherly light, he would eat his hat.

He guided her from the church. The scents of rain-damp street and mutton pie baking at the pub settled upon him. He never tired of the aromas of life upon land, of comfortable, simple terrestrial habitation. Much as he never tired of pitch-sealed planking beneath his boots balanced against the rolling sea. As in all things, he was a man split.

"Did you come by the path from the rose garden, my lord?"

"I did, indeed. And a charming descent it was."

"Do you really think so? I would have thought you far too sophisticated for that sort of rustic diversion."

"I am full of surprises, it seems."

"It is the quickest route to the Hall, and your boots are already dirtied. Would you mind returning by the same route?"

"Not with such a companion upon my arm."

"Oh, no," she said, drawing away from him. "The path is too rough and narrow here." She set off before him. Alex was on the verge of arguing the point. Then she stepped up the stair to the churchyard gate, allowing him a fine view of her enticing backside. He acquiesced silently.

"What has brought you back to the country in the midst of the season in town, Miss Carlyle?"

She halted, turned to him and placed her hands upon her hips.

"You won't like the reason and I should not tell you."

Unexpected. She never did or said what he anticipated. In that way, she was a great deal like ocean wind.

"Then do not, madam. I shouldn't like to disappoint you already."

"Already?" She looked as though she wished to laugh. Then she sobered and started up the path again. "I have come home to stop the smugglers from plaguing our coast. I am determined to do so, with or without assistance from you and my father."

Just as he'd guessed. The path widened and he came abreast of her. Butterflies and bees and motes of late day sunshine busied the warm air, the grass knee-high and berry hedges wild to either side of the path. She looked perfectly at home, a country maid on a country path.

Alex had bedded duchesses and diamonds, seduced courtesans and *contessas*. But he had never seen anything as lovely as Miss Serena Carlyle at the present moment. He stared, realized he was staring, and made himself speak.

"You have appealed to your father and he rejected your request for aid?"

"He says they bring valuable goods to the coast and do not harm anyone." She took her full lower lip between her teeth. "But I know differently."

"And how do you propose to discourage them single-handedly?"

"I do not. I intend to contact the *Cavalier*. I am persuaded Captain Redstone will help me if I make my case convincingly enough."

Alex hid his astonishment behind smooth tones. "Redstone? That ridiculous pirate?"

"Yes. I daresay you think I am foolish."

"I think you don't have any notion of what your plan entails." None, whatsoever. Imagining her upon his ship, amidst the rough men of his crew, Alex's heart beat unaccountably hard.

"I may not, but I haven't any alternative, have I?"

"You could forget about the smugglers and focus your attentions upon more pleasing endeavors."

They reached the edge of the gardens. She turned to him, surrounded by green and riotous blossoms, a question in her speaking eyes. Alex could not resist the temptation, and he had absolutely no reason to. He was not betrothed to her stepsister, nor had he any intention to be now. Even scoundrels had their limits.

He stepped close.

Her eyes widened as she tilted her head back to meet his gaze. "By that, you do not mean endeavors such as helping my sister plan her wedding, do you?" Her voice quavered. A gentle flush stole into her smooth cheeks.

"One would be unwise, Miss Carlyle, to labor at plans for an event that will not come to pass."

Her lips parted upon a tiny exhalation. "An event that will not involve *you*, that is?"

"Clever girl," he murmured.

"I am not a girl. Not by many years."

He lifted a hand and stroked her velvety pinkened skin with a fingertip. "Perhaps not. But you blush like one."

She drew in a quick breath and backed away. "But, my stepsister will—"

"Find a suitable groom. As you said, she is an incomparable, and well dowered."

Ivory brow slightly drawn, she stared at him for a long moment during which the breeze stirred strands of honeyed hair against her cheek. She brushed it away, but her studying gaze did not waver.

Abruptly she turned and started through the garden. "The milliner said sailors from the *Cavalier* came into the village a fortnight ago." She spoke somewhat quickly. "They were extraordinarily well behaved, Mrs. Hatchet assured me."

They better have been. "The milliner's name is *Hat*chet?"

The corner of her mouth twitched, irrepressible. "I once thought that was amusing too. When I was still in the nursery."

Alex smiled. "Now I am to understand you think me immature as well as unpredictable and unprincipled?"

"I never said you were unpredictable."

"Ah. But unprincipled stands."

"Well." Her gaze remained pinned upon the house ahead. "You are."

"But I do have principles, Miss Carlyle. They are merely different from yours."

She halted once more, setting an uncertain gaze upon him. "I wonder."

For the first time in his life with a woman, Alex's mouth went dry.

Hoofbeats sounded at a distance, the clatter of heavy carriage wheels accompanying them. A traveling coach appeared upon the drive from beyond the tree line.

"Oh," she said, her brows lifting.

"Are you expecting visitors?" Damned inconvenient interlopers.

"It is my stepbrother's carriage. But he had intended to remain in town until my stepmother wished to return. That must mean, my lord," she turned to him, "that my stepsister is home." She smiled, an uneven curve of lovely lips, but in her eyes the question lingered.

She continued toward the house with a quick step, as though relieved to be going. Unaccustomed to allowing anyone else the lead in anything he did, Alex could only follow.

Chapter 7

I have a house, and I have some land,
and I have a daughter that shall be at your
command.

—"Turkish Revelry"

Serena greeted her family in mixed relief and consternation. A less dramatic excuse to escape the earl's warm gaze and suggestive words would have sufficed. Her time without Davina had been too brief. But perhaps this was to be her punishment for being such a wretched sister.

"It's good to see you here, my lord," Tracy said, shaking his hand.

"Forgive me for intruding upon your homecoming," the earl replied.

Davina swept out of the carriage.

"Lord Savege, how kind you are to welcome us home." She offered her fingers in a grand gesture so that he was obliged to bow over them. Tracy handed Charity out of the carriage. With marked pallor, she curtsied, not meeting the earl's gaze.

"Miss Lucas." He offered her a gentle smile. Charity's lips looked gray, her eyes wide as china blue saucers.

Serena linked arms with her. "Come, darling, you

must be fagged from the journey. We will go inside and have a cup of tea."

"Charity, remain here," Davina said down the length of her straight nose. "Serena, go ahead of us and command Bess to have tea laid out in the green parlor at once. My lord, I hope you will join us for dinner."

"Thank you, ma'am, but I am expected at home shortly. I must take my leave of you now."

Davina's face drooped into a pout. "We are devastated to lose your company so soon, my lord. Do come inside for a cup of tea while the coachman fetches your carriage."

"I came upon horseback, and as we are in the country now, I'm well able to find the beast myself," he said pleasantly, bowed to all and strode away toward the stable.

"Come, Charity," her mother sniffed. "This sea air will ruin your complexion."

Serena squeezed her sister's arm and released her, glancing back toward the earl's retreating form.

"Well, that's a surprise, to meet with the fellow here when we aren't even in residence," Tracy said. "Not all of us, at least. Must've come over to speak with your father about the settlement. Something pressing, I suppose."

"He said he has business to attend to here." She could not believe the earl's astonishing suggestion that there would be no wedding—not without greater confirmation. He was a rake, and he had met with her father in town the very day they left it, to discuss the contract. "But what are you doing home already?"

"Last night at the club I heard Savege had decamped to the Park. Mama wouldn't have anything for it but to hound him down." He grinned ruefully. "She's determined nothing will stand in the way of Charity's advancement."

"Oh. Naturally."

"Ain't nothing natural about it, haring off to the country before the season's out. I saw you in the garden as we came up the drive. The two of you taking a stroll?"

"I was cutting roses. Papa was engaged." The unsettling intimacy of the meeting in the church and walk up the path closed her lips upon the entire truth.

"Seems like a good enough fellow to wander about in the garden with you while waiting. What do you think of him now?"

Serena chewed upon her lip. "I wonder if Charity can like him."

"Do you like him?"

"I hardly know." Her skin heated when he touched her, all the way through her blood to her marrow. That wasn't liking, though. It was sheer Judas wickedness.

"Well, he's to be family, so you'd better get to liking him if you don't." Tracy's voice quieted. "I've never seen her so determined. Do you think he meant to hint at his disinterest by leaving town so abruptly like that?"

"I don't think the Earl of Savege hints about anything, Tracy. If he does not want Charity, I have no doubt he will say so to Papa directly."

"Still, I'll wager we'll have a wedding before the summer's out if Mother has any say in it."

Serena entered the house and searched out the housekeeper. Bess stood before the linen closet in the corridor, chewing upon her fingertips.

"My stepmother and Charity have returned, Bess. Sir Tracy as well. We must make up their rooms at once." She reached into the cabinet for the best bed linens. Bess snatched them from her arms.

"Now don't you go pretending you don't have other matters to be about, Miss Serena. The maid will help me with this. But if you want to be helping, you might tell

John I've need of the stable boy to run down to the village and fetch me a brace of capons and a bag of beans from Mrs. Cobb. Lady Carlyle has got to have her beans and I've none in the pantry and no hope of them till market on Wednesday," she grumbled between closed lips, "not knowing she was coming home so abruptly like, chasing after earls and such."

"Good heavens, news travels quickly in this house." Serena paused. "And in the village as well. Bess, Mrs. Hatchet told me that sailors from the *Cavalier* recently came to the village. Do you know anything about that?"

The housekeeper pursed her thin lips.

"Now why would you be minding the back and forth of common sailors, miss? They haven't anything to do with a lady."

"I am not so much interested in the common sailors as in their captain. I wish to send him a message but I haven't a notion as to how I might do so."

"Lord, that's worse! Miss Serena, you stay clear of that Redstone. For all he's a good one, pirates are a nasty lot. They can't be trusted."

"Bess, you have lived your entire life in and around Glen Village. How on earth can you know anything about pirates?"

The housekeeper gave her a grim look. "I know what I know, ma'am. A lady's virtue isn't safe with the likes of that man."

"I haven't any desire to actually meet with him, only to send him a message. But I must know it will reach him."

A queer light stole into Bess's eyes. She turned toward the cabinet.

"Don't go mixing up with pirates, miss. You'll find yourself in boiling saltwater."

"Thank you for that advice." Serena headed toward

the stable. But by the time she returned from her task, frustration had gathered in her, and she was feeling rather foolish for having dashed all the way back to Devon without a plan. How on earth could she communicate her purpose to Redstone if she did not know how to find him?

She spent the remainder of the evening stewing upon her futile intentions. Davina rhapsodized about Lord Savege's magnanimity in calling upon them immediately upon their return, Charity said and ate practically nothing, and Tracy and her father spoke of the shooting to be had after a month away from the best coveys. No message came from Savege Park calling off contract negotiations, or even indicating that the earl would call upon her father soon. Serena's skepticism had been justified. Rakes would be rakes.

Before she climbed into her down-covered bed, she went to the window and opened the sash wide. The air was warm and damp, tinged with brine. She drew it into her lungs and wished that imagining a pirate standing before her could actually produce one.

By all accounts Redstone was not terribly old, quite fierce, and a thoroughly horrid character. His pursuits spanned the Atlantic, from the waters of the West Indies in which a decade earlier he had harried rich planters, to the Channel where more lately he bested a good number of French men-of-war before Bonaparte finally met his just deserts. The pirate had killed any number of men, and if rumor were to be believed, each one an actual villain. He left innocents alive and released cargo and ships he did not absolutely require back to their owners.

Redstone, captain of the swift and crafty *Cavalier*, was a figure of pure fantasy. But he was also a real enough man. He must have some residence upon land, or at least a dock where he frequently berthed.

Serena fell asleep exasperated and awoke much the same. After church she spoke with both the pub master and the vicar, neither of whom had anything useful to say concerning the sailors. The vicar, however, noted that he had it upon excellent authority that another donation had been made to the orphans' asylum in Exmoor, as well as to the home for soldiers' widows in Bideford. Mrs. Hatchet added her two cents to the exchange, a handful of other villagers joined the conversation, and soon all were trading self-congratulatory stories about how Redstone had chosen for three years in a row now to make berth upon the north Devon coast, as though he liked it better than anywhere else in the world.

A good number of folk, apparently, had seen the *Cavalier* several weeks earlier, close to shore—or claimed it was the pirate ship. That not one of them considered taking out a boat and following the vessel to learn which inlet or cove it dropped anchor in frankly astounded Serena.

But she hadn't ever cared for those details before either. The locals were proud to be important to Redstone, and the authorities had not yet come looking for him due no doubt to the aid he gave in the war.

Serena pursed her lips, climbing into the carriage. Everyone knew of him but no one had ever set eyes upon him. He was more ephemeral than a ghost. In comparison, the Earl of Savege, thoroughly disinterested in the smugglers, seemed a much more likely potential ally. At least she knew she would see him again, and when she did, she could argue her case.

The thought of sharing sufficient privacy to do so

sent nerves through her belly. She tamped them down and forcibly brought to mind her sister's innocent face. Then for good measure she conjured up the scoundrel to whom she had so naïvely given her maidenhead and who immediately thereafter married another girl.

Rakes, like pirates, were not to be trusted.

"Ah," Davina said in sharp delight as they entered the house, brandishing an embossed card. "It is an invitation from Lord Savege. He is to hold an open house in the grand style." She beamed and turned to Serena's father. "Do you see, Charles? I knew the moment he saw Charity's beauty and charm he would be grateful you approached him."

"An open house, Mother?" Tracy peered over her shoulder.

"All the county is invited, with an al fresco luncheon and gifts for the gentry and farmers alike. No doubt he wishes to present his betrothed to the country." She petted Charity's cheek.

"She is not yet his betrothed, dear," Serena's father said. "He has not agreed to the terms."

"Hasn't asked her to marry him either," Tracy interjected with a wink at Serena.

"He will not until he is satisfied with the agreement, of course," Lord Carlyle replied.

"Certainly taking his time about it," Tracy added. Serena's gaze darted to her father. He was looking at Charity thoughtfully.

Her stepsister's cheeks colored and her eyes lowered. "I am sorry, Papa. Perhaps he does not like me."

"Of course he likes you," Davina clipped. "You are young and virtuous and beautiful."

"I have little conversation," she mumbled.

"A woman needn't have conversation to appeal to a gentleman," Davina pronounced.

Or an identity, apparently, Serena considered. At least not initially.

She turned toward the stair. She would ask the earl for his assistance at the open house. He might be disinterested now, but he could not hold fast against her plea when she told him her story. Any man with an ounce of compassion, not to mention care for his dependents, must agree with her reasoning.

Except her father. She glanced back into the foyer, but he had already retreated to his study, to his plants and fossils and books of nature, all that seemed to truly interest him now. Since her mother's death he was a shadow of a man. Davina's rule at Glenhaven Hall only served to sink him further into retirement. Sometimes when the fog rolled over the coast, Serena imagined that if her father were to go out in it, he would simply vanish—as Viola had—the daughter he never spoke of, as though she had not existed, as though he had not loved her so well as Serena knew he had. Loved her as he had loved his first wife. The loss of them both at once had broken him.

She climbed to her bedchamber, went to her writing table, and dipped her quill into the inkpot.

Dear Captain Redstone,

We have never made one another's acquaintance, but I have the imperative need to speak with you concerning a topic of great importance.

Her pen faltered. Of course they had never made one another's acquaintance, and needs that required hasty introductions were always imperative. She crumbled the foolscap and began again.

A scratch came at the door.

"Serena," Charity whispered at the crack. "Are you at leisure?"

"Come in." Serena released a frustrated sigh and covered her work. Charity entered, her eyes awash in unshed tears, fingers twisted together.

"Dearest," Serena exclaimed, and moved to her. "Your hands are frigid. Whatever is the matter?"

Charity's exquisite face crumpled and the tears descended.

"Oh, sister, I am so unhappy."

Serena drew her to the bed and reached for a lace kerchief.

"Dear me, darling. Don't cry, we will discover a solution to whatever distresses you. I promise it."

The blue eyes opened wide, streaked with red.

"Then you will break your promise, for there is no solution to be found. Mama is set upon it. I may not escape my fate." The tears flowed. Her tapered shoulders shook upon a delicate sob.

Serena's stomach did an odd turn about.

"What fate is that, darling?"

"M-M-Marriage," she whimpered. "To *him*."

"To Lord Savege."

Charity sobbed harder. Serena patted her sister's hands and chewed upon her lip. Perhaps her stepsister knew more of the earl's reputation than she had assumed.

"I see," she murmured, caught between the inevitable will of Davina and her knowledge of a certain rake. "But whyever, Chare? I should think being the Countess of Savege would be a lovely thing." She scrabbled to find reasons her sister could appreciate. "You will have a luxurious dressing chamber and private parlor, no doubt, decorated precisely in the manner you would like. And your hothouses will produce fruits and flowers all year long." This was ridiculous. "Then of course there are the gardens, so pleasant to stroll in. Also, the housekeeper at the Park, Mrs. Tubbs, is an unexceptionable person, and you know she is our own John Coachman's sister. She is wonderfully friendly and competent, and not at all a gorgon as one sometimes hears of in great houses. You would never have to do a thing to keep the place in fine condition, for I suspect she would do it all for you."

"But I do not wish a large dressing chamber or garden. I could be happy with a modest compartment and a small garden. And—And—" She buried her face in the lace. "I will have to be *his* wife!"

Serena wrapped an arm about Charity's shoulders and drew her head upon her breast.

"Yes. But I daresay that would be quite nice." Thrilling, if he kissed her the way he kissed strange women in darkened parlors. Serena's stomach turned again, this time with nausea. She forged on. "He is quite handsome and has such a gentlemanly address," when he was not teasing inappropriately and making otherwise unsubstantiated statements. "And—"

Charity's head popped up, her eyes fraught with distress.

"He frightens me, Serena. Terribly. I am barely able to breathe when I meet him."

Serena had that same reaction. She wished fear caused it.

"He frightens you? Whatever for, dearest?"

Charity shook her head. "I wish it were not so. I want so very much to please Mama, and Papa too. But—But— When he speaks to me, I—" She dissolved into crying once more, the sobs coming harder now as her emotions seemed to gain momentum. "There is no hope."

"Of course there is hope. You must simply come to know him better and you will see that he is all that is amiable." And each sunset as the moon rose, the cows in the pasture leapt into the sky and flew over the silvery crescent.

Except that he *was* amiable. To Serena's misguided sense of amiability. Distractingly so.

This was impossible. But in seven years no one at Glenhaven Hall had thwarted Davina's will—not Charity, Tracy, or her husband. And the second Lady Carlyle had the bit between her teeth now.

Charity sniffled. "He is not amiable."

"Darling," Serena tilted her head. "May I venture to suggest something of a delicate nature?"

Charity nodded, dabbing at her watery nose with the soaked lace. Serena handed her a fresh linen.

"Is it possible that your fear of Lord Savege springs not from him, in particular, but rather from a trepidation over marriage?"

Charity's face went blank.

Oh, good heavens, hadn't Davina told her yet about a wife's intimate duties to her husband?

"What I mean to say is—"

"I am not afraid of gentlemen, if that is what you think," Charity said shakily.

"You aren't?"

Charity shook her head. "I danced a quadrille with Mr. Markham at Lady Godson's ball last week and did not mind his company in the least," she stated as though that were all the evidence Serena could possibly wish to prove the truth of her assertion.

"Mr. Markham?"

"Oh, yes. And a fortnight ago Mama allowed me

to drive in the park with Sir Peter Pickford. I enjoyed it very much. It was nothing like that drive with—with—" She stuttered into weeping again.

Serena stroked her arm. "I see. What do you think, then, makes Lord Savege different from those other gentlemen?" Perhaps that he breathed sensuality and laughter at once. Or that he looked at a woman as though he could read her thoughts, and touched her as though he knew precisely where it would wreak the most havoc within her.

"He is so large," Charity whispered. "And—And—frightening."

"Yes, dear. We have covered that already."

"He is not anything like his brother. I thought he might be. But he is not."

"His brother? Are you acquainted with Mr. Savege?"

"He paid a call last summer while you were at your aunt's home in York, to ask Papa some matter of business." She wiped her nose and her brow relaxed. "He was quite gentlemanly. Mama had gone shopping for the day to Clovelley, and when Mr. Savege saw that my hands shook as they do sometimes when I meet with strangers, he offered to pour the tea. He told me of how he learnt to do it in the West Indies when he was a boy because at his uncle's house there were no ladies, so the housekeeper taught him." She smiled, then her pleasure faded. "I hoped the earl would be like him, but they are not alike in the least."

"I daresay." Serena tried to imagine Lord Savege pouring tea and nearly laughed aloud.

Charity's shoulders shuddered and she dropped her face into her hands, weeping anew.

"There now," Serena consoled. "You must not ruin your face. My stepmother will be displeased to see you all splotchy at dinner."

"I know, but I cannot help it. I thought of running away." Her eyes held a wild glimmer Serena had never seen before, like a rabbit trapped in its warren by the fox. "But I could not go through with it. I would miss you so, and our sisters. Then I would be forced to work as a governess or lady's maid, I think, and I do not believe I would like that very much at all."

"No doubt."

"So, you see, I must marry him." Her tapered shoulders drooped in thorough despair. Serena watched, and her heart began to patter swiftly. Perhaps the earl had not been speaking untruths. Perhaps he did not intend to wed Charity.

She set her jaw and shook her head. "No, sister, you mustn't."

Charity's head shot up. "I mustn't? But—"

"You mustn't. Not if you cannot abide him. That would not do at all. You must simply tell your mother you will not and she will be obliged to accept it."

"I cannot. That is impossible."

"More impossible than marrying a man who terrifies you?"

Charity's tearstained visage crinkled again, but her head bobbed in one pathetic nod.

"She is your mother. She must understand—"

"I cannot. Do not ask it of me."

Serena understood. She had only a mere seven years of Davina's shrewish mothering compared to Charity's eighteen, and was only now beginning to crawl out from beneath the heavy blanket of disapproval and censure.

"Then I shall." She must. It all seemed perfectly clear now. Charity's misery had wiped away the last of her foolish loyalty and dangerous timidity. Davina would not win this battle.

"No!" Charity gripped her fingers. Hers were icy. "Promise me you will not."

"Why not? I am an independent woman now, and she cannot harm me no matter how I displease her."

"I am so glad for it, for I love you very dearly. But if you tell her, she will know you do it out of affection for me."

Serena met her sister's surprisingly aware gaze.

"I understand." She furrowed her brow. "Then we shall simply have to stop Lord Savege from offering for you."

Charity's shoulders drooped. "It *is* hopeless."

"It is not. He has not offered for you yet. Papa seems to think the delay is unusual, and yesterday I—" She bit her tongue. "I agree with Papa. Perhaps the earl will not offer."

"But Mama is convinced."

"Papa is not."

"Tracy is."

"Well, Tracy and your mother may be wrong. We must hope so," and trust in a rakish lord after all. Perhaps. "In the meantime I will think of some method of putting a stick in the spokes if Lord Savege should decide he likes Papa's offer."

"Will you? Serena, you are the most wonderful sister!" Charity clutched her fingers and her eyes shone with gratitude. "When will you begin?"

"The open house at Savege Park on Saturday. I will devise a plan, and if Lord Savege has not come to terms with Papa's offer before then, we will put it in motion. How does that sound?"

"Very good! Thank you. Thank you, dear, dear sister."

Serena smiled, a coil unwinding inside her, the corkscrew of guilt that had spiraled tight the moment she heard the Earl of Savege's voice in a crowded ballroom. A weight seemed to lift, like the world from Atlas's shoulders.

Her sister did not wish to marry him. It did not matter that Davina expected it, or even if contrary to his words in the garden the earl wished it. Serena would halt the alliance. Charity's misery in anticipating the marriage was so extreme that Serena would not feel any guilt in effecting the ruination of it.

She might even enjoy it.

Chapter 8

Stay here in charge of what is yours;
you have no need to suffer ills on the barren sea
and go wandering.

—HOMER, *ODYSSEY*

Alex sat astride his horse at the apex of the hill stretching down in fields of sheep and wheat to the town of Avesbury two miles distant. His steward rode away upon a sturdy cob up the ridge toward the stables.

"And so, brother," Alex said, turning to his twin in the gig beside him, "now that we have finished bringing me up to date on business, I have a mind to head to the Cork and Barrel for a plate of shepherd's pie and some conversation. Care to join me?"

"Conversation with farmers and cobblers?" Aaron grinned fondly. "Won't you have enough of that tomorrow at the open house?"

"It's those damned democratic principles of piracy. They get under a man's skin after too long." He chuckled. "I am famished. Come on along."

"No, I'll pass today." His brother's brow creased and he shifted upon the hard seat. His leg pained him. It always did after a hard rain like the one they'd had the night before, a night Alex had spent largely awake for no good reason, listening in the darkness to the heavy fall of drops upon the window.

He had only been home five days and already noticed a difference in his brother. Aaron seemed sober, even more pensive than usual. Alex suspected the reason, and shied from the certainty of knowing.

"Suit yourself." He pressed his knees into his mount's sides and headed toward town. As boys, he and Aaron had raced this hill to Avesbury a thousand times, upon foot and horseback. Alex usually won, but Aaron had given him hard pursuit. Now, thanks to Lambert Poole and Napoleon Bonaparte, his brother could not run a single step. But the true villain of the piece was Alex.

He rode along cobbled streets between the rows of gray stone houses built along the flanks of the inlet. Reining in before the tavern, he left his horse and a coin with the proprietor's young son. The place was nearly empty of patrons at that late afternoon hour, farmers and artisans finishing their work before dinnertime. A pair of wrinkled ex-soldiers playing chess in a corner tugged their caps. A gentleman sat at the table nearest the entrance to the kitchen, a mug of ale before him. The stranger nodded. Alex returned the gesture and sat by the window.

The proprietor strode in from the back.

"G'day, milord. Pie today? The missus pulled a fresh one from the oven not a quarter hour ago."

"Thank you."

The fellow clunked a tankard upon the rough wooden table. "Everyone's glad to come up to the Park tomorrow, milord. Some's here haven't been in a dozen years, I'd say."

"Then it's high time we opened the doors, isn't it?"

"Yes, sir." The man smiled and retreated to the

kitchen. Alex glanced out the window at the late afternoon sun falling in slanting angles upon the muddied street. He should have opened the Park to the public years earlier. If Aaron were earl, he would have. During all those years when he raised hell through the West Indies and London, Aaron had continually reminded him of the behavior due his consequence as heir, then again after their father died and Alex inherited but continued living as he had before. But Aaron had never chastised him. Lambert Poole took care of that well enough.

When he turned to his ale again, the stranger stood before him.

"My lord, may I join you?"

He spoke with the same Cambridge accent as Alex, but there was a foreign character to his face and the cut of his costly coat. His eyes, a peculiar amber shade, conveyed more than mere civility in the request. They required assent.

The hairs on the back of Alex's neck stood on end. Avesbury did not sit upon his land, but he didn't like men he knew nothing of handing him orders, especially not so near the Park.

He nodded. The gentleman lowered himself to the bench opposite, setting his glass upon the table.

Alex regarded him without expression. "To what do I owe this pleasure, sir?"

The man reached across and offered his hand. "I have been looking forward to making your acquaintance for quite some time, Lord Savege."

Alex took his hand. The stranger's grip was firm, his palm as rough as Alex's despite his appearance of gentility.

"I am afraid you have me at a disadvantage, sir."

"I am Ashford."

Alex's gaze narrowed. The name was familiar. A peer.

The fellow smiled ever so slightly and waved a nonchalant hand.

"Viscount. My seat is in Kent, but I am rarely there, as you are rarely here." He sat back, folding his hands upon his lap in another gesture that bespoke some origin other than England. "I captain a vessel called the *Blackhawk*. Do you know it?"

Alex's muscles tensed. "Why should I?"

"Because your own ship nearly outran it a year ago in the Channel."

For an instant, vertigo spun Alex. Ashford regarded him steadily, his feline eyes glimmering, but not with malice.

"Who are you?" Alex said, his voice lower than he intended.

"Precisely who I have said I am, a man much like yourself who lives his life in several worlds, not all of which are compatible with one another. Did your ship recover quickly enough from the shot we put across her bow, by the by? I didn't like to do it, but we had to shake you. We'd other quarry to track down and no time for courtesies . . ." He paused. " . . . that day."

Of the two ships the *Cavalier* had not managed to outrun in her life, the *Wasp* engaged in activities like his, but entirely for profit. The *Blackhawk* was something much different. When it had run him down that foggy spring morning while the war still raged, he'd been glad to escape with only a nick to a foremast yard and a perforated sail.

"But you have time now?" Alex asked. "A year later? I cannot believe this visit is to proffer an apology."

Ashford chuckled. "No indeed. And in truth, you might have bested us if you'd found us quicker in that fog. The *Cavalier*'s speed is legendary."

The pub master trundled from the kitchen, set a plate of meat and potatoes on the table, and disappeared again. Alex did not touch the fare.

"My lord, why are you here?"

"Ah." Ashford nodded. "As clever as your reputation recommends. You will not ask me how I know you."

"Being a done thing, it seems less relevant than to understand why you have sought me out. Given your revelation of both your name and ship, I suspect you harbor a mistaken notion that I may be trustworthy." Alex hadn't known until this moment the identity of the man who captained the *Blackhawk*, a ship dedicated to hounding down and destroying slaving vessels in the Atlantic. Upon the ocean, Ashford went by another name, just as he did.

"Not so mistaken, I think," Ashford murmured. "We have been watching you for years, you know."

"Have you? And who are 'we'?"

"My associates and I."

"All of you with the same purpose, I suppose?"

"Not entirely." He flicked a speck of lint off his elegantly tailored sleeve. Alex recalled now how he had heard the Viscount of Ashford occasionally spoken of in society. The gossips called him a dandy, even a fop.

The man sitting across from him was anything but. Shrewd intelligence glinted in his unusual eyes, his brow that of a man who had suffered. Each morning at Savege Park, Alex looked at such a face across the breakfast table. But Ashford's slight smile suggested he had left that suffering behind. Unlike Aaron.

"What do you want of me, to turn my ship to the work you do?" He shook his head. "I have no interest in vigilantism of that sort."

"Only the sort that hurts wealthy bloods where it bothers them most?"

"Something like that."

Ashford's gaze did not waver. "I have a proposition for you."

"I suspected as much. But if you know me so well, you know that I am unlikely to take you up on it, whatever it is."

"A smuggling vessel captained by a man named Dunkirk commands this coast of late."

"The *Cavalier* commands this coast."

"And yet its master seems not to understand the danger the *Osprey* poses to his interests. All of his interests."

"By which you mean my estate?" Alex settled back in his seat. "Dunkirk has steered clear of it. He is not so foolish to traffic with a lord. He limits his activities to villages and towns."

"So, you have been watching him."

Alex set a hard stare upon the man. "Your proposition?"

"Find the *Osprey* and sink her."

Alex frowned. "She is a smuggler, not a slaver. Even so, I don't care for that business." He stood. "I am not interested, Ashford."

But Serena Carlyle was.

It seemed like a month since he'd seen her in that church. He had spent the week planning the open house, his mind still wrapped around the peculiarly enchanting woman. But now his worlds seemed to be crashing into one another, the one he sought so eagerly to escape colliding head on with the one he was beginning—for the first time ever—to be able to imagine.

"Regrettably," the viscount said. "You are mistaken, my lord." He came to his feet with catlike grace, his gaze watchful.

Alex's jaw tightened. "A man who tells me I am mistaken had better be able to defend his words," he said with silken calm.

"The *Osprey* has worked in the West Indies for some time now, only coming to these shores a year ago. Her regular cargo is slaves. But lately Dunkirk has taken to smuggling arms."

"For what purpose? The war is ended."

"We cannot be certain, but a noble patron controls Dunkirk's actions. I suspect that patron is near, and I wish to discover him."

"You think the *Osprey* berths here because her patron is close." Alex regarded him steadily. "You do not suspect me."

Ashford shook his head.

"Then why involve me? Take the *Osprey* yourself. Your ship is more than capable of doing so."

"Other matters detain me at this time. But more importantly, this coast belongs to the *Cavalier*, as you have said." The viscount bowed. "Also, I believe it will be to your advantage to become involved."

"Why?"

Ashford stepped back and picked up his hat from the seat. "Consider it, my lord."

"I already have. I gave you my answer."

"Then I must be content with that." He donned his hat. "Good day, Lord Savege."

The pub's door swung shut behind him. Alex looked down at his dinner, his appetite gone now. His hand stole to his waistcoat pocket and he pulled out the letter. He sat, pushed aside the plate, and unfolded the missive.

Dearest Alex,

I hope you are going along well. Mama says she hasn't any idea why you returned to the country so abruptly. I admit I was surprised as well. We miss you dreadfully already and hope you will return soon, and you must bring our brother to town too.

The news since you departed is as to be expected. Mama lost three hundred at whist two nights ago then made it up again the very next evening. She has the most astounding luck. I attended the opera and I have no idea what you see in that faux Italianesse. She is horrid, all hair and bosom and little voice. But I daresay gentlemen do not care a fig about talent.

In other news, Lady Coakley is increasing, despite her estrangement from her husband. Lady March's salon this week was particularly stimulating; Mama won a wager with the countess that Wilberforce would attend, despite all the colonials clamoring that he caused the revolt on Barbados last month with his talk of abolition. The Earl of Poole was present and attempted to speak with me, but I gave him the cut direct. Finally, Emily Vale has lopped off all her hair, renamed herself Athena, and joined the Ladies Regiment. Mama says she is glad I am not of the same peculiar disposition. If only she knew the truth of it, la!

There it all is. I have nothing more of interest to report. Hurry back to London, darling. It is never the same here without you.

Your devoted sister,
Kitty

Alex rubbed his hand over his face. Kitty never wrote to him, and he had barely seen her or their mother during his time in London, despite residence in the same house. Buried in the missive was the real reason for this unusual communication. He could only be glad she hadn't written Aaron about it instead.

Her shame dug as deep as his own. Shame and regret.

If he had not been so thoroughly engrossed in drink, game, and women that year in Barbados, he might have been sober enough to see through Lambert Poole's false courtship. He might even have noticed Kitty's nervous guilt.

Then, when she came to him and Aaron to tell them the truth, he would not have grunted and sank back into his rum with a dismissive wave of his hand. He would not have allowed his brother to demand honor from the cad, only to lose face instead. And when Aaron returned from Poole's plantation a chastised man, Alex would never have cooked up a uniquely original form of retribution.

But even that had not sufficed to cure either of their disjointedness. So when their father died and the shackles of Alex's inheritance clamped about him, he finally told Aaron everything that had burdened his heart since boyhood.

In response, Aaron went off to war.

Off to war for adventure and glory—what Alex had always desired but could never have because his birthright determined his destiny—what Aaron had always abhorred but sought nevertheless, trying to fulfill his brother's dream.

For months now, though, Alex only wanted it over. His love for the sea would never fade, but he no longer wished to hide from his guilt in London or upon the ocean. He didn't give a damn about smugglers, no matter what cargo they carried, and he had no desire to go chasing after slavers. He wanted distraction. A flirtation with a uniquely pretty woman he could not stop thinking about provided that nicely.

But Kitty's letter proved his self-deception. Anger still burned in him alongside the ever-present regret.

Lambert Poole's continued lack of remorse over his behavior with Kitty all those years ago, evidenced by his taunting at the salon, dug at Alex. Jin had warned about Poole's recent interest in the *Cavalier*. The piece in *The Times* the previous week confirmed it. Well settled into government now, and with the war over, Poole could finally pursue his eight-year-old revenge upon his pirate nemesis.

Alex fished a coin from his pocket and deposited it upon the table. The old veterans glanced up from their game, brows creased. He gave them a nod and left the pub.

He looked down the sloped street toward the harbor below. The setting sun cast the water into gold, pink, and violet stripes. Boats dotted the coast, most fishing vessels, a few larger craft. Nothing like his own sleek schooner. His prize and his punishment.

He set his jaw.

Let Poole come for him. Within a month Alex would reboard his ship to prepare for the summer cruise. If Poole wanted Redstone, he would be there to greet him with cutlass, pistol, and a wide, welcoming smile. In the meantime he would play the earl in grand style at the open house. If he worked very hard at it, some might even believe he deserved it.

Chapter 9

> *Hail, stranger; in our house you shall find*
> *entertainment,*
> *and then, when you have tasted food, you shall*
> *tell what you have need of.*
>
> —HOMER, *ODYSSEY*

"Y ou look lovely, sister." Charity smiled as she scanned Serena's apricot muslin frock and simply plaited hair.

Serena suppressed a swell of satisfaction and took up her reticule. She had dressed for the gathering at Savege Park carefully, with an eye toward pleasing a rake into helping her drive away smugglers. But the bright expectation in Charity's face pushed away all other plans.

"Don't worry, darling. I will take care of everything."

"I know you will." Charity's eyes were round with complete trust.

By the fashionably late hour at which Davina deemed it acceptable to arrive at the open house, the Park already overflowed with people. Farmers and tradesmen, gentlemen and servants, crowded the estate's dozens upon dozens of chambers, its lawns and formal gardens. As though fashioned for the event, the day shone bright, a clear sky stretching over the ocean beyond the terraced gardens, reflecting its azure glory.

Inside the house, guests strolled through the public rooms, marble busts and oil portraits of the present earl's predecessors, furnishings and paint, silks, and rugs gracing walls and floors. Arm linked in Charity's, Serena followed her father and stepmother through the place. Savege Park reflected its master, elegant and tasteful with an underlying aura of opulence and unmistakable masculine authority.

But her attention was focused upon finding the earl himself. Her nerves fairly sizzled in anticipation.

Exiting the house through a drawing room onto a broad patio paved in slate and railed with Italian marble, Serena looked past tables laden with delicacies for the gentry and hardier fare for the farmers and onto the cliff above the sea. The air smelled of salt, sunshine, and freshly cut grass.

Upon the lawn, laughter arose from a group of young people playing Blind Man's Buff. Nearby, a cluster of weather-tanned farmers rolled bowls, and ladies shot arrows at targets placed carefully beyond blankets spread for children with jackstraws and blocks. A handful of musicians beneath a pavilion played country dances. It was a picnic such as Serena had never seen, something like Vauxhall but in simpler, less frantic style. Then again, for most of the single occasion when she had visited Vauxhall, she was hidden in a corner of the walks, losing her virginity to Robert Bailey.

A gentleman separated from a group and came toward them. Tall, with hair the color of autumn leaves just fallen off the branch, and similar eyes, something about him struck Serena familiarly. The heavy cane supporting his lanky frame and his awkward progress across the terrace explained it.

He smiled as he halted before them and bowed.

"Welcome to Savege Park, my lord, madam," he said to her parents, then turned to her. "You must be Miss Carlyle. How do you do?"

"It is my honor, Mr. Savege."

He shifted his attention to Charity, and the kindness in his gaze turned gentler still, but the corners of his mouth seemed to tighten.

"Miss Lucas, it is good to see you again."

Charity smiled prettily and dropped a curtsy, never breaking their gaze.

Serena stared in astonishment. In six weeks in London she had not once seen her stepsister greet a gentleman with such clear pleasure.

"May I escort you to the refreshment table for a glass of lemonade?"

"Thank you, sir," Davina said in affected tones. "Naturally my daughter would be honored, but I would like to pay our respects to Lord Savege. Is he anywhere about?"

"I saw him last at the archery yard, but he seems to have gone elsewhere since," the gentleman said with perfect ease, ignoring the bald insult. Serena blushed for her stepmother, then for her father, who said nothing to cover up the gaff. "May I assist you in finding him?"

"No, thank you, sir," Davina said. "I will seek him out myself. Come now, Charity, Serena."

"Mama," Charity peeped, her eyes downcast. "I should very much like a glass of lemonade."

Serena's gaze darted to Davina.

"Very well." Her stepmother's lips thinned. "You are all graciousness, sir."

"Miss Carlyle, will you join us?"

"Oh, thank you," Serena said, "but my stepbrother

asked me to find him straight away. He came over upon horseback earlier. It seems he could not wait to have a go at your billiards table." She smiled encouragingly at Charity, watched the two walk away, and without further delay escaped her father and stepmother. She had no desire to talk with Tracy now, only to find the earl and make her case—or cases, as it were. Charity's future and the future safety of all local girls depended upon it.

Serena searched the lawns and gardens, making slow progress through the local gentry and villagers she'd known lifelong, until she began to despair of ever encountering the earl upon his vast estate crowded with guests. Extricating herself from conversation, she rounded a hedge and halted abruptly.

Charity sat upon a scrolling iron bench beneath a flowering peach tree, a lacy parasol twirling in her hands, her white skirts spread upon the seat nearly touching Mr. Savege's leg. His hand rested upon the bench between them, the other gesturing as he spoke, his cane forgotten beside him. Charity laughed, the tinkling sound drifting to Serena upon the sea breeze. The gentleman smiled, and Charity's parasol twirled faster.

A tiny fist curled around Serena's heart. She must find the earl straightaway and make her case on her stepsister's behalf.

Smugglers all but forgotten, she turned to seek out Lord Savege. Familiar russet taffeta flashed at the edge of her vision. She swung back around.

Davina approached the peach tree, her face grim. She spoke, and Mr. Savege and Charity came to their feet, he with the assistance of his cane, now clutched in his fist. Charity dropped her gaze, Davina took her arm, nodded to the earl's brother, and drew her away.

Mr. Savege turned about and lurched toward the terrace, his shoulders stiff.

Serena pulled her gaze from him and sought out her stepsister again. In the shade of a pavilion awning, Davina loomed over her daughter's shrinking form, lips moving swiftly. Charity's eyes grew wide, her mouth opened, only to close again instantly. The brim of her lace-trimmed bonnet ducked, the parasol wilted.

Serena could no longer bear to watch. She whirled about and strode toward the house, determination renewed, and crossed the patio into the drawing room. The air was cooler inside, fragrant of cut flowers and dark compared to the lawns. She scoured each chamber. How on earth could a man so effectively disappear in his own house?

She paused in an alcove near the kitchen. The scents of freshly baked tarts and roasting meat came through a heavy closed door. It seemed unlikely the earl could be within, but Serena tried the handle. It held fast.

Frustration bubbling beneath her skin, she pivoted and met the Earl of Savege's interested gaze. With one broad shoulder propped against the alcove's doorjamb, and arms crossed over his finely clad chest in an insouciant attitude, he radiated aristocratic, masculine ease.

Serena's heart slammed against her ribs.

"My lord," she said, rather more tottery than she liked, "I have been looking for you."

His delicious mouth curved up at one edge.

"How flattering," he said, his voice as deep and wonderfully smooth as she recalled it every night lying fitfully in her bed. "Or perhaps not." He gestured to the door behind her. "That is the back door to the pantry."

"Um, yes. Well, I looked everywhere else first. You are a difficult man to find."

He unfolded his arms and stepped into the shadowed alcove. His presence filled the tiny space.

"If I had known you were looking for me, my dear, I would have happily made myself found sooner."

She took a steadying breath and squared her shoulders.

"My lord, I wish to speak with you about a matter of great importance to a number of people. I am glad to find you in private so that I may."

"Is that so?" His smoky eyes glimmered in the dim light.

She narrowed hers. He would not make this easy. He was a scoundrel, and she had given him plenty of reason to believe she preferred shadowy encounters to otherwise.

"Yes, it is so," she said firmly. "I hope you will hear me out and sincerely consider my words."

"I am all ears, madam." And compelling eyes, and gorgeously firm jaw, and satiny hair, and muscular arms, and a great many other body parts she should most certainly not be staring at and wishing to touch.

"There is something you do not know that could alter your attitude about—"

"Smugglers?" His gray eyes turned dark.

"Oh, no. I mean to say, well, yes. But that is not what I wished to—"

"Miss Carlyle, allow me to be clear upon this matter." His voice still rumbled beautifully deep, but unyielding now, the teasing tone abruptly absent. "I have no intention of becoming involved with that ship."

"But if you would only listen—"

"Your father is correct. The smugglers will complete their commerce here and be gone before long. I advise you to stay out of it, madam."

Serena's stomach clenched.

"You do not understand."

"I understand perfectly well that an unthinking female can get herself into great trouble by concerning herself with matters which do not concern her." His perfect jaw hardened and he seemed to loom larger in the close space.

"I—"

"You are not accustomed to being told what to do. Your father suggested something like that the other day."

"My *father*?" Serena's chest filled with heat, and not at all the thrilling kind this man typically inspired in her. Vexation, fast and sticky, climbed through her limbs, tangling in her throat and surging onto her tongue.

"My lord," she said, not now minding the slight unevenness of her voice, "I am not an unthinking female, as you say, but rather have a personal interest in smugglers coming to this coast. Perhaps you were away from home at the time, or do not recall."

"At the time?"

"Thirteen years ago, the summer smugglers came into Clovelly harbor and—" Her voice broke "—abducted my sister."

His expression was unreadable.

"Miss Lucas?" he asked after a moment.

Serena shook her head. "My true sister. Her name is Viola. She is two years my junior."

"Why have I never heard of her? Is she not in society?"

"No. She is still gone."

His gaze flickered.

"They never brought her back, and no one ever believed me. They said she fell from the cliffs into the surf and was lost. I tried to tell them the truth of it, I insisted, but they would not listen, and so no one pursued the ship when it left the harbor that very same day. After they called off the search, my mother continued looking. She believed me. She alone. A storm blew up, but Mama stayed out all night upon the bluff. When they brought her home, she took a fever. A fortnight later she perished."

He regarded her steadily while her heart beat a staccato rhythm. Her mother's death was not her fault—she had long ago reconciled herself to that, despite the pain of losing her. Smugglers *had* taken Viola. But she had blamed her father for not pursuing the kidnappers, and for allowing his wife's liberty upon the cliff that night. Perhaps part of her still did. But who was she to imagine he could control his wife when he could not even control his eldest daughter from staging her own ruination?

"You still believe your sister is alive?" the earl finally said.

"I know she is."

He reached out and took her hand, encompassing her in his warm strength. Serena gulped in a lungful of air. She hadn't told her story to anyone since that year.

"Do you see now? I cannot simply allow that ship to sail blithely along our coast."

"I begin to see." His thumb stroked across her palm.

Abruptly, the desperation slid from Serena's body. So many years had passed since that horrible day, and where memories remained vivid, grief had aged. Now only conviction drove her desires. And his touch . . . *distracted*.

Lovely distraction.

She tried to smile but chewed upon her lip instead. "I suppose 'beginning to see' is a start."

He moved closer, setting his fingertips beneath her elbow to draw her toward him.

"You had quite a time of it, and tragedy leaves memories that cling."

She lifted her gaze to his, the smoky eyes warm now. He seemed to know how she felt. He also seemed to know precisely where to touch her even casually to make her joints weak.

"Have you a loss in your past, as well?" she breathed unevenly.

He bent his head.

"Perhaps for the time being, my dear, we might set a comparative discussion of personal tragedies aside."

She should resist the alluring tenor of his voice. She should pull free and step into the light of the corridor or wherever it was she had come from. She couldn't recall. She could not even recall what they had been speaking of.

"In favor of what topic?" she uttered.

"As a gentleman, I must allow you to choose." He stood very close. How he'd gotten so close, Serena did not quite know.

"*Are* you a gentleman?"

"Occasionally." His thumb caressed her palm again. Frissons of pleasure leapt through her, like silvery sunshine dancing upon ocean.

"Now, for instance?"

"Not now." His knuckles stroked along the side of her breast.

Serena struggled for breath. "What are you doing?"

"Touching you." His voice sounded husky.

"You should not."

"Tell me to stop, then."

"My lord, I fear that I have conveyed to you the wrong impression of my character."

"You have conveyed to me precisely the impression you wish to. An accurate impression, I'll merit."

"No," she said wobbly.

"You have not yet asked me to stop."

Because she simply could not make her mouth do so. Her lips seemed frozen in a perpetual parting of breathless anticipation, her tongue a useless organ awaiting activity more satisfying than mere speech. His hand stroked again.

"I wish to, but you are very good at this." And now no impediment to her enjoyment of him existed. Charity would not marry him. Serena would make certain of it. "You have had a great deal of practice, I daresay."

He bent to her ear, his breath stirring the tendrils of hair escaping her braid.

"And yet at this moment, Serena Carlyle, it seems as though you are the first woman I have ever touched." The tip of his tongue stole along the sensitive edge of her earlobe, his hand covered her breast, and Serena sighed at such length that her lungs emptied entirely of air. His words, kiss, the warm dampness of his mouth—she did not know which precisely caused this reaction, or all. She only knew she wanted it to continue.

"Perhaps my character is not so pristine, after all," she offered upon a quaver, lifting her hands to grip his arms.

"To my great good fortune," he murmured, setting soft caresses beneath her ear then along her throat, descending slowly, tantalizing and satisfying both at once. He was all hard, contoured muscle beneath her hands and a shadow of whiskers against her skin. She stretched to allow him easier access as he took her waist in his strong hands and pulled her closer. Inside, deep in the well of Serena's innermost being, a spark ignited, seeking fuel. She wanted his mouth upon hers, for him to kiss her like he had before, to fan the spark into a flame. His lips upon her neck held her spellbound, a willing captive to his attentions.

He slid her sleeve off the curve of her shoulder, laying kisses delectably in the gown's wake.

"What are you doing?" she gasped.

"The same that I was doing before." His voice was muffled, undoubtedly by the fabric of her gown.

"This is more than a mere touch, my lord." She threaded her fingers through his marvelously satiny hair. "You truly mustn't."

"But I truly must." His mouth met the exposed swell of her breast, hot and damp. Serena choked upon a staggered breath. He licked her flesh along the edge of the bodice, gripped her waist tighter, then licked again, taunting, tickling. Serena foundered, sinking into pleasure, into burning, blissful wickedness. He stroked, and warmth rose in her, and an aching far and away the most wonderful she had ever felt. She strained for breath, wishing, hoping, fearing.

It all came true. With a single, smooth movement he lifted her breast free of her garments and set his mouth to its taut tip. His tongue circled, tasted, then claimed.

"Oh, *no*," she moaned, thoroughly subsumed, completely abandoned to his touch.

He paused. "No?"

She gripped his neck. "No— *Yes*! Yes . . ." Words fled. His tongue stroked, his lips caressed, and she was lost. Lost to the final ounce of modesty she possessed, no longer now, and happily so. Lost to every last shred of rationality. Lost to even her own hard-won sense of self-preservation. How could she allow him to do this? How could she be so foolish? How could she be such a heedless wanton?

She wanted more. More of him sucking upon her until she thought she would die from pleasure.

She slipped her hands to his shoulders and pressed him away.

"No," she uttered. "I was mistaken. Please stop."

He did so with unflattering immediacy. But when he straightened and lifted his gaze, his eyes were hazy with the same desire that careened through her. He was beautiful, and through his eyes, she was too.

"No," she groaned, turning her head away. "This cannot be happening." She snapped her face back to him. "Do you intend to marry my sister?"

He blinked. "No."

"No?" she spluttered, stuffing herself back into her clothes. "Then what is this—" She gestured toward the corridor in vague, frantic motions. "—all about? Davina says you planned this event to present your new bride to the neighborhood."

Astoundingly, the corner of his mouth lifted.

"I planned this event, as you say, in order to find an opportunity to be with you alone. I have, Miss Carlyle, been thinking about you quite a lot lately."

Serena stared. Words stumbled from her mouth as a breathless utterance. "Inviting everyone within twenty miles to one's house is a peculiar way to talk to a single person alone."

"I don't particularly wish to talk." He looked at her lips. "I can talk with you in a crowded drawing room." He bent his head and his breath brushed over her sensitized skin. "But in a drawing room I cannot do this." He covered her mouth with his.

Chapter 10

Shall I disguise my thought, or speak the truth?
My heart bids me speak.

—HOMER, *ODYSSEY*

His lips urged hers open instantly, and she gave way without hesitancy. He claimed her thoroughly, pressing her into his palm, cupping her head, and Serena welcomed it. Welcomed his tongue moving in her mouth, against hers, drawing pleasure through her body, making her hungry for more. He tasted of warmth and something rich and spicy and perfect. He tasted like her fantasies.

But that was the definition of a rake, she supposed. A wayward woman's fantasy.

She dragged her mouth away and dashed the back of her hand across it.

"No," she said over her palm, holding it up as a shield. He did not move to close the distance again, but his hands did not release her.

Her throat tightened.

"I cannot seem to prevent being attracted to you. You are odiously handsome and clearly have perfected seduction to an art form. But I am not so thoroughly abandoned to all propriety and fidelity as you seem to believe. My family expects you to offer for my sister."

"Your family's expectations are mistaken." He stared at her as though he wished to kiss her again, his smoky eyes half lidded. She fisted her hands and sucked in breath.

"Oh, why can't you go find a willing widow or some other lady more suited to dalliance?"

"Do not fool yourself, my dear." His voice was low. "You are perfectly well suited to dalliance. And I do not wish to find any other lady at present. I wish to dally with you."

"Well, I do not share that wish."

"That is a bald-faced lie." He stroked her cheek. To her horror, she leaned into the caress.

But why not? Why not feel again what she longed to feel? She might never have another opportunity like this one, and certainly not with a man like the Earl of Savage. There simply weren't other men like him. Men with soulful eyes and devastating smiles. Men whose barest touch turned her knees to jelly and her convictions to chalk.

Men who could make love to a woman while courting her sister, whatever he claimed when he was trying to make her kiss him. With wretched *success*.

The purpose of her mission in seeking him out flooded back to her. She closed her senses to his perfect good looks, his alluring voice, his enticing scent and hardness, and blurted out, "You are wholly unsuitable as a husband. You would make Charity quite miserable, you know."

He stiffened and drew away. Serena nearly followed, but caught herself upon the balls of her feet and locked her stance.

"In fact I have said I shan't make her any kind of husband at all. But you are impressively protective of your stepsister," he said in a strange voice. "It is unusual to be so attached to siblings one acquires so late in life."

"I *am* protective. I was already eighteen when our parents married, but she was still quite young and needed my attention."

His brow lowered. "She has a mother who might give her that."

"A horrid one."

His eyes narrowed.

"I know I should not say that," she conceded. "But it is true. My stepmother is awful to her daughters, and Charity is horribly frightened of her even while she loves her."

"Frightened? Does she beat her?"

"One needn't suffer physical beatings to be beaten in spirit, my lord."

He nodded thoughtfully. "So you seek to waylay such abuse."

"I seek to make it less painful for both of us."

His eyes grew darker yet, pools of murky intensity.

"Does Lady Carlyle abuse you as well?"

Serena shook her head. "I stopped allowing her cruelty to wound me years ago. But when she hurts Charity, I—I—"

"You feel her pain as though it were your own." The words came hollowly in the small space between them. Serena had the urge to reach out and touch his face, to press her cheek against his chest and feel his arms tight around her. It was nonsensical. She knew so little of this man, and what she did know should appall her.

"You see," she said to cover her confusion, "I am responsible for her."

A spark seemed to glimmer once more in his gaze, but not an easy one.

"Shouldn't her father or brother be?"

"They should. But I am."

"Because she lacks other champions."

"Because I failed at it once before, and after that I refused to fail at it ever again."

A long pause, then finally, "You failed?"

"I was there when they took Viola. I watched them bind my little sister in ropes, gag her, and drag her away, and I could do nothing about it. I tried, but I failed." She drew in a deep breath and set a firm look upon him. "So you see, my lord, I am obligated to make it quite clear to you that you are not the ideal husband for my stepsister, and as such it would be best if you did not offer for her after all."

Storms seemed to pass across his eyes, then abruptly they cleared.

"You are a remarkable woman, Miss Carlyle," he said without any hint of teasing to his tone.

Serena furrowed her brow. "Have you heard what I just said?"

"Of course. Have you returned the favor?"

"What?"

"I have said I will not offer for your stepsister. Thrice now."

She set her hands upon her hips. "You said so to me. But I understand that you have not yet made that clear to my father."

"Then I shall have to do so without delay." His gaze lingered upon her hips. Despite her resolution not to be moved, Serena squirmed beneath his regard, delicate shivers starting at each point of her skin upon which his slow perusal paused. "Your parents have no notion of this conviction of yours, that Miss Lucas and I would not suit?" he asked, following the line of her body back to meet her gaze.

"No. Only my sister and myself."

"She is not amenable to the match either?"

Good heavens, the man must be a consummate actor. He looked perfectly unaffected by the information that Charity did not care for him. But it must at least prick his pride, if not his sensibilities. He was a great lord, after all, beset by wanton widows and hopeful mamas alike, assuredly unaccustomed to being countered.

"My lord—"

"Call me Alex."

Serena's heart tumbled over. She righted it and folded her hands before her. "That is rather too familiar, isn't it?"

He shifted his weight onto one foot, crossed his arms over his broad chest and regarded her with a lifted brow. His cravat was crushed, his hair extra tousled by her fingers raking through it, and his eyes danced. He looked good enough to eat.

"I daresay it is a bit too late to claim that excuse," she mumbled.

"A bit," he drawled.

Her cheeks flamed. "You know, my lord—"

"Alex."

"—your teasing can be horrid at times."

"Astute, as always, madam." He bowed.

"You cannot marry Charity."

His mouth curved up at one edge. "Not when I wish to remove each piece of her stepsister's clothing with my teeth. No."

Heat flooded Serena from brow to toes, gathering low in her abdomen in tiny lapping pools.

"You do?" she whispered.

He nodded with wicked certainty.

"Of course you do," she stated. "You are a rake."

"So they say."

"Accurately?"

"I am considering reforming." He grabbed her wrist and pulled her against him in one swift motion, clamping his arm around her waist. "But not quite yet." He bent his head, and Serena allowed herself to be kissed. The hard length of his body, his heat, and the deliciously firm caress of his mouth filled her with longing.

She would let him seduce her. She was more than halfway seduced already, and no one could be hurt by it. This time she would be prepared. She knew perfectly well what a rake could do to her heart, and she would never allow such a man close again. Or anyone. When she loved, she inevitably lost.

But why not take a little wicked pleasure while she could? Why not, for one brief, glorious moment, dream and live again?

Alex tasted the sweet, hot desire in her kiss and wanted more. His hands itched to touch her fully, to explore the curves and planes of her lovely face, graceful neck, regal shoulders, and the beauty below that moments ago he'd brought to enticing peaks with his fingers and tongue.

Then he would explore further.

He wanted her naked and spread wide for him upon his bed, and he had little patience to wait for it. He was harder than he'd been in months. Years. She pressed her soft hips to his, innocently seeking satisfaction, and he slid his hands down and held her against him. She sighed, her neck arched, and he delved into her damp mouth—partially, temporarily, feeding his craving the only way he could at the moment.

But later . . . later he would have her alone behind locked doors, and he would take her as he wished.

Her hands slipped up his arms to his neck, grasping delicately. He imagined licking her palms and sucking upon each finger in turn, then upon the prize between her slender thighs. She would be eager for him, he had no doubt, coming like an angel against his tongue.

He groaned in frustration.

Alex never had to wait. Women came to him flaunting their wares like street vendors selling pasties, and he took as he pleased. Now this woman, with the lightest of touches, the most unpracticed caresses, was driving him mad with need.

She rubbed up against him, mewling whimpers of anticipatory pleasure, and he plunged into her mouth deeper, locking their tongues in a battle of raw want. He could take her here. But someone might interrupt. Too many curious eyes filled his house. It would be foolish. And he wanted more than quick satisfaction from this damnably alluring woman. He needed hours with her to rid himself of his insane preoccupation. He needed an entire night.

She twined her fingers into his hair and her foot about his ankle, cradling his erection against her belly.

Perhaps a few nights.

He wrapped a hand about her jaw and separated their mouths.

"Serena . . ." His voice sounded peculiar to him, far too rough, far too breathless. "Serena, we must stop this."

She nodded, her eyes glazed with desire. Lips reddened from his kisses shaped the words *We must,* but no sound issued forth. Then her gaze seemed to come into focus and she said audibly, "We must?"

He grinned.

"For now," he murmured, pressing his mouth to hers again, then again, parting her lips and filling his senses. He couldn't get enough. She was like strong rum and sweet brandy and fresh water all at once.

She slipped her hands to his chest and pushed. Alex broke the kiss, swallowing hard. The novelty of being repulsed by a woman twice in the same hour—rather, *at all*—lodged uncomfortably in his chest despite his own suggestion that they should not carry on at the present.

She met his gaze, hers now unsettlingly clear. Intelligence winked in it, and wariness.

"What do you mean, 'for now'?"

He stroked her cheek. Her skin was soft, lightly flushed.

"I intend to make love to you, Miss Carlyle."

A rippling shudder seemed to pass through her body. Her lashes fanned out from her unique eyes. She blinked.

"Do you?"

He nodded.

Her lips curved up.

It was nearly Alex's undoing. He struggled, reining in the desire to haul her against him and have his way with her here and now and damn the consequences. But he had to content himself with brushing the pad of his thumb over her swollen lips, marking the sensation of her upon his skin.

"Indeed I do." With effort, he stepped back and released her.

Behind him a throat cleared.

"My lord," his valet said in monotone. "Your presence is required upon the patio. One of your guests has suffered an incident." Tubbs bowed and withdrew.

Serena's expression shuttered, her mouth set in a firm line. Unlike her. But he would have her smiling again soon enough. Then shouting his name in ecstasy.

He bowed. "If you will excuse me, ma'am."

She curtsied.

A jaunty swagger lifted Alex's steps as he made his way toward the other end of the house, images passing through his mind of a pretty woman pinned beneath him, honey-colored hair spread about her creamy shoulders, her beautifully mismatched eyes hazy with passion. He crossed the drawing room to the French windows his mother had installed a year earlier, claiming they allowed more light into the place. Until now he hadn't noticed how right she was. Sunlight streamed through the opening, bathing the room in blue and gold as he'd never seen it before.

By God he felt good. It must be the anticipation of having a woman in his bed after such a lengthy hiatus. In his new fastidious depression of character, he had not partaken of feminine flesh in over a month. Since just before he met Serena Carlyle.

He stumbled over the patio threshold.

Good Lord, he hadn't been so agreeably distracted since he was a boy and that redheaded tart in Bridgetown made him a man. But Serena was not a tart. She was a lovely, respectable daughter of a country baron. And he had kissed her to within an inch of her virtue, then propositioned her.

He ought to be hung from a yardarm.

He did not dally with virgins. Not for years now. But as long as he was a pirate for a few more months, he might as well behave as one. She certainly wasn't resisting. His smile broadened.

A handful of guests, mostly women, clustered at the far edge of the patio, their attention fixed upon one spot. They moved aside for him, revealing Miss Lucas reclining upon a chaise. Childlike eyes round, she stared at her mother perched at her side. Around them the collection of women—ladies, shopkeepers, farmers' wives—seemed to be offering advice as the baroness chafed her daughter's hands.

"Ma'am, may I be of service?" Alex moved near. The girl's gaze shot to him, then back to her mother, alive with dismay.

"My lord," Lady Carlyle said, her voice less affected than usual. "My daughter has fallen down the stairs and turned her ankle." She gestured toward the steps descending to the garden. "I believe she may have sprained a joint." Her hands seemed to grip her daughter's pale fingers harder. "Now she has taken a megrim from it and feels quite unwell."

"I am stricken to hear this. I will send for a physician at once." He caught the eye of a hovering footman and gestured. The fellow hurried off.

"Thank you," the baroness said with a moue of gratitude. "She must have quiet and dark, or she will undoubtedly become ill. Have you an out-of-the-way chamber in which she may rest?"

"Of course. Miss Lucas, are you able to stand?"

The girl's porcelain brow creased and her lashes fluttered but she did not meet his gaze.

"I do not know, sir." Her words were barely audible.

"Come, let us give it a try." He grasped her gloved hand. It was cold as the dogwatch in a winter squall. She shifted her legs over the edge of the chair and released a little cry of distress.

"My dearest," Lady Carlyle said, twisting her hands together. "Perhaps a litter could be fashioned to carry her inside, my lord, or a footman called?"

Alex nearly sighed aloud. The woman's fretful gesture, her uncharacteristic tone and ridiculous suggestions, were tailored for maximum effect. He had been the target of such histrionics before. He kept himself aloof from polite society largely to avoid such entrapment.

But this conniving mother would not succeed. He had no intention of offering for this taking little bundle of lashes and nerves. With remarkable clarity born in him by the flash of a simple beauty's eyes, he considered it amazing that he had even briefly considered marrying Miss Lucas. He might deserve a lifelong penance, but he would not impose it upon himself willingly.

He must be very careful now.

"Miss Lucas, may I summon your brother or father to carry you within, where you can be made more comfortable?"

"They have already departed," Lady Carlyle said.

Of course they had.

"Then, will you allow me to assist you?" he asked the girl.

Eyes wide as a capstan, she nodded, fraught gaze flickering to her mother. With a scratchy dislike in his chest for women who terrified their own progeny, Alex slid his arms behind her back and beneath her knees and lifted her, light as a child, her arms demurely tucked away from him. He carried her inside and prepared to set her upon a couch in the drawing room. The crowd dispersed upon the patio.

"Oh, this will not do," the baroness said. "Have you a darkened chamber? I cannot expect that a gentleman like you would know what it is to suffer a megrim, of course, but strong light exacerbates the condition."

So much for French windows. Alex was of a mind to drop the girl and see whether her dubiously injured head and ankle could bear it. But she seemed genuinely wretched, her eyes closed, face turned away from him, fingers twisted together.

"Of course." He moved toward the corridor and to a

small interior parlor his mother used for letter writing when she stayed at the Park. A footman opened the door, and Lady Carlyle followed him and his dainty burden inside the chamber, lit only by a tiny round upper window. He lowered Miss Lucas to a chaise. Her mother fussed about her, arranging her skirts over her ankles and a pillow beneath her foot.

"I will call a maid to attend Miss Lucas until the doctor arrives," he said. "Or would you prefer my housekeeper?"

The baroness came to his side.

"Thank you, my lord, a maid will do. We are ever so grateful for your condescension. I should like to speak with your housekeeper myself, in fact. I know of a receipt for a poultice that will draw the swelling away from the ankle. I would very much like to make it up in your kitchen, if I may."

He bowed. "Certainly, madam. Allow me to bring her here and she will assist you."

She laid a firm hand upon his sleeve.

"No, no. I could not drag you away from your guests again." She moved to the door more swiftly than Alex could have countenanced for a woman of such stiff dignity. "I will return in a moment."

The door snapped shut behind her, and Alex knew himself for the greatest fool alive.

He strode forward and grasped the knob. It fell off in his palm. He stared at the useless hardware, his pulse pounded, and a series of curses descended from his tongue that had only ever been heard upon his ship's spar deck.

"My lord?" the girl across the chamber peeped.

He bent to fit the knob into the hole. It wiggled without taking. That woman could not have planned this. This was his house, damn it. He would murder whichever footman left this door handle broken. He would murder his butler, housekeeper, and his mother as well, if any of them were at fault.

"There seems to be some trouble with this knob," he said in calm tones. Of course he sounded calm. Since he had disembarked from the *Cavalier* weeks ago, the only moments in which he sounded anything other than perfectly urbane, he'd had Serena Carlyle in his arms. Now it was looking blasted certain that would never happen again.

He placed the useless knob upon a piecrust table and knocked on the panel.

"Milord?" a footman's curious voice came from just outside. Listening at the crack, no doubt.

"The doorknob is broken. Fetch the locksmith from town at once. And the blacksmith as well. Be quick about it."

"Yes, sir." Rapid footsteps retreated along the corridor.

Alex took a slow breath and turned to the girl upon the chaise. She was sitting up.

"Feeling better, ma'am?" He tilted his head.

She shook hers.

"Your mother planned this."

She remained silent, her gentian gaze replete with distress in a face as white as the *Cavalier*'s bleached canvas.

"Are you in fact injured, Miss Lucas?"

Her rosebud lips trembled, neither confirming nor denying. Alex battened down the anger rising like a wave against the hull of his self-control. He rubbed a hand across his face.

"Is the door truly broken?" she whispered upon a quaver.

"Serendipitous, hm?" He folded his hands behind his back and leaned his shoulders against the door.

Her delicately winged brows questioned.

"Fortunate accident," he murmured, adding, "for some," and turned his gaze to the portrait of his father hanging above his mother's escritoire. The sixth Earl of Savege stared at Alex like he always had in life, disapproval and chastisement writ upon his lined face, the harsh oil strokes doing him thorough justice.

Damn him for not allowing his heir to follow his dream of purchasing a commission and going to war. Damn his father for believing him when he pretended that to be sent to the West Indies to assist his uncle with the plantation was a punishment. Damn Aaron for insisting upon sharing his repairing leases, and for possessing more loyalty and honor than sense. Damn himself for learning far too late that he could not deny his true character. And damn Serena Carlyle for welcoming his kisses and making him think for a brief, curious, astounding moment that he might finally be allowed a taste of real happiness.

He returned his gaze to the girl.

"Forgive my candidness, ma'am, but I suspect you are as unsatisfied with this circumstance as I."

She did not reply. But she stood up, upon two apparently perfectly hale ankles. Alex suppressed a scowl of distaste. Serena had made it clear that her stepsister feared Lady Carlyle. He should not blame this girl. She was a pawn in her mother's quest for status and connections. The baroness would be unhappy to learn, no doubt, that his closest companions were a half-breed Egyptian pirate and three score ex-slaves and criminals. Of course, his brother was unexceptionable *ton*. He just never left Savege Park.

Poor, misinformed Lady Carlyle was doomed to disappointment.

"Milord," the footman said breathlessly from the other side of the door.

"Where is the locksmith?"

"Under the old oak by the south well."

"Under the oak?"

"Dead drunk, sir."

"Blast," Alex muttered.

"Milord?"

"What about the blacksmith?"

"In the hay wagon."

"Same condition?"

"Yes, sir." The man sounded sincerely contrite, as though he himself had handed the fellows the whiskey punch. Bless his heart.

Alex's fists curled, his fingertips driving into his palms.

"Fetch my mother's smelling salts and a pot of coffee, and pour them both into that locksmith. And send to Clovelly for the carriage maker. He might have appropriate tools. Bring Mrs. Tubbs to me, as well."

"Yes, milord."

Alex took a long, deep breath. Just as her husband did in the dressing chamber, his housekeeper worked miracles in the rest of the house. After all, she managed to keep his unhappy brother eating and breathing in his absences. She might have a magical key that would solve everything.

Not precisely everything. He gazed at the incomparable across the chamber and a sinking sensation crept into his chest.

"Charity!" Lady Carlyle's distressed tones rang through the door. Alex moved into the center of the chamber to make way for Miss Lucas to approach, but she remained immobile as a Greek statue—white gown, white skin, whites of her eyes prominent. The stare of fear and submission.

Alex's lungs filled like a drowning man's.

"Daughter, are you all right?"

Miss Lucas's gaze darted from the door to him.

"She is well," he responded. "We are both well, awaiting release with happy anticipation."

"My lord, I am here." His housekeeper's no-nonsense greeting came through. Good. Let this farce be ended and the farce of the remainder of his life begin at once.

"Mrs. Tubbs," he said pleasantly, "have you, by chance, a key or other tool worthy of this challenge?"

"It will take some time, my lord, but I think it will do."

"We will be within in moments, Charity dear," her mother called.

Alex turned to the girl.

"Our liberation is at hand, Miss Lucas." He smiled.

Her lashes fluttered yet again, apparently attached to butterfly wings.

No. He could not go through with it. This silent simpering would drive him mad. Although, of course, he deserved any discomfort fate visited upon him, if not for the wrongs he had done his twin, then for the girls like this he had once used so abominably, however willing they believed themselves at the time.

"My lord, I am sorry," she whimpered. Tears pooled in her eyes. "Dreadfully sorry."

He lifted a brow.

"You needn't apologize, Miss Lucas. It was a mistake and will all be sorted out shortly."

Alex straightened his shoulders. Society accounted him the worst sort of rogue when it came to women. He might have turned over a new leaf years ago, and another even fresher leaf recently, but he would not be such a bottlehead as to choose this of all moments to become a man of actual character.

The baroness would not have her way in this. If he were a gentleman, he would offer for the girl. But as he'd told her sister an hour ago, he was not a gentleman upon all occasions. And if Lady Carlyle caused a fuss, he would take this chit by the hand and instruct her to report upon precisely what did not occur while locked in this foolish closet. According to her sister's testimony and Miss Lucas's own behavior, she did not want this match and would undoubtedly be eager for the opportunity to avoid it.

Unless, of course, Miss Carlyle had lied about her stepsister's wishes. Unless she was as calculating as the baroness, her passion earlier all a show to entrap him.

It could not be. He had seen enough female falsity to recognize sincerity when it gazed up at him with eyes the colors of the sky over the Atlantic at dusk.

"Do not fret, Miss Lucas," he assured, his chest somewhat looser. "All will be well."

She dabbed at her damp cheeks with a scrap of lace.

"I've got it, my lord," Mrs. Tubbs announced. A key rattled in the lock and the workings visibly moved.

"You see?" He gestured. "Freed before dinner—"

She hurled herself at him. In his surprise, Alex barely knew whether to look at the girl pressing her lips against his or the door bursting open.

He grasped her shoulders and peeled her off his chest, but the damage was done. Faces filled the doorway—her mother, his housekeeper, the third footman, the local squire's wife, the curate, Sir Tracy who had apparently not yet left the Park, and Aaron, his brow drawn tight.

And Serena.

Her cheeks were gray as ash, bewilderment awash in her lovely eyes as she stared at him. Then her gaze shifted to her sister.

Despair palpable as tar crossed Serena's face.

"My lord, what is going on here?" Lady Carlyle hurried into the chamber, her son at her heels. Miss Lucas clasped her gloved hands and ducked her chin.

"Nothing whatsoever until the door handle turned," he said tightly.

"Lord Savege!" She gaped at him, then her daughter. "Charity, what have you done?"

"In point of fact, she—"

"Charity, this is insupportable!"

"Mama," the girl whimpered, "I did not—"

"And you as well, my lord," Lady Carlyle cut in, as though she'd no idea of the possibility of such a heinous act. "I am horrified at this lack of propriety."

"No more than I, ma'am." He directed a clear look at the girl.

Miss Lucas shrank into the sofa, the portrait of delicate misery. Titters sounded in the corridor from more bystanders, fortunately for them none of his servants.

Serena moved to her stepsister and wrapped an arm around her narrow shoulders, putting her body directly between Lady Carlyle and the girl. Protecting her sister. Her chin was high, but tears trembled in the violet and blue eyes. Jaw and fists clenched, Alex watched her tending to the girl's palpitations and his chest hollowed entirely.

"Lord Savege," the baronet said stiffly, "may I have a word with you in private?"

"I would be astounded if you did not insist upon it." Alex barely recognized his own voice. He nodded and gestured for Sir Tracy to precede him out the door. The guests and servants stepped aside, Mrs. Tubbs offering him a resigned look as he passed. He ignored it, as well as the abrupt pounding of his heart and head as he walked to his study.

The distress in a pair of unique eyes had decided it for him.

In the thrall of her mother's power, Miss Lucas could not be depended upon to tell the truth. As such, she barely deserved his consideration. But Alex could no more vilify the girl now than he could publish a broadsheet declaring her ruination. If he did not now offer for Miss Lucas, the baroness would make her suffer.

Any suffering on Miss Lucas's part would be Serena's as well.

He knew what it was to bear another's pain. He could never wish that upon anyone, least of all a woman whose heart seemed so firmly in the right place, a simple beauty with mismatched eyes.

And now, among his other desires regarding Serena Carlyle, he had the most astounding urge to protect *her*. He could do so for the moment by going along with this. But he was by no means resigned. A way out of the mess would be found that would save the chit's reputation and assure her mother's satisfaction. He would discover it as soon as could be, then he would be free to pursue her sister as he wished. For the time being only, his dreams of Serena Carlyle spread upon his mattress must wait.

He suspected she was worth it.

Chapter 11

Up to her upper chamber she went . . . and then
wept.

—HOMER, *ODYSSEY*

W hy did you do it, Chare?" Serena whispered
through the door of her stepsister's bedchamber.
Everyone else had left the house for the day, Davina
and Diantha to Clovelly to shop, Tracy and her father to
ride. She could talk freely to Charity now from the corridor, her only option for conversation. Not that Charity
would take part in the dialogue.

"I cannot speak of it," her stepsister whimpered.

"You cannot remain in there forever, darling. You
have been crying for three days. Let me come in and
we can talk it all over. I promise I will understand." She
had understood even as Charity had fallen from the
lips of the man who had told her minutes before that
he wished to make love to her.

Rakes could not be trusted. It proved her enduring
foolishness that for a moment, numbed into delirium by
his caresses, she thought this rake might be different.

"Darling, won't you tell me what happened? Then
together we may devise a solution to this problem, as
we have always done together in the past."

"The contract—" came the muffled reply.

"It is not signed. The earl has not yet returned it to Papa." Serena chewed on her lip, delving deep groves in it, as she had for three days. "Charity, do you wish to marry him after all?"

The sobbing grew louder.

"I will take that as a no." Serena slid down against the wall upon her behind, releasing a wavering breath. Apparently, twenty minutes alone in a parlor with Lord Savege had not scrambled Charity's wits as thoroughly as they had her own.

She closed her eyes, forcing back the tears prickling behind her lids. But the empty ache in her middle would not abate.

Footsteps sounded on the stairs and her father appeared.

"I thought you had gone riding with Tracy." Serena climbed to her feet, dusting off her gown.

"The weather turned unexpectedly."

Like Lord Savege's intentions. Serena clasped her hands together to hide their unsteadiness.

"She still will not come out except for breakfast and dinner, which she attends without speaking to any of us."

"Or eating a bite," her father said. "Lord Savege will take a skeleton to the altar if your sister persists in this foolishness." He shook his head. "But none of us have been eating, it is true. You have not finished your plate in three days."

"Papa, can nothing be done?"

His pale brow wrinkled.

"She made her choice, daughter. She must now live with it." His eyes spoke the seven-year-old sympathy his tongue could not. Serena had made her choice at one time as well. And just as then, her father was now allowing matters to run their course without protesting. For thirteen years he had been a man broken, without a will of his own, only his wife's instead.

"You do not believe Lord Savege voluntarily compromised her, do you?" she asked. Within the bedchamber, the weeping intensified.

Her father's brow crept up. "Do you?"

"He is a libertine. I told you that the moment my stepmother proposed the alliance. But . . ." She twisted her fingers in her skirts. Wishes were not the truth, not when men of a certain stamp were involved. "I don't know, Papa."

"What motive, Serena, would a man of his stature have to rush his fences at this juncture like he did in that chamber?"

Serena had no satisfactory response. And it hurt less not to think on it deeply. She didn't know why it should hurt at all. Except that when the earl looked at her in that particular way, his smoky eyes alight, it seemed he knew her thoughts—both the admirable and the wicked—and approved of them all.

Her chest hurt, and the place behind her eyes where the tears would not cease gathering. He had promised her. *Nearly* promised. And she, lost to his caresses and woefully naïve, had believed him.

"Your stepsister is a very pretty girl, and together her brother and I have settled a sizable dowry upon her. But Lord Savege can be as choosy as he likes in the matter of finding a wife." Her father wished to speak the truth of his wife's perfidy at the open house. Serena could see it in his soft eyes. But he would not. He never had.

She tucked her arm into his.

"I suppose my stepmother is planning the engagement party now." The party that must not happen for a wedding she herself would not allow. *Could* not allow. She would kidnap Charity to her aunt and uncle's house in York before the day arrived if she must.

Her father's hand shook covering hers. "You are a good girl, Serena."

But her father did not really know her. Not like the Earl of Savege did.

"I want Charity to be happy," she mumbled. "And this is not the way of it."

He ignored her words now. "I am certain your stepmother would be delighted if you offered help."

As delighted as a wasp could be. Serena went with her father, pondering the notion that while she was not to enjoy the attentions of a handsome knight after all—however briefly—at least she had a wicked stepmother to serve. Sometimes fairy tales did come true.

Alex rounded the corner of the stable corridor and his strides faltered. His brother stood at a stall door, one hand gripping his cane as always, the other stroking the neck of a roan mare.

"She is still in fine condition," Alex said, starting toward his twin at an easy gait. "You ought to give her a ride."

Aaron's brow furrowed.

"You know I cannot." His voice was uncharacteristically short. "Why do you suggest it?"

Alex leaned a shoulder against the wall.

"Have you ever tried?"

Aaron swung his gaze around. Hardness shone foreign upon his features.

"When I am in London, and not here to see," Alex pressed, "have you ever had her saddled and asked a groom to assist you up? Have you even considered the possibility?"

His brother's jaw tightened. "Why are you taunting me?"

"I am merely asking." Alex gestured languidly.

"Well don't ask again. It shows your arrogance."

Aaron clutched his walking stick and shuffled to the opposite side of the stable, away from the horse he'd bought just before Alex purchased a commission for his twin. She was a prime goer, all long legs, strong withers, and tapering head. A beauty. Before he departed for the front, Aaron declared laughingly that he'd finally fallen in love as he always hoped. They drank a toast to the mare with a full bottle of brandy, and continued laughing through the night. It had all seemed wonderfully clever at the time. Now Aaron could have neither horse nor real love.

Nevertheless, the angry, sullen man with whom Alex had shared the Park for the past three days was not his brother, at least not the man of the past two years. Something else was wrong.

"If a fellow cannot be comfortable revealing his baser nature to his closest kin," Alex drawled, "then the world has come to a sad state indeed."

"You cannot impress me with your affectations, Alex. I was there when you learned them." The tip of Aaron's cane echoed as he clunked toward the door. Alex followed.

"I have always wondered why you did not learn them as well. Not your taste, I daresay. All those lessons in your prosy books of sermons suited you better."

"Cheese it, Alex. I'm not in a humor for this today."

Alex grasped his arm, easily pulling him to a halt. Aaron was careful, always so careful, not to fall. Not to disgrace himself, even in front of his twin.

"Then what are you in a humor for today, little brother? Shall we have the gig hitched up and trundle over to Glenhaven Hall to call upon my lovely bride?" His voice sounded tinny. "A taking little thing, don't you agree? Why, you've barely congratulated me upon winning such a prize."

"I congratulated you."

"Oh, did you? I must have missed it for all the racket of coins clinking in my coffers from Carlyle's and Lucas's bank accounts." He released his brother's arm and plucked a strand of hay from a bin. He twirled it between thumb and forefinger. "Rich little filly, Charity Lucas. And quite pretty. Not to my usual tastes, of course, but that won't matter after the heirs are begotten." He chuckled. "Or before, for that matter. A man must do what he must do, after all." He allowed his mouth to curve into a sly grin.

"Do you mean to bait me, Alex?" Aaron's voice was flat.

Alex lowered the strand of hay.

"What on earth do you mean, little brother? Why would I possibly bait you, and about what, pray tell?"

Aaron's mouth thinned to a line.

"Stop with this 'little brother'-ing. Stop with it all." His hand upon the cane shook.

Alex dropped the strand of grass and straightened his shoulders.

"I will stop with it when you come clean, Aaron. With me, and yourself."

His brother's brown eyes flared, a combination of anger and panic that dug into Alex's gut. But guilt and regret still reigned in Alex, and he knew they would never be conquered until his twin lived his life again fully. Until he found happiness.

"You haven't any idea what you are saying."

"Don't I?" Alex took a hard breath, steadying his stance. "Then listen to this, brother, until you are honest with yourself you will never have peace."

Aaron's face paled. "That's rich. You don't want that ship any longer, do you, Alex? Then why do you still own it? Why didn't you sell it to Jinan before you came ashore last month?"

"You know perfectly well why not." Because it was all that had kept Aaron living for over a year after they carried him off the battlefield, half a man. When doctors, his mother and sister, had despaired of him, lying abed day after day, eating nothing and saying little, reports of the *Cavalier*'s journeys lit his dulled eyes, got him talking.

Once talking, he ate. Eventually he climbed from bed. Finally, he walked again. He took his first steps to the balcony to search out the schooner upon the horizon, a prize barquetine in tow and a hold full of swag. The next day Alex came ashore, and then into the night, as he recounted stories of the cruise, he and Aaron drank together again. And they laughed.

"I'll tell you why you haven't given it up," Aaron said, his voice low. "Because you have a death wish. You're waiting for Lambert Poole to come at you, guns blazing, so that you can stand on deck as arrogant as ever and take one in the chest just to prove you can."

"Don't be absurd."

"Well, you know what, big brother, contrary to popular belief, you are not immortal. And in my estimation, one cripple in the family is more than enough." He jolted away, each shuffle-clump of his walk scraping across Alex's guilt like sand on a raw wound.

His twin wanted the girl.

The moment Alex first spoke with him about it in private, after the last guests had gone home and a message was sent to Lord Carlyle, he saw it in his brother's transparent gaze. He wanted Charity Lucas, and as

Alex explained to him the events that had passed in the parlor, Aaron's gaze turned from dismayed to pained, then lifeless.

Perhaps he and the girl had an understanding, a secret agreement that Lady Carlyle's intervention ruined. Alex would never know. Aaron would never tell him. He read the shame in his brother's eyes just as easily as the pain.

And now his own intended escape was ruined. Within moments of the debacle he had determined to convince Carlyle to offer his stepdaughter to another suitable fellow, one who would enthusiastically take his place. He would enlist the aid of his mother and sister; they knew everyone in town and could not fail to discreetly find a worthy groom. Miss Lucas was a beautiful girl, and well dowered. If it could be effected swiftly, few in society need ever know of this foolish betrothal, and Lady Carlyle could be satisfied.

But now he was hamstrung. He could not offer Charity Lucas to another man when his brother wanted her. And so he was holding onto the contract, not signing or rejecting it. Better the devil one knew—and he knew with a certainty he would not wed Charity Lucas. But if he threw the girl off, she would be ruined. He could not do that to Serena. He could not allow her to be hurt.

He would instead convince Miss Lucas to bring an end to it. And in the meantime, he would do what he must regarding his brother. When pricked deep and often, a man would eventually fight back.

Alex stared after Aaron's slowly retreating form. His twin's shoulders were as square, his spine as rigid as his, despite his crutch.

Arrogance and pride. They both possessed bushels of it. Aside from Savege Park, it was their father's greatest legacy.

* * *

Serena walked down to the village each day in
search of information about the smugglers and Redstone. Meeting with complete failure in her attempts to
encourage Charity to explain or even speak, she vowed
to be prepared with a plan the moment her stepsister
finally emerged from her despair. *What* plan, precisely,
Serena hadn't any clear idea. Her thoughts were completely muddled.

Contrary to all hope—and his stated intentions—the
earl had not backed off of the betrothal. She could not
trust him. She *did* not trust him. The responsibility now
rested upon Charity. So while Serena was composing
yet more speeches to convince her stepsister to end the
thing, she made herself useful to her previous project,
the project that had her scouring London ballrooms a
month ago for the Marquess of Doreé—the night the
earl had kissed her in the dark and started her dreaming once again.

Delicious dreaming.

Reckless dreaming, heedless of reality.

She would meet him again at the betrothal ball at
the end of the week. Imagining the encounter made
her stomach twist.

"I haven't seen those sailors since the first time, Miss
Carlyle." The blacksmith shook his sheep-shorn head
and ran his thick fingers atop the stubble.

"You have cut your hair, Joe, haven't you?"

He blushed beneath a layer of soot.

"I suppose it is safer this way, with all the fire in your
shop here." She smiled.

The flush deepened.

"Me new wife bade me do it, miss. Said she wanted
to be able to see me mug better." He grinned from cauliflower ear to cauliflower ear. Serena smiled, bid him

good day, and swallowed down the lump in her throat, caused no doubt by a seasonal complaint. Why Lord Savege's handsome visage should pop into her head when Joe spoke of his wife with such affection, she had no idea.

Yes, she did. And she hated herself for it.

She ought to find another handsome gentleman to be wicked with as soon as possible. Then the memory of *his* warm voice in her ear, *his* touch, would be overcome by another's.

The idea held no appeal.

She did not *care* for him. How could she? Unless that martial light she had seen in his gray eyes when Tracy had insisted upon speaking with him meant something significant. Unless his apparent hesitation to sign the betrothal documents signified his lack of true acquiescence. And unless his assurances to her had not been lies, and now he only stood by the betrothal to protect her stepsister's reputation. The reputation he had placed in jeopardy.

They had been *kissing*.

Somewhat, at least. And not at all like he had kissed her, it appeared. In point of fact it had appeared very much like— *No*. It went against every rational notion to believe Charity had initiated the embrace.

Someone was not telling the truth. The girl whose weeping had not ceased in days. Or the rake.

Serena wandered through the churchyard gate and between berry hedges where the two of them had strolled, and wondered what it would require to wrest him from her thoughts. And *deeper*. Perhaps it only needed her beloved sister, festooned in wedding finery, marching up the aisle upon his arm?

She arrived at the house in a foul humor, with nothing to show for her research efforts but more aching and a peevish mood. Davina waylaid her in the foyer.

"You must assist me with your sister's gown. That hack of a *modiste* I hired in town ruined the lace, and Charity must shine tomorrow night."

"Charity shines in whatever she wears." Serena followed her stepmother into the sewing room. "She is a true diamond."

"A diamond that must impress an earl."

"He already offered for her," Serena replied. "She needn't impress him." Yet here she sat, sewing lace upon a gown for a betrothal ball to celebrate a wedding neither bride nor groom wished. Or so he had said in a shadowed alcove while she clung to him like a limpet upon stone.

The needle jabbed Serena's finger, her throat tight and thick.

"Fustian." She sucked upon it, watching her stepmother plying an embroidery frame. "Why must you persist in pressing this match? Why is it so important to you?" The words popped out. He had done this to her. With his soulful eyes and teasing smile, the rogue had encouraged her to do and say things she should not. Could she prevent it if, now that the dam was cracked, water continued to flow through?

Davina's carefully coiffed head came up slowly. She pinned Serena with an icy stare.

"Are you questioning my decision, daughter?"

Serena's cheeks heated. She hated it when Davina called her that. Davina knew it.

"Charity is a beautiful girl with excellent connections," she said more choppily now. "She needn't marry a man she does not like. She might attract any number of gentlemen of means and fashion if she went about town a bit more." Or about Savege Park, under flowering peach trees.

"She is best settled here," her stepmother said coldly.

Serena bit down on her lip, her very insides trembling. Good heavens, how could she expect Charity to withstand her mother when she herself could barely do so?

"They are unsuited to one another."

"You know nothing of it. The Earl of Savege will make my daughter an excellent husband."

"If he ever bothers to call upon her again, or sign the contract," Tracy said from the doorway. He lifted an apple to his mouth, his gaze sharp upon his mother. "Good afternoon Mother, Ser. What are you making there, Charity's burial shroud?"

"He will come here for the betrothal ball tomorrow evening." Davina snipped a dangling thread. A shred of crimson silk clung to her palm. She swiped it off irritably. "All the best families in the county will attend."

"Disappointed you cannot host this route in London, Mother dear? Savege holds such an advantage upon his own land, doesn't he?"

"Everything is for the best." An edge cut Davina's voice.

Tracy bit into the apple. It cracked in two. An odd, satisfied smirk shaped his mouth. He proffered one half to Serena.

Serena's brows knit. She tied off her work and stood.

"Are you engaged now, Tracy?"

"At your service, sister." He bowed, his thin-lipped grin faltering.

"Thank you. I wish to go to Avesbury. I should like your company and I have need of the carriage. Will you drive?"

"Of course."

"What business do you have in Avesbury?" Davina

asked without looking up from her work. Tracy studied his mother's bent head.

"I ordered a gown at the dressmaker's. It is ready today."

"What sort of gown?"

"A ball gown," purchased with her own money, her mother's dowry, Serena's first gift to herself for attaining the austere age of twenty-five in Davina's house without losing her love of laughter.

"Why didn't you have it made up by that *modiste* in London?"

Serena forced a look upon her face that mimicked her name. She curtsied and left the chamber.

Tracy drove, chatting the few miles to Avesbury about inconsequentials. Serena drew in the honeyed scents of early summer and gazed out at the sloping fields dotted with sheep and interspersed with wildflowers, the pears and peaches and nut trees alongside the road dropping petals to make ready for fruit. The perfection had once soothed her, before she had seen the perfection of a wicked earl. And tasted it.

"You are quiet, Ser."

She glanced at her stepbrother. He held the ribbons loosely, his gold hair reflecting the sunshine.

"Am I?"

"You never talk much when Mother's around, but I expected a bit more from you on this ride. You did ask me to come along, after all."

"I did. But I have nothing in particular to discuss, I'm afraid. I only wanted company."

"That's not like you. Happy enough on your own. Always have been. What's bothering you?"

Her conscience. Her lax morality. Her pathetic weakness in the face of Davina's wrongful resolution.

Her very unwise heart.

"I suppose I miss Charity's companionship. She is always, well . . . *there*, if you understand me."

"Like a lapdog."

"Of course not."

"A stand-in, then." He glanced at her, brow lifted. Only Tracy had ever asked her how she got along after Viola and her mother were gone. But after the first few queries, he had not asked again. He had not believed her either. They all knew her to be a dreamer.

"A faery."

"A faery? Doing it a bit too brown, aren't you, sis?"

"Charity is as lovely as a faery."

"Not nearly clever enough to be one, though. Or mean-spirited. Nursed my father on his deathbed for months, and she was only a little girl."

"Some faeries are good-willed." She chewed on her lip. "And such faeries ought to be allowed to marry gentlemen of their own choosing."

"She's done for, Ser. You'd better become accustomed to the idea."

"You don't seem so resigned to it." She turned fully to him, the breeze brushing across her cheek beneath a dapple of tree branches overhanging the road. "I don't think I have ever seen you speak to your mother like that before, Tracy, just now in her sewing parlor."

He set his jaw but did not respond.

"Tracy?"

"Listen, Serena, you needn't press me about this. I'm doing what I can."

Her pulse jumped. "To end the betrothal?"

"I cannot speak further about it. Just know I have it in my sights." He was silent a long moment. "Savage wasn't best pleased with it either," he said, almost as though speaking to himself. "Very decent of him to do the right thing by her, but I don't think he wanted to."

The rumbling road beneath the carriage wheels echoed Serena's thoughts and emotions, scattered and rocky. *He wasn't best pleased.* Her belly stung with tingles of hope.

"Serena?"

"Yes?"

"You are a fine person. A good friend." He paused. "I admire you."

"Good heavens, Tracy, what has brought this on?"

"Don't tease, Ser. A fellow's got to say what he must while he's able."

"Why, are you going somewhere? Don't tell me you have volunteered for the Foreign Office?"

"No," he scoffed. "Nothing like that. But I mean it. Don't forget that."

She folded her gloved hands upon her lap.

"Then thank you."

They reached Avesbury in short time. Tracy went on to the pub to order tea for Serena and stronger refreshment for himself while she visited the dressmaker. It was a gown fit for a princess, pale blue and sparkling with sequins and crystal beads upon the bodice. Charity's ball costume of white, tissue-thin silk and an overskirt of pearl-studded tulle was much more fashionable, and her stepsister's beauty would enhance it all the more. Serena hadn't any notion of outshining Charity, but her throat grew tight imagining wearing the gown—even for such an occasion. She had never owned anything so beautiful.

The dressmaker wrapped it carefully in paper and gave it to her assistant to load into Tracy's carriage. Serena was thanking the *modiste* when a woman in serviceable gray taffeta and a mobcap atop her shining gray curls came through the door.

"Miss Carlyle!" A smile creased the woman's round

face. "It's a pleasure to see you. What brings you to Avesbury?"

"Good day, Mrs. Tubbs. I am picking up a gown Mrs. Shepherd made for me." She gestured to the dressmaker stepping into the rear room. "I hope you are well."

"As well as can be. How are those nieces and nephews of mine getting along at the Hall now?"

"Growing swiftly. Your brother has already taught little Johnny to ride."

"John is a fond papa, and a fine coachman."

"The best. I hope he and Bess conveyed to you my compliments on the spectacular event you orchestrated at the Park a sennight ago. The open house was a great success, it seems."

"Oh, not at all." Mrs. Tubbs waved her hands as though batting away flies. "My master was the one who did it all."

"Did he? How fine of him." Exceptional. A London rake planning a country party for hundreds of people? "But I suspect Mr. Savage assisted."

The housekeeper shook her head. "I'm afraid he's rather low these days, miss, on account of the usual complaint, of course."

Serena nodded.

"But my master being who he is, he won't stand for it. He had Master Aaron hopping mad about some thing or other the other day. Always trying to stir him up, bless his soul. Of course, I shouldn't tell you that, but you're such a lovely young lady and my brother and his wife have always said such good of you. You care for that family better than any newcomer could, I'll merit."

Davina, of course. Seven years was not enough time for country folk to accept a stranger into their midst.

"My sisters are very dear to me, Mrs. Tubbs. I would do anything for them."

A string of beads upon a rack glimmered in a ray of sunshine piercing the window. The housekeeper's gaze seemed to flicker in the rainbowed light.

"My master said that very same thing to me about you not three days ago."

Serena's stomach tightened. "Did he? How singular."

"Don't you say so?" She lowered her voice. "But he is a gentleman amongst gentlemen, miss, even when he's on that ship of his, sailing off to the good Lord knows where, all for the orphans and widows' sakes. Softhearted to the core, though those folks in London wouldn't know him from Satan. But we do, don't we?" She smiled conspiratorially and shook her head with fond tolerance, apparently thoroughly oblivious to the wild shock coursing through Serena.

It could not be.

It *could* not be.

He—

Mrs. Tubbs must be mistaken. She had only been housekeeper at Savege Park for . . . twenty-five years.

No.

Oh, dear God.

"Of course," Serena said upon a little choke of desperate air. "Mrs. Tubbs—"

"There's that rascally brewer now." Peering out the window, the housekeeper bustled toward the door. "He's a new fellow over from Clovelly, Miss Carlyle, and up to all the tricks. I'll have to ask Mr. Haycock to take him in hand if he doesn't start giving me what I pay for."

Serena's heart raced, damp palms soaking through her kid gloves.

"Naturally," she managed. "Mrs. Tubbs—"

"Wasn't it a pleasure seeing you today, miss?" She pulled the door open. "And I am glad to know you didn't take a chill from that awful alcove. I've told Mr. Haycock we must have that old pantry doorway walled up once and for all, but with the sheering and planting and repairs, it's forgotten again. Perhaps in the fall after harvest. Good day to you now."

The door jingled shut.

Serena swallowed repeatedly, head reeling, dizzy with mingled panic, astonishment, and sheer exhilaration. She could not believe it. But there it was, insisting upon being believed.

Perhaps Mrs. Tubbs was misinformed. Or inventing stories. Servants always thought too highly of generous masters, especially if they knew them from childhood.

It explained so much. And from what she knew of his history—*both* men's history—it was easily explainable if one only thought to align the clues.

Serena's brain raced. So many clues. Too many coincidences. Only the vastly differing characters of the two men, their divergent habits and attitudes, drew a screen over the obvious. A care-for-nothing, pleasure-seeking, town-loving rake and a callous, merciless, hero of a pirate could have nothing in common.

Except, perhaps, everything.

Serena drew in long, slow breaths, forcing steadiness into her quivering body while her mind spun. But a quarter hour later when she met Tracy for tea, she could not control the frantic beating of her heart that sealed her lips so effectively she could not manage conversation despite his concerned looks. And when she had reviewed and reviewed again Mrs. Tubbs's words, her own housekeeper Bess's comments about sailors, and so many other subtle hints passed to her through the mouths of servants, she wondered at her blindness, and at the blindness of the rest of polite society who had absolutely no idea that the Earl of

Savege and the pirate captain Redstone were one in the same.

Recalling Alex's firm insistence that she should not concern herself with smugglers and pirates, Serena's skin prickled with the thrill of his secret. Then, without breaking its galloping stride, her mind turned to the only firm conviction she could muster from her confusion of thoughts and emotions. The single insistent thread of certainty in the whole.

Charity must not, under any circumstances, marry this man. Whatever that required, she herself would assure it. Nothing had changed.

And yet everything had.

Chapter 12

About his shoulder he slung his sharp sword, and beneath his shining feet bound his fair sandals, and went forth from his chamber like a god to look upon.

—HOMER, *ODYSSEY*

Alex adjusted the snowy cuffs of his shirt peeking from a fitted black coat more suited to Carlton House than Glenhaven Hall. With steady hands he affixed a diamond solitaire pin within the fall of his cravat and met his valet's gaze in the mirror.

"What is it, Tubbs?" His arms dropped to his sides. "Go on, come clean. You have been gawking at me for an hour. You disapprove of my coat?"

"No, my lord. It suits the occasion well."

"Then you disapprove of the occasion?"

"I cannot say, sir." His mouth set in a prim line. All his servants were behaving peculiarly. It could only be their concern over the changes they imagined would take place when a new mistress moved in.

Over his dead body.

Alex met his brother in the hall at the base of the stairs.

"Ready, old chap?"

Aaron gave him a steady look. "My dancing shoes are laced."

A ball, for God's sake, for a man whose twin brother could barely walk. The Baroness of Carlyle was as cruel-hearted as conniving. But Aaron's spirits seemed, oddly, to have improved as the week wore on and the night of the blasted betrothal party neared. Alex had hope.

They took the coach in grand style, arriving early so that they might stand in a receiving line. Ridiculous affectation in the country. He hadn't done such a thing since the route his mother threw in town to celebrate his twin's departure for the war. He'd been too foxed to recall any of it very well the following day.

He saw her first among a cluster of servants. She spoke, nodding her glistening head and addressing each maid and footman in turn, her eyes meeting theirs directly, a gentle smile upon her generous lips. The servants dispersed, she turned and met his gaze, and heat rushed from his chest into his groin.

Clearly this would be a great deal more difficult than he had imagined.

A gown of summer blue caressed her gently, sparkling over her breasts and tracing the line of her hips and slender legs. Around her neck a thin gold chain dangled, a single teardrop sapphire hovering above the cleft between her breasts where he most wished to lay his tongue now. She stared at him, her glorious eyes wider than he had seen them before. Pink stained her cheeks, a remarkable show of modesty for a woman of such ready passion.

He must find the girl immediately. His betrothed. No time could be wasted.

Alex turned from Serena and met her stepmother crossing the chamber, her daughter upon her arm.

"Dear Lord Savege, how lovely it is to see you here. We have missed your company this week."

He bowed. "Good evening, ma'am. Miss Lucas, would you care to take a stroll upon the terrace before your guests arrive?"

"Your guests, as well, my lord." The baroness's lips curved like a carriage whip in motion.

He offered his arm to the girl. "Madam?"

Flickering a dull gaze at her mother, she placed her hand upon his sleeve like a moth alighting. Her fingers trembled. He drew her toward the garden path he had first walked with Serena that day that seemed like a lifetime ago, when he had been so struck by her vibrant beauty. In comparison, the female at his side seemed the mere shade of a woman.

"Miss Lucas," he said gently when they reached the slate paving winding through thickets of early summer flowers, the perfect English garden lit with Chinese lanterns for the occasion. "I have neglected calling upon you these past several days in the hopes that I would receive a visit from your father instead, asking me to withdraw my suit. That is usually how it is done, as I understand it."

Her lashes fluttered but her mouth remained a pale line, her gaze downcast. Tiny striations of red laced the plumps of her cheek, and the whites of her eyes appeared ivory. The same marks had scored Kitty's face for weeks after Lambert Poole used and abandoned her.

Miss Lucas remained silent.

Alex covered her frigid hand with his palm.

"I know you cannot be happy with this match," he persisted, maintaining a soothing voice despite his rising frustration. "Your mother has clearly driven you into it as successfully as she forced my hand."

Her lips parted, then she ducked her head.

"Miss Lucas?"

Her gold curls shook back and forth, two agitated jerks.

"No, sir."

"No, sir, what?" He bent to peer beneath her brow. "My dear, you must tell her the way of it. If left to me to do it, you would be ruined."

Her head came up swiftly. "You will not?"

He regarded her for a steady moment then shook his head. Her shoulders slumped, in regret or relief, he could not tell. He released her hand.

"If you cry off, Miss Lucas, I will support any justification you give for it. I give you my word." Another nick would not effect his reputation. Nor did he care if it did.

Her lips parted. "I—I—" she whispered, her eyes brightening. Hope sparked in Alex's chest. "I *cannot*." She pressed a kerchief to her mouth. "I cannot," she repeated through the lace. "My mother— You cannot understand the— She—She—" She sobbed.

Alex took her hand.

"Do not cry. You must greet your guests with a clear face." He patted her fingers, an avuncular gesture. Good God he was only thirty-one years old. How could his life have come to this? And why did he feel as aged as Methuselah now? Or perhaps he was merely weary. Weary like the sailor Odysseus who day after day sat upon the shore of a beautiful goddess's lair, despairing of ever finding his way home again.

But in the end Odysseus did go home. After twenty years at war and in exile upon the sea, he found his way back to his Penelope.

Alex guided his betrothed toward the ballroom where her family and Aaron greeted guests. Serena kept her gaze averted, her countenance pleasant to the collection of polite society found in the country at this awkward time of year—those who had returned early from London to see about their crops and herds, a good number of elderly ladies and country squires, few people of high fashion but all perfectly correct. No smell of shop about Lady Carlyle's gathering.

It was all the same to Alex. He only cared for the company of two persons in the place, and one he was no longer permitted to pursue. The other remained noticeably erect and impressively calm, much like the sea in a dead wind. The dead wind of his brother's soul.

When all guests were welcomed, chandeliers lit, ratafia and champagne tasted, and violins and celli tuned, Alex requested the honor of his betrothed's hand in a dance. Once again she proved a wearisome partner, with no conversation and little grace. He chatted of superficialities for the benefit of spectators, she replied in monosyllables, then he was free of her.

He stood up with as many ladies as the orchestra provided sets. He could not recall ever doing so before in the course of his dozen years in society. But tonight he welcomed any diversion from his brother's increasingly blank stare, his betrothed's pallid visage, and her mother's haughty mask of triumph. Curiously, the baron was hardly to be seen.

"You should ask Miss Carlyle to dance," Aaron said as Alex handed him another glass of champagne. He needed brandy, both of them did, but this must suffice. "She has endured the attentions of old men and dullards all evening, and you slight her by not taking her down a set."

"Thank you, brother. When I wish your advice upon etiquette I will make certain to ask for it." His eyes narrowed. "But she is very pretty." Beyond lovely. "Why don't you ask her to dance?"

"Bastard."

"Coward."

Aaron limped away. As he came to a doorway, Miss Lucas appeared in it. Aaron bowed. Her lips curved into a shy smile.

Alex took in a tight breath and sought out her stepsister among the array. She stood in a shadowed corner, her back to the wall, gaze trained upon him. He moved toward her. She stepped forward to meet him, unafraid, unabashed, with perfect serenity of face and form. He had, perhaps, underestimated her experience with gentlemen of his sort. She smiled placidly, no hint of rosiness about her cheeks now.

"Miss Carlyle." He bowed and reached for her hand—he should not, he knew—and touched perfect, trembling bliss. The air went out of his lungs.

"My lord." She curtsied and withdrew her quivering fingers, her eyes a study of curiosity and, astoundingly, mischief. Alex's chest loosened.

"Do you find something to amuse you in this august event, madam, or is it I that causes your mirth?"

"Oh," her eyes flashed dark with strands of candle-light, "I could never express amusement over one of my stepmother's parties. They are far too impressive. This is a fine example, don't you agree?"

"Of course. Would you care to dance, Miss Carlyle?"

"Thank you, I prefer not, Lord Savage." Her tongue seemed to linger upon his name. A fortnight ago he would have taken her hand, led her to a secluded spot, and kept her there until she was unfit to return to the ballroom. He should have done so at his house a sennight since. He should have dragged her to his bed-chamber, disappeared from his own party to make love to a beautiful woman, and so forfeited his role as host as well as the opportunity to become leg shackled to her stepsister.

Regrets abounded. Alex suspected he was, at this point, comprised of little else.

"And why must I be disappointed in this, madam? Are you weary of dancing so early in the evening?"

"It is after midnight, far from early by country standards. But you are no doubt accustomed to town hours."

"No doubt. You have not answered my question."

"I have no satisfactory excuse, at least that I care to share." Her eyes danced, but behind the lively hue, questions swam. Alex's pulse quickened.

"Serena—"

"It would be best if you addressed me formally."

"I am not so much of a cad as you believe me to be. Not for years now, at least." He smiled softly.

"And how much of a cad is that, my lord? A mediocre one, or an infamous one?"

"Infamous, I suspect." If he could touch her again, upon some common pretext, he could at this moment die a happy man. Or at least a painfully aroused one. "A week ago behind that broken door, contrary to appearances—"

"And reputation."

"—I did not—"

"As well as my own experience."

"—voluntarily—"

"Don't." She closed her eyes, drawing her shapely lip between her teeth. A rigid current ran up Alex's spine. She lifted her gaze again, conveying all. "Sir, my loyalty to my sister—however misguided she is now in pursuing this match—does not allow me such a disclosure from you. Not—" Her lashes flickered. "Not now."

He nodded. "You are justified in silencing me." But he would extract himself from this betrothal, and then she would hear him. "I am once more chastened it seems."

Her eyes seemed to retreat. "I do not intend chastisement. You are doing the right thing, I think, although—" The opening strains of a waltz captured her faltering voice. He imagined taking her in his arms for the dance. He could do so without fear of detection by her family and others. His skills at playing a part were extraordinary, honed through years of practice.

"Although?" he prompted.

"Although I do not entirely understand why, and certainly not how."

"Don't you understand why?"

Her brows dipped. "*How* is rather more to the point, sir. But I suppose you will do as you may." Her gaze flickered. "As will I."

"Then we must hope that one of us will meet with success." He could dance with her. He could act for the assembly. But as soon as their hands touched, she would know.

Now, however, he would not abuse her so. He could not show her a glimpse of that which he could not offer her fully.

Yet.

Serena sucked in wisps of air. It filtered into her rushing blood, buoying her. Astonishing, given the murky confusion of her thoughts.

"I suspect you have good reason for pursuing your course in this manner." The very best. He was a man of conviction, decision, yet compassion. Unusual to say the least for a rake. But not so for a hero. Not for Perceval or Galahad or Arthur. Not for Robin Hood.

It made no sense whatsoever for the Earl of Savege to respect an alliance forced through a manipulative mother's trickery. By his own admission and generally accepted knowledge, he had ruined any number of young ladies, though not in recent years. He needn't accept Charity now.

But a hero would. Lancelot had married Elaine, after all. And the Greek warlord Odysseus remained with Calypso for ages. Of course, that was because he couldn't find a boat to sail home, and anyway he thought the goddess would kill him if he left.

A giggle welled up in Serena's throat. She must be hysterical, or plain silly. His sultry gaze and familiar address did that to her, as though they knew each other well already. But in truth they knew little more than the flavor of each other's lips, the texture of hands and face, and he was still betrothed to her sister.

Until he made an end to that—or Charity did—they must play this game of pretense. It was a single thread of sanity amidst the clamor of uncertainties, and Serena needed it. She could not yet allow herself to truly believe.

"Will you remain at the Park this summer, my lord? The season is nearly concluded, or you would certainly return to town, I guess."

"I have little interest in town now, in fact."

"Really?"

"Less and less each day." His warm gaze stole along her throat to her exposed shoulders, heating beneath her skin like a bath.

"Oh," she grasped at breath. "But I suppose you travel a great deal in the regular course of things, in any event."

He regarded her carefully. For the first time in their acquaintance, he seemed uncertain of her intent.

"Do you enjoy traveling, Miss Carlyle?"

"I enjoy sea travel." Foolish gamble. But the words were already said, and she could not confront him point-blank. Her daring did not extend that far. He was—for heaven's sake—*famous*. A dangerous man.

"Have you done much of it, then?"

"Only—" She faltered, her courage slipping.

"Only?"

"Only in my imagination." Her heart beat in frantic tempo. The corner of his mouth stole upward.

"I am a careful man, Serena. I do not make the same mistake twice. This time, I applaud your imagination. It serves you well to dream of the sea."

Her name upon his tongue, his words, drew her into his secret, flooding her with longing and rendering her dumb. His gaze slipped to her mouth, traced the line of her jaw to her hair, then back to her eyes. She read everything in the smoky depths, all the desire coursing through her, the sweet agitation of potential and hunger that could not be satisfied. It left her awestruck.

"Madam," he bowed, "good evening," and strode away.

Serena did not know where to look, her heart and mind atumble. She cast her gaze about for distraction.

Charity sat upon a silk-covered chair at the edge of the dance floor, Mr. Savege beside her. Her eyes were soft, his smiling, neither untoward, both perfectly unexceptionable. Anyone observing would think what fond siblings they were soon to become. Serena knew her sister, and she knew better.

Frustration twined through her, and a niggling fear that perhaps, despite all, Charity would not release him and then where would they be? He would be forced to cast her stepsister off, Charity would be ruined, and she herself would have nothing—not Charity's happiness—not delicious seduction.

The memory of Alex's hands upon her would not die. They were not the hands of a gentleman, but a sailor's, rough, capable, strong. Beautiful hands that made her insides shimmer.

She sought him out again with her gaze across the chamber. As though he anticipated her regard, his gaze lifted to hers and for a moment he caressed her more intimately than his hands ever had, or his tongue, deep inside her, and Serena knew that in the world of dreams, heaven and hell must be entwined.

His handsome face sober, he shifted his gaze to Charity and his brother.

Around Serena the music scratched out of tune, candles sputtered, and headdresses and cravats sagged. She swallowed a sigh and went to find her father. It was high time to end the festivities. The betrothal celebration had run its course. No more amusement could be had this night.

The following day Charity appeared at breakfast weary and drawn once more. The gentle pleasure in her face while she spoke with Mr. Savege had departed. In its place shone renewed misery.

Serena swallowed a mouthful of dry muffin and set down her coffee.

"Charity, I should like your assistance in cutting flowers this morning. The heat from the candles last night wilted everything the gardener cut yesterday, and today is his holiday." She stood, ignoring her stepmother's suspicious regard and Diantha's curious look. Her father did not lift his attention from his journal. "Will you help me?"

Eyes rimmed in red, Charity nodded.

In the garden, Serena linked arms with her and drew her along the path, a basket tucked over her elbow.

"How did you enjoy your ball?" She made her voice light.

"Well, thank you."

"It seemed you enjoyed one part of it greater than the rest."

"I danced with him," she said dully. Serena would have preferred tremulous. Her sister seemed to have lost even the will to be distressed.

"Of course you did." She paused to snip a full pink bloom. "Charity, you must tell your mother you cannot marry the earl. You simply must. You are doing yourself a disservice to continue in this, and you will be very unhappy with the outcome." Another flower fell into her basket. Grasshoppers zigzagged through the warm air, their wings and the songbirds in nearby branches sending up a symphony discordant with Serena's nerves.

"I wish to tell her." Charity spoke the words so softly Serena barely heard. Her breath caught, hand arrested upon the shears.

"You do?" She met her stepsister's gaze. Charity's eyes seemed like whirlpools. "Charity, do you have feelings for another gentleman?"

Her silvery-gold head jerked up and down in tiny movements.

Serena drew in a deep breath. This was better than she had hoped.

"Do you believe he returns your admiration?"

The girl's chalk cheeks colored up.

"You must tell your mother," Serena said. "It would be wrong not to do so."

"I cannot," she whispered.

Serena dropped the basket and grasped her sister's hands.

"If I stand beside you, can you? I know how difficult it can be to speak one's mind to her. But we will hold hands." She laced their fingers together tight, her sister's soft and cold. "Just like this. Can you do it then, Chare?"

Tentatively, she nodded again. Serena grabbed the basket.

"Let us go now. It is best to tackle unpleasant tasks without delay."

Charity walked half a pace behind despite their joined hands, but she went voluntarily. They found Davina in the drawing room.

"Stepmother, Charity has something she wishes to speak with you about."

Davina cast Serena a sharp look, then a glance at the footman. He withdrew and closed the door.

"What is it? I am quite busy and must begin writing invitations for the wedding. I have little more than a fortnight to prepare everything. Do be quick about this."

Charity's fingers stiffened between Serena's. Serena pressed her forward, her insides churning with mingled hope and unease.

"Charity?" Davina frowned.

"Mama. Mama, I—I—" Her bow-shaped lips barely moved, her fingers viselike upon Serena's. "I do not wish to marry the earl. I—I like another gentleman."

Davina's eyes opened like an angry mare's, the whites showing all around blue centers.

"You have no right to like another gentleman. You are betrothed to Lord Savege and will devote yourself to him."

Charity shrank back. "Yes, Mama."

"No!" Serena exclaimed. "No, she must not. She is not yet officially betrothed to him and does not like him. In fact, she is terrified of him. Anyone can see that."

Davina's eyes flashed. "You know nothing about it."

"I do indeed." Serena's heart pounded. "My sister could be perfectly happy with a gentleman of her choice but you seem to be so intent upon social advancement that you blind yourself to her misery. How can you be so unfeeling?"

Her stepmother advanced, her whole person seeming to grow larger, narrow face flaring with fury. Charity retreated, tugging away from Serena.

"Do not gainsay me, Serena. You have put her up to this, thinking you could best me. But my daughter will wed whom I choose and when I choose it. You are not mistress of my children or of this house, no matter how your father tolerates you."

"I am not, it's true." She trained her tongue against her body's shaking. "But I love my sister and wish to see her happy. Why don't you?"

"There is a great deal more to marriage than happiness. If you had not made yourself unsuitable for a respectable union as your father hoped for you, you would know that by now."

Charity whimpered. Serena struggled for breath. Davina had never spoken of it in seven years, not since that horrible day. It should not bother her after so long. That it cut so freshly sent alarm through her. She should not care that she was unmarriageable. She *did* not care.

Oh, *she could not.*

"You are wrong," she uttered, twisting her hands together. "You are damning your daughter with this, and I"—her voice dipped low—"I hate you for it." She whirled around, grabbing Charity's limp hand and dragging her from the chamber.

In the corridor, Tracy caught up with her.

"Whoa there." He drew her away, gaze flashing to Charity's tear-streaked cheeks. "What's happened here?"

"You must take Charity driving, Tracy. She needs air immediately. Please." Serena pressed her stepsister's hand into his and fled.

But there was no place to flee to. It would not matter if she hid in a cottage away from Davina's hard rule. She wanted only to live in her dreams, but lately those had far outstripped sense and reality. Convinced she did it for Charity, she had brought down Davina's wrath instead. Charity would suffer for it.

Someday, when her own dreams finally disintegrated to ash, she might learn to endure a life without a gentleman's touch, without a heart devoted to her. But she could not bear a sister's suffering. Never again.

Chapter 13

How I love my rolling sailor when he's on a rolling sea.

—"Rolling Sea"

Alex twirled the scrap of foolscap between thumb and forefinger.

"Poole has his go-ahead from the Board of Admiralty. He will be here within a fortnight."

"Not here, and not in person, surely." The summer evening without stretched into night. Aaron sat with his back to the library window, his face draped in shadow. Better for both of them. This way Alex could not see the expression of resigned misery his brother had tried to hide all day.

"I would not put it beyond him to come himself," Alex said. "He is a capable sailor."

"You are much better, and he has no ship of his own here. He will be at the mercy of whatever naval officer the Admiralty chooses. Braverton, probably, or Halloway. Neither of them have been happy with you, even when you were sinking French men-of-war."

Alex studied his quartermaster's note again.

"Poole will come here. Jin has it upon good authority that our fine earl knows the *Cavalier* is in the region." He paused. "He asks permission to haul away."

"Without you?"

"Why without me? It's nearly June. I had planned on going, or have you forgotten?"

No response met him. Alex stared out the window.

"I will return in ample time for the harvest." And he would remain at the Park. Weeks ago he'd had little desire to return to London in the fall. Now, with Serena Carlyle a few tantalizing miles distant, forbidden as an apple in Paradise, he had no desire whatsoever to leave Devon.

But as yet he had no foolproof plan either. The chit would not budge. He was at *point non plus*.

"In case you have forgotten, Lady Carlyle is planning a wedding for a fortnight from now," Aaron said slowly. "A wedding at which you are to be the groom. Mother and Kitty are already on their way home to assist in the preparations."

Alex waved a negligent hand and stood.

"You know how I hate ceremony, little brother, especially the matrimonial sort. Why don't you take my place? Wedding vows would ring so much truer upon your tongue than mine." He strode for the door and out before his brother could respond.

In his study, he poured a glass of rum and swallowed it whole, the burn in his throat nothing compared to the hard heat in his chest that had settled there the previous night when she met his gaze across the ballroom. He was an absolute imbecile, finally ensnared by a woman simply because he could not have her.

He carried the crystal decanter to the terrace, stretched out upon a chaise, and poured another glass, then another, until the stars tilted into one another and he lost track of the constellations.

"Milord," someone mumbled, "would you like dinner brought here?"

Alex brandished the empty decanter.

"More rum."

He awoke in blackness to the chatter of birds, harbingers of the dawn. Head heavy, he climbed to his bedchamber, filled a saddlebag with smallclothes and starched linens, and scribbled a note. He addressed it to his brother, depositing it upon the dressing table for Tubbs to deliver.

Before the first gray of early morning stabbed the dark, he had saddled his horse and rode toward the hidden dock. The notorious libertine earl was a living, breathing scandal, second only to the pirate Redstone in his flagrant disregard for law and morality. But the man Alexander Savege was a coward, pure and simple.

Night wind came off the cliff side, enough to drive Alex's single-sailed craft away from the inlet at a clip. Ahead, the *Cavalier* rested upon the horizon, canvas dull behind the veil of morning. Just as he anticipated, Jin was holding the ship close to shore, still waiting for his reply. But his messenger boy, Billy, would sleep the morning through in the wood house at Savege Park, unaware he had missed his boat. Jin must welcome his captain instead.

Alex came alongside the hull. A figure appeared at the rail and a rope swung down. Alex tied the boat and the ladder descended. Slinging the saddlebag over his shoulder, he climbed aboard his ship.

"All attention, cap'n on deck!" Big Mattie shouted from the helm where he was polishing the oaken pins.

The smattering of sailors atop halted their work to tug at caps and offer him a "G'day, Cap'n," or "Welcome back." Not one batted a lash at Alex's clean face and gentleman's clothing.

Alex paused, then crossed the deck to the hatchway, scanning the spars, rigging, and dozen furled sails.

No breeze stirred and the ship drifted, anchor stowed, sweeps at the ready. Jin would not risk being taken dead in the water, not with the British navy out hunting for them.

His lieutenant met him upon the stair. Jin reversed direction, gaping a moment then shuttering his expression when they passed a cluster of crew members cleaning the guns. Alex nodded, the sailors greeted him unremarkably, and Alex and Jin passed into the captain's quarters.

Jin closed the door.

"What are you doing here?" He did not ask the obvious: after eight years, why had Alex chosen to appear aboard as the Earl of Savege? Alex didn't quite know, only that his crew's loyalty and discretion stunned him. A rough, weathered lot, they had never failed him, like his servants and tenants at the Park whom he continually abandoned yet who held him up like a hero, a title he had never deserved.

He threw down his pack and went to the basin to wash the sheen of rum-redolent morning mist from his face.

"Giving you a holiday," he said into the towel. "I want you back here in a fortnight to put to sea."

"You are not concerned about Poole, then?"

Alex folded the linen and laid it aside.

"If he finds us, I will stand him down."

"And if he brings friends? How many frigates can you handle at once?"

"You know precisely how many."

"Why not head for the Channel now?"

"Because," Alex smiled without mirth, "I am expected at Avesbury Chapel in fifteen days."

"The chapel?" Jin stared again, his light eyes disbelieving. "You are not marrying that girl, Alex."

"So you know." As Alex expected. Little got past Jinan Seton—former slave, master seaman, the cleverest son of a bitch he had ever known. "Then you also know that my intended balks at withdrawing from the agreement." And other considerations impeded. The pride of a scarred gentleman. The tender, steadfast heart of a winsome lady.

"Alex." Jin's brow furrowed, his aristocratic face taking on an attitude of impatience. Only this man could regard him with such a patently critical expression and remain in his good graces. They had been through far too much together. "What are you thinking?"

"Nothing that would interest you, certainly." Alex went to the door.

"There is a woman involved."

"There is always a woman involved, Jinan. I know you know that. I taught you to read with classical literature, after all."

Jin grinned. "Point taken." He sobered. "But not for you."

"Still not for me. The fair flesh tempts me only insofar as I may escape it when the deed is well done."

"You are lying."

"You haven't any idea. Now leave. Your chariot awaits you portside."

"Aye aye, Captain. But, news first. Matouba sighted the *Osprey* a sennight ago, off the larboard side, but so far out it wasn't worth a look-see. Running shallow."

Then, not loaded down with cargo.

"Any other neighbors trawling about?" The Viscount of Ashford's visit in Avesbury a fortnight earlier scratched at Alex.

Jin regarded him curiously. "A few merchantmen. Should we have seen someone else?"

"Only the British navy." Alex shook his head and waved his friend through the door. The day was rising cool and clear upon the water, a tickle of breeze stirring the sheets. He watched his quartermaster onto the boat and away across the blue-green expanse, disappearing toward shore. Then he turned his face to the deck. His helmsman stood amidships, awaiting orders.

"Cut the sails, Mattie. Let's take a ride."

If Ashford's vessel, the *Blackhawk*, still stalked the coast, Alex wanted to know. And if he bumped into Lambert Poole and a fleet of men-of-war in the meantime, at least he wouldn't have to find a way to escape the parson's noose.

Serena awoke for the sixth morning in a row with a megrim, this time to wails. Bolting upright, she cast off the covers, dragged on a wrapper, and ran to the stair.

In the foyer below, a maid clutched Bess, sobbing, the housekeeper patting her back. Both footmen and another maid stood nearby, huddled and whispering. Diantha peeked from the drawing room doorway, chestnut curls bouncing around wide blue eyes.

Serena's father moved into the foyer toward his housekeeper.

"Bess, John has the cart ready to take Penny home."

Bess drew the girl around with a snug arm and walked her away, murmuring comforting sounds. Serena's father gestured to the other servants and they dispersed. Serena clutched her wrapper about her.

"Papa, what has happened?"

He looked up, his face drawn.

"I am afraid the news is poor. Penny's sister went missing from her family's farm two days ago and has not been seen since. This morning they discovered her cloak by the inlet bridge."

Chill crawled up Serena's spine. "Have the smugglers been sighted?"

His gaze darted to Diantha. Serena's stepsister retreated behind the door, but her hem showed.

"Serena," he said quietly.

"Papa, Penny's family are *our* tenants."

"Your father's tenants," Davina said coolly, moving into the foyer, "Not yours, Serena. Diantha, go help Nurse prepare Faith for our visit to Clovelly." She snapped her fingers. The fifteen-year-old ducked from the drawing room and up the stairs past Serena, eyes full of excited agitation.

"Clovelly?" Penny's family's farm bordered the estate closest to the port town. "To look for information about the smugglers?"

"What smugglers?" Davina's lip curled. "You are excessively foolish, Serena. Penny's sister was a wild girl, the precise reason I refused to employ her in this house. She has run off for an adventure—"

"And left her cloak upon an inlet bank?" Serena shook her head. "*Papa.*"

"Daughter, there is nothing to be done," he said without feeling. "The girl made a foolish choice and her family must now suffer for raising her poorly."

His words staggered Serena into silence. Davina lifted her gaze, icy blue and triumphant.

Serena rushed to her bedchamber, called for a maid, and dressed. Then she hurried down the hill. Glen Village was astir with the news.

"Mr. Cobb said he saw those smugglers the other day in Clovelly harbor," Mrs. Hatchet said breathlessly, hands fluttering about a tray of silk flowers.

"Clovelly harbor?" Did her father know this, or Davina? "When?"

"Not three days ago. As soon as the *Cavalier* disappeared from sight those nasty fellows returned, it seems."

"The *Cavalier* was sighted?" Serena's heart turned about.

"Yes, miss, been here and gone, leaving that poor girl to be filched by a fox at the henhouse."

"Oh, good heavens," she whispered.

Serena's father had sent a note over to Savege Park three days earlier requesting a reply upon the issue of the contract. Mr. Savege returned a message indicating that his brother had been called away suddenly to check upon one of his estates in the north. Lord Savege would return within the fortnight.

Now Serena suspected the truth.

While she had slept fitfully, waking each day to her family falling apart inch by inch as the wedding drew nearer, he had escaped. And, just as the milliner said, he left their little stretch of coast unprotected. As he had said to her on the London street, he did not believe in the threat the smugglers posed any more than her father or stepmother.

But he would be forced to believe it when she'd had her say.

Serena's chest throbbed with anger, purpose, and dangerous anticipation. Frustration cloaked it all. She had thrown away her opportunity the night of the ball, rashly cowed into silence by desire and futile dreams. Now how could she speak with him, leagues away?

But he would return, and she would give him a piece of her mind. Distance made the reality of the pirate Redstone much less awesome—distance, and the memory of his thundercloud eyes sparkling with delight, telling her without words that they shared something. That she *might* dream.

She did not know whether to trust him.

"They left a fellow behind," Mrs. Hatchet said, eyes bright.

"Who? A crew member off the *Cavalier*?"

The milliner nodded, curls bouncing beneath her cap. "All's likely. He's been sitting in the pub for two days, taking all his meals and drinking modestly. Paying like an honest man, of course."

"Is Mr. Cobb certain he's from the *Cavalier*?"

"He said he's a sailor on furlough enjoying the countryside, but if he's off a merchant or fishing vessel. he's the finest midshipman I've seen. He even stabled a horse at Jack's for the night, and he talks like a gentleman, the vicar says."

"He did? He does? Is he still there?"

"I haven't seen him leave, but I've been busy in here with these bergères only just arrived from—"

"Oh, yes, thank you, Mrs. Hatchet. I am much obliged." Serena hurried across the street. Nerves twisted into bundles, she didn't care now that she shouldn't enter the pub without a gentleman escort. She pulled the heavy door wide and met the cool, ale-scented interior. It was empty of all but the pub master.

"G'day, Miss Carlyle." He bowed from behind the tap, smiling. "Come in for a cuppa?"

"Hello, Mr. Cobb." Her gaze darted around. "I understand a gentleman, a sailor, spent some time here during the past few days. Is he still about?"

"No, miss." His brow furrowed. "Jack brought his horse around an hour ago, right after news came about that poor girl. Tragic happenings."

"Wretchedly tragic. Good day, Mr. Cobb." Serena dragged herself from the pub, anticipation curdling as she set up the path toward the Hall, and aching desperation taking its place. It was useless. All of it. What could she do to ensure anyone's safety when she could not even control her own heart?

Branches rustled aside the path and a horseman emerged from the shade of a willow. Serena stumbled to a halt. He dismounted and walked toward her.

"Good morning, ma'am," he said, and bowed as though strange young gentlemen encountered ladies upon country paths every day of the week. He was tall and somewhat lean like her stepbrother, with dark hair and pale blue eyes, his skin tawny with exposure to sun. But his garments were a gentleman's, well made and costly. An onyx pin hid within his cravat, a thick gold ring set with a dark ruby upon his left hand.

"Good morning, sir. This is my father's land, the house not a hundred yards distant. May I assist you in finding your way?" Best to be safe. Her hands shook. As a girl, as many times as she dreamt of encountering a handsome stranger on an impressive steed in a dappled glade, she never imagined he would study her with such critical intensity. Or that he would not look particularly happy about it. He must be the sailor from the *Cavalier*. But then why would he be lurking along this path, of all places, miles away from Savege Park?

"Thank you," he said, an edge to his gentlemanly address. "I have found what I seek, Miss Carlyle."

Serena swallowed around her bubbling fear.

"You must be acquainted with my father, then. Or perhaps my brother. Allow me to guide you up to the Hall. I believe Tracy is still in this morning."

"I am not interested in speaking with your father or brother. I wish conversation with you."

She reached for something to hold onto, or a weapon, her hands meeting only the prickly branches of blackberry bushes. His eyes seemed to smile, though not his lips, then he shook his head.

"I seek only your counsel, ma'am. I am upon an errand of importance to both of us, I think."

Sudden stillness washed through Serena's veins, loosening her constricted throat, dashing apart the fear.

"Have you come from him?"

His mouth turned up at the edges. "Not with his knowledge. But, yes."

Her blood sang. With a few words, a stranger's grin, her world shifted, quaked, and turned upside down. "Who are you?"

"Jinan Seton. I am pleased to make your acquaintance, ma'am." He bowed.

She stared. "What do you know?"

"Enough."

"How?"

Now he smiled fully. "Miss Carlyle, I have been a slave, a servant, a sailor, and a wanted man. All that gentlemen and ladies in their ivory towers do not know of the world seething beneath their feet would astound them."

Serena's hands shook, Mrs. Tubbs's knowing glance passing through her memory. She took a hard breath. "I must speak with him."

His brow lifted. "Must you?"

"You must know about the smugglers. Did they take that girl?"

"I suspect she is with them, yes."

Serena's stomach clenched. "What do you wish to speak with me about?"

"Your sister."

"My sister?"

"She must not hold him to this betrothal."

"Of course not. I have been telling her that for weeks

already but she won't make an end to it, for reasons—" Serena bit her lip. She *must* do it. It was patently clear she could no longer trust Charity. Words her father had spoken in London weeks earlier pressed at her, a reckless idea coming to full fruition. The Earl of Savege needn't hold a monopoly on depravity. If behaving as shamelessly as he were the only way to halt this marriage in the eyes of her family, she would make it so. A rake and a pirate would not resist seduction, and she had nothing to lose.

Except, perhaps, the remainder of her foolish heart.

"Take me to him," she said before prudence could halt her tongue, "and I will convince him to break it off."

"He does not intend to return until the wedding."

The man whose kiss in the dark had scored her soul with bravery was hiding out until the last minute.

"But you know where the *Cavalier* is now, don't you?"

He nodded, his eyes narrowing.

She chewed upon her lip, courage the same as she had once felt in Alex's arms swelling within her. "I can be ready by sunset."

"With what excuse to your family?"

"I will think of something." Her heart racketed. She set off quickly up the path then swung around. He stood perfectly still, watching her. "Can we return by morning?"

"That depends."

It was enough for Serena. "Meet me here."

He nodded.

She turned and flew.

Chapter 14

Way, hay, we roll an' go.
And we roll all night, and we roll all day.

—"SALLY BROWN"

The *Cavalier*'s bow turned slowly behind the gentle landward breeze, yardarms swinging like choreographed dancers, working the ship around to face the newcomer.

"She's hoisted her hanky, Cap'n," Big Mattie grumbled in obvious disappointment. The men were spoiling for a fight against an equal, and nothing like the vessel tacking toward them through the placid sea had come their way all week. They'd picked up a free agent privateer, a twenty-two-gun brig hanging about the mouth of Bristol Channel with a hold full of some honest merchant's goods. But that only whet their appetite for a scrimmage. "Should I tell the boys to stand down the guns?"

"No." A white flag was a white flag. But it was not a guarantee. Alex's heart beat to the rhythm of the *Blackhawk*'s sweeps sending ripples along her path. "Hold them at the ready, but tell them to take care. No mistakes."

The helmsman's chest puffed in affront, but he remained silent.

"Master's on the quarterdeck, sir," shouted Matouba from the crow's nest, but Alex could already see it. Ashford stood at the highest point of his ship before the mizzenmast, hatless to be known at once by sight. Alex nodded to Mattie. The sailor lifted a speaking trumpet to his nearly toothless mouth.

"Advance no further, sirs, or we'll be blowin' your hides down to Davy Jones."

Ashford signaled to his mate, the fellow shouted in French across the deck, another holler sounded beneath, and the oars stilled then reversed direction a few strokes. On deck, sailors hauled the lines, turning canvas through the negligible wind, and the *Blackhawk* slowed to a halt. Late afternoon sunlight cut across her rigging, casting a net of shadows upon the ocean.

Alex filled his lungs. "What business do you have here, Captain?" he shouted across the still water. "Commerce or conflict?"

"Conversation. Invite me aboard."

Blast it, the knave had confidence. But Alex knew he would be a fool to do otherwise. If he died anytime soon, he'd rather it be in a fight with a seventy-gun ship of the line than damn abolitionists.

He signaled for the ladder to be let down and made his way to the rail. Ashford came over in a boat, two oarsmen with no visible weapons. The viscount wore only a saber at his hip, no pistol. But Alex knew well enough of the skill of the *Blackhawk*'s captain with a sword. Rumor traveled swiftly over the salt seas.

Ashford climbed onto deck and glanced about, a quick, professional assessment. Alex would have done the same.

"Pretty little boat," Alex said in greeting, gesturing to the sleek craft drifting fifty yards off the *Cavalier*'s bow. She was shorter than Alex's vessel by ten yards, and with a half-dozen fewer guns. Still plenty lethal. "Your lieutenant won't think of coming around to stern while you're here, will he? Because if he does I'll be obliged to fire upon him," he finished pleasantly.

Ashford grinned. "I am not interested in harming your ship. Or have you forgotten our conversation?"

"Another place, another time." Alex waved a hand.

"Ah. A wise man."

"So some say, but they are sadly misled. What is your purpose here, sir?"

Around them, Alex sensed his crew perched at the ready. One false move from Ashford or his men upon the *Blackhawk* and a dozen lead balls would be lodged in the viscount's flesh within an instant. But Ashford knew that already.

"To restate my offer." The amber eyes studied Alex.

"Offer for what? Unwanted trouble? I'm not a man to change my mind. Your efforts are wasted here."

"Sailors from the *Osprey* took a girl off Carlyle's land, a farmer's daughter. The next time it could be your land."

"When it is, I will be certain to make note of it." Alex imagined Serena walking the secluded path from Glen Village to her father's house and his blood went cold.

He wiped the image away.

"You might forestall the event," Ashford said quietly.

"You might return to your ship and take yourself off. I've given you my answer. Twice now."

Ashford turned and moved toward the rail. He paused and looked about again, this time with obvious admiration.

"Your ship is a beauty, Savege. But she is meant for better work. Don't sell yourself short."

"I'll sell you to the devil if you don't hare off my deck within the next thirty seconds. And if I see your colors again flying toward me, I won't stop to ask your business before I fire."

"I do not doubt it. Good day, Captain."

Alex watched the fellow reboard his ship and the *Blackhawk* turn her bow into the sunset.

"Mattie, when did we last sight the *Osprey*? And where?"

"Long 'round Clovelly harbor, sir, not ten days ago."

"Why do you imagine she's hanging about?"

"Don't know, Cap'n. P'raps she's got a stash some-wheres nearby, and confederates."

"Perhaps." Alex stared at the horizon. "Make our course for the coast. At a clip."

"Aye aye, Cap'n."

Mattie shouted the orders along the length of the deck shining ochre-colored in the fading light. Sailors set to their tasks, sheets swished, and sails hoisted. Alex took the wheel from his mate and leaned into it. The deck swayed beneath his boots as the ship came about, lines creaked, water rolled over the polished hull, and he felt it as though she were his own body. All of it, sounds and sensations, were so familiar, comforting.

But he didn't want comfort. Anger simmered be-neath his skin, the creeping fingers of hopelessness tugging at his chest.

He did not belong here. He loved it, breathed it in like the gods drank ambrosia. He had convinced him-self he'd come to sea this time for the clarity he could only find upon the ocean, to devise some course of action that would save the girl's reputation and his brother's hopes. But Ashford, damn him, was right. He was using it as a hideout, Robin Hood taking cover in goddamned Sherwood Forest.

They carved the dusky water, restless now with the breeze that sprang up at evening. Rain scented the air, clouds moving out from the land darkening the twilight. After some time, minutes without measure upon the ocean, land came into sight. His land.

Alex gave the order to lie to as soon as they reached boat distance, and he put the helm into the hands of a mate. He moved toward the stair, the darkness nearly complete atop. Far forward at the bowsprit a sailor lit a lantern. The men would stay up late, eat, sing, and drink by it. At one time Alex had enjoyed such simple diversion. But no longer.

Tomorrow he would return to Savege Park. The wedding was still more than a sennight away, long enough to halt the betrothal. And when that was settled, he would decide what to do next—about his brother, his ship, a lady he had not stopped thinking about since the moment he set foot to planking.

"Ho, Cap'n!" Matouba shouted from the lookout. "Skiff riding bow-fast at a league. Looks like Master Jin and Billy. And—"

The cloudy twilight cast the ocean's surface into murk. A pinpoint of light hovered over the black water and the dim outline of a boat.

"And?" he called up to the crow's nest.

"I dunno, Cap'n. He's wearing a cloak."

Alex moved toward the rail, peering into darkness. The boat came into view below, a lantern tied to its bow, the figures within barely visible against the craft's white boards. Water slapped the hull between the ship and tiny craft. The sailors to either side of Alex threw down line, and Billy tied her tight and climbed onto the rope then flew hand over fist like a monkey up to the rail.

"Evenin', Cap'n," he said, barely out of breath, tipping his cap. "Gave me the slip back there th'other day, but I'll forgive ye for it." He grinned.

"Billy, who's our guest?"

Jin offered his hand to the cloaked figure. Alex's gut clenched, the hairs on the back of his neck standing up.

Billy screwed up his freckled face. " 'S'a lady, Cap'n."

Big Mattie pushed the boy aside. "What's Master Jin doing with a lady? He knows the articles 'spressly state no sailor should bring aboard a woman. Wrote them up himself."

The woman put her hand into Jin's, the hood of her cloak slipped back, and lamplight shone in her dusky gold hair. Alex shook his head to clear it, the heat of anger, astonishment, and something much more vital, alive, rising in his chest, setting his heart beating fast.

He opened his mouth, closed it again, took in a sharp breath, hoping that oxygen could accomplish what reason was failing at as his worlds collided.

"Hang the articles."

Serena gripped the rope ladder, moisture seeping through her gloves. It did not help that Mr. Seton was right behind her in case her half-boots slipped and she fell. The higher she clambered up, the farther down she could tumble, and she couldn't see a thing in the pitch-black. Good heavens, who knew a ship could have such tall sides? As they had approached, the *Cavalier* loomed like a black forest across a plain. Climbing aboard it did not make it any less formidable.

But none of it really mattered, because what truly had her heart racing was its master.

A hand from above gripped her wrist and hauled her aboard. She scrabbled, staggered, and her feet met solid planking. She righted herself and sucked in breath, peering at the figure before her. She had the impression of a bulky body, and none too clean from the odor.

"Welcome aboard, miss," the sailor grunted, and backed off. "Evenin', Master Jin."

"Where is the captain, Mattie?" Mr. Seton brandished the lantern he had brought onto their little boat at the dock. The light served only to brighten his face and the other sailor's heavy visage, casting the remainder of the deck into darkness except for another lamp quite far away. Creaking sounds, a few clanks here and there, and boot steps.

"I am here."

Serena whirled around. Yards away, visible only by the glow of the distant lantern, a shadowed figure stood at the rail, tall and broad shouldered. Her pounding heart climbed into her throat. The three words had not sounded anything like Alex's voice.

God help her, what if she'd mistaken it? She didn't know Jinan Seton from Adam, and they had neither once said Alex's name.

"Captain," Mr. Seton said behind her, "I ask permission to bring a lady aboard."

"Seems you've already done so, haven't you?"

Serena's blood warmed with mingled relief and exhilaration. It was not his voice precisely, too rough and hard, and with a Celtic hint to it. But she would recognize its rich timbre and teasing tone anywhere, even disguised. Those were imprinted upon her soul.

"I offer my apologies, sir," Mr. Seton said. "She carries an urgent message for you."

A message from herself: rid the coast of the smugglers or she would tell the world exactly what she knew about the notorious Captain Redstone.

Silence streamed across the deck, the lapping of water against the ship's sides and ropes complaining the only sounds now except her raucously beating heart.

"Mattie," he finally said in the same grating murmur, "take the lady to my day cabin and have my steward see that she is made comfortable. I will be along shortly."

"Aye aye, sir," the hulk grunted. Mr. Seton passed him the lantern. "Miss?" He motioned her forward.

Serena didn't bother glancing back. With the light before her, she could not see Alex's face anyway. The sailor led her to a narrow strip of stairs, the hatchway thrown back, and he extended the lamp for her to descend. At the base of the steps the ceiling beams hung just above her brow. Mattie slumped his shoulders, ducking his head, and led her along a deck empty of humans but hanging with empty hammocks. At the shuttered door at the deck's end, he knocked and a sailor opened it, this one dark-skinned.

"The lady's to have tea, and water to freshen up," Mattie grumbled. "Good evenin', miss." He tugged at his cap brim and retreated, leaving her looking upon a beautifully furnished chamber lit by a single lamp. She should have expected such luxury. The man was an earl, after all, not some common sailor.

"Ma'am, the washroom." The steward gestured toward another door, this one letting onto a small chamber with a sloping wall and lead-lined compartment, a basin and jug of water set upon a shelf.

"No. No, thank you." If she tried to wash, she would surely spill water everywhere. Her hands shook like a blancmange. "But I should like some tea." The rum Mr. Seton had plied her with on the little boat as they crossed the endless, fathomless, and increasingly black sea had left her dry-mouthed and a bit dizzy.

"Yes, ma'am." He took her cloak and departed through another door.

Serena stared at the elegant furniture—a winged-back chair upholstered in brocaded silk, a similarly fine sofa, a carved table with matching chairs—and turned away from it all to pace. Would he make her wait long? Would he release his quartermaster from service for bringing her aboard? Did pirates release misbehaving crew members or simply keelhaul them?

Good heavens, what on earth had she been thinking to do this? She didn't really know Alex Savage, Redstone even less. She listened for every sound, every step upon deck, with painfully strained nerves. When the steward reentered the cabin, she jumped.

"Your tea, ma'am." He set a silver tray with cup, saucer, teapot, and sugar dish upon the table. Serena stared at the elegant china, hysterical laughter rising in her throat.

"That will be all, Juan."

Her gaze shot up. He stood in the doorway, shoulder leaning against the door frame, arms folded across his chest. The shadow of a wide-brimmed hat obscured his face.

"Aye aye, sir." The steward bowed.

"Juan." His voice rumbled rough. "Take that lamp with you."

Serena's throat closed. The sailor unsnapped the lantern from the table. Alex did not move, light from the retreating lamp casting him in shadow then disappearing up the stairs. A cloak of darkness wrapped about them. Somewhere a window stood open, cool night air drifting across the cabin and the hush of the ocean beyond.

"Why did you tell him to take that?" she said.

"What are you doing here?"

Sharp heat darted through her, twining sickly. Anger laced his menacing tone, and unspoken threat. The shadows closed around her, not the tantalizing dark of the parlor that night in London, but frightening, alien, like the man standing before her.

"The smugglers, they—" Her tongue faltered, twisted. "They took a girl from my father's lands, a farmer's young daughter. Well, sixteen, I think."

The door shut. Serena's heart jerked.

"What business is that of mine?"

"You must—" She stuttered to a halt as he moved forward, visible as a shadow now as her eyes adjusted.

"I mustn't do anything I do not wish to do," he replied.

She gripped her hands together to still their shaking. "I need your help. We all need your help. Isn't that what you do, help people in need?"

"You've been reading fairy tales, ma'am. This . . ." He paused. " . . . is reality."

"I—I know that. It is only that—"

"No."

She sucked in breath. "No?"

"No." Still guttural, but with a rounded edge. He halted before her, so close the heat of his body seemed to reach out and wrap itself around her trembling limbs. Salt air tangled in her senses, laced with lavender and fresh tobacco, weakening her. This was Alex, the man who had held her and gazed at her as though he thought she was beautiful, with longing in his smoky eyes.

Yearning deep as the ocean swamped her.

"Well, if you will not help me with that," she breathed, hardly knowing how she would say the words, desire alone now driving her tongue, "you must help me with another matter."

"Another matter?"

She stared into the dark. He had removed his hat.

"You—You—"

"I?"

"You haven't the pox or anything awful like that, have you?"

On the deck above, a pipe sounded a tune, followed by the quick rhythm of palms striking a drum and a fiddle's raspy response.

"I beg your pardon?"

She could hear his breaths in the space between them, discern the outline of his shoulders and face. She swallowed fast, repeatedly, nerves tumbling over her tongue.

"You sound remarkably like an acquaintance of mine when you say that. Arrogant, too sure of yourself by far."

"Do you realize to whom you are speaking, woman?"

"I daresay, no," she quavered. "But have you?"

"Have I what?" he growled.

"The pox . . . or some such thing."

He laughed, a low rumble of amusement. "No, I haven't." His smile soaked into the abruptly altered tone of his voice.

Serena's joints turned liquid. "That s-seems remark-able."

"And yet there it is."

"Pirates are not known to be discriminating."

He moved nearer, closing the space between them to a breath.

"I discriminate well enough."

"Some gentlemen, you know," she barely managed to utter, "will kiss nearly anyone, anywhere, even a stranger at a ball in a darkened parlor. Or—Or, in a pantry alcove."

"Then there is no basis for comparison."

"I don't understand."

"I am not a gentleman." He touched her face, curving around her cheek, strong, callused warmth penetrating her skin, and Serena wanted to sink into him. "This is not anywhere; it is my ship." He bent his head. "You are clearly not nearly anyone, or you would not be here."

She sucked in a breath, his scent, touch, and the salt air unraveling the shreds of her reason.

"And . . . ?" she breathed.

Moonlight sliced through the windows, a cloud parting above revealing, at last, his beauty. Silver-blue sparks lit his eyes, his gaze fast upon her lips. Serena's heart constricted.

"And?" she whispered.

"And you have not come here," his voice was husky, gloriously familiar, nothing like the pirate's, instead like her dreams, "for a mere kiss."

Heat flooded Serena, from the center, up, down, then everywhere. His other hand circled her jaw and she leaned toward him, as though drawn by a tiny thread attached to the dead center of her chest. His gaze never left her mouth.

"Do you know what you have come here for?" The lock of his hair brushed her brow. She struggled to form words.

"Yes." Not for smugglers. Not even for Charity.

For *him*.

"How is that so, maiden fair?" His words played, but his tone was deadly serious.

"Because I—I am not a maiden," she stumbled, then hurriedly added, "There was a man, years ago, he—"

"I don't need to hear it," he said, gravelly again.

She swallowed, her throat as thick as her heartbeats racing like the heavy gallop of a plow horse.

"But it was only that once. I am not like—" *Your other women.*

"You are like no one else." His voice was a deep caress, scoring her senses, stealing thought until all she wanted was his kiss and touch upon her, *everywhere.* Her need frightened her, fashioning her unsteady response.

"This is only tonight," she whispered. "One night." One night to hold as collateral her father and stepbrother could not ignore. But she trembled, and she knew that it was much more. In truth it was everything.

His fingers slipped into her hair, his body grazing hers.

"Of course."

"No one must know of it." Unless necessary. A last resort.

His hands stilled, the only movement the gentle sway of the ship and the deep, fast filling of his chest against hers.

"What passes in the dark," he whispered, "remains in the dark."

"And you will not marry my sister?"

"No." His brow creased, his gaze lifting to meet hers so very dark and—oddly—questioning. "No."

She went onto her tiptoes and pressed her lips to his.

He gathered her toward him, his hand around her face, his arms encompassing her. She opened her mouth to him and breathed in his heat, drank his flavor and texture, and lifted her hands to his body.

Firm muscles rippled beneath her touch, and he kissed her deeper, claiming her mouth fully as she ran her palms over his chest, weakening at the thrumming of raw power beneath leather and linen. She sighed and let him kiss her, carry her to heaven with the decadent union of lips and tongues.

He broke the kiss and pulled away. "Have you been drinking rum?"

"Mr. Seton gave me a small amount."

"He did, did he?"

"He saw that I was quite anxious."

He kissed her mouth, her brow, one closed eye then the other, then returned to her lips. He urged them apart, skimming the tip of his tongue over one then the other.

"You needn't be now." His hands slid down her waist and thighs. He crouched, removing first her half-boots and then, with the lightest, headiest touch, slipping beneath her skirt, unfastening her stockings and sliding them down her legs. Serena's breath hitched hard.

"Yet I must admit I still am," she rasped. "Somewhat."

He straightened. "Allow me to make you more comfortable."

"Since you are the cause of my nerves, I don't see how— *Ohh.*" She gasped, his hand covering her behind and drawing her against him. She clutched his waistcoat and shirt, twisted them in her fingers, the hard length of his desire against her belly washing longing through her, a craving she had held at bay for weeks. He surrounded her buttocks, tilting her face up to meet his mouth again.

"Here is a beginning," he murmured against her lips, shifting his hips into her tender need and drawing her thigh alongside his, washing her with sensation. All else ceased to exist, everything but his body, his kiss. "And—" Her bodice sagged forward. "—another." He gazed at the exposed upper swell of her breasts, appreciation in his silvery eyes. "Let us see if we cannot make you more comfortable yet." His voice was beautifully uneven, as though it affected him to see her in dishabille. His fingertips ran along her spine and loosened the laces of her stays.

She let him draw her gown and petticoat off, setting his lips to the tender inner curve of her elbow, freeing her hands then lifting her arms, holding her wrists together as he pulled the corset over her head. His touch remained gentle, this pirate-rake caressing her as though she were something delicate.

Moonlight illuminated her white shift in ghostly

hue and his gaze remained upon her partially concealed breasts. Shame trickled through Serena, and she wanted to cover the plain linen garment. She'd had so little time to prepare, to invent the story that would allow her privacy in her bedchamber all night. She never thought to don something alluring, even if she owned a garment that would tempt a man of his experience.

His palm cupped her, his thumb circling her nipple through the fabric, tightening the linen until the peak stood out unbearably taut.

"Beautiful woman," he whispered, as though he truly believed it, as though her average breasts and unadorned clothing intoxicated him as his touch did to her. She closed her eyes and turned her face away, her breaths heavy and uncontrolled, at the mercy of her mounting desire. Heat gathered between her legs. If he could do this to her with his gaze . . .

"Touch me," she whispered. "Please."

His thumb passed over the strained peak and shudders rippled through her. She throbbed, damp at the crux of her thighs, her wanton desire for him ignored for so long now loosed by his hands upon her. He drew her face to his and kissed her, soft and beautiful, then growing firm, urgent like hers in return, his hand caressing her as though this alone could satisfy him. Then he bared her, pushing the fabric of her shift away.

His breaths seemed to come faster, but she knew her imagination invented it. He had seen so many women's bodies. Touched so many. His hand holding her hard against his hips, his hot, thick erection against her—she mustn't mistake it.

But his gaze seeking hers now, awe flickering in it and strange uncertainty, told her perhaps she was wrong. Perhaps she did to him what he did to her, deep within. Perhaps she made him fear. And dream.

Watching her eyes, he curved his palm around her breast. Serena moaned softly, arching into his touch. He bent to her ear.

"Has another man tasted you?"

"Only you." The words were barely a breath. His fingers teased, dragging her into further captivity. He bent and took her nipple into his mouth. She gasped, sank her fingers into his hair and pressed her body to him. His kiss echoed everywhere inside her at once. He caressed, licking, circling, and she wiggled against him, awash in sensation, need building in her like boiling honey in danger of spilling over. She ached with such sweetness, but it did not suffice. She wanted to touch him, to do to him what he was doing to her, to make him ache. He gave her pleasure and she needed *more*.

"I don't know what to do," she whimpered, moaning as he pulled away.

"I will show you." His voice at her ear was rough, breathless, his hand stealing along her hip wonderfully sure.

"No—I mean to say, yes. *Yes.*" He caressed the inside of her thigh. She loosened her knees and squirmed in mingled pleasure and shame at her body's ecstatic reply. She wanted him now, inside her. Wanted him so badly. *"No."* She grabbed his hand. "I—I am too—" Humiliation filled her.

"Too what?" He nuzzled her neck and she dragged in air, clutching his fingers tight.

"Too hungry," she uttered so softly she barely heard it.

He stilled.

"Davina said I am immodest, tempted by the devil. I don't believe that, but I don't think I am normal. I want it so much," she said in a rush. But it was far too late to turn back. "I have always wanted it. But somehow, I don't know why or how, I want it even more with you. Al—"

His fingers slid across her lips, muting her. She gripped them and pulled her mouth free.

"No, I must speak. I mean to say, *this* is not me. *Me*. I do not do this sort of thing. I want to, but I don't. But ever since that night in London when you—"

He jerked her tight to him, hands gripping her beneath the arms, and kissed her hard. She clutched his shoulders, dissolving into the beauty of touch and scent and heavenly sound, their breaths fusing as their mouths met in a frenzied dance of desire and secrecy. He cupped her head in his powerful hand and pulled back only enough to press his brow to hers, to murmur above her lips, his voice husky and low.

"Tonight there are only the two of us, my beauty. Cast off any identity that does not attend to the passion within you."

She trembled. "But, I—"

"You are a unique, exquisite woman. Let me serve your body as an acolyte serves a goddess." He held her tight against his arousal, possessing her with his hands. "Let me worship your need. It is beautiful to me."

She released a long, quavering sigh and wrapped her arms around his neck.

"Yes." If he wanted to pretend anonymity, she would give him that. And she would do the same. Tonight she would forget obedience once and for all. Forget propriety. Forget Davina's cruel words when all those years ago she went weeping to her new mother, seeking comfort only to get cold censure. Forget her father's woeful disappointment. Tonight she would say goodbye to falsely proper Miss Carlyle and allow herself to be merely a woman in the arms of a man who knew how to please her. "Please teach me how to touch you."

"Yes." He kissed her neck, dazzling kisses that made her heart and blood sing. "I was just getting to that. And you needn't say please."

She laughed, but it did nothing to dissipate the twining need in her body.

"Now, pl—" She bit her lip. "Oh, don't wait. But—"

He curved his hands around her thighs to shift his arousal snugly against hers, the sensation of soft fabric against her aching flesh a fantasy. Pleasure rocked her. Her eyelids fluttered.

"But?" His voice was beautifully rough.

"But do not go too quickly."

"Never." He took her mouth and slid his hand between their bodies. Serena melted.

Alex groaned against her teeth, and kissed her again deeper. His touch was heaven, firm, direct, meeting her need instantly and filling her with more. He caressed her, stroking perfectly then stealing back, light around her entrance then hard where she needed it most.

"Al—" she choked, swallowing his name just as he uttered hers, "*Serena*," so deep, so familiar.

Her heart keeled, came about, and careened into the maelstrom.

Alex lifted her in his arms and pulled her onto the sofa. She clutched his neck, shaking her hair free, and it tumbled half out of its pins as she reached for him again. He stared at her naked body illuminated by moonlight, his eyes fevered.

His voice came forth strangled.

"Serena, I lied."

Chapter 15

So he spoke, and her knees were loosened where she sat, and her heart melted.

—HOMER, *ODYSSEY*

Panic shot through Serena. She struggled to cover herself with her hands.

"You lied?" This could not be happening. Not now. Not like this, when it felt so right. Not again. *But so much worse.*

He gripped her wrists and pushed her onto her back. He bent her arms upward until her breasts jutted, the hard peaks begging for his mouth.

"I lied." His hungry gaze consumed her. "I cannot go slowly." He tore at his waistcoat and shirt then his breeches until he wore nothing and Serena's insides turned molten. She barely had time to take in his arms, corded with strength, his muscular chest and alarmingly thick male part, before he brought his powerful body over her. "Not this time."

He brushed against her intimately and she trembled, needy and petrified at once. She breathed deep, his eyes so hot as he reached between them.

"*This* time?" she whispered.

He pushed inside her. She gasped at the pressure,

then moaned, matching the sound of pure satisfaction coming from his throat. He paused and her breaths sped like the beats of hummingbird wings, her every muscle paralyzed.

"Sweet woman," he rumbled, dipping his mouth to hers, "let me in all the way." He kissed her, his tongue delving into her tender flesh, his hands tangling in her hair. The breath washed out of her. Her neck arched, thighs opening to him, and with a single thrust he penetrated her fully.

Serena moaned, long and abandoned.

"*Serena.*" Her name was rough, deep in his chest. He moved carefully, caressing slowly, stretching and shaping her to him. He closed his eyes and bent his head to hers, his breaths taut. "Serena, you are exquisite. Outside and in."

She ran her hands down his arms, feeling him everywhere. With slow, rocking thrusts he fit his thick shaft deep into her. And with every invasion she needed more. Much later she would understand fully what he did, rather than forcing her, instead coaxing. Now her body understood. Where he took her again, and again she grew pliant, responding as though fashioned to capture him, to hold him like this. Need built, coils of yearning as he stroked in perfect rhythm, the firmer and steadier the more she wanted.

"Yes," she whispered, then pleading, "*Yes.*" He delved so far in, so perfect, and when he met her center and she ceased breathing, he pulled back then went deeper still. Her hands flailed, her body reaching. Alex gripped her hips and dragged them downward, arching her back as he thrust high into her.

He groaned. Then another high thrust, more urgent. Ecstasy shimmered in her, into her breasts and throat. His fingers slid from her face to her peaked nipple, twining the desperate ache against his thrusts. It almost hurt, building too tight but agonizingly sweet. He bore into her harder, faster, his hand around her buttocks dragging her against him now.

"Serena, *my God.*"

She sought, lifting tight to him, to make whatever was coming come faster but wanting it to last forever. Her fingertips dug into his shoulders. "It's too much," she gasped. "Too— *Ohh!*"

It broke, her body jolting, a concourse of honeyed fire licking, burning, abandoning her to joy. She cried out sounds she had never heard before, pleasure rippling through her as Alex rose in her, straining forward. His whole body hardened. Serena gripped him, sinking her fingers into muscle, shaking through her pleasure as he released himself into her. Her name fell from his lips in a deep moan.

For a moment of divine stillness, that was everything—they two, perfectly fused.

His brow tipped against hers, his hair falling across her eyes, and Serena's reality had never felt so much like a dream. Alex scooped her into his embrace, pulling her chest flat against his, and buried his face in her hair. She clung, struggling for air beneath him, his heavy breaths compressing hers. But she was willing to suffocate and die now, a happy, deliriously happy woman, if it must be. She opened her lips to his shoulder and tasted his skin, salt and rich, spicy man. *Alex.* Her eternity of imaginary bliss shimmered into truth.

Up on deck, music vibrated, feet clomping on the planks to the rhythm of the tune stretching out over the ocean. They must be able to hear it on shore.

He pulled away all too soon. She gulped air and turned her face aside.

Now came the horrid part.

Nothing about making love to Alex was like her experience with Robert, all frustrated grunting and florid haste. But Serena understood well enough that in one manner all men were alike. When they had gotten what they wanted, they left. Or they threw a woman out, if the woman happened to be an interloper on their ship.

He stood, and she could hardly bear to look at his glorious masculine beauty revealed in crystal moonlight. His gaze traveled over her body, unreadable. She drew her knees together and chewed her lip. *Attractive.* What a prize she must seem after all his stunning courtesans and seductive widows.

He crouched, touched her chin with his fingertips, and kissed her—a simple, slow kiss—then pulled back and gazed at her anew, his eyes beautifully soft. Serena could not breathe.

His hand found hers and he drew her up. Standing, he slipped the back of his fingers along her cheek and throat to her collarbone, lingering there. Then he ducked his head and seemed to inhale, his jaw rough with the day's whiskers brushing her cheek. She savored it, knowing she would never again experience anything so wonderfully intimate as this small, incidental detail of his body, this texture.

"Come to my bed, my beauty," he murmured, and touched his lips to her neck.

She froze, warm tingles soaking into her skin from the kiss all the way to her toes.

"To your bed?"

He drew away, the corner of his mouth tilting upward.

"Unless you would prefer to spend the remainder of the night upon that couch. It seems rather small for two, though."

"The remainder of the night?" she repeated dumbly.

"The part that is dark until the sun rises. Yes."

He was laughing at her. Rather, with her, his soulful eyes drawing her into his teasing as always. She swallowed around the thickness in her throat. Her clothing lay strewn upon the floor, his atop it.

"You are not real." He was some sort of fantasy. Her fantasy. *Any* woman's.

He lifted her palm and placed it upon his chest. Beneath taut skin, his heart beat steady and rather quick.

"I am indeed real. Quite. Come, lovely woman."

Serena yanked her hand away and scampered backward, her heart pounding again.

"No."

His brow creased, discernable even in the dim light. The fiddle scratched above, an agitated tune now, drumbeats following.

"No?"

"Yes. No. Now I am the one who gets to refuse you something."

"Not if you are wise." His voice dipped low. "Come here, Serena."

"No."

His eyes narrowed, a predatory light illuminating the gray. Like a wolf.

"What, pray tell, do we wish to prove with this rather tardy show of defiance, madam?"

Serena's palms went damp. She grabbed her chemise off the floor and dragged it in front of her.

"*We* wish for you to do something about those smugglers." She could barely mouth the words of her blackmail. Good heavens, this was the most foolish thing she had attempted yet, even more foolish than thinking she could seduce him, which really she hadn't done at all because he had done it, and anyway she had wanted him more than anything ever in her life.

He crossed his arms, the gesture no less threatening with all of his skin showing than when he wore clothing.

"And what are we intending to do about it if I do not?"

"Te—Te—" Oh, Lord, she couldn't do it. "Tell everyone who you are."

The grin that curved his lips was the most wickedly handsome thing she had seen in all her twenty-five years.

"Really?" he purred deep in his chest.

She nodded, her teeth chattering.

"You would tell everyone?"

"Everyone. I will post it to *The Times* if I must."

"And that's all?"

Her brow wrinkled. "That's *all*?"

"You do not attach any other threats to my lack of action against those smugglers?"

"No. Er— What do you mean?"

"No other restrictions or hazards I must bear with if I refuse to comply with your demand?"

"What other threat *could* I level?" Astonishment colored her tone.

"You would not . . . withhold?"

"Withhold?"

His gaze scanned her body again, hair, bare shoulders, hands clutching the linen in front of her breasts, a partially exposed leg, her ankles and feet.

Serena's eyes went wide. "You mean, withhold *me*?"

He nodded slowly.

"Tonight, or upon future occasions?" she breathed.

"Yes." The predatory grin widened.

Heat gathered between Serena's legs so swiftly it shocked her. She blinked. He was mad. But she wanted him still, and the message in his eyes shaped the word upon her lips.

"No."

He moved forward so swiftly she hadn't time to retreat, and swept her up in his powerful arms like a rag doll.

"I can live with that," he said huskily, and carried her to his bed.

He made love to her again, not particularly slowly as he had promised, but nevertheless punctuated with wonderful lessons in which he taught her several clever things. First he showed her quite nicely how a man might encourage a woman's pleasure with his mouth in places Serena had never, ever imagined anyone's mouth could be. Then she learned how easily a woman could make an unquestionably virile man actually sigh, with the smallest effort and a few carefully chosen gestures involving her lips and tongue.

Practicing this new amusement, she went over and above what was required, swiftly earning reciprocal treatment that had her nearly tearing the bedclothes off the mattress and calling out his name repeatedly. Alex silenced her with his talented mouth, not because every man on board did not already know his true identity, but because, she thought, he simply wanted to kiss her as he drove her over the edge of ecstasy again. She sank onto him, her hair falling across his chest as she covered his damp skin with open-mouthed kisses, grateful, awed, trembling with satisfaction.

She slid off him and curled around his side on the narrow mattress. He tucked her beneath his arm and laid his other across his face, his lazily grinning mouth still visible.

Finally he took a deep breath and cocked his elbow behind his head, closing his eyes.

Serena wished she could sleep. But her blood sang

with happy agitation. Her fingers drifted down his chest and flat belly, around his navel to the dark, slender line stretching lower. She trailed her fingertips to the side, toward the mark on his hip she had noticed earlier when she was far too busily engaged in wonderful wickedness to comment upon it. The black ink shaped a simple set of crossbones. No skull. She traced it lightly.

"Have you had this since you began pirating?"

"Only three years."

"You know, it is amazing the way some people talk about you—Redstone, that is—as though you were a god, or something akin."

"You know better, of course." His voice rumbled low, near sleep, his hand tucked around her hip.

"Lady Effington praised you in public, roundly, right after you sank Lord Effington's yacht."

"She had good reason," he mumbled.

She circled the tattoo with her fingertip again, then ran her hand to his chest. "You are."

"Hm?"

"Not a god, certainly." She smiled against his skin. "A hero."

His breathing stilled. "I am not the man you believe me to be, Serena."

"You are." He would end the betrothal without hurt to her stepsister. Of this she was now certain.

"I am a pirate. Not a rear admiral."

Silence stretched amidst the creaking boards and the pipe's whistle atop, the drum's patter, and a brace of voices. Serena's heart tightened. But a principled man did not pick and choose where he would act heroically. Nobility of character must always prevail. She still harbored hope.

She breathed in the scent of his skin. "What are they singing up there?"

His chest expanded in a breath beneath her.

" 'Farewell and adieu to you, fair Spanish ladies.' " His song came like the rumble of thunder upon the horizon, quiet, deep and melodic, at once soothing and powerful. " 'Farewell and adieu to you ladies of Spain. For we've received orders for to sail for old England.' " Through her cheek and belly, his voice stole into her body, moving her as though pitched perfectly for her pleasure, growing the ache within once more. " 'And hope very shortly to see you again.' "

"You sing," she whispered. "You sing sailor songs."

" 'We'll rant and we'll rave like true British sailors,' " he continued, a Celtic lilt stealing into the phrases. " 'We'll rant and we'll rave across the salt seas.' "

She grinned against his skin. " 'Rant and rave'?"

" 'Till we strike soundings in the Channel of Old England.' " Now his tone seemed to smile too. " 'From Ushant to Scilly is thirty-five leagues.' "

"Do you hide your ship there, at Scilly?"

He did not respond. She ran a fingertip along the line of one rib. He reached down and grasped her hand, entwining her fingers with his, palm to palm, the simplest gesture. Serena's heart fluttered hard.

"Spanish ladies?" She spoke to prevent him from discerning the betraying beat. "I have heard they are quite beautiful."

"Of course." He sounded perfectly serious.

"Then there must be other sailor songs about them, I suspect."

"You suspect rightly."

"Sing one."

" 'First I had a Spanish girl,' " he sang, this time a long, rolling, swagger of a melody, " 'But she got fat and lazy.' "

Serena cracked a laugh. "That is absolutely vulgar."

"Well I didn't write it, madam, and you requested it."

"Oh. Of course." She bit her lip upon a grin. "Then do continue, please."

His voice dipped low. " 'Now I have a Devonshire girl,' " and slowed, " 'she damn near drives me crazy.' "

Her hand within his trembled. Her entire body. She lifted her head. Moonlight dashed across his features in silvery swaths, highlighting the strong planes of his face as though he were a fairy-tale prince painted by a master artist. But his skin, his touch, were alive, warm, and real.

"The lyrics are not truly 'Devonshire girl,' " she said, trying to make her voice even, without a great deal of success. "Are they?"

He rolled onto his side, rising above her, and she leaned back against the pillow. His dark gaze scanned her face.

"They are now," he murmured, and bent to her. As he kissed her, Serena's heart expanded, moved by his touch, his gaze. When she could no longer bear the swelling inside her, she drew her hand to his cheek then passed it between their lips. He kissed her fingers one by one, then her palm, then laid it down, took her in his arms and held her.

He slept in moments. She stared into the darkness, the ache of loneliness within her never greater.

Alex woke her in the thick gray just before dawn. Salt mist clung to her skin as he feathered kisses across her eyes, the bridge of her nose, her mouth. His hand curved around her breast then smoothed down her belly to her hip, drawing back the bed linens to bare her.

"There is no time to do to you what I wish to do now," he murmured, his warm lips on her brow. "Your boat awaits."

He climbed from the bed and pulled a pair of breeches over his contoured behind, then disappeared into the larger chamber, returning with her clothing. The garments were abominably wrinkled. She pulled the shift over her head. He grasped her wrists to still her, and tied the ribbons himself, so neatly she almost laughed. Then his hands slid over her breasts and she gasped instead.

"No time," he uttered hoarsely.

The corset proved no obstacle for the London rake. Serena's cheeks burned as he tightened the laces with the expertise of a lady's maid. Robert had not bothered to remove her stays. No man had ever seen her as Alex had. Like he had seen dozens, probably hundreds of women.

But she refused to become foolishly maudlin. She had accomplished what she wished. The sore heart she won as a consequence must be hers to bear.

With the pale glimmer of first light stealing through the shutters, Serena went to the door. Alex followed, drew her to him and kissed her, his hand upon her face, arm around her waist. She grasped his taut waist, imprinting the feel of him onto her palms, the heat and flavor of his mouth.

He released her and opened the door, his smoky eyes unreadable.

"Good day, madam." The corner of his mouth tilted up.

A sailor leaned against a barrel several yards away. He came to instant attention, and Serena followed him onto the top deck. Mr. Seton met her, gave her a brief good morning and guided her to the little boat they had arrived in.

Serena could not bring herself to feel ashamed. She had chosen, she was glad of her choice, and they were all sailors, no doubt accustomed to even more flagrant exhibitions of immorality than her single, breathtaking night of debauchery. As the shallow boat pulled away from the *Cavalier*, the ship receded into the mists, beautiful, shapely and polished, strong and powerful like its master. She had not gotten what she wanted regarding the smugglers, but she was certain now about his intentions concerning the betrothal. And if by some madness he did not stand by his promise to find an end to it, she possessed a weapon greater than any Davina could produce. The ends justified the means. With that, she could pretend she was perfectly content.

She had pretended the same thing for thirteen years. This time it cost a bit more effort.

Chapter 16

*He hid himself under the likeness of another . . .
and all of them were deceived.*

—HOMER, *ODYSSEY*

Serena paced the rose garden, buds springing into full glory with summer's heat, her cheeks and chest equally hot. Six days remained until the wedding, yet Alex had not called at Glenhaven Hall to put a stop to it.

"Care to take a ride, Ser?" Tracy strolled toward her along the path, the cut of his coat too fine for the country but his smile genuine.

Genuine she appreciated right now. *Tardy* she could do without. But Alex had told her plainly he was not the man she thought him. He was talking about his pirating then. Still, her fantasy had made him into Galahad when perhaps he was more like Lancelot, the hero to win all contests in avoidance and prevarication.

Her confusion of thoughts and feelings could not be greater. He was a rake, and with her he had done precisely what rakes did. She would be a thorough hypocrite to blame him for that. She long ago learned that men could not be depended upon. Robert Bailey had not come through. Her father had not. Why should this man, merely because she wished it so desperately?

She must tell them about her night with him. Tracy and her father. Whatever Alex planned—if he indeed did plan anything—now he was giving her no choice.

"I would be glad for a ride, Tracy." Glad for an opportunity to reveal her utter degeneracy to her dearest friend and only confidant. Except the Earl of Savege. Wrapped in his embrace, she'd confided in him, and he had accepted her.

She hadn't thought this could hurt so much.

Why did he wait? What reason on earth could he have to delay? A man of such experience in the world must have any number of methods for extracting himself from an undesirable connection. Perhaps he had never been so entangled with a spotless innocent like Charity, though. It would no doubt prove especially tricky to handle matters discreetly. But for heaven's sake, he was a pirate. He must be able to come up with *some* clever solution.

Unless he did not truly wish to.

No. She would not carry her doubts so far. She could not be that mistaken in him.

She went inside and dressed in her riding habit, then met Tracy in the stable.

"Let's go over the bluff," she said. "It is such a fine day." She might as well enjoy her last views of her beloved home before she was exiled to York, or perhaps that little cottage in her imagination, to spend the rest of her life alone.

Mounted, they ascended the hill and the sea came into view. It stretched to the horizon, blue and unusually calm, like the night she had spent upon it in the arms of a rogue.

"Your father received a note from the Park," Tracy commented as they meandered along the crest through scraggly trees mostly bared of their leaves by the ocean wind. "Lady Savege has some questions about the wedding celebration, it seems. She's paying a call this morning with Savege."

Serena's heart turned over. She found her tongue. "I—I suppose that is to be expected."

Alex was coming to break it off.

With *his mother*?

This was not the behavior of a perfidious villain. Nor a rogue. At least, she didn't think so.

"Mother has the maids polishing the stair rail and dressing Charity's hair like she's off to the queen's drawing room. You don't want to hang about the house for that, do you?"

And see the man who had catapulted her into ecstasy—*multiple times*—casting off his innocent bride-to-be, his mother in tow? Nausea wrapped around Serena's insides like the claw of some dreadful mythological beast. This was not turning out as she had imagined it.

Oh, God, she had not imagined it at all. She had just ached, and wanted—wanted the best for Charity, and wanted Alex.

"We must turn back, Tracy. Charity and Papa will need us there."

"All right. There's a turn-about just ahead." He seemed to release a pent breath. "You don't seem yourself lately, Ser."

She could not even mumble an assent or denial. It was true. She was not herself. And yet for the first time in years, only a handful of nights earlier for a few breathtaking hours, she had been utterly, entirely herself.

"Still worried about Charity and Savege, I guess." He glanced carefully at her. "Aren't you?"

Serena's eyes widened, sudden hope stirring.

"You told me not to ask, I know, Tracy, but have you made any headway in your efforts with my stepmother to halt the wedding?" Alex might not need to do it. Perhaps he already knew something she did not. Perhaps his delay—

"No." Her stepbrother frowned and glanced out at the ocean, regret shading his vivid eyes. "It came to nothing, I'm afraid. I am sorry, Ser. I wish I could have succeeded."

"Oh, well." Serena's heart thudded. "You did what you could."

His gaze remained troubled. Serena's mount tossed its head, jingling the bridle. On the hill ahead, riders approached.

"Looks like the earl and her ladyship had our same idea to come along this path," Tracy said.

Serena's hands convulsed on the reins and her horse danced about the path as Alex and his mother approached.

Tracy greeted Lord and Lady Savege with a hearty "Good day."

"Good day, Sir Tracy," the dowager said. "That is a very fine mount you have there. I won something like her from Drake last year. Lost her again to Chance, though, the young sharp."

"Thank you, ma'am."

"Miss Carlyle," Alex said smoothly, "I would like to make you known to my mother."

Serena dredged up a reserve of calm and lifted her gaze to the dowager countess. Lady Savege was a modest looking woman, elegantly dressed, with hair streaked brown and gray and lightly powdered beneath her bonnet, a severe cheek, but soft eyes.

"My lady, it is my honor." Every mote of blood in Serena's veins, every hair on her body, was aware of Alex. But she could not look at him. For the first time since making his acquaintance, she turned craven. She did not understand him. She did not understand what was happening to her. And she did not think she could hide it. Not any longer.

"How do you do, Miss Carlyle?" The dowager studied her. "Sir Tracy, will you and your sister change direction and continue with us to your parents' house? I should very much like to have a chat with the young lady who, as I understand it, helped rear my son's betrothed."

Serena's hands were slippery on the reins.

"Of course," Tracy said affably, and fell in beside the earl's big black horse. Atop it, broad-shouldered and so handsome, Alex looked like a prince, the hero he claimed he was not.

Serena wanted to sink into her saddle like a miserable puddle. She had spent weeks convincing herself she only wanted an end to Charity's unhappiness. But deep in her secret heart she wanted a beginning of her own. The rakish peer sitting so elegantly upon his blooded saddle horse would never be that, no matter what he had whispered to her in the moonlight. He might dally with her gladly, but he would not remain long.

"Miss Carlyle," the dowager said as the gentlemen took up the path behind them, "I understand your sister remained in town only a short time. I did not have the opportunity to make her acquaintance, of course. What is she like?"

"She is kind and gentle, with a lovely disposition and a great deal of patient understanding." And a horrible fear of her evil mother.

"Very beautiful, as well, I understand."

Serena nodded.

"Well, at least in that last they will make a fine pair. My son is a handsome devil. So is your stepbrother, by the by. Sir Tracy is young, but has he begun looking about him for a wife?"

"I do not believe so. He is always quite busy with business, managing his estate since his father died."

"Seven years is more than enough time for a man to see matters settled," Lady Savege said dismissively.

Their horses clopped along, the sea wind stirring bonnet ribbons, manes, and cloak trims. The back of Serena's neck prickled with warmth.

"Why are you unmarried, Miss Carlyle?"

They were the exact words Alex had said to her in that London alleyway.

"I never found the opportunity." And now she feared that even if given the opportunity, she would not have the will. She wanted to cry, to curl up in a ball beneath some thickly shading tree far from the ocean and weep her eyes dry and her soul out with the tears.

But she was made of sterner stuff. Viola's disappearance, Robert Bailey's turn-about, and Davina's cruelty had forced that upon her. No libertine earl's smoky-eyed seduction would break her. Not, at least, forever.

She radiated beauty, the vibrancy of life shimmering just beneath her silken skin and in the dusky gold locks escaping her bonnet, twisting about her lovely face in the breeze, catching the sunlight. Chin high, she avoided his gaze. Idiot that he was, it made Alex want her more.

"We didn't expect you to return until the nuptials, Savege."

Alex pulled his gaze from Serena's rounded back-side settled neatly in the saddle, her shapely leg tucked around the front pommel defined by the drape of a gown the precise shade of her left eye. He met her step-brother's curious regard.

"I did not expect to have returned yet." But he could not remain at sea while this woman walked upon land. And he had work to do. His mother was a sturdy horse-woman, but this stroll along the winding coastal road hadn't been her idea, nor the visit to Glenhaven Hall today.

"I am curious, Tracy. You know I don't bother much with matters here—"

"Your Haycock is an exceptional steward, like my own Shepherd, no doubt. Don't need to do a thing for Shepherd to keep Lucas Manor running in tip-top con-dition," the young man said with pride.

"Glad to hear that," Alex murmured. "But lately I have heard rumor that a few miscreant smugglers are trifling with some of the farmers. Shook up a family on your stepfather's estate recently, didn't they?"

Sir Tracy's brow beetled. "You heard right. But I don't think you need have concern over that. They made such a success of it during the war, some of these coastal folks are still running goods despite the lifted embargos."

"I daresay." Some noncoastal denizens, as well. Alex's groom, Pomley, had offered an intriguing morsel of information three days earlier. On a visit to the car-riage maker in Clovelly, Pomley noticed Sir Tracy's personal man by the docks chatting up a handful of sailors. Later in the pub, Pomley found the valet em-broiled in an agitated conversation with a pair of out-of-work soldiers. "Which goods?"

The baronet slanted Alex a sideways glance, his eyes the same bright blue as his young sister's, but the expression in them rather more acutely aware. Like Serena's.

"I suppose brandy, lace, the usual luxuries from Belgium and France. Fellows don't seem to realize a man can purchase all of that legally and for a fair price again." He chortled, but the sound held a false quality.

"They will no doubt discover that soon enough." Alex's gaze flickered to Serena. She had a fine seat in the saddle, her spine straight and shoulders tilted back and low, a bit like she'd sat while riding him that final time, her skin glistening, lovely eyes half lidded with passion. In all his years at sea and in London, he'd never made such an effort contrary to his desires as when he let her step off his ship wrapped in the cloak of dawn.

He forced his gaze to the coastline, the bluff dropping here to narrow pebbly beach below. In the miles of rocky path he'd tread alongside his mother before meeting Serena and her stepbrother, he had not seen any evidence of an entrance to a smuggler's cave, on his land or Carlyle's. But that didn't mean it was not there.

"Don't suppose you know of a seaman by the name of Dunkirk?" he asked casually.

The baronet's expression did not flicker. Rather too steady, it seemed.

"Can't say that I do."

"He is captain of the vessel that's been seen around here these past few months, apparently. Did they find the girl who went missing from your stepfather's tenant's farm?"

"No, but it seems to have been a single incident, perhaps only a runaway, my mother believes."

"Ah, yes. Peasant girls can be so unruly," Alex murmured with blue-blooded disinterest. Billy and Adam—a strapping Exeter linesman handy with his tongue, not to mention dagger—were still searching for the girl in the coastal haunts. Alex had ordered them not to return to the *Cavalier* until they found trace.

Tracy laughed again. "Aren't all women troublesome? Except my sisters, at least Serena and Charity. Diantha is a handful, but she's still a girl."

Serena was most certainly not a girl. Every inch of her pleasure-loving body breathed mature woman. But she was not as innocent as Tracy imagined. Of all possibilities, Alex had not expected a cool reception from her today.

Perhaps Miss Carlyle was up to something beyond what she professed.

But so was he. He would not tell her of his investigations into the smugglers' activities, not until he discovered something of merit to tell. In the meantime, he would free himself of this ridiculous betrothal. Thus his mother's presence today.

Glenhaven Hall appeared below the bluff, tucked into the hill.

"I have always admired your father's house, Miss Carlyle. It is so shockingly irregular," his mother said with such amiable grace as they dismounted, he had to smile. Precedent demanded that he take her arm to lead her inside. Probably for the best. The more he watched Serena's simple, graceful movements, sensuous in a way he hadn't quite noticed before, the more difficult it became not to undress her with his imagination. Touching her, even casually, would be sheer folly.

Lady Carlyle and her daughter awaited them in a sunny parlor that enhanced the girl's guinea looks. Alex bowed to Miss Lucas while the baroness made obsequious gestures to his mother. The girl's cheeks were sunken and eyes dull.

"Do have a seat and I will ring for tea," Lady Carlyle said, the macaw feather in her hair arrangement quivering. Serena curled her hand around her sister's and drew the girl onto a sofa. Her lashes lifted and finally she met Alex's gaze. Her eyes glimmered, but with what thoughts behind them he could not read.

"My dear Lady Carlyle," his mother said, "I cannot be happy with the plans you have for celebrating this union of our son and daughter. I must host the wedding luncheon at Savege Park."

"You are too kind, my lady." The baroness smiled thinly, pouring out tea and passing it to her guest. "I would not dream of imposing upon you."

"Then we shall have an intimate dinner beforehand," she said above her teacup. "Just our families, cozy and comfortable. Tomorrow evening. I will not accept a refusal."

With a controlled smile of satisfaction, the baroness bowed her carefully coiffed head. "Of course. We would be so pleased."

"That, my dear girl," the dowager patted Miss Lucas upon the knee, "will allow you opportunity to become acquainted with my son's staff. There are only just over fifty of them now, far fewer than when my husband lived. But I am certain Mrs. Tubbs—that is his housekeeper, although I daresay you know that already from that unfortunate incident you suffered upon your previous visit to the Park . . ." Her gracious regard never faltered. " . . . I am certain Mrs. Tubbs will assist you in hiring more help. But you will not be entertaining often at the Park, I suspect, unless you choose to remain there while my son is in town."

She rested her dimpled hand upon her breast. "How I abhorred it when Lord Savege went up to London to enjoy his amusements, leaving me all alone in that cavernous place. I could not wait to return to town and friends and entertainments. And the grand fêtes I threw! You will want to do precisely the same thing, of course. My daughter Katherine and I will help. We adore lively parties. The grander the better." She chuckled.

Alex could have kissed her. He hadn't needed to say a thing. She was as good as guineas all on her own.

"My daughter will be content wherever you wish her to reside, my lord," Lord Carlyle said, looking as uncomfortable as Alex had ever seen the fellow.

"Oh, I daresay wherever she chooses." Alex's mother waved a careless hand. "My son won't care a fig where she sets up house if it isn't London, will you, Alexander?"

The girl's miserable gaze did not rise.

"Wherever my sister settles in," Sir Tracy offered, "she'll have Serena's help in getting used to the place. Won't she, Ser?" A look of grateful affection crossed his face.

Serena returned it, a slight tightness to the corners of her mouth but no other indication of the outrageousness of the request. She nodded then glanced at Alex. Her gaze shifted to his mother, then back to him again, seeming to question now.

"Yes, of course," she only said. "Whatever Charity prefers."

Miss Lucas's gentian gaze turned to her stepsister, filled with devotion. Alex's chest felt inordinately tight. They adored her. And well they should.

Perhaps she played no game like the games he was so accustomed to enacting with his brother, his friends, and all the world. Perhaps sibling love alone drove her actions. If Lucas was involved in this smuggling business, as he suspected, perhaps Serena's pleas for his help sprang from a wish to protect her stepbrother, to confine the knowledge of his criminal activities within the family whilst bringing them to a halt.

If that were not the case, Alex would soon discover the truth of it. But if she did simply hope to protect her family, and she was the woman he believed her to be, he of all men certainly did not deserve her.

He would, nevertheless, have her.

Chapter 17

Truly you are a rogue.

—HOMER, *ODYSSEY*

Serena closed the door to the cottager's stone and thatch house, tucked the empty basket over her elbow, and leaned against the exterior wall. She released a shallow breath of nervous excitement.

Penny's sister, Sissy, had not been taken. Within the hut, Penny's family was now unpacking the food Serena had brought over as a sympathy gift. But they had given her a great deal more in return.

Sissy had run away, not alone, but with her brother, they told her. A sailor. Last night they received word from her. They were so overwhelmed with relief they hadn't even thought to halt their bubbling tongues while Serena asked question after question.

The girl was now in Clovelly putting up in a rented room with another sailor's wife, a Mrs. Dunkirk, but planning on leaving for Bristol shortly. In the meantime she had sent a purse of coins home to assure them of her safety and well-being. In a hastily scribbled note, Sissy foolishly boasted that if they must contact her and could not find her immediately, they could leave a message at a dock hidden at the edge of Savege Park in the shadow of a cave.

Serena's hands shook. The girl and her brother must be involved in this smuggling business. Unless she had hired herself out for favors in Clovelly, there was no other way to explain the money, and Serena suspected that even girls of ill repute did not amass that sort of coin in such a short time. Perhaps Penny's siblings acted as land runners for the smugglers.

Serena set off across the sheep pasture toward the Hall, renewed purpose in her steps.

This only confirmed her belief that some local man of wealth and position guarded the smugglers' safety. Perhaps one of the aldermen of Clovelly, or a magistrate. Or someone of even greater influence. The damning evidence of the hidden dock's location forced her to consider the obvious candidate.

But why would a wealthy earl with his attentions fixed upon London, and captain of his own successful ship, allow smugglers upon his lands? He was an inveterate gambler, of course. Perhaps he had lost his fortune to the tables and sought to recoup it this way. It would explain his refusal to help her rid the coast of them.

Ridiculous. The *Cavalier* had to be loaded with gold from its conquests in the Channel during the war. But if Alex were involved, her father must agree to calling off the wedding.

She had been a fool to imagine she could reveal him publicly. Piracy was a hanging offense. He certainly did not deserve her loyalty. But she had no wish to see him dead. The idea of it made her ill.

Serena entered the house, threw off her muddy boots, bonnet, and spencer, and raced up to her chamber. Charity sat upon the bed. Red rims ringed her eyes, her pert nose like one of the strawberries now bursting along the path to the village.

Serena fell to her knees and drew her sister's hands to her cheek.

"Darling, don't cry. I promised to free you from this match and I will. Only give me more time." Her pulse quickened at the thought that Alex seemed to be making his own efforts at frightening Charity off. Or at least his mother was trying to do that. But she herself still held her ace, and would use it if need be.

"At th-the party tonight—" Charity stammered.

"No, dear, you will not be required to meet his staff. And I daresay Lady Savege exaggerated the number of them in any case." To what end, she could only hope.

"No, I—" Charity dissolved into a flurry of flapping hands.

"You what, darling?" Serena slipped onto the bed beside her. "What troubles you about this evening?"

"H-H-*He* will be there."

Serena nodded, her belly tingling just like Guinevere's must have every time Lancelot walked into a room.

"Yes, well, the party is for the two of you, of course."

Charity's fingers spasmed.

"Not Lord Savege." Her voice became very soft, reverent. *"Him."*

Serena released a breath of relief. "His brother?"

Her stepsister lifted her bright blue eyes, replete with feeling. Serena could not help smiling at the unmarred devotion there.

"You like him a great deal, don't you? He is the gentleman you spoke of before?"

Charity nodded, her cheeks coloring to ripe peach.

"Well then, you must dry your eyes, don your prettiest gown, and enjoy his company this evening."

"Do you think I should?"

"I don't see why not." Serena stood up. "Charity, I

have a suspicion that this betrothal is nearly at an end, so you have nothing to fear concerning your feelings for Mr. Savege." Except, of course, if the brothers were more alike than she suspected. But she doubted Charity would give her heart so easily to a man who did not deserve it. She, fortunately, didn't have a fantastical imagination that made princes out of libertines.

Shortly alone again with her reckless sighs, she donned a silk frock of rich green-blue she'd had the dressmaker in Clovelly design, her mother's sapphire teardrop pendant, and arranged her hair simply. Her nerves jittered in anticipation of seeing the earl again. Fortunately she had plans for her night that distracted her attentions from that a bit.

Just above an hour later, in the light, airy drawing room of his vast mansion, he greeted them elegantly, his gaze resting upon Serena for a moment longer than it probably should. After managing to settle her stepsister beside Mr. Savege, Serena found herself sitting alone with the dowager.

Lady Savege glanced across the chamber and assessed Charity critically.

"Your sister is not in Alexander's usual style."

Serena schooled her features. Women of great consequence, she understood, often felt at liberty to say outrageous things.

"I daresay," she murmured.

The dowager's gaze came to her. "Neither are you."

Serena forced a smile to her lips. "Fortunately, my lady, that is immaterial."

"When was it?" The dowager's eyes narrowed. "Recently, or years ago? You are not young, but my son no longer pays any attention to chits just out of the schoolroom, except of course with this mysterious travesty of a betrothal." She waved her hand dismissively.

Serena's mouth went dry.

"I beg your pardon, ma'am?" she croaked.

"He was uncharacteristically fidgety before we called upon your family yesterday, and again earlier this evening. I thought it due to his dislike of social niceties. He has never been one to suffer fools, and I fear your stepmother quite comfortably meets that definition." She pursed her lips. "But in observing the two of you together, I begin to understand matters."

Serena feared her mouth hung rather wide. "Together?" They had barely spoken since aboard his ship.

"So that's the way of it, hm?" the dowager said thoughtfully. "Has he tried to inveigle you into indiscretions despite this arrangement with your sister? That is too bad." She shook her head. "He is a thorough rogue and I am ashamed of his libertine ways, but I love him as any mother loves her son, and in any case I haven't the slightest bit of influence upon his life. He does what he wishes, whether others say naught or aye."

She placed her hand upon Serena's.

"Do not let his teasing make you any less of what you are, Miss Carlyle. If you want him, tell him so. But do not allow him to trifle with you. Men do not respect weak women."

Serena's mouth snapped shut.

The dowager stood. "Now I will speak with your stepmother and attempt to throw a wrench in Monday's program. Perhaps I shall complain about the location of the ceremony. The chapel here at the Park is in horrid condition and needs a thorough restoration to make it worthy of the wedding of an earl. He must be married in London's St. George's, of course." Her gray eyes twinkled. "This should be great fun."

Serena stared at her back.

He had been *fidgety*?

She tried to tamp down her own sudden fidgets, but they would not be tamed. Her gaze crept up.

Alex was watching her, his eyes alight. She frowned. His delicious mouth curved into a grin. Tightness gathered in her chest, then elsewhere. As though he knew the reaction he inspired, his gaze warmed, and she nearly squirmed in remembered pleasure. He had given her precisely that look before he put his—

"Dinner is served, my lord," the butler intoned from the doorway.

Serena slid a hand over one hot cheek, took a steadying breath, and moved toward the dining room, her shoulders back. She might not be able to control her response to him, but she could have a say in other people's destinies—her sister's and a boatful of smugglers, for starters.

It proved as easy for Serena to steal into the stables and saddle her horse without detection as it had been the night Mr. Seton took her to the *Cavalier*. John Coachman was already abed, and the stable boy slept like a kitten in the loft, entirely oblivious. She had needed John's help in London when she wished to confront Lord Doreé outside that gambling club. At home in the familiar haunts of the bluff and coastal paths, however, she could easily make the short journey to the beach by herself.

But alone upon the path barely lit by a waning moon, the route to the dock seemed different than the night she had ridden it with Mr. Seton. The wind crept beneath her cloak in invidious fingers, and every bend in the pebbled track offered ominous shadows her horse seemed as reluctant to traverse as she. Twice she thought she might be lost, but the whoosh of waves upon the shore ahead encouraged her.

By the time she reached the short dock jutting from an indentation in the cliff's rock face, Serena had several times been forced to convince herself it was better she came tonight and did not wait until daylight. This way she would certainly not encounter anyone who could question her about the note she left tied to the dock for the smugglers.

As soon as she dismounted, she discovered her mistake.

A figure emerged from the shallow cave, dark and large. He stumbled forward, unsteady upon heavy-booted feet. Serena sucked in a breath and stepped back, her horse tugging the reins. The man's head swiveled around.

"Well, well, boys, what do we have here?" he slurred.

Boys? Her heart racketed.

Another man sauntered from the cave, weaving a bit, and a third unfolded from the rocky ground in the shadow of the dock, rubbing his face.

Serena's gaze darted around. The closest place to remount was the dock post, but the heavy fellow had already moved between her and the water. She must run for it. Perhaps these men would be too inebriated to follow. She let the reins fall, preparing. The thought sped through her mind that these might be sailors from the *Cavalier*. Then the skinny fellow on the ground loped up with a grating laugh, and it didn't matter who they were. Her pulse raced, flight her only impulse.

"Pretty thing, ain't you?" the skinny one said with the unmistakable singsong of an Irishman, not at all pleasant in this case.

"Why don't you take off that cloak so as we can get a better look at ye, little girl?" the big one said.

"This is a mistake, gentlemen." Serena's voice shook. "I will leave you to yourselves now."

"Oooh! A regular captain grand, ain't she, fellas?"

"More like she's puttin' it on." The Irishman wavered upright, black eyes gleaming. "What are ye, girl? An upstairs maid?"

"Had me an upstairs maid once," the third ruffian leered. "Smelled like peaches."

"Let's see what this one smells like."

Serena swung around. The heavy one grunted and threw his arms forward, missing as her horse bolted. A hand clamped around her wrist, slamming her back against the big one. He pinned her arms against her body, and the skinny ruffian released her wrist. Her horse's hoofbeats retreated up the path toward home.

"Unhand me this instant. You will be in a great deal of trouble if anything untoward occurs here."

"Un-to-ward?" The third one let out a guffaw. "Hell, boys, we'll be in trouble if anything un—" He swayed as he moved toward them. "What did she say?"

"Shut up, Andy," the skinny fellow grumbled, leaning forward and sniffing. "No peaches, Glen. Smells more like biscuits."

"Ach! I've ate enough biscuits to last me a—"

The Irishman slapped Glen across the face, his palm whisking past Serena's cheek.

"Not hardtack, ye knuckleheaded brute." His brows wiggled at Serena and he sniffed again. "Like me mum's soda bread wi' currants she makes at Easter. Must be the holidays, boys. You got a present for us wrapped up in that cloak, little girl?"

She swallowed her rising gorge. "No. But you have got a ship full of illegal goods. Don't you?"

The skinny one's hand stopped at the edge of her cloak.

"What's she talking about, Cian?"

"I said, shut up, Andy. She don't know a thing."

"I know you are sailors from that smuggling ship. You are here waiting for a message, aren't you? From whom?"

"Hell, Cian, let's get out of here." Glen released her.

The Irishman grabbed her arm and dragged her toward the dock.

"We're taking her with us."

"You're dicked in the head, Cian. We can't take her. She'll scream."

"I will. I'll scream right now unless you unhand me."

"Nobody'll come for you. Girl like you, going out in the middle o' the night for a spot of adventure. Just like Sissy, that saucy wench." He spat, and pulled her along the dock planking.

"Aye, but Sissy come by her own will," Glen muttered.

Sissy, Penny's sister. These must be the smugglers Sissy had gone with her brother to meet in Clovelly. Perhaps these men thought she was just another profit-seeking wench?

A little boat rested at the end of the dock.

"This one looks better'n Sissy," Andy commented blearily.

"Get in, girl."

"I will not!"

Glen hung back, but Andy advanced behind the Irishman.

"Get in now, wench." Andy pushed, Serena lost her footing, Cian's hold slipped, and she fell. Her head smacked the side of the boat, her stomach rose fast and she leaned over, the world titling, the men's faces abruptly blurry.

"No—No, take me back—" Her tongue felt thick.

Fingers padded at her head, her own, and she flinched, meeting hot flesh, peculiarly numb.

In an instant the pain set in. The boat jerked away from the dock and Serena nearly tossed up her accounts. She swallowed hard and gripped the bench.

"Thinking with yer nuts, as always, Cian," Glen called from the dock, his big form a thick black mark in her tortured vision.

"Luck gettin' back to the ship on yer own, Glen," Andy taunted and sucked from a bottle, plying the oar with his other hand.

"What about her orders? She said to wait here till Serle brought word," Glen called across the widening breech.

"Tell her to stuff her orders up her arse." Andy laughed. Cian slapped him and plucked the bottle away. Andy's rowing paused, he leaned over to spit into the black water, then plied the oar once more.

Serena tried to get her bearings, but pain racked her head abominably. She was about to be treated to attentions even Penny's wayward sister hadn't liked, apparently. Cian gripped her wrists as though she might make a break for it, but with her head swirling, she would certainly drown if she attempted that.

"Don't be stupider than you are, Andy," Cian grumbled. "This one's good for the night. We'll take her to the covey and when I'm done with her you can have her. Then we'll pick up Glen in the morning."

"No one's s'posed to go to the covey till we get word."

"Is this how you sailors treat women?" Serena gulped back the terror clamping her lungs. "I understand there are ships upon which women aren't even allowed aboard."

"Oh, ye unnerstan' that, missy?" Cian dragged her

against his bony hip. He wasn't much taller than her, but all wiry force.

"Captain Redstone does not allow a woman upon his ship." Except upon occasion. "And certainly there are not women upon naval ships. You must be some sort of misfits." Dear Lord, she hoped this tactic worked.

"Shut her up, Cian. She's gettin' on me nerves." Andy's oars moved slower.

"Ye hear that, girly? Yer gettin' on Andy's nerves." Cian pinched her arm. "But I still like ye." He reached into her cloak and grabbed her breast.

Serena's vision abruptly went crystal clear.

"My father, Lord Carlyle, will see you both hanged."

The Irishman snatched his hand away.

"Ye lyin' bitch."

"I am not lying. I am Serena Carlyle, and you will drop me upon the shore this instant or—" She cast about for a threat. "—or the gentleman I was to meet at the dock will have your friend Glen at the end of a pistol and your ship's location within the hour," she finished haughtily.

"Gor, Cian." Andy's oars went still. "What if she's tellin' the truth?"

The Irishman's black eyes narrowed. "What gen'leman?"

"That is none of your business." Her head pounded, but she forced hauteur into her tone. "Now put me ashore."

"We better take 'er back, Cian." Andy's oar cut the water with sudden enthusiasm. "If 'e finds out—"

"If who finds out?" Serena swiveled to him.

"Cork it, Andy!" Cian's black eyes narrowed. "All right." He sounded anxious. "I suppose we can do that, if ye promise not to mention any o' this."

"I'll do no such thing. But if you harm me any further, my gentleman friend will have the story from Glen and your necks in nooses."

"I dunno about that," he said, gaze darting about the boat. "And ye seen our faces and know our names—"

Andy blustered. "But we'll be gone off to Bristol before she can find us—"

"Bristol?"

Cian's face seemed to pinch. "If we're gonna put you off, here's as good a spot as any." He grabbed her arm. Serena fought, the boat thrashing from side to side. Andy yanked her shoulder and she tumbled over the edge.

She went under, the water surging around her cold, driving beneath her skin and into her nostrils and eyes. Her feet hit the bottom and she struggled up, pulling against the weight of her garments. She gulped in air, bobbing at shoulder height, her boots scrabbling sand. She opened her eyes, the salt stinging her skin and washing from her hair over her face.

The shore sat not ten yards distant. Behind her the slap of oars and Andy's cusses whispered across the water in the still night.

She thrust her arms forward and parted the water, pushing with her legs wrapped in muslin and wool and thanking God for the calm tide assisting her in. A wave smacked at her back, throwing her to her knees and into the swirling froth. She heaved to her feet and dragged herself shallower until the water eddied without menace at her ankles.

She sank to her knees, then her palms, and a thick sob escaped her. Water streaming from her body, she closed her eyes and sucked in shaking breaths.

How unutterably foolish she had been. She should have waited until daybreak, asked Tracy to accompany her to the dock. A note deposited then would have served its purpose well enough, and she could have told her stepbrother all her worries, even her plans. Perhaps he would have helped her.

Serena fell onto her elbows, cradling her face in her hands, and forced her thoughts into order as her breath came back to her. One by one she reviewed the clues the smugglers let drop, filing them in her memory. Then she pushed onto her hands again and crawled the rest of the way out of the ocean. Casting off her sodden cloak, she struggled to her feet and looked up.

Her shaking limbs went weak.

The beach was nothing more than a thin crescent of rocky sand at the base of a moss-covered cliff, some fifty paces across. At its northern end, a trail led into the rocks, the moonlight revealing a path up the steep rise between scrubby trees, narrow steps carved almost like a ladder into the stone. Just beyond, no more than a quarter mile distant from the top, Savege Park rose like a pillar of dormant strength. In the silvery darkness of midnight it looked like paradise.

Dragging her cloak behind her, soaked gown clinging to her legs, Serena crossed the beach in labored steps and started climbing. She had climbed the rocky bluffs and hillsides of her father's estate often in childhood, and as she struggled, memories of those happier moments urged her to continue when her feet slipped on pebbles and she lost her balance.

Exhausted, knees bruised and hands scraped, she scrabbled to the top of the trail then sat to regain her breath. She could not go to the house in her present condition. The outbuildings sitting somewhat back from the bluff within a cluster of trees were closer.

The wind, stronger at the summit, crept through her sodden gown. Serena shivered and glanced at her cloak, then took it up and slung its weight over her shoulders.

She trudged toward the closest buildings. Dogs barked, but she was too exhausted to care. With a flurry of panting, a trio of animals appeared, scampered around her, sniffed at her drooping hem then darted away. A pinpoint of light became clearer as she approached the trees. It jiggled at hip height, and a high voice cut the darkness.

"Who be there? Friend or foe?"

She recognized that voice. *"Friend."*

The lantern swung upward, revealing a boy's face already weathered by life upon the sea she had just climbed from. She nearly wept.

"Billy, I must see Lord Savege."

Chapter 18

A bold man does better in all things.

—HOMER, *ODYSSEY*

Alex sipped his brandy, swirling the liquid on his tongue but not enjoying it. He needed a stronger spirit. Rum. But he could not drink that now, not after tasting it in Serena's hungry mouth. Not until he had her again.

He set the glass on the edge of the billiards table alongside the proof of Tracy Lucas's involvement with the *Osprey*: a letter from the baronet to the smuggler's captain, Dunkirk, arranging a transfer of cargo from an undisclosed location onto the ship several days from now.

"That's all we found, Cap'n," Adam said, pulling at his cap. "Sissy ducked out soon as Billy marked her. A regular captain sharp, that girl. Knows it when she's in too deep. Her brother hung around, though. Once we pumped him full of Ruin, he talked. Bloke was right sick of his sister." The linesman grinned. "Said she was a bag of trouble for setting him up with them smugglers and showed us the letter to prove it. When he dropped off from the gin, Billy filched it. Thought it might be enough."

"It is. You have earned your furlough, Adam. Billy as well." He didn't bother disguising his voice. His crew, tenants, the villagers—they all knew. It seemed the only people who did not were the commissioners of the Board of Admiralty and the *haut ton*. Serena had not, as promised, revealed it. The thought of her threat almost made him smile. The image of her when she had uttered it, half naked and bleary eyed from making love to him, stirred primal heat in him.

"I'll be off now, Cap'n, if that's all right."

"Pass through the kitchen on your way. Mrs. Tubbs will have something for you and Billy."

Adam ducked from the billiards room, shoulders hunched, ill at ease in the great house.

Alex snapped the cue stick against the palm of his hand and took the shot the sailor had interrupted. The ball met its mark, just as Adam and Billy had found theirs. It seemed Sissy had used her brother's connections at the docks in Clovelly to get in cozy with the smugglers, then shacked up with Dunkirk's wife, probably to curry favor with the captain. Alex couldn't worry about where the girl went now; that sort never failed to land on their feet. The letter she'd let slip into her brother's hands and then Billy's was all he needed.

He leaned a hip into the table and lifted his gaze to the doorway. His valet stood there.

Alex frowned. "What is it, Tubbs? I thought you turned in hours ago."

"My lord, a visitor awaits you in the stable. The boy discovered her upon the grounds, and she requested to speak with you particularly."

"She?"

Tubbs cleared his throat and lowered his voice. "A lady, my lord. I might venture to say *the* lady."

Alex's throat went dry. Without pausing to grab his

coat, he thrust the cue at Tubbs and moved into the corridor, suppressing the urge to run.

Serena. In his stable. In the middle of the night.

Something must be wrong. She had barely spoken with him earlier that evening, clutching her sister's hand like she was saving a drowning woman—when Miss Lucas's hands were not hovering inches from his brother's. Never touching, though.

Aaron and the girl were deuced fools. But the terror in her eyes when his mother spoke of London and hosting balls and routes, and Aaron's besotted gaze when she spoke with him, must be having their effect upon her. That left Alex as good as unspoken for again.

He reached the rear drive and ran the remainder of the way. A lantern's amber light filtered onto the drive from the stable interior, the door open a crack. Pomley waited outside.

"Is anyone else within?" Alex caught his breath.

"No, milord. I sent the boy to the carriage house, and the others are already there abed."

"I will call you if I have need."

"Yes, sir." Pomley set off into the darkness.

Heart in his throat, Alex pulled the door open.

She stood huddled against a stall door, a blanket wrapped about her, hands clutching it white as vellum. Her wet hair straggled down her back and her eyes were wide.

He took four strides and wrapped her in his arms. Her face pressed to his chest and he held her tight, the trembling of her body washing cold dread through him. He stroked her hair, his fingertips sinking into the salt-crusted tresses, and pressed his cheek to the top of her head. He had wanted her in his arms every moment since she left his ship, but not if it meant this.

"Serena," he murmured, masking his fear in comforting tones. "Serena, what has happened?"

She drew in a deep breath, fists unclenching against his ribs, and pulled back. For a moment she stared at him, her eyes impenetrable in the dancing lamplight.

She pushed out of his hold.

Alex nearly grabbed her again. But she stood straight-backed, proud and determined even in her obvious distress.

"I went to the dock tonight."

Alex shook his head. "To the dock?"

"I learned that the smugglers use your dock as a place to deposit and receive messages. I went to leave one of my own."

"Your *own*?"

"To encourage them to reveal the location of their covey, so that I might send the authorities after them."

"Serena, the authorities around here don't give a damn about smugglers. They are too busy keeping workless seamen and soldiers from trouble to bother with merchants, even illegal ones." Why was he arguing with her when he should just drag her back into his arms and kiss away her grimness? Her beautiful mouth beckoned, the cast of her cheeks and jaw exquisite in the flickering shadows.

"I had to do something." She clenched her hands, dropping the edges of the blanket. "You will not."

His gaze dipped to her body. Beneath the clinging gown, her nipples were aroused, her slender belly rising with short breaths, her thighs pressed together.

With effort he steadied his voice. "What happened?"

"There were men there when I arrived. Three sailors, smugglers. My horse bolted." She swallowed her words, her gaze skittering away.

Spiky heat licked across Alex's shoulders. He moved forward but she retreated a step. He halted, his heart pounding.

"Serena, what did they do to you?"

"Nothing. They took me on a boat ride. I told them my name and they released me."

"Did they put you off nearby? Is that why you came here?"

"It was not by choice." Fire sparked in her gaze, a combination of wariness and heat that tightened Alex's chest and groin at once. More and more it astounded him that she remained unwed. Why hadn't men before him seen the passion in her eyes or her strength of will, and fallen under her spell?

Perhaps they had. Perhaps—the notion nudged him for the hundredth time—she did not actually wish a husband. Or perhaps she did. Perhaps she still wanted the man to whom she first gave herself, but could not have him.

"Why are they using your dock, Alex," she asked in an eerily even voice, "the one by which you access your ship?"

"I haven't the slightest notion." He stared. "You believe I have something to do with the *Osprey*?" Clearly she had no idea of her stepbrother's involvement.

"Is that the name of the smugglers' vessel? How do you know it?"

"I captain a ship in these waters. But perhaps that escaped you the other night while you were busy in my quarters."

Her jaw set, but beneath the thick blanket her body seemed to shake.

Anger overcame him, sweeping like a wave, directed toward her stepbrother and father, the men who had not only the right but also the duty to protect her.

"What were you thinking, looking for them in the middle of the night?" he demanded. "Are you wholly devoid of sense?"

"No. Merely assistance," she hurled back. "I have had to search for them and paste clues together by myself. And yes, I have entertained the idea that you may be involved. You are certainly in no hurry to halt their activities."

"I appreciate your trust, madam."

"You shouldn't be surprised. I haven't any reason to trust you. You lied to me."

"I did not." Never. And he never would.

"You said you would not go through with this betrothal."

"I told you I would not marry your sister, and I will not, as you know perfectly well, don't you?"

Her eyes went round. "The wedding is four days away, Alex. When do you plan to break off the engagement, on your twentieth anniversary?"

"Very clever. Were you this clever with the smugglers who abducted you?"

"You are a beast." A sob escaped her. She dashed her palm against her lips, her eyes swimming with distress. His chest felt like it imploded.

"Serena." He reached for her, but she twisted from his grasp, the blanket falling to the straw-strewn floor. His throat tightened. "I cannot be the one to end this foolish engagement—not without your stepsister's full consent. She would be ruined. You know that. You must know it from the show my mother is putting on."

"And what if my sister does not oblige in this tactic?" Her voice hinted at desperation.

He searched her fraught gaze, his heart pounding. *Goddamn* his brother, and damn the girl. "Then I will break the thing off cleanly tomorrow, if that is what you truly wish."

A war of emotions crossed her lovely face, confusion and pain.

"She will protest. She is frightened of this—of you—but so much more of her mother." She blinked as though battening back tears. "You may be the master of your ship, Alex, but you are not the master of everyone's hearts." She sucked in breath and thrust her chin up, the lamplight revealing a darkening bruise upon her temple just beneath the fall of her damp hair.

Blood washed across Alex's vision, unfocused anger twined with panic so blind and wholly unfamiliar his knees weakened. He grabbed her, clamping his hands around her arms and dragging her to him.

"Am I not?" His voice sounded unfamiliar. His hand wrapped around her jaw, forcing her face up. Her gaze met his, filled with longing, and Alex's anger, burning like a bonfire, wavered. Thoughts, words, abandoned him. None could suffice for what she did to his soul, for what he wanted to give her if only he possessed something truly worthwhile to give.

Alex covered her mouth with his, instantly wrapping Serena in secure, vital heat. It was too perfect, too wonderful and familiar, as though she had never been out of his arms.

But in the days since she had, he'd done nothing to prove he was anything other than what society painted him. Her fantasies, fueled by his touch and alluring gaze, confused her into mistaking his character. His actions spoke loudest.

She yanked free. "*No.* I love my sisters, my family. I must help them and the innocent people under my father's protection from this danger."

His hands surrounded her face. "Don't you understand that I know that? Better than you can imagine."

"Then why aren't you giving me your aid? Why am I left to do this alone?"

"Because—" His fingers threaded through her hair, tilting her head back. His eyes looked like rain-heavy clouds in the flickering light. "I am no hero, Serena." Her name scraped across his tongue. "I am only a man. A very flawed one at that."

Beneath his exposed gaze, the fight whooshed out of her, frustration, fear, all submerged in yearning. Her hands sought his arms, gripping solid man.

"You were right," she said. "I think I don't know who you are."

His mouth met hers, seeking and as bewildered as she, but completely, commanding and possessing, spinning her world into a vertiginous spiral of longing and luxuriant hope. He pressed her back into the stall barrier, and she welcomed his urgency, his hands upon her molding her to his body. He caressed her everywhere, as though needing to feel her as she needed him, her face, hips, breasts, the curve of her back, even her hands, shedding blazing light beneath her skin.

Fingers tangling with hers, he bent his mouth to her throat and forced his leg between her thighs. Heat assailed Serena, almost painful in its intensity, ratcheting higher with each stroke of his tongue upon her tender skin. She rocked against him, her body tightening like it had that night, like it did each time she had touched herself in the nights since, remembering what he had done to her. Wanting him.

He lifted his head, his breath heavy, eyes bright with desire. Everything inside her reached for him.

"Who was he, Serena?" His voice was rough.

"Who was who?" She twined her hands in his thick locks.

A muscle flickered in his jaw. "The man who took your virginity."

"It doesn't matter." She pulled his face down and covered it with kisses. He smelled like brandy and clean linen and that ineffable scent that was Alex alone. "I don't even remember him now."

He went immobile.

"You *don't remember him*? Were there others after him?"

"No. Except *you*. And I do remember him, I simply do not care to discuss it." She pressed her breasts to his chest to feel him with the sensitive peaks, her wet garments heightening the pleasure. Her head ached but his nearness breathed life into her. "But isn't this rather a case of the pot calling the kettle black again? How many women have you been with since you lost your virginity?"

"You are a lady." His voice was strangled, his hands maddeningly still now.

"No, I am a wanton, which of course we have already established to everybody's perfect satisfaction. Kiss me, Alex."

He gripped her waist. "Who was he?" he ground out.

"A friend of my stepbrother. He courted me. I thought I was in love with him, then he went off and married someone else without mentioning it to me first." She smoothed a hand across his cheek. The day's growth of stubble rasped against her fingertips, sending tendrils of delirious anticipation through her as she remembered that roughness upon her thighs and belly and the curve of her breast. She stared into his beautiful eyes where perfection seemed to meet heaven and shook her head in wonder. "He never made me feel the way you do. Never. He didn't make me want to scream, or to eat him alive."

Alex swallowed jerkily, bent and captured her mouth again. She met him fully, the man she had craved since the moment he first touched her. More so since she saw him smile. He played with her, nothing gentle in the hungry strokes of his tongue this time, and she ached for the sweet pleasure of taking him inside her.

She spread her thighs and he hiked up her damp skirts and reached between them, cupping her so hard she cried out, the sound cascading to a moan as he caressed her tender flesh. She was liquid and hot and thrillingly alive.

"Alex, make love to me," she uttered. "Now. Here. I need it."

He thrust his finger into her and she gasped at the shocking intimacy. It felt so good. So hard and him. She wanted everything about him, his touch, his voice, how he made her feel like she could never tire of this, never tire of sublime joy.

"What do you need?" he said roughly against her mouth, and stroked in and out, his palm massaging her to frenzy. She moved herself against him.

"It. I—I need—" she panted, swamped in desperate yearning.

"What?" he growled, pushing two fingers inside, now pumping into her steadily, faster, as though he was satisfied taking her this way, wanted her only like this. Sharp longing built in her blood, shook, built again, carrying her to the edge of delirium. But it wasn't enough.

"*You.* I need you."

He lifted her onto her toes, hitched his hands beneath her thighs and bent to her ear. "You have me," he whispered, and guided his shaft into her.

She pulled him in completely, and for a moment Serena pretended she did have him. As he gripped her hips to settle her around his need and she laughed with the ecstatic happiness hiding inside for years, she made believe he was hers. He wrapped her thigh about him, sank deep inside her, and she knew this would last forever. Nothing so perfect, so alive, could ever die. Someday, after he put her off, it would become a dream. Now she cried from the beautiful pleasure of his touch, Alex moving inside her, and tried not to think that this would be the last time, if after this, or soon, he would finish with her. Now it must last.

"Serena, come to me, love." His body was all around her, arms holding her, straining against shirt fabric as his thrusts quickened. All of him, large and powerful, hers for a single, perfect moment. "You drive me mad, sweet Serena," he whispered against her cheek, his voice harsh. "I cannot continue like this. Come now."

"Make me," she uttered on a strange sob.

He kissed her hard, deep, and completely.

"I want you," he uttered against her lips. "More than I have ever wanted a woman. I want you on me day and night, to possess you like this every hour. Now come, or I shall embarrass myself and then where will we be?"

She arched against him. "Embarrass? But how—"

"It is too long since the last time." His jaw seemed to harden, his shoulders to grow stiff, his thrusts coming less steadily but so deliciously.

"A sennight?" Her body reached for him, need tightening.

"Didn't—" He caught his breath. "—you hear what I just said?"

"Yes, but I—"

"*Serena.*"

"I don't believe you! I don't believe the things you say to me."

He went perfectly still.

"Well this is having the desired effect," he said into

her hair. He spread his hand around the side of her face. His gaze was bright, intense, his voice rough. "Then believe this, foolish woman, I am furious with you for putting yourself in danger tonight, and the other night when you followed a sailor you do not know onto a ship you had never seen to meet a man renowned for violence."

"Stop it. I am not a child to be chastised." She gripped his neck and bore down upon him.

He grunted and shifted inside her. "You behave as one."

"I did not go to see any man." Need shimmered through her like a living creature. "I went to see you."

"You should not have."

"I spent years being obedient to others' wishes, and now I will do as I please," she circled her hips, feeling him, angling so he drove shivers of pleasure through her, "whether you like it or not."

"Does this please you?" He forced her against the wall, bringing him hard against her tender core. "Because I like it." His voice grated with anger.

She clung to him, startled, a little frightened, her body burning.

"It does. Yes. Alex, please—"

"Be silent, woman, while I use you." He gripped her hips, his fingers digging into her flesh, and drove up into her, no beautiful caress but a fast, brutal stroke, pinioning her to the boards. Then he did it again, pulling out entirely then thrusting hard and high. And again. And again, forcing her open, but never enough. She whimpered, a desperate edge of pleasure consuming everything but his rough touch, his scent of sin, and the wild need inside her begging to be satisfied. He lifted her knee and pounded hard, then with a moan his sinews strained and he flattened her against the stall, halting abruptly but for the flexing deep inside her.

"Alex, *please*," she sobbed, on the edge of ecstasy, trapped between his body and the stall door and trying to twist her hips on him. His chest heaved against hers in labored breaths. He drew back, made their gazes lock, and panic seemed to glint in his dark eyes.

"Serena." He kissed her with new urgency, her mouth and throat, his hand curving around her face then her shoulder, drawing down her bodice, baring her sensitized nipples.

"Oh, Alex, help me."

"Yes," he murmured and covered her with his tongue, then his teeth, nipping. She moaned, grabbed his hand and guided it to the crux of her aching.

He dropped to his knees in the straw, pushed her sodden skirts to her waist and took her with his mouth. She cried out, melting to his tongue, quivering and contracting as he consumed her, drowning in pleasure, needing him inside her again yet wanting this delirium never to end. He caressed and all doubt within her fled, this possession all she desired.

He slid his fingers into her, touched her with his thumb. Then his tongue.

Her hips jutted forward. "*Alex*," she moaned, coming in a staggering agony of fulfillment.

Her head fell back and she dragged in air, his hands wrapped around her thighs like a dream now except for the muted pull within, echoes of pleasure, and the hard, hurried beat of her heart. That painful beat spoke to her, telling her that something had changed and she should run from it before someone stole it away again while she watched.

Alex let her skirts fall and spread his hands on her back, pressing his brow to her belly, his shoulders rigid.

She sifted her fingers through his hair, satiny dark against the pale of her skin.

Finally he drew away and climbed to his feet. She grasped his shirt, twisting it around her fingers to hold him close.

"You did that at first—before—" She touched his lips. "—to show me what it might have been like had those smugglers not released me. To teach me a lesson."

"I did," he said tightly. "And to have you. At the moment the two were inseparable." His jaw clenched and he looked away.

"It had rather the opposite of its intended effect. It was you, after all."

He took a deep breath. "I do not control my actions where you are concerned. You make me insane."

"The experience is mutual."

His gaze slewed back to her. "No. That is false. I was wrong before to accuse you of rash behavior. I see now that your every action is carefully calculated. Your judgment is not always clear, but you choose all you do with great decision."

His tone was severe, but Serena did not think he intended to accuse. Even as he spoke, his gaze scanned her features as though he might find something in them that he sought. With tender fingers, he touched her hairline where her temple smarted, his jaw taut.

"Yet my actions are all for nothing," she whispered, foundering beneath the emotion in his eyes. Or did she imagine it, wanting to see it now like she wanted air? "I fail."

"You merely overestimate your capacity to succeed." Like sunshine bursting through a thundercloud, the firm line of his mouth tilted up at one edge. "In that manner, you would make a fine pirate."

"Alex." She met his gaze squarely. "I did not calculate this. I hadn't thought—"

"No," he interrupted, his eyes sobering once more. "I know that." He released her waist, moving away. "I will saddle my horse and take you home. I suspect you prepared your absence tonight as you did before. You will not have been missed?"

She shook her head. "Wedding plans have exhausted everyone. They will not notice when I return."

"All the same, we will walk when silence becomes necessary. Are you able?" His gaze scanned her, dispassionate now upon the surface, but it seemed to cost him effort to make that show. He desired her, but he did not want to. It showed so clearly in his rigid stance, in his words. The teasing, care-for-nothing rogue was entirely gone.

She nodded. He disappeared around a corner. Her breath slipped away, her lungs compressing as though he took the air with him.

He held her close but did not speak as they rode the dark miles. Beyond the first grove of trees beneath the bluff at Glenhaven, Alex pulled his horse to a halt, dismounted, and drew her down. He wrapped a lead tether around a branch.

Serena set off on the road and immediately stumbled. Alex caught her, curled his strong fingers around her arm then slipped his hand into hers. He paused. Stepping close, he drew her palm into a ray of fading moonlight. Scratches crisscrossed her skin, rusty with dried blood. He lifted her palms to his lips, first one, then the other, and kissed them with devastating tenderness.

"I suppose now I have the hands of a pirate too." Her heartbeat throbbed in her ears.

"You are well on your way," he murmured, a flicker of light in his eyes, then released her. He remained close as they walked, but without touching her. At the porter's gate at the end of the short drive, he halted.

"Tomorrow I will return," he said quietly. "Until then."

Serena walked the remainder of the way as steadily as she could, knowing he watched. She entered through the servants' entrance, stole up the back stairs on torn stockinged feet, and slipped into her bedchamber.

A single candle lit the dressing table, more than enough to illuminate the harsh planes of her stepmother's face.

"Hello, daughter. Where have you been?"

Chapter 19

Do not rebuke for this your flawless daughter
. . . for we are quick to anger, we tribes of men
upon earth.

—HOMER, *ODYSSEY*

Davina's gaze pierced Serena, assessing her hair, gown, and face in one contemptuous sweep.

"Answer me." Even as low as a whisper, her voice cut through Serena's exhausted defenses.

"At the beach."

"In the middle of the night?" Her stepmother's nostrils pinched. "You look like a trollop, and apparently are still behaving as one. Who did you go to meet? A farmer's son? Or, no. It must be a married gentleman."

"What?"

"It explains your impatience to return from town and your distraction these past weeks." Davina's eyes narrowed. "Yes, I have noticed. And I have been waiting for you to make a foolish misstep." She stood and walked to the door, pulling a key from her pocket. "As soon as your sister marries, you will no longer reside in this house, Serena. When I tell your father of this—" She gestured contemptuously. "—he will agree with me that Diantha and Faith will be better served without your poor influence upon them."

"He will not. My father would never cast me out of his house. Never." Serena's voice shook with certainty.

Davina's eyes narrowed. "He has indulged you far too much. But no longer. Until the wedding you will remain in this locked bedchamber each night after dinner until I summon you to breakfast."

"You are locking me in?" Serena's eyes widened. "In my own house?"

"For the safety of my daughters' reputations."

"And after that?" Fire burned in her belly, humiliation beyond anything Davina had made her feel before.

"I do not care where you go. But you will no longer be welcome here. Perhaps you will be able to convince your lover to set you up in a house of your own, or an apartment in London." Her face grew waspish. "It is no more than a man's plaything deserves, after all. That is what you made yourself years ago, Serena, a toy for men who do not respect you, who want only one thing from you. Despite my reservations I have made an effort to keep you respectable." Her gaze traveled over Serena's ruined gown and hair again. "But you seem happier in this role."

She closed the door quickly behind her, the key clinking in the lock.

Serena sank onto her bed, curling her battered hands beneath her chin and her bruised knees up to her chest. Her father would not disown her, and a tidy sum waited in the bank ready to be spent upon a comfortable little spinster's cottage if needed.

Yet she wept.

A horseman galloped up Savage Park's long tree-lined drive through the dawn mist. Alex watched from the window of his bedchamber and shrugged into his coat. He walked the dark corridor to his brother's door, knocked, then continued to the breakfast parlor. The footman entered just before Aaron.

Alex took the message from the servant's hand. "That will be all."

The footman bowed and retreated. Aaron, standing just inside the parlor, closed the door after him.

"So what's so important that you've woken me so early?" He glanced at the pinkish-gray light filtering in through the window.

"You were already awake," Alex said, pouring a cup of coffee and setting it on the table near his brother, then another for himself. He didn't care if Aaron minded the gesture. He didn't care about much of anything this morning.

Hours earlier he had descended to his lowest, playing upon a woman's passionate nature to force himself upon her. That she had not despised him for it, that she wanted him and enjoyed it, did not exonerate him. The action was not the crime. The reason for it was. Anger. And the need to control that which was not in his power.

As always.

Today, however, he would begin anew. Through the remainder of the dark night the images of the bruises on her body worked through his conscience, tightening his lungs until he could barely breathe. Some matters were within his power to address.

He snapped open the wax seal and unfolded the missive.

"As I suspected," he said, passing it to his brother. Aaron lowered himself into a chair awkwardly and set his cane against the edge of the table. He perused the sheet.

"They are sending Halloway and the *Command*, with Poole along for the ride." Aaron placed the message from Alex's contact in Portsmouth on the table. "You were right."

"I am always right, little brother." He studied Aaron's pallor, his sunken cheeks so much like Miss Lucas's lately. "I expect they will be here within the week."

"What will you do? Send the *Cavalier* back to the covey in Scilly?"

"Did you read the whole?" Alex gestured.

"He notes that *White Lady* and *Titan* are being fitted out at lightning speed, as though they'll ship out before planned next month, but he's heard no news to confirm or deny that rumor. What do you think?"

"One or both will accompany Halloway here."

"Weren't they meant to head to the Barbary Coast as soon as they're finished?"

"Plans can alter."

"They say *Titan* is faster than that American, *Wasp*, the one that outran you two years ago. They used a similar design, smaller vessel, more guns."

"The *Cavalier* is fast too, and she has plenty of guns."

Silence stretched across the chamber.

"Alex," his brother finally said, "you cannot be thinking of taking on three British naval vessels at once."

Alex shifted his gaze to his brother's somber face. "Why not?"

"Because you will die doing so, and every man on board with you, unless they live to be hanged at the gibbet."

Alex pushed out his chair and stood.

"Naturally the crew must come first. Well then, perhaps I'll send a note around to Jin to ready the ship to put out to sea. The wedding will be over and done with by then, and my little wife installed here. She'll no doubt be glad to be rid of me swiftly enough." He cast his brother a glance as he moved toward the door.

"We'll head down to the West Indies for a spell, make it a lengthy cruise this time. Sure you don't want to come along?" He paused. "On second thought, perhaps it would be better if you remained here to help make the new Lady Savege comfortable. I'm sure she will be glad to have a friend in the house, and the two of you seem to get along so well."

Aaron's face went white, his lips a compressed line.

"As you wish, Alex."

Alex leaned his shoulder against the door frame casually, disappointment cutting through him like a knife. Again, as always.

"Well then, if you leave it up to me, I'd like your company. Her family is close enough to provide comfort if she needs it while I'm gone." He turned to leave.

"Alex, after—"

He swiveled around.

"After the wedding," Aaron continued, his voice tight, "when you return from the cruise, will you and Lady Savege go up to London, as you usually do for the winter, or remain here?"

"I haven't given it a thought. Why do you ask?" Alex's heart beat fast. Aaron's brown eyes were awash in silent desolation, his breaths shallow. Alex waited, refusing to hope but hoping nevertheless.

Aaron dropped his gaze. "Merely curious."

"Ah, of course." Alex nodded, emptiness filling his heart, pressing aside the nascent, barely tested sliver of something else, something new. The old wounds were too strong to give way.

His brother sipped his coffee, eyes averted, hand unsteady upon the bone china. Alex watched, and without warning a chamber of his ancient edifice of regret crumbled.

Fate had chosen better than he always imagined,

after all—if not perfectly. This man, his twin, intelligent, kind, and unalterably honorable, should not have been born first. With the curse visited upon Aaron by the battlefield, and Alex's own self-serving behavior, he could never truly know what his brother lived with every day. But Aaron's cowardice now was his ruination. He was not meant to lead.

But Alex *was* meant to lead—a peerage, a ship full of rowdy sailors, even a strong-willed woman. He imagined Serena's lovely face, her passion and steadfast courage. She was not another man's now. But even if she were, that would not stand in his way.

He smiled and moved into the corridor.

"Where are you going?" Aaron's voice came thin behind him.

"For a ride." It was high time he paid a call upon his bride. First, however, he had business to attend to.

Serena passed slowly from the walled garden into the park, trailing her light shawl on the ground. The morning was fine, already warm, gull cries upon the wind and songbirds astir in the trees, the fragrance of roses, lilac, gardenias, and lilies tangling in the air.

Her head ached, her eyes were fractured with red, and her hands and knees still smarted. But she could not remain within the house, not during the daylight hours of freedom Davina allowed her. Her father had gone out early, and now she must wait to put her case before him.

Hoofbeats sounded on the turf. Her heart stumbled and she turned toward the sound. The big horse's coat shone like polished ebony in the morning light.

Alex pulled it to a halt, bowed from the saddle and tipped his high-crowned hat. Elegantly arrayed in a loose coat and breeches befitting the country, clean-shaven and sparkling-eyed, he looked as beautiful as he had in the lamplight hours earlier, tousled and unkempt. Always he stole her breath.

"You said you would return today," she managed with credible calm. "But isn't this rather early for a London n'er-do-well?"

He smiled wide and her heart lurched. She had not entirely expected this greeting. She hadn't known exactly what to expect.

"I told you." He held her gaze. "I aim to reform."

Her insides tingled.

"I suppose it is already quite late in the day for a sailor."

"Just so."

He remained on horseback. Serena curtsied properly. Ten of Glenhaven Hall's broad high windows looked out onto the gardens with fine views of the park. If Davina had already returned from her trip to the village, she would get no satisfaction from this interview.

"There is something I wish to show you," he said.

"Now?"

"Tonight."

"I cannot. My stepmother discovered my absence last evening." Shame for her impossible predicament burned hot as a lit taper in the pit of Serena's stomach. "She will be vigilant now."

"Discover a method to evade her detection." A shadow crossed his eyes. "I believe you will want to see this."

She nodded. "I will try." The blacksmith might have a tool for picking locks. She would run down to his shop as soon as Alex departed. Laughter welled in her, unbelievable and deliciously breezy. Davina could lock her in, tell her twenty times she was soiled goods. But beneath Alex's smoky gaze, anything seemed possible, everything right.

"Your groom will have your horse readied at the end of the drive," he said.

"You have already spoken with John? I could have."

"Yes, but now he also understands that if he allows you to ride off again at night without an escort, I will dismiss his sister from my employ."

Serena's eyes widened. "Mrs. Tubbs? Your house-keeper? But—"

"If he were my servant, after that stint in London taking you to meet the Marquess of Doreé in that alleyway, he would have long since been sent on his way."

She stared in astonishment.

"That is rather high-handed of you, isn't it? And ruthless."

His eyes took on a dubious light.

"Serena . . . *pirate*?"

Her laughter tumbled forth and she slapped a hand over her mouth.

"Of course." She should not laugh, or smile, or feel so full of him. She lived a fool's paradise. But paradise for a short while was better than no paradise at all. The sunshine sparkled and she had no tolerance at the present for gloomy forecasts of her future alone. Open-eyed, she had chosen to dally with a rake. She would gather rosebuds while she may.

The horse sidestepped, and Alex turned toward the house.

"I am off to call upon my intended, then."

"Are you?"

"I am indeed. Do you think she would be more comfortable with her sister at her side for this particular interview?"

Serena's heart slid into her throat, pattering fast.

"I suspect she would, but—"

"Then don't keep the animal waiting, my dear."

The horse's head bobbed, a trick of its master's skill no doubt. "Your sister has need of you forthwith." He removed his hat and gestured with it toward the house. She turned hesitantly. He replaced the beaver, winked, and set off toward the drive, his mount's heavy hooves tossing up divots of grass in its wake.

Serena nearly picked up her skirts and ran. Tamping down her nerves, she walked carefully along the path to the back door. Then she tore off her spencer and bonnet and flew up the servants' steps to the upstairs parlor.

Charity sat like a specter upon the window seat, looking down onto the drive through filmy islet curtains. She lifted her sad gaze to Serena.

"He is here." Her voice was a whisper of hopelessness.

"Don't fret, darling. I am with you."

"But you will not always be with me. After Monday, I will be alone."

Serena swallowed thickly. The mere notion of being alone with Alex—indefinitely—dizzied her.

A silent minute became two. The door opened and a footman entered.

"Lord Savege," he announced then departed, closing the door behind the earl. Serena came to her feet beside Charity.

"Good day, Miss Lucas." He bowed. "Miss Carlyle, thank you for attending your sister as I requested."

She nodded.

"Ladies?" He gestured for them to sit, so smooth, so relaxed and nonchalant, the supreme gentleman, consummate rake because he never had to work at it. But Serena had seen his anger and felt his urgency. She had shared his laughter. Perhaps she did know him. Perhaps a bit.

Charity sank to her seat and Serena sat upon the edge of a wooden chair.

"Miss Lucas, I asked your sister to be here at this time because I have a matter of a delicate nature to discuss with you and I hoped you would be more at ease with her present."

The white fichu over Charity's perfect bosom palpitated. "My lord?"

"I find it my unlucky task to require you to put an end to this engagement which has now become impossible for me to honor."

"Re-Require, my lord?"

"It has come to my attention that my brother holds a considerable affection for you. I believe he fancies himself in love." His steady gaze never altered. "As this is an unprecedented occurrence for him, I must acknowledge its significance and act upon that."

Charity's knuckles stood out white around the handkerchief clutched between them. She did not respond, but her lips looked uncharacteristically firm.

Alex leaned forward and his voice softened.

"Unfortunately, aside from our betrothal, for reasons that I cannot disclose at this time, my brother is unable to extend to you an offer of marriage."

Charity's hands jerked.

"He and I are quite close, however," the earl continued. "As you may imagine, under such circumstances it is not advisable for you and me to marry. You must, Miss Lucas, finally release me from this arrangement."

Charity's lashes flickered, fluttered, then beat like the wings of a moth frantic to escape a spider's web.

"I must," she replied, her tone remarkably steady.

"If you wish to retain your unimpeachable reputation, yes."

The door swung open and Davina swept in, Tracy sauntering behind. Charity popped up, the earl following more elegantly, and Serena nearly screamed.

It was too soon. She never imagined Alex would take this tack, wonderful and horrible at once, but it was brilliant. Charity now knew Mr. Savege loved her in return. But why wouldn't he offer for her?

"My lord," Davina purred, "What a pleasure to see you here. How do you do?"

"I am well, thank you, ma'am." He bowed. "I have been discussing a matter of great importance with your daughter which I must address with you now."

Davina's eyes narrowed but her thin smile remained fixed. "But of course, my lord. You are soon to be family. You may say anything to me."

Charity stepped forward. "Mama, I wish to tell you, rather than Lord Savege. I—I must."

Alex looked down at her, his gaze gentle. Serena's heart hammered.

"What is it, dearest?" Davina drew off her gloves, setting them upon a table with her discarded bonnet. "About what do you wish to speak to me?"

Spots of color dimpled Charity's ashen cheeks.

"Go ahead, Chare," Tracy murmured, glancing at Serena then the earl. "Tell us."

"Miss Lucas," Alex said quietly, "pray allow me to—"

"No. Thank you, sir." Charity's eyes were bright. "Mama." She pulled in a deep, quick breath. "I—I will not wed Lord Savege. I will not."

Davina's gaze went icy calm.

"You have not broken it off with his lordship, have you, daughter?"

Charity's entire body quivered, but her shoulders did not slump. Alex stood like a solid rock of confidence beside her. Serena held her breath.

"I have, Mama. We—We will not marry."

Tracy's gaze sought Serena's again, eyes wide and filled with anxiety. Serena's heart went to him. He loved Charity as much as she did, and perhaps knew even better than she how his sister would now suffer for her courage.

Davina's face had turned white, livid red rising high on her cheeks. "But this is entirely unacceptable."

"Lady Carlyle," Alex said with perfect calm, "your daughter and I are agreed upon this. The arrangement was made in error, as most present at the time must have been aware. If it should become generally known, however, I am assured none will fault Miss Lucas for withdrawing now. A young lady of breeding and modesty such as your daughter would be better suited to a gentleman of less worldly interests than myself." His gaze did not even flicker. Serena struggled to maintain an even façade, caught between euphoria and hysteria.

"No, my lord." Davina's eyes were wide. "I simply will not accept this. For weeks now you have allowed my daughter—my *family*—to believe that you wished this alliance."

"I beg your pardon, ma'am, but I gave very little indication of that. You must forgive me for insisting upon the truth, but it was largely your doing."

"You were guest of honor at a betrothal ball that the whole county attended."

"I had hoped not to be obliged to, I will admit. However, the thing was done. But it can now be undone with sufficient discretion."

"The wedding is three days away." Davina's voice shook elegantly.

"And yet the banns have yet to be read, haven't they, Mother?" Tracy spoke low. "Jumped your guns on that one, didn't you?"

"That matters nothing," she snapped. "Lord Savege will have purchased a special license. I depended upon it."

"You know I had no intention of doing so, madam." He held her gaze steadily until finally she withdrew hers, looking down at her fingertips pressing into the table, lips pinched and nostrils quivering.

Alex turned to Charity. "Miss Lucas, perhaps you wish a breath of fresh air. May I escort you to the garden?"

She shook her head, her gaze trapped on her mother. Serena ground her teeth. *The widgeon.* But perhaps Charity was wise to seek her punishment immediately rather than await it in terror.

Alex's brow creased. "Are you quite certain, ma'am?"

For the first time in weeks, Charity met his regard squarely. She nodded.

"Then, if you will pardon my departure from you now, I will search out your father and apprise him of the situation." He turned to Davina. "My lady," then Tracy, "Sir." His gaze came to Serena. "Miss Carlyle." He departed.

Serena's heart raced, her insides twisted with excitement and profound relief. He had ended it.

And now for the consequences. But a glimmer of defiance sparkled in Charity's eyes.

"You have disobeyed me, Charity," Davina said in dark tones without lifting her gaze. "Do my wishes mean nothing to you then?"

"Oh, no, Mama." Charity twisted her fingers together. "I only—Mama, I never wished to marry him, to be a great lady, and he did not—"

"Silence." Davina's cold blue gaze slewed to Serena. "You encouraged her to it. You prompted her to do this, you filthy, disloyal *cocotte.*"

"Mother." Tracy stepped forward. "You mustn't."

"Tracy, leave us."

"But Mother—"

"Leave us now, or you will shortly regret defying me as well," she snapped. Tracy's jaw went white. Casting Serena a look of agonized apology, he backed toward the door. Davina closed it behind him with a deceptively soft click.

"My son, the dear boy, thinks so highly of you, stepdaughter," she said over her shoulder, then turned to face Serena. "It would be difficult for him to hear the truth about a woman who gave her innocence to a philanderer and continues to do so, apparently, while she lives beneath my roof."

Charity's gaze flew to Serena.

"But I expected as much from that woman's daughter," Davina added. "I only hoped my own children would remain clear of her sullying influence."

Prickling heat flooded Serena. "Leave my mother out of this. She was a person of greater character and goodness than you will ever be."

"Viola was not my husband's daughter." Davina spoke with silky ease. "That girl you called your sister shared only half your parentage. Ah, you were not privy to that information, were you? Your father did not tell you everything after all, I guess. How awful for you to discover his lack of faith in you now, after so many years."

A fist clutched around Serena's heart.

"You are lying," she uttered. "You haven't any idea of what you are talking about."

"But I have." Davina stroked her fingertips along the gloves on the table. "After you allowed yourself to be used by that man your first season, my husband told me the truth of it, how when he was in town for the session she allowed a sailor—a common sailor—into her bed."

"It is not true."

"Your father was absent from home for quite a few months then, your mother insisting upon remaining in the country with you, her darling firstborn. But all the while she was cuckolding him." She spoke the words with relish, her tongue twining about them as though caressing each syllable. "When the child came to term, it was obvious your father could not have sired it."

"She—"

"She told him. She could not hide it, of course." Davina tsked, then her gaze came up sharp. "And she passed on her sluttish ways to you, with which you have now infected my daughter."

Serena stepped forward, bringing herself within inches of her stepmother, pulling in a steadying breath.

"My mother does not concern any of us at this time. You will honor Charity's decision now, and treat her with the dignity and consideration she deserves. She does not merit your censure." She clasped her stepsister's fingers. "Charity, your mother is angry and disappointed in her hopes now, but in time she will see that this is best for you. You have only done what your heart tells you is right. You must trust that."

Charity's eyes swam with gratitude, tears sparkling. She nodded. Serena urged her toward the exit, and her stepsister went.

She turned back to Davina.

"I will remain in this house until my father tells me I may no longer, or until I choose to leave it. You have no power over me, Davina, nor will you ever again. Your spiteful words and bilious treatment cannot wound me." She moved toward the exit, shaking, and not at all certain of herself.

"You will go to your bedchamber tonight and remain there as arranged."

Serena swiveled about. "But there will be no wedding."

"Yet I still have the key, don't I?"

Nausea filled Serena's stomach. If Davina could threaten her with indefinite incarceration, she could do the same to Charity. Or Diantha, so spirited already at fifteen. Even four-year-old Faith. She herself could escape to a cottage, or to her aunt's home in York, but she could never leave her stepsisters now.

Against the crushing weight of Davina's revelations, she lifted her chin and strode from the chamber. As she came into the foyer below, hands and legs shaking, Bess was closing the front door.

"Milord Savage is a fine one, isn't he, Miss Serena? So pleasant and kind to all."

"Has he left already?"

"Just now, miss." She cast a glance behind Serena, dropped a curtsy, and bustled away.

Serena pivoted and met her father's gaze. Brow creased, skin hanging beneath his pallid eyes like used tea leaves, he seemed much older than his years.

"I have spoken with Lord Savage. He informed me of Charity's wishes."

Serena grasped his hand. "It is for the best, Papa. You do know that."

He nodded. "I will not cause him trouble."

"Papa." She could not remain silent. Looking upon him, her heart churned with compassion and pity. "Davina said that my mother had a lover and that this man was Viola's father. Is this true?"

His shoulders seemed to sag further. Gaze empty, he met hers and only nodded.

"Is that why you blame yourself for my mother's death? You were still jealous. Or perhaps angry with her after all those years."

"She still loved him." The words slipped from his tongue as a breath.

Serena's eyes went wide. "Oh, Papa."

He turned away, looking out the window of the door as though onto the bluff.

"After your sister was gone, and your mother became ill, I think in her heart she believed he would come."

"Papa, I don't understand. Did she—"

"Serena, do not ask more of me." His shoulders shook. "I cannot bear it. I never could."

She touched his arm, but he was cold, defeat marking his every aspect. She struggled in her emotions.

"Daughter," he said so quietly she barely discerned it, "you are a good girl." He reached into his waistcoat pocket and pressed warm metal into her palm. She opened her hand. A brass key rested upon it. "Your stepmother has Bess's key. She does not know of the additional set I keep."

Serena's pulse tripped.

"Papa, tonight—"

"I will make certain she does not check up on you."

"But hasn't she told you of what she accuses me?"

He clasped both her hands. His trembled. It seemed he would speak. She waited, but he remained silent. Serena pressed her cheek to his knuckles, mouthed the words *Thank you*, and slipped the key into her pocket.

Tonight, after all were abed, she would slip out of the house to meet her lover, just as her beloved mother once had. She was everything Davina claimed.

Chapter 20

I was not deaf, I was not blind
When I left me two fine legs behind,
Nor was it sailing on the sea
Lost me two fine legs right down to me knees.

—"MY SON JOHN"

John walked Serena's horse to the end of the drive, hand around the bridle. The earl waited, seated upon his mount in the cover of a grand elm stretching its black limbs above. He moved forward, his features starkly handsome in the light cast by the thinning moon. The night was warm with the scent of blooming jasmine and the faintest hint of ocean breeze.

The coachman tugged his cap, and Alex moved toward the road. Serena nudged her horse forward to catch up.

"Good evening, Miss Carlyle." He glanced aside, swiftly scanning her from hood to the hem draping over her horse's haunch. "I trust you are well."

"Not as well as you, I'll merit."

He cast her a questioning look.

She lifted a brow. "Your reacquired freedom?"

"Your father met with the news as though he expected it. How is your stepsister?" His voice seemed stiff, his whole demeanor so different from earlier in the day.

"Well enough. My stepmother is incensed, of course."

"And you?"

"Me?"

"You had no difficulty coming out this evening?"

"No." She fiddled with the reins. "Alex, where are we going? What do you wish me to see?"

"Trust me." He spurred his mount into a canter. Serena followed, unease heavy beneath her skin. They rode more than a mile, passing onto his land and heading in the direction of the shoreline. The terrain grew rocky, then steep. Alex drew to a halt, dismounted, then came to her and lifted his hands to her waist.

"We will walk from here."

Serena placed her palms on his shoulders and dropped into his hold. They stood motionless, hip to hip. She slid her hand to his face. He grasped her fingers, his eyes impenetrable, and drew away. He tethered the horses to a branch and continued toward the shore.

Serena's breath came tight and her belly felt hollow as she moved after him. Was this the sadness that had often lit her mother's eyes, wishing for a seafaring man who would not have her? But she had loved her father too. The four of them had shared so much happiness together, days of adventure and warmth until Viola disappeared and her mother spent her final hours staring hopelessly out at the ocean as fever ravaged her, the wasting sickness of despair in her gaze.

The terrain sloped off. A whistle sounded from the darkness above the rolling hush of waves upon the beach. Alex responded, and a figure stepped from behind the shadow of a scrubby tree. No more than Serena's age, the man's clothing was worn from the elements, his brows and hair jutting from beneath his hat bleached. In one thick hand he wielded a crowbar.

"This is Adam," Alex said quietly. "You are already acquainted with Billy"—the boy appeared at her side—"and Mattie." The hulking man who had greeted her upon the *Cavalier* approached from behind.

"Gentlemen, open it up," Alex said.

Mattie doffed his cap as he moved past her, then bent and brushed at the sandy ground. Billy went onto his knees and did the same, and Adam set his tool to the beach.

"They found this early today, quite a bit farther away from the dock than I expected, and closer to the water than is advisable."

"This?"

Straight edges appeared in the ground, about four feet square, a broken iron padlock attached to one side. Adam heaved at the crowbar, and a thick hatch jutted upward. Billy and Mattie dug their fingers beneath it and hauled. It came open and fell back on the beach with a thud.

"The smugglers' cache," Alex said. "A storage cellar, years old, it seems, but the cargo is recent, no more than a month or two." He bent his dark gaze to her. "Would you like to see it?"

Wordless, Serena nodded.

"Unfortunately, the nature of the cache makes the use of lamps somewhat perilous," he said, taking her hand as Billy climbed into the hole, his feet clunking on hollow wooden steps. "But as you are an adventuresome sort, I suspected you would not mind it."

Mattie picked up a lantern and lengthened the wick, and light shone across the black square in the ground.

Billy poked his head out of the hole.

"All clear, Cap'n."

"Come out of there, Bill."

The boy leapt up onto the sand. Alex took the lamp and drew Serena forward. He set a foot upon the first step.

"We will take a look, then I have news for you to hear."

Serena followed him, his grip steady as they descended. Lined in planking sealed with pitch, the cellar smelled mostly of dust, with an underlying scent of something acrid. It was surprisingly dry. She reached the floor, a tiny space of sandy planks. The lamplight illuminated crates the size of horse troughs stacked to the ceiling, obscuring the actual size of the chamber.

"What is it?"

"See for yourself." The lid of one crate rested ajar. Carefully, he lifted a board aside and Serena leaned forward. Shining black metal winked up at her, rows of muskets, strands of yellow straw twining through their elegant menace.

"Are all the crates the same?"

"Those we have investigated, yes. Also pistols, ammunition, quite a few barrels of gunpowder, and other supplies."

Serena glanced aside to an open barrel of iron chains and manacle cuffs.

"Why would smugglers store arms here, upon this coast and your land? And why now, when the war is over? I had heard such commerce was regular years ago. But since?"

His grasp on her hand tightened.

"Let's get away from that gunpowder, shall we?" He drew her up the stair.

Once clear of the hole, he gestured for the sailors to close the hatch. Billy whisked handfuls of sand over the door, hiding it once more.

"Thank you, gentlemen. You may go now."

Mattie and Adam sketched awkward bows to Serena, Billy offered a grin, and the three set off along the beach.

She tugged her hand free.

"Alex?"

He shook his head. "I don't know. My business is not in this sort of cargo, Serena."

"But you have encountered such cargo before?"

"Upon legitimate vessels of war and merchant ships, yes." But something strange glinted in his eyes.

"How did you know to find it here?"

"I suspected it."

"Here, precisely?"

"No." He paused. "I made an initial study of the coastline the day my mother and I rode to Glenhaven Hall. But I found nothing. The boys searched quite some time this morning before coming upon it."

"You looked for this three days ago and failed to mention it to me before now?"

"I was preoccupied."

Her eyes went wide.

Finally his glinted. "I brought you here tonight, Serena, to encourage you to cease your investigation into the *Osprey*'s trade. Now that you know the stakes of this game, I trust you will understand the necessity of steering clear of it."

Her fists balled.

"The stakes of the game, Alex, are human lives. If you hoped for my voluntary retreat after seeing this, you hoped in vain."

"I hoped you would show a modicum of sense. Clearly I was mistaken." He did not seem angry, rather his gaze shone with a peculiar sort of desperation, so unsuited to this man of power and authority. Serena blinked, wishing away the intensity of his regard.

"I must do what I can," she muttered.

He grasped her hand and pulled it toward his chest, then abruptly dropped it.

"Serena," his voice was low, "you will not bring back Viola with this misguided crusade. She is gone."

She fell back a step. His eyes flashed and he grasped her shoulders.

"*No*. Let go of—"

"No, Serena. I know these men, their kind. I have known them for years, how they live and of what they are capable. I will not allow you to fall into their hands as well."

She struggled to breathe. "You believe me?"

"About your sister's disappearance? Why wouldn't I?"

"No one ever has."

"Now someone does." His gaze remained steady, his grip on her strong and secure. "Serena, give up this search for her."

Emptiness swirled in her, but a cold claw still clutched, a fantasy unwilling to relinquish its hold.

"She is gone, isn't she?"

He frowned but did not respond. Stillness seemed to settle over the beach, the waves quieting, even the stars above ceasing to twinkle in the velvet black.

She stepped out of Alex's hold, harsh irony biting at her that this man should be the one to bring her to this point. The man her heart fought so hard not to admit, her sailor-lover, like her mother's. He would leave her just as everyone she loved left—her sister, mother, even her father who took his heart away when she was twelve then sat back and allowed hers to be crushed again six years later and every day since then beneath his wife's heel. Alex wanted her now, but he would never be hers the way she needed him. Dreams of shining knights and enduring love were for foolish little girls.

"Alex." Her voice was barely a whisper. "How did you start upon this life?" She gestured toward the sea. "Why did you begin it?"

He did not answer immediately. Finally, he spoke.

"Revenge." His voice was flat.

Serena shivered.

"Not a heroic motive, you see," he said, studying her face. "The basest."

"Revenge for what wrong?"

"A man—a gentleman by title and breeding—took advantage of my sister's innocence." His eyes shone with a hint of renewed fierceness.

"It happens," she said, meeting his gaze directly. "Sometimes willingly."

"She was not yet sixteen. A servant discovered them in time to salvage my sister's virtue, but the man left her heartbroken. I told her she would recover from the hurt soon enough. My brother did not respond so sanguinely. He went to demand satisfaction."

"He challenged the man to a duel?"

"And was shamed for it. Aaron knew little of swords or pistols, only of books and sermons. He wanted a career in the Church." He drew a deep breath. "The blackguard laughed in his face. When my brother returned home, I saw the toll the beating had taken upon him and determined that together we should mete out punishment to the cad, but with my own form of justice. It seemed . . ." He paused. " . . . a great lark at the time."

"You were young."

"Old enough to know better."

"That was when you bought the *Cavalier*, in the West Indies. But after, when you had suitably chastised the fellow, why did you continue?"

He shrugged. "We enjoyed it. *I* enjoyed it, so much so that when word came that my father died, I resented him for it." He laughed without mirth then quietly repeated, "I resented him for it. And because I felt cheated once more, still hankering for adventure, I encouraged my brother to go off to war."

Serena sucked in her breath. His gaze shifted to her.

"I bought him a commission and sent him away with a 'Bon voyage' and a hearty pat upon the back. I hated the idea of returning here to this captivity," he gestured inland, "and so if I could not remain with my ship, my brother should act as my proxy in an endeavor equally dangerous. Three years later he returned disfigured and destroyed."

The wind kicked up with the deepening of night, stirring a lock of hair over Alex's brow. Serena's fingers tingled to brush it aside and to lay her palm upon his cheek and hold him.

"Charity is in love with him," she whispered. "But you knew that before you called this morning."

"I suspected as much."

"If what you said about his feelings for her is true, why won't he offer for her? They seem well suited to one another."

He met her gaze. "In all ways but one."

"Which one?"

"Aaron's injury did him great harm, to both his mind and body, beyond what may be readily discerned."

"Beyond?"

Waves lapped at the sand, reaching higher as the tide rose.

"My brother, Serena," Alex said slowly, "no longer functions fully as a man. He is physically incapable of it."

Serena's heart gaped, swallowing Charity's dashed dreams. She closed her eyes.

"Serena."

She lifted her gaze. The moonlight bathed him in iridescence, emphasizing his masculine beauty. He was no more real to her now than his brother could be to Charity. Beneath the weight of the day's revelations, that stark truth bore upon her too violently.

"Your stepbrother is involved in this." He gestured to the cellar. "I intercepted a communication from him to the captain of the *Osprey*. Tracy is the smugglers' noble patron. The ship is his."

Chapter 21

I am not like the immortals, who hold broad heaven, but like mortal men.

—HOMER, *ODYSSEY*

Her cheeks had turned chalky when he told her about Aaron. But now the animation in her lovely eyes receded, leaving dull flats of color. Her lips opened, her breath uneven.

Alex reached for her. "Serena—"

She swiveled away. "I wish to return home now." She moved swiftly toward the horses.

He followed. She evaded his gaze as he helped her mount, silent and stiff, then set her horse into quick motion. He wanted to drag her off that damned saddle and make her look at him, speak to him. But he could no more force her confidence now than he could run down her stepbrother's ship and put it upon the ocean floor.

Her groom waited outside the stable, weary-eyed yet obviously relieved. Alex drew her down, but she pulled from his hold and made for the rear of the house without a word. Halfway along the path she halted. Her father stood in the dark at the garden gate.

Alex moved forward, their footsteps on the pebble

pathway crunching amidst the soft chatter of crickets.

"Papa, have you waited for me all this time? Just like my stepmother?"

"No, daughter, not like that," he said quietly, and turned to Alex. "My lord."

Alex nodded.

"You needn't be concerned, Papa. Lord Savege and I have merely been upon a hunting expedition this evening discovering evidence of smugglers that you apparently haven't a care for." Her voice was brittle, not like her. "And even if this did compromise me, I am certain you would not feel the need to defend me, as you did not once before when I would have given anything for your protection." She put her hands to her face and her shoulders sagged. "Oh, Papa, I feel so deceived."

The baron bowed his head. "Serena, I am sorrier than you can imagine."

Her face came up, a single tear staining her cheek. Alex's hands curled into fists.

"What are you sorry for, Papa?"

"For your stepmother's part in this villainy."

"My stepmother." Her eyes burned. "Of course."

"Years ago, when I first learned of it, I tried to make her see reason. Our income was more than sufficient, but she wanted more, influence especially, I think. And she was already so deeply involved in her business interests when we married. I had no idea."

"Business interests?" Serena shook her head. "Papa, tonight I saw muskets, and iron manacles." She turned to Alex. "Am I wrong?"

He shook his head. "The *Osprey* was a slaving vessel until recently."

"Papa, importing slaves has been illegal for years. And these weapons cannot be meant for good if they are being stored here as contraband."

The baron's face looked ghostlike in the fading moonlight.

"How could you allow this, after Viola—" she stuttered. "And Mama. I cannot believe it of you, but you have already said it is true. Oh, Papa, say something!" Her voice broke.

He remained silent. Her body seemed to shake, but she held her head high.

"Then I must be content with that," she finally said. "But at least tell me my sisters have no idea of it all. Tell me Charity and Diantha remain innocent."

The baron nodded his head. "I believe so, but I know little of it all now." He lifted his gaze to Alex's. "I suspected, my lord, that my wife so avidly wished for your marriage to my stepdaughter because she hoped to watch your comings and goings more closely through such a connection, and to gain easy access to your lands. The bluff falls steep upon my estate, and we haven't such an easy route to the sea."

"Well, there at least she met with disappointment." Serena's voice dipped, quavering. "Papa, I wish to remove to my aunt's home in Yorkshire as soon as possible. Permanently. I would like to take Charity with me. She has never been fond of Devon, and in York, I believe she may make a good match."

Alex drew in a tight breath. Carlyle's attention shifted.

"My lord," the baron said, "I might ask what intentions you have regarding my daughter."

"You might." Alex managed to contain his anger behind a hard tone. "But you would be overstepping your bounds. In my estimation, sir, you long ago relinquished any claim of authority you held over your family, this daughter in particular."

Serena's eyes went wide. Her father seemed to

shrink in upon himself. She saw his weakness, and her face fell.

"Papa," she uttered, "please go. I cannot speak with you further tonight and I must settle matters with Lord Savege now if I am to depart for Yorkshire soon."

He nodded. "We will speak together tomorrow." He turned and crossed to the house. The air seemed to leave Serena, her body to deflate as she stared after his retreating form.

Alex touched her arm. "Serena, your father—"

"Lied to me for years, as everyone has." She pivoted away. "Tracy. *Tracy.*" She shook her head, as though unable to believe it. "Even Charity, who told me she would be brave and then allowed that woman to control her."

"Not everyone has your strength of character. Sometimes lies are easier."

Her gaze lifted to him, alight with betrayal.

"For the great pirate captain Redstone too, it seems," she said, her eyes shuttering. "Or, perhaps I mean to say the notorious Earl of Savege."

Cold slithered up his spine.

"Serena, don't do this."

"Do what?" Her body seemed to sag anew. "Alex, please go. I cannot see you now, or I daresay again."

It was sheer foolishness. Her eyes shone with hurt and confusion. But she believed her own words. The set of her jaw told him that.

"You do not truly intend to remove to Yorkshire," he said.

"Why not?"

"Why not? *Serena.*"

"Alex, as much as I am attached to Glenhaven Hall, it is long past time for me to leave it. I cannot remain with my father, and Charity will be better off away from here, where thoughts of your brother cannot be far from her."

"Why are you talking about your damned sister? Are you incapable of thinking of yourself first for once?"

Her lips tightened. "Astoundingly, it is possible for a person to wish for the happiness and welfare of others. I beg your pardon if that notion is not included in your lexicon of scandalous behaviors."

He knew he should not quarrel now. He should return home and call upon her tomorrow after they'd both slept and she had time to come to terms with all she had learned of her family. But Alex never did what he should. The blood spinning hot in his veins, and her nearness, alluring in a way he had never dreamed even as she held herself aloof, assured that he would not do so now.

"Serena, I want you."

"I know that." She fisted her hands at her sides, as though afraid she might use them otherwise.

"And you want me."

"I cannot bear any more of this." Her eyes flashed with a hint of panic. "You lied to me too!"

"No. I already told you I did not. I never intended to wed your sister, not from the very night I made her acquaintance."

That seemed to arrest her. "That night, at the ball? You didn't?"

Alex stared at her wide eyes, parted lips, the gown pulling across her breasts with quick breaths, and he ached to grab her. His thoughts had never been so contorted, his tongue so tied. Dear God, it was a good thing none of his crew or servants or tenants or anybody else was here to see him like this. None of them would believe it.

But he didn't care what those people thought of

him. He never had. The only person whose opinion meant anything stood before him, her eyes awash in confusion.

"Of course I didn't," he uttered. This woman, her voice, her sincerity, her unstinting devotion to those she loved—he had seen that perfection the night they met, and he'd wanted it. All of her.

She shook her head as though she did not believe him. Alex clenched his jaw.

"Damn it, Serena, why are we discussing this again? My brother cannot be my heir, and although I did not always, I now take the responsibility for my lands and dependents quite seriously. That I even considered for a moment marrying anyone was because with an heir assured I would be free to pursue my life as I wished it." He paused and looked at her closely. "You must know that by now."

But she seemed to draw in upon herself with his last words.

"Alex, please leave now."

He grasped her hand tight, all the contact he would allow. If he took her in his arms, he would not release her.

"Serena, what has happened?"

"Nothing. I don't trust you. I told you that before but you don't seem to believe me."

"How can you not trust me now? I have told you everything. *Everything.* It isn't pretty, but you know it all. I am who I am."

"I started to believe in you. To believe that for once I might—" She broke off, her eyes suddenly wild. "Don't you see? You are just like them. You live your life as two men, or three if you include this lord-of-the-manor you have been mimicking so credibly these past weeks."

"Well, if I am, you haven't complained of it. You have

been playing along perfectly smoothly. For God's sake, I don't even know how you learned of it all."

"Your housekeeper told me."

His jaw went slack. "Mrs. Tubbs?"

"At first I thought she assumed I knew already, but then I don't think she did. I believe she intended to reveal your identity to me." Her hand was cold in his. "Alex, I don't know what those muskets are for, but people will die because of them."

He went perfectly still.

"Of course they will," he said. "People die every day."

Silence stretched between them, her gaze steady, speaking his last, single, greatest fear. She wanted him to go after her stepbrother. Now, after all she had been through, she needed him to be a hero.

"Serena, you don't know what you are asking. People *will* die." And if her stepbrother were one of those people, she would hate Alex for it. He stepped closer. "This is not make-believe."

She blinked rapidly, tears glistening.

"How well I know it. I was foolish to imagine you as something you are not. Alex, I cannot see you again. I want you to go, and not to return."

He released her hand and stepped back, sickness like he'd never felt upon the ocean rolling through his body.

"If you hold by this," he heard himself say as though through a tunnel, "you will be making a great mistake."

"We will both be better off for it, undoubtedly."

"You cannot believe that."

"I do. Please leave, my lord."

"Not yet." He seized her, pulled her close, and took the stubborn, tight, dishonest line of her mouth between his lips. She resisted for the space of a breath only, then opened to him, parting upon a sob, her hands wrapping around his neck. Then she was in his arms, pressing against him, driving thought and argument away and leaving only his need to be inside her, to be encompassed in her beauty, her strength and generous heart.

The sliver of moon slid behind clouds and darkness wrapped about them. But Alex did not need sight to feel her, to know her, and know she was his. He should have known it the moment he first touched her without seeing, tasted her without recognizing his life changing in an instant.

Trailing caresses into her hair and along her throat, he spread his palms over her soft behind and fitted her snugly to him.

"I could spend the entire night kissing you like this," he murmured, running his tongue along the tender edge of her ear, breathing in her cinnamon and woman scent, at once exotic and as familiar as home, but like no home he had ever known. He caressed the undersides of her breasts with his thumbs then across their perfect swollen peaks. She trembled.

"When I have you next in my bed," he whispered, "not an inch of your skin will go unkissed before I am inside you again. I want to do that to you, to give you pleasure, to touch you every way you desire for as long as you desire it."

She twined her fingers through his hair and dragged his mouth against hers. The flavor of salt clung to her lips, silken and damp.

Alex touched his fingertips to her cheek. His heartbeat stilled.

"You are crying? Serena—"

She yanked out of his embrace, twirled about and ran across the garden, to disappear into the house. He stared at the closed door for endless moments, then turned and strode into the darkness.

Alex woke late to his valet drawing open the bedchamber curtains. He slung an arm over his eyes to shut out the anticipated glare, but rain pattered on the panes, obscuring the daylight.

He hadn't known it would rain today. For weeks he had not paid attention to anything except Serena.

"The boy returned here an hour ago, my lord," Tubbs said, his lips tight.

"Billy?" Alex shrugged out of the covers and put his feet on the floor. He accepted a dressing gown and tugged it over his bare chest. "Any news?"

"The cache is gone, the cellar emptied of its contents early this morning, apparently."

He froze. *"You say?"*

"He and Adam went by the beach again before coming here for your orders. Adam chose to remain at the cellar to guard it."

Alex rubbed his hands over his face.

"What good is a damned guard upon it now when it's empty? Blast it, Jin should have let me know the *Osprey* was nearby."

"Perhaps the muskets were loaded onto another vessel, my lord."

Alex waved away the comment. It wasn't Jin's fault, whatever the case. Alex should have ordered Mattie and Adam to remain at the cache overnight. But he'd dismissed them, more concerned about Serena than anything else.

But Serena did not care about anything other than those muskets, and protecting her loved ones. Now the two were intertwined, the weapons on her brother's ship, heading out to God only knew where with a crew of miscreants who seemed to think preying upon the local population an acceptable pastime.

Alex moved to his writing table and scratched a few lines on a sheet of foolscap.

"Call Billy up here, Tubbs. And take this to Pomley. He will know what to do." Lucas had forced his hand, but he still held trump cards, and he would not give them up without a fight. It was high time he donned his captain's hat again.

Alex met the Viscount of Ashford on an unremarkable street corner in Clovelly overlooking the hillside sloping to the harbor below. Gulls circled the rooftops, their cries matching his mood.

"I was surprised my messenger found you so quickly," he said, accepting Ashford's hand and shaking it, appreciating the gesture this time. "I've had no news of your ship in these parts this last fortnight."

"Ah, but you warned me not to come within sight." Ashford tapped his walking stick on a cobble in a staccato rhythm, an affectation that suited his elegant European appearance. It also had the advantage of making him look uncannily nothing like the ship captain Alex had recently met. "And your long nine-pound guns are rather a deterrent," the viscount added with a grin.

"Is that all?" Alex started down the street, Ashford strolling along beside him.

"That, and I was paying a visit to my wife and son at a fine little cottage I recently purchased just south of here." He waved the brass-tipped stick in a general southerly direction.

"Did you?"

"Seemed the thing to do, don't you know."

"I am afraid I don't."

"You will."

Alex shot him a sharp glance, but the man had paused to peer into a storefront at a garish display of marzipan and chocolates behind the window.

"Fond of confections?" Alex asked mildly.

"No. But my wife is." Ashford straightened his hat, and with another light grin began walking again.

"I am prepared to assist you in sinking the *Osprey*."

The viscount nodded. "I suspected that was the reason for this meeting."

"Her cargo includes at least twelve-score musketry and several hundred pounds of powder in forty-pound casks."

"This is not a guess on your part, I am to assume."

"My crew found the cache upon my land, but I failed to post guards and Dunkirk retrieved it. I suspect the powder is intended for cannons."

"Ah."

"She'll go up like an inferno when she's taken."

"And when do you anticipate that might be, my friend?"

Alex slanted the fellow a curious look. "I thought you might know. I've several people watching, and they haven't seen her here in Clovelly harbor or elsewhere for weeks. A message I intercepted indicated another date for the loading, two days from now. Still, if she got past us somehow, she's likely on her way south already and we've missed her. I'll have to track her down."

"Then go tracking north, my lord."

Alex frowned.

"To Ireland? Are these French muskets, then?"

"Not so far north. To Bristol only."

"Bristol? With an arsenal suitable for an army?"

Ashford's gaze shifted to the ocean laid out beneath

the sky in broad, whitecapped strokes of azure and cerulean.

"Her patrons hope to raise an army."

"In Bristol?" Alex's steps slowed. "Where hundreds of former soldiers and sailors wait in bread lines for their next meal," he answered his own question.

"Some of our most honored members of Lords would have us believe that those poor unfortunates, if given sufficient encouragement, would stage violent revolts against their betters in hopes of a new day to come," the viscount said smoothly. He came to a halt, tapping the cane against the inside of his boot. "Those same alarmists would also like to convince us that slaves, similarly encouraged by talk of abolition in the hallowed halls of Parliament, would do the same."

"As they did in Barbados several months ago."

"Hm, yes. I believe that is how the rumor went."

"Are the muskets meant to actually arm a rebellion in Bristol, or to merely give the appearance of one?"

"Either, with the result that the outspoken members of Parliament who support reform will find themselves heartily unpopular come the next election. Perhaps even in danger of their lives. Some of the king's wealthier subjects, you see, cannot abide by the idea of change."

Alex had never been one for politics. But this was treason. If Tracy Lucas was involved in it, he had to learn the whole story.

"Are the antireformists targeting anyone in particular?"

"Since the revolt in Barbados, they see Wilberforce as the greatest threat to their interests. Anyone associated with him, lords included, will suffer for it."

Kitty had mentioned Wilberforce to him recently. In the same breath as Lambert Poole. She'd written of her encounter with Poole at a political salon in town at which Wilberforce was also present—the Earl of Poole, who for years had worked to gain the trust of the Admiralty, who even now was on his way to the Devon coast with at least one man-of-war in search of an unruly pirate.

It could all be coincidence.

"If you go after the *Osprey*," the viscount said quietly, as though aware of breaking into Alex's thoughts, "I would advise you to be discreet."

"To let it be known that I've no interest in her, that she is free to leave as she pleases." As he had done for months already. Serena's frustration with him from the beginning, her finely controlled anger that night in the London alleyway when he stepped between her and her quarry, sprang from that. Everyone knew Redstone had no interest in smugglers, only reprobate lords and their pleasure ships. It would not be difficult to make certain that message circulated again.

It would hurt her to hear it.

"Then when you come upon her," Ashford added, "she will not take fright until it is too late."

Alex could not wipe the image of Serena's distressed eyes and tearstained cheeks from his thoughts. He understood why she had taken fright in the garden. The information he was about to put about to the world at large would only make her run faster.

"The *Osprey* boasts a mere fourteen guns to our combined twenty-two," he suggested.

"Ah, in for a penny, in for a pound? I like that in a fellow." The viscount smiled. "The infamous Captain Redstone, friend to all, enemy to none except those lords who most deserve it, willing to be seen abreast of an antislaving ship? Astounding."

Alex ignored the foolery. "The *Cavalier* will set off at nightfall day after tomorrow."

"I shall be there with bells on, my good man, and happy to support your endeavor if need be." The viscount bowed with pretty grace.

Alex nodded, and crossed the street toward his curricle. He paused then swiveled about.

"Tell me, Ashford, is the Marquess of Doreé involved in any of this business?"

The man's uncanny gaze did not flicker. "Would a simple assent or denial satisfy you?"

Alex grinned, pride for a clever, determined woman swelling his chest.

"Then I have my answer." He tipped his hat and left Ashford upon the street corner alone.

Chapter 22

Mrs. Hatchet says the *Cavalier* is being fitted out to weigh anchor for its summer cruise," Bess said. "Two of those nice young sailors visited the village yesterday, this time to purchase a cap for the boy's mum. He said she makes the prettiest hats in England."

Serena did not lift her eyes from the pile of linens. She folded another napkin, frayed at the edges and worn thin in spots. Like her heart. She placed it atop the stack.

"You seem to have changed your tune regarding sailors, Bess."

"Seems some sailors are better than others, after all, aren't they, Miss Serena?"

"These will do well for wash rags. But don't let my stepmother see them or she will make you throw them out."

"So high on the instep, even the scullery maid's got to be clean behind the ears."

Serena made the mistake of looking up. Bess's smiling eyes narrowed. Serena's gaze skittered away.

She should not have allowed Alex to kiss her in the garden, so close to the house. For three days she had endured Bess's grinning, curious glances and John's uncustomary scowls. The head footman and her father's valet had cast her several meaningful looks as well. Fortunately none of the other servants seemed to know, nor her stepmother and sisters.

She should not have allowed him to kiss her at all, not once he had said those words about pursuing his life the way he wished, confirming her fears. Like a dark incantation, his admission had dashed her foolish dreams to pieces.

He had also said he wanted her.

Perhaps . . . perhaps she had been too hasty in thinking she understood him. Grief over learning of her father and Tracy's betrayals colored everything Alex said that night, and fashioned all her accusations. And confusion over the truth about her mother had made her wary. But now more than anything, she did not trust her own judgment. Alex had searched for the smugglers' cache, despite his strong feelings about not becoming involved. Perhaps she had gotten it all wrong. Perhaps the only person she could trust was the one she most feared trusting.

But she had told him to leave, and now apparently he would. She set the stack of linens in a basket.

"Have you seen Charity this morning, Bess?" Avoiding Davina had become Serena's primary purpose. With the wedding canceled, Tracy had gone off to Bristol upon business. Until he returned and she could confront him, she could not see her stepmother. Her father, hiding in his study all day, made avoiding his sorrowful, guilt-filled face easy. At least he'd told Davina not to lock her bedchamber door.

Now, of course, she didn't have anywhere to go at night.

Her heart hurt, as Alex had prophesied. Unhappiness for her stepsister, even for her father, weighed like an anchor upon her. But the pain on her own behalf was so much worse. She had lost a trusted friend, her beloved stepbrother. But that was nothing in comparison to the ache of missing Alex.

"Miss Charity is in the park with Nurse and Miss Faith," the housekeeper replied. "You might tell the little one that Cook baked shortbread not an hour ago."

"I will."

"Miss Serena?"

Serena looked over her shoulder.

"They say the *Cavalier* will make a pass by Clovelly harbor tonight after sunset, before she sets off. Captain Redstone is bound to throw up a show of skyrockets for pleasing the spectators, like he did when they set out in the spring."

"Your purpose in telling me this, Bess?"

The housekeeper's round cheeks lifted. "Will you be going over to Clovelly to see them off, then?"

To watch the man she had foolishly fallen in love with sail away?

"No. I haven't any interest in pirates."

She found Charity with their sister and Nurse at the edge of the garden, not far from where Alex had kissed her and told her he would do to her whatever she desired. Scattered gray clouds spread patches of shade over flower beds and trees, opalescent light casting Charity's pretty form gowned in white into gentle relief against the emerald backdrop.

Serena kissed her youngest sister on the brow and twirled her fingers through the four-year-old's brown curls, so like Viola's. She bent and whispered, "Cook has a treat for you in the kitchen, warm from the oven."

The child's eyes opened wide. She bussed Serena on the cheek and ran to clasp her nurse's hand.

"All right, Miss Faith," the old servant said with a smile, heaving off the bench. "What did you say to her, Miss Serena? That she'd find a pirate inside the house if she hurried?"

Serena froze. "Good heavens, Nurse, what is that about? Faith doesn't have any notion of pirates yet."

"She does since Miss Diantha's been filling her head with stories these past three days." Nurse nodded knowingly.

Serena willed her cheeks not to burn. They all knew. But they were all wrong.

"Nurse, you are too slow!" Faith insisted, her whole diminutive body bent to the task of dragging her caretaker across the lawn.

Charity moved beside Serena. "She is a great deal like Diantha, I think. Not at all like me and Tracy." She turned to Serena, a gentle smile on her berry lips. "Or perhaps she is simply like you."

"I don't know how. Not through Papa, certainly. I suspect I mostly resemble my mother."

Charity's gaze remained soft. The haunted look had disappeared from her lovely eyes in the past several days, but no brightness enhanced the blue. Still, Serena welcomed the smile.

"I will leave for my aunt's home in Yorkshire in a sennight." If Tracy returned in the next several days. She must speak with him before she left. "I would very much like for you to go with me, Chare. I think we should have a fine time there, and I always miss you when I am away. This time I won't have to."

Charity linked elbows with her. "I think I would like that." She sighed and turned her gaze north, in the direction of Savege Park.

Serena tucked a stray lock into her stepsister's bonnet. "There, now you are even more perfect than ever.

The gentlemen in York will fall over themselves in pursuit of your hand."

"I suppose it is better that he will not offer for me," Charity said, as though Serena had not spoken. Her gaze remained distant.

"Why do you say that, darling?"

"Because I am unfit to be a dutiful wife."

Serena pulled back, touched a fingertip to Charity's chin and drew her face around.

"You are the fittest person I know to be a dutiful wife to a good man. Do not allow this betrothal fiasco to convince you otherwise."

"Oh, but you see, I am indeed unfit." She slipped from Serena's hold, clasping her hands together. "I am unable to be a wife in the complete sense. Or—Or rather, I do not wish to."

"What do you mean, darling? That you do not like the idea of it? I know when your mother first introduced her plan for you to marry Lord Savege—"

"No." Charity's lips compressed. "Please do not speak of that."

"It still distresses you that greatly? But, why? You are free of that marriage and can now make another more suitable match."

"But, I cannot. I—I—"

"Charity," Serena said more firmly, "cease this stammering and say what you will. You clearly wish to tell me something important, and if I can do anything to help, you know I will."

"I was always afraid." The words poured out. "When Mama first told me how a married gentleman— What I mean to say is, the *act* of marriage— The idea of it frightened me so. Then after that time with Mr. Baker, Mama told me I was useless in that way."

"Who? What time?" Serena grasped her sister's fingers. "Chare?"

"Mama wished me to marry a man, Mr. Baker, enormously wealthy, a Cit." Her eyes were bright, but not with tears this time. "He seemed to have so many ships, and plantations, or at least one, I think, but I do not understand any of that."

"Good heavens, when was this? How do I not know of it?"

"You were in York." Charity dropped her gaze. "Two summers ago, that time when Papa remained in town."

Serena swallowed through the thickness in her throat. For two years Charity had kept this from her. She battened down the fresh sting of duplicity.

"What happened with Mr. Baker, Charity?"

"It all happened so quickly, I hardly remember it, except the humiliation."

"Humiliation?" Cold certainty crept into Serena's limbs. "What did my stepmother force you to do, Charity?"

"To lie with him." She closed her eyes, gold lashes fanning onto her cheeks. "She said her business with Mr. Baker was tremendously important, but that he refused to sign a contract with her unless he had me as his wife. But he wished to—to—"

"To?"

"He wished to know if we would suit one another before he married me."

"Suit one another in the bedchamber?"

Charity nodded. "I did not understand. Aren't all ladies suited to the gentlemen they marry?"

Sick fury filled Serena. "Your mother is a wicked, wicked woman. She made you lie with that man and then he would not marry you after all?"

"She was wicked." Charity's eyes glinted with something Serena had never seen in them before. It almost looked like defiance. "But it was my fault, truly. I could not do what he told me to do. I— He became very angry and Mama called in a physician. She told Papa I was ill."

"With what malady?"

"A female complaint, she said. The doctor examined me. He found nothing amiss, but Mr. Baker would not have me. It was horrible."

"I imagine it was."

"I disappointed her," Charity said in a low voice, "but I could not be sorry. He terrified me and his— his— It. I cried and he—" She squeezed her eyes shut. "No, I mustn't think about it ever again. I told myself I would not." She lifted a direct gaze to Serena. "I know I shall never be courageous enough to marry, or if I do, my husband will despise me."

Serena studied her stepsister, the newly straight set of her shoulders, the unusual clarity in her eyes.

"Your mother must have believed you could be a suitable wife to Lord Savage. But it does not fadge, Chare. If you had married the earl, he would have annulled the marriage when he discovered your—that you would not produce heirs." He would not have forced her, Serena was certain of that.

Charity nodded. "Mama said that was to be expected. But an annulment takes enough time, she said."

"Enough for what?"

"I don't know. But she said that as soon as he discovered my—my—"

"Reticence."

"He would go off to London and leave me at the Park waiting for the annulment to pass through Parliament."

Plenty of time for more caches of illegal arms to be ferried across his lands, more wealth to pour into Davina's filthy hands. Perhaps Baker had been part of this scheme at one time, and Davina had prostituted her daughter to win his alliance.

"Her greed knows no bounds," she muttered. "How she could have exposed you like that, knowing Lord Savage would be forced to repudiate you to assure the annulment, that it would become public. It is not to be borne."

Charity's eyes took on a sorrowful look once more, dreamlike upon her beautiful face. Serena's anger dimmed, her heart squeezing for her sister.

Then tripping.

Then speeding.

A miracle born out of tragedies seemed too unreal, too fantastical. But Serena had always believed in fairy tales, in magic and wonderment, in knights in shining armor who wished no more from a lady than her hand and heart. Serena now knew enough to laugh at that ideal. But for Charity, afraid, in love . . .

Perhaps?

"It is for the best." Charity released a wistful breath.

"I don't know that." She fixed her stepsister with a firm look. "Charity, if Mr. Savage did not wish that duty of you in marriage, could you be happy with him?"

Her stepsister's eyes glistened. "I think I could be happy with him even if he did."

Serena kissed her on the cheek then hurried inside to her escritoire. She sat to write with guarded hope. This was no fairy tale. A man's pride was involved, a considerable obstacle. But as confused as she was about Alex's intentions toward her, Serena knew one thing for certain: he wished for his brother's happiness as much as she wished for Charity's. And if she had learned anything in the past weeks, no obstacle seemed too great for a pirate.

A carriage arrived from Savege Park near noon. It trundled up the drive in stately elegance, and Davina hurried to the drawing room to receive her guests. None descended, only an impressive footman in black livery with gold piping on the sleeves. With enormous consequence he proffered an invitation to Miss Carlyle and Miss Lucas to join the dowager countess and her daughter, Lady Katherine, for luncheon at the Park.

"This is unheard of," Davina fumed after her husband sent the footman back to the carriage to await his passengers. "She intends to insult me."

"She intends to entertain our daughters," he said quietly. "No doubt she is uncomfortable with the outcome of the betrothal between our children and wishes to mend fences."

"She ought to. She orchestrated the outcome," Davina spat. "And you." She pointed a finger at Serena tying her bonnet in a bow beneath her ear. "You did as well, and now you hope to auger favor with Lady Savege and her daughter."

"Of course I do, stepmother," Serena said with a hard-won pacific smile, her pulse pounding. "I daresay, who wouldn't?"

She linked arms with Charity and together they walked to the carriage. It was a splendid vehicle, all shining wheels and butter-soft squabs. The footman rode with the coachman atop, but Serena could not gather sufficient calm to speak a word to Charity, even to ease her stepsister's nerves. She had thought never to see Alex again, or perhaps not for a very long time and then only in passing by accident. But two lines of hastily scratched prose upon a sheet of paper, and here she sat in his carriage behind four gorgeous horses speeding along the road to his house.

After entering Savege Park, she did not see him for nearly two hours.

Nerves on edge throughout luncheon, during which she forced herself to sample from each remove, and afterward at tea in the drawing room, she struggled to make conversation with the dowager and Lady Katherine sufficient for both her and her tongue-tied stepsister. Serena had spoken briefly with Alex's sister at the betrothal dinner. She seemed quick-witted, exquisitely fashionable, but not at all snobbish, with a sparkling smile and gray eyes like her eldest brother's.

"Will you remain in the country for the summer, or return to London, Lady Katherine?"

"Dear me, Miss Carlyle, do call me Kitty. I am ever so fond of you already and friends should not stand upon ceremony. May I call you Serena? It is such a beautiful name."

"It suits the lady," Alex said from the doorway.

Serena's heart stopped.

Kitty chuckled. "My brother is a great flatterer. Do not pay him any attention."

He bowed, a quirk of a smile shaping his beautiful mouth. "Ladies, it is a pleasure to see you here again, and under such happy circumstances."

"What circumstances are those?" his brother said as he entered the chamber then stopped short, the tip of his cane snapping against wood. "Miss Carlyle, Miss Lucas—good day." He bowed, his handsome face pale. Serena's heart cinched. She had assumed Alex would prepare him for their visit.

Mr. Savege's gaze slewed to his brother, awareness abruptly glinting in the light eyes.

Perhaps Alex had prepared him after all.

"Mother, I would like to show Miss Carlyle the gallery," the earl announced. "I do not believe she had opportunity to visit it at the open house, and the portrait by Lawrence of you and my sister is well worth viewing. Will you join us and regale us with stories of the sitting?"

The dowager stood. "That sounds like a capital idea. Come along, Kitty. Alexander will lend Miss Carlyle his arm and you must give me yours. My joints plague me dreadfully today."

Lady Katherine's gaze darted back and forth between Charity's pink cheeks and Mr. Savege's unusually bright eyes. She leapt up.

"Yes, of course, Mama. A stroll in the gallery seems just the thing now."

Serena followed them to the doorway where Alex stood beside his motionless brother. Mr. Savege squared his shoulders and turned toward Charity.

Alex shut the door behind them.

"Don't say a word, Kitty," he murmured as they moved along the corridor. "Thank you, Mother."

"You are quite welcome. I will have your brother's head upon a platter if he does not do what he should in there. Don't you agree, Miss Carlyle?"

"Well, yes, although not the platter part, of course." Her heart beat almost too quickly to allow breath for words. "But if they cannot come to an agreement, I will be astounded. My lady, thank you for your assistance in this. You are tremendously kind."

"She is a dear, sweet girl and deserves my son. My other son, that is." Her eyes twinkled. "But you must direct your thanks where they are deserved, including toward yourself. If Aaron declares himself to your stepsister, it will be because you brought her here, and his brother encouraged him to it."

"*Alex* encouraged Aaron to declare?" Kitty exclaimed. "What on earth do you know of that sort of thing, you roué?"

"At least I am not a spinster," he said with urbane indifference.

Kitty's laughter cascaded through the corridor.

"Now you truly mustn't pay them any attention," the dowager said, patting Serena's hand. "They tease one another mercilessly. It is the way they show their love. Kitty, come along and we will ask Mr. Button to bring a bottle of champagne from the cellar to celebrate."

"Mama, you cannot. It will ruin their chances entirely."

"Don't be superstitious, Katherine. It is unbecoming." They disappeared down the corridor.

Steeling herself, Serena lifted her gaze.

Her blood turned to honey, her tongue to wool batting. Alex's eyes were as warm as ever, his nearness filling her as always with both longing and a sense of completeness. She sucked in breath and reached for support. Her hand wavered by the doorpost inches away. Alex watched, silent, his gaze so careful upon her, as though waiting.

She forced her feet to move into the gallery. "Thank you for responding so swiftly to my message."

"Astounding what a small revelation can accomplish, isn't it?" He was not far behind her. Serena could not bear to turn and look. She pretended to study the portraits, dark with swatches of color and light, faces that vaguely resembled Alex's, or his brother's, his sister's, the picture of the dowager and her daughter, others. She barely saw.

"I understand you will be leaving tonight," she said. "What excuse do you give your family when you go?"

"None."

Her steps faltered. "They do not wonder, or ask?"

"Perhaps, and yes." His voice came close at her shoulder, deep and peculiarly tempered. Heat curled down her spine into her thighs and through the palms of her hands. She ran a fingertip along the edge of a picture frame, seeking distraction, any sensation to still the tremors rising in her.

"Do they ask when you will return?"

"Occasionally." His warmth seemed to reach out and caress her arms and neck where he had kissed her and made her ache for him, steeling along the length of her back and legs. She knew his body, how he held her skin-to-skin, the rasp of his callused hands upon her a glorious joy.

"When will you?" she said unsteadily. Her tongue would not obey. She should move away. She had told him she did not wish to see him again. "Return, that is?"

"It is difficult to say." He seemed nearer yet, his head bent, and now she heard the unevenness of his breath, heavy and short. "In time."

She could succumb so easily. She could be with him for as long as he wanted her and at least be happy in those moments. She could lie to her heart as everyone she loved had lied to her for so long.

"For what?" she whispered, her voice as tight as the coils winding inside her of need and pain.

If she reached back, she would touch him. Touch him and be part of him for a moment, a fleeting fantasy.

"In time for what?" she repeated, the air barely stirring.

His hand, large and beautiful, moved toward hers. Serena's heart stuttered.

With a hard exhalation, he let his arm drop. She squeezed her eyes shut and tried to breathe, to think. She wished only to be in his arms forever and nothing else now mattered—Charity, Tracy, her father's grief, her mother's folly. Only this man. Thick desperation rose in her throat and she choked it back.

"Alex?"

"Serena." His deep voice trembled upon the whispered syllables.

She pivoted around. Her breath caught. His eyes were like storms, dark and shadowed, his brow fraught with restraint. He met her gaze, and everything she felt, everything she longed for, seemed to tumble between them.

She tilted her face up, leaning toward him, and he came too, bending to her, drawn by the same steel cord wrapped about her heart and attached to his. His gaze consumed her, making love to her without words, without touch, as though needing this closeness, seeking in her eyes that which she would give him so readily if he asked. She could not have disguised her emotion if she wished to, not from herself and not from him. His warmth reaching out to her, his breath upon her cheek, his scent encompassed her, laying her heart naked and replete with him.

"Alex, I—"

"No." His voice was rough, low, his shoulders rigid and gaze raw. "Don't, Serena. I am leaving, and this time I may not return."

"Not return?" Panic coursed through her. "How can you 'not return'?"

"There are—" He waved an insouciant hand, his throat working. A taut, farcical laugh escaped his chest, "—adventures to be had."

She stared, her pulse streaming.

"*Alex,*" she whispered.

"I am not my brother. Though I might desire it, I haven't the bravery for—" His jaw hardened and he gestured between them. "This. Not now."

It was like a fist knocking into her, grabbing her lungs. But she had to speak. It could not end like this. Oh God, *it could not end*. What had she done?

"I was mistaken about you." She fought to gather her quavering voice. "I was overset the other night, but I understand now how searching out the smugglers' cargo went against your inclination. It was generous of you. And today what you have done for Charity and your brother proves it further."

"You were not mistaken. I have little honor and less concern for others. Helping to bring them together merely relieves my guilt of complicity for Aaron's unhappiness. I did it for no other reason than that."

"I don't believe you."

"That is no surprise to me whatsoever, my dear." Distance echoed in his tone.

"You are not the care-for-nothing rogue you pretend to be."

"I am indeed."

No. Her heart could not be so misguided. "Prove it."

"Easily." He grasped her shoulders, a simple binding so powerful, tears rose in Serena's throat. She thought he would kiss her, his body so close his heartbeat sounded in her very soul, careening into hers as his chest rose in a tortured breath against her breasts. Endlessly he held her, his mouth nearly upon hers, bathing her parted lips with unspoken words.

He swallowed hard, bent to her ear and murmured in a voice like pebbled satin, "I am lying to you now."

She wrenched from his hold. His eyes, cool now like winter rain, as she had never seen them before, seemed to confirm his words. Confusion shook her. She gulped back the thickness in her throat, shaking her head.

"I do not understand you."

"Perhaps that is for the best."

Dashing moisture from her cheeks, she hurried from the chamber. She met Lady Savege in the corridor outside the drawing room, a footman in her wake bearing a tray of glasses and a bottle.

"There you are, Miss Carlyle. How did you like the portrait? I daresay I appear twenty years younger in it, but who wishes to be that age again, all confusion and distress? Except you, dear, of course." Her gaze lingered upon Serena's flushed face, and she added in a murmur, "You are such a sensible girl." She gestured the footman forward then glanced behind Serena. "Alexander, Miss Carlyle requires refreshment. You ought to know better." She swept into the drawing room.

Charity and Mr. Savege stood by the mantel, hands joined. Her face shone, his a display of gentle masculine happiness. Their heads came around. Charity's lips parted on a tinkling laugh and she threw herself across the chamber into Serena's embrace.

"I am happy for you, darling," Serena whispered, not trusting her voice for more. Charity grasped her hands, her countenance wreathed in a beatific smile.

"Thank you, sister. Thank you so very much." She lifted a shy face to Alex. "Thank you, my lord."

"Have I missed everything?" Kitty called out from the doorway, and entered, arms wide. She wrapped them around Mr. Savege. "Aaron, you devil. Stealing our brother's betrothed right out from under his nose."

Charity's cheeks ripened, but her glow never dimmed.

"I am a fortunate man indeed." Mr. Savege accepted his sister's affectionate kiss with grace. She released him and he looked to the earl, gratitude written upon his face. Alex tilted his head in recognition. A muscle ticked in his tight jaw, then his gaze slid to Serena.

She dragged hers away.

"We must have a toast to the bride and groom," Lady Savege announced, taking up a glass.

Serena sipped hers as expected, smiling at her sister and her new betrothed, aching so hard inside with love and loss she could barely breathe, and knowing from the heat on her skin that he watched her still. It was as though only they two were in the chamber, yet an ocean gaped between them. They all sat and Serena made the appropriate remarks, although afterward she did not know of what they spoke. Finally the earl excused himself, claiming business matters to be addressed before he departed Savege Park.

"I cannot fathom how you can still be planning on leaving tonight, after this," his sister complained. "Always flitting off somewhere just when things become interesting."

"A man of my consequence does not flit, madam," he said evenly.

"What does he do, then?"

Serena lifted her head. His gaze held hers.

"He makes carefully calculated decisions," he said, "and acts upon them, hoping for the best outcome."

"I daresay." The dowager pursed her lips. "Son, come kiss my cheek before you go."

"I am not leaving until this evening, Mother." But he complied.

"Yes, but I miss you already, and a woman must take her comforts where she may."

He turned to Charity.

"My felicitations, ma'am." Then his gaze came to

Serena again. "Miss Carlyle, your servant." He bowed and left the room.

Later, Serena did not clearly recall the drive back to Glenhaven Hall with her stepsister and Mr. Savege, or even her stepmother's reaction to the news. At the first opportunity she extracted herself from her family and went into the garden, then climbed up the bluff. Cresting the hill, she sank down upon the grass and stared at the empty ocean, grayish blue beneath the cloud-scattered sky.

The sun dipped in a pink and lavender haze toward the water. Serena finally stood, patted the wrinkles from her gown and turned toward the house. Unlike her mother, she would not wait in vain for her beloved to return, wasting away, imagining the impossible. Years of practice tamping down her dreams would stand her in good stead now.

Chapter 23

The more I think on you, the more I think long,
If I had you now as I had once before . . .
—"BONNIE PORTMORE"

The *Cavalier's* departure was much discussed among the servants, who all seemed to think Serena wished to know every detail of the spectacular show Captain Redstone and his crew gave the people crowding Clovelly's docks. Tracy returned two days later, appearing at dinner, face drawn and eyes weary. But he greeted the news of his sister's betrothal with pleasure.

"I like him very much, Chare. Glad to know we will be seeing him around here, at least until the wedding," he said with a kind smile.

"Oh, no." She blushed prettily. "He was obliged to make a journey to one of his brother's estates. Lord Savege will give it to us as a wedding gift, as it is not entailed."

"That is very generous of him," Serena's father said, not lifting his attention from his almond custard.

Serena could not bear to look at her own plate. Her stomach, far too twisted to accept food, protested at the very scent, and at her father's words, the same ones she had said to Alex days ago.

"Tracy." She folded her napkin and placed it on the table. "I know you must be fatigued from your journey, but would you walk with me now? It is such a fine evening."

Her father's head came up. He glanced at his wife. Lips tight, Davina cut into her soft custard as though it were leather.

"Of course." Tracy rose.

They went into the garden. She took his arm.

"How did your business in Bristol proceed? Well, I hope."

"I am sorry to say, no." He drew a tight breath. "But I don't wish to bore you with details. What has everyone here been doing without wedding plans to busy them?" He chuckled, but the sound seemed strange. "Ah, but there is a new one to replace the old, fortunately."

"Tracy, I know of your involvement in smuggling. I learned of it the very day you left for Bristol. I saw the storage cellar and the muskets and ammunition on Lord Savege's beach. I also know that in the past your ship has illegally traded slaves."

He did not look at her for many moments. Gradually he drew to a halt.

"Then you know it all."

"I know your mother and you have been engaged in horrible business for years. Charity told me about Mr. Baker—"

"Baker? Who is that?"

"You don't know of Davina's attempt to marry Charity to a tradesman named Baker?"

"No. I thought she wanted her to marry the earl so she could use his lands freely as she's hoped to do for years." He gripped her fingers. "I tried to halt that, Serena. As soon as I saw how unhappy Chare was, I begged Mother not to force it. She wouldn't listen to me. She never listens to me. She even threatened to turn me in to the authorities if I—" He whirled away. "I've been trying to make her see reason, to convince her this must all end. For years, Serena. But she's like a dog with a bone, biting harder the more one tries to pull it from her mouth. Her thirst for power grows with each success." His eyes looked haunted. "Sometimes I think she will stop at nothing."

"What do you mean, Tracy? Haven't the two of you already done enough awful things—traded slaves illegally, smuggled armaments, and allowed sailors in your employ to harass and injure innocent people?"

"I deserve your censure for those things. But you don't know the half of it. This time, Ser, this time she—" He wrung his hands.

"What, Tracy? What will she do?"

"I went to Bristol to call it all off. Even before that I contacted Poole, but he hasn't returned my messages."

"Poole? The Earl of Poole? What does he have to do with it?"

Tracy turned away, brushing his palm across his eyes. His shoulders slumped, the fine wool of his London-tailored coat crumpling like paper.

"It's all for the best now, I guess. The Admiralty has sent ships here. It won't be long before they come upon the *Osprey* and discover what we've done. What she hoped to do. We are all done for, but at least it will be over finally."

Serena's throat constricted.

"The Admiralty has sent ships here? To this coast? Why?"

He met her gaze, exhaustion and defeat written on his face, so unlike the usual happy countenance she had depended upon for years.

"They've been spoiling for Redstone for months

now," he said. "Finally got around to making the decision to run him aground. It's in all the papers, you know. Sometimes I think they made such news of it because they hope he'll hear of it and run. But . . ." He looked away again. " . . . perhaps they will be too occupied hunting him down to go after the *Osprey*. Though I suppose with that many ships, they can do both. Redstone is a clever fellow, and he's got a fast vessel, but the navy's well armed, and enough folks want him stopped for them to keep at it now that they've started."

Serena's hands trembled.

"How many?"

"How many what?"

"Naval ships? How many are going after the *Cavalier*?"

"Three at least. Some of their fastest, apparently. Best commanders in the navy and all that." He waved a hand. "Ser, I have been the weakest man alive."

And Alex was being the strongest.

Like clouds parting to reveal a tempestuous sunset, it all became perfectly clear—his cryptic words six nights earlier in this very garden. He'd said she did not know what she asked in wishing he would pursue the smugglers. Then at the Park two days ago, looking at her so steadily while he said he hoped for the best outcome.

He had lied to her, and to everyone, but only *now* at the last. He must be aware of the navy's threat. He had been dodging the authorities for a decade. But despite the British men-of-war coming for him, he was going after the smugglers. He did not want her, or anyone, to know, because he was not certain of success. He'd made that clear enough when he said he might not return.

But he had tried to tell her nevertheless. He had held her and whispered the truth.

Tracy laughed, an awkward crack of distress.

"Perhaps they will find Redstone with my ship and blame him for it all. Wouldn't that be marvelous?" he uttered, grimacing. "I could bring down a hero as well as the family."

Serena gripped his arm.

"You cannot allow him to take the blame for this."

He stared down at her hand as though it were a manacle. His gaze came up then flickered back to her fingers digging deep dents in his sleeve.

"Ser? What's going on?"

"Alex—Lord Savege is Redstone. I believe he has gone after your ship in spite of the navy's threat. You cannot allow him to come to danger because of what you and your mother have done." Her voice strained and she grasped him tighter. "You cannot."

Tracy stared at her and said the last thing she expected. "You love him."

She could not respond. Yes, she loved a rake and a pirate. Of course she did, desperately, magnificently, completely. How could she do otherwise?

Tracy's brow furrowed, his eyes awash in regret.

"But he will not have you, will he? Because of my cowardice and weakness."

Serena shook her head in astonishment.

"Tracy, at the present I am not interested in discussing your cowardice and weakness. He is now in mortal danger because of you, and you must go out there and find him before the navy does."

"I knew about what Rob did."

She released him.

"Rob? *Tracy*—"

"I knew. Mother didn't need to tell me. I told her before you even did. No one else knew, though she wanted you to believe you would be ruined in the eyes of society. She ordered me not to demand that he marry you. She didn't wish scandal attached to our family. She took money from him instead."

"Money? She paid him off not to marry me?"

"His betrothal to that other girl was already a settled thing. I think he paid over the money out of guilt." He turned his distressed gaze away. "I should have called him out. I should have defended your honor."

"He was your friend."

"He was a cad to use you so."

"He did not force me, Tracy. I was young and naïve, but I made the choice." Just as she had with Alex, although not the choice to love him. Fate had decreed that, beautiful, kind fate, more generous than any magic spell or potion. Fate that would not be thwarted.

"Did you tell Savage that? You did," he answered before she could speak. "But he must have a pristine bride to bear his heirs, the hypocrite. His consequence deserves it, I suppose, or why else would he have agreed to marry my widgeon of a sister?"

Serena set her jaw. "Tracy, I love you and I always will, but I do not like you now, nor will I for a long time to come, I suspect. You of all people have no right to speak of either Charity or the earl in this manner."

"Fall out of love with him, Ser. He will break your heart just like he's broken the hearts of other respectable ladies for years."

"Thank you for that advice," she clipped, impatient. "But I would much prefer your immediate action to recommendations. You must sail out and find the *Cavalier* at once and tell him to flee, to Spain or the West Indies or wherever he will be safe." She thought fast, her pulse speeding. "Or you could intercept the navy's ships and waylay them, tell them anything, lie, offer up the *Osprey* or your horrid mother. You must do *something*." Her voice hitched. "I am trapped upon this wretched coast without any way to contact him, and my heart is breaking because I think he loves me and is doing this because I asked him to."

Tracy's chest rose and fell in hard breaths. His eyes, no longer haunted, looked alive again.

"I haven't a ship."

"Then hire one at Clovelly harbor, with a captain to go along with it." She grasped his shoulders and tried to turn him toward the house. "There were at least three good-sized vessels there last I saw, and there must be dozens of sailors waiting at the docks looking for work."

"Mother will crucify me."

"Your mother deserves to be thrown into a shark-filled lagoon. What are you waiting for? Go!"

He wrapped her in a crushing embrace and kissed her upon both cheeks.

"Thank you, Ser. You and that reprobate earl may make a man of me yet." He set off toward the house. "If Mother asks where I've gone," he called back, "tell her she can read about it in *The Times* next week beneath the heading 'News of the Admiralty.'" He laughed, the sound of open, relieved mirth drifting to her on the sea-scented breeze.

Serena's heart squeezed, for everything she had known and everything she loved.

Next week . . .

How long would she have to wait to learn if Tracy reached the *Cavalier* in time? When would she know if her world of real-life dreams was about to begin, or end before she could tell her shining knight everything in her heart?

* * *

Alex stood at the most beautiful oaken helm upon the most beautiful yellow pine deck of the most beautiful ship on the sea and sucked in a lungful of salty air. He never tired of life on the ocean. Just as he never tired of Serena Carlyle.

She did not despise him. Or if she did, she'd done a fine job of hiding her disgust in the gallery, her eyes simmering with desire and something much deeper. Staggering. He'd wanted her so much, to taste her kiss and make her his. Not hauling her into his arms had proven an act of will worthy of sheer madness.

He didn't begin to deserve her. Not then. Not yet. But by God, he would taste her kiss again. He would become worthy of the greatest endeavor of his life or he would die trying.

Still, he couldn't deny it felt damn good to stand upon his deck, the breeze fresh and sails trim, watching the whitecaps dash by, with a mission at hand.

Making love to Serena felt better. And he planned to do so for the remainder of his life. If he didn't die shortly.

"Crack on, Jin," he said easily. "Let's run for a bit."

The quartermaster shouted out orders. Alex's crewmen leapt to decks. Sheets hissed and sails filled, carrying the wind in a lover's embrace.

Perhaps in heaven a man could simply make love to the woman he loved over and over, without ceasing. Then again, if he died soon, perhaps it wasn't heaven he'd be going to. Lying was one of the Seven Deadly Sins, or a Ten Commandment. Thou shalt not lie to the woman thou lovest, and thou shalt also not lie to her about lying to her. The yardarm needed a noose with his neck in it. If he lived through this and she forgave him, it would be a miracle.

He was insane, deeper in love than he had ever imagined a man could be, certainly not a man like himself. In love for life and the oceanic eternity beyond.

"Ship ahead!" Matouba's clear alert shot out over the deck.

Alex's blood sizzled with sudden tension. A vessel had breached the horizon. This was one of the parts he enjoyed the most, the mystery of discovering if a neighbor would be friend or foe, prey or predator.

Mostly they turned out to be prey.

"Who's borrowing our breeze today, Matouba?" he called to the crow's nest. "Someone interesting, I hope," he added under his breath. After nearly a sennight afloat, their most fearsome encounters included an American privateer he'd let pass without molesting, a fleet of herring boats, and a gentleman's wedding cruise out of Lynton. They fished with the fishermen for a few hours, trading rum for tackle. But for the newlyweds Alex hoisted his colors. The bride fainted straight away and the groom turned white as ash. Alex called out his congratulations to the happy couple as the *Cavalier* breezed by, Big Mattie falling over laughing, barely able to hold the helm, and Jin rolling his eyes.

But on the fourth night out, just before sunset, Alex had caught a whiff of rocket smoke on the westerly wind. He turned his bow into it and tacked close-hauled toward the source. White sails flickered on the horizon for an instant then his quarry vanished into dusk. She did not show the following morning.

Probably the HMS *Command*, most likely waiting for the *White Lady* and *Titan* to arrive from Portsmouth.

If Halloway wanted him, he could jolly well come get him. Alex hadn't seen the *Osprey* yet, and the fishermen hadn't either in the fortnight they'd been out. The smuggler's best course to Bristol lay along the coastal channel. Perhaps she was in hiding until the men-of-war left the area, or she had stopped to pick up more cargo. But until he saw her and sank her, he would continue trawling back and forth across this damned coast no matter who challenged him.

"Looks like a merchant vessel, sir," the lookout shouted.

"Her sails are patched," Aaron said behind him.

Alex swiveled about. He hadn't heard his brother approach. Happiness seemed to be making Aaron especially light on his feet and cane. Yet he'd come, nevertheless, to take their final cruise together, just as they had taken their first.

"Mm." Alex looked out at the ship following leagues away in the *Cavalier*'s wake, the wind behind her. "Do you remember that British frigate we came across off St. Croix in 'ten?"

Aaron nodded. "The one with the patched sails?"

"Those wily naval officers will do anything for a prize. Bring her around, Jin. Let's see who's coming to tea, shall we?"

Jin called the orders, sailors hauled lines, the yards swung, and the schooner luffed, casting a wide arc through the gentle blue swells toward its pursuer.

"It's a barquetine, sir," Matouba called. "Four guns only, uncommon shallow in the draft."

"Four guns?" Not the *Osprey*. "Then what is she doing bearing down at me like a nun in heat?"

"Expecting any visitors, Alex?"

"Other than the Royal Navy? Not today, little brother."

"It's not Ashford's ship, is it?"

"No." The *Blackhawk* hadn't shown its masthead yet. So much for help when needed.

"Beat to quarters, sir?" Jin asked, gaze pinned upon the newcomer.

Alex studied the swiftly approaching vessel riding high in the water, a light-loaded merchant ship by the looks of it, but chasing after him? It seemed unlikely. Perhaps she did not know precisely whom she chased.

He nodded to his quartermaster. "And hoist the colors."

Jin hollered, the drummer perched at the deckhouse snapping the beats fast and loud even before the order was done. Alex's crew, well rested after more than a month ashore, and bored stiff for the past sennight, leapt to the task of readying the ship for battle. He would not take any chances, not with his crewmen's lives, and not with a particular lady sitting at home waiting to hear good news. At least he hoped she was waiting.

Remembering her hot mouth, her supple body under his, her unique eyes overflowing with emotion, satisfaction filled him.

She was waiting.

As the barquetine neared, Alex ordered the *Cavalier* brought around to her larboard, preparing a neat target for his chase guns. Presented with the clear threat, the merchantman did not change course, sailing clean within range of the schooner's cannons.

"Is she passing us by?" Aaron asked skeptically.

"Her captain's telling us he wants to talk. Or to be boarded."

"Odd," Jin murmured. "She's letting fly." The barquetine's sails shook, bringing her to an uncomfortable halt.

"Hail her," Alex said.

Jin hefted the speaking trumpet and called over to the merchant vessel across the low rolling swells. "Hoa! Where are you bound?"

A hoary looking fellow in a faded naval officer's coat came to the rail, trumpet in hand.

"I've a passenger aboard wanting to speak with your captain," he called over.

"This passenger's name?"

A man stepped up beside the captain and took the trumpet from him. Alex's heartbeats slowed, the inevitability of it feeling oddly clean.

"Tracy Lucas," the baronet called across the water. "Redstone, I've got to speak with you."

"Let him come," Alex muttered.

Jin dropped the trumpet and gave orders. Within minutes a boat was in the water, rowers pulling Serena's stepbrother swiftly toward the *Cavalier*.

"Is this entirely wise, Alex?"

"He wouldn't be here, Aaron, unless she'd told him. Are you still glad you made the decision to come along and not remain with your pretty little bride?"

"I must say, I am awfully curious now. And, yes, I'm glad." He smiled like Alex hadn't seen in years.

The boat came alongside and Lucas climbed aboard, dusting off his coat and breeches as he straightened from the ladder. He looked more like he'd gone out for a drive in Regent's Park than a cruise through the Celtic Sea.

Alex broadened his stance and set his fists on his hips.

"Sir Tracy Lucas, what a pleasant surprise. What cargo are you carrying on this fine craft? Cannon and pistols? You've already got enough muskets on the other to trick out an army."

"Nothing." The man's gaze darted about, taking in Alex's crew spread across the deck, surprised then relieved when he saw Aaron. "The ship is empty except for fresh water and shot, but only as ballast. I don't even have powder for the guns."

"Well then either you're a fool or you have a death

wish. Turn about and head home before someone with less patience than me kills you. But first tell me where to find those goods you've got heading to Bristol."

"I cleared the hold so I could catch up with you."

"Catch up with me? You know you ought to be running from me, rather. Don't you?"

"Serena said I had to come."

Alex's world stilled to a single, horrifying thought.

"Do not tell me, boy, that you have that woman on board that vessel with you right now."

Lucas's eyes went wide. "Of course not! What do you think I am?"

"A scoundrel who would sell his sister to an even worse scoundrel for a well-located storage cellar."

Aaron cleared his throat.

"That wasn't me," Lucas said, directing his words at Aaron; to his credit, Alex thought. "It was my mother. I tried to stop it, you know. But here, Savage, you've got to listen. The navy's on its way here looking for you. You must get clear of the coast fast, head over to Ireland and hole up for a spell, or to America. I'll waylay my ship and send it packing."

Alex regarded the younger man steadily.

"You are wading in deeper waters than you know, Lucas," he finally said.

"I do know. But you've got to get lost. I'll find the *Osprey* and throw its cargo overboard if you'd like. I promise."

"Strange promise from a man who's bound to lose a bundle—"

"Look alive!" Matouba shouted from above.

Alex's gaze snapped to the horizon. Leagues distant, a three-masted, square-rigged brig cut across the eastern sea, her colors flapping.

Lucas's face screwed into a peculiar expression. "There's my ship now."

"Topsails unfurling, sir. She's seen us," Jin said.

Alex shouted toward the rail. "Cut loose the boat! Mattie, make chase. Go large."

Jin started calling out orders, hands ran to the lines, and the *Cavalier* swung around with the wind. Lucas waved frantically for the merchantman to follow, his shouts drowned out by the swishing of sails, the hissing of sheets, and Alex's own heartbeat.

Aaron came up beside him. "How long until we reach her?"

"An hour or less. We have the wind, and she's carrying a heavy load." He turned to the baronet. "Will he turn and fight, or give over?"

Lucas drew in a tight breath, the sunlight glinting in his bright hair.

"For any other pirate or privateer I suspect he'd surrender and ask for quarter. But, Savege . . ." His gaze flicked to the gold and black flag tied to the *Cavalier*'s mast. "The Earl of Poole is in on this, and Dunkirk is his man. If he sees your banner, he'll open fire on you."

"Then we'll have to be very careful, won't we?" Alex suspected he shouldn't feel such a rush of satisfaction at this confirmation of his suspicions about Poole. But it all seemed so neat and clean. If only Poole himself would show with Halloway, he could tie it all up with a little bow.

"You, careful?" Aaron murmured.

"Captain," Jin said, uncharacteristically releasing a pent breath, "the *Command* has arrived."

"Royals in the water, Cap'n sir!" Matouba shouted from the shrouds, having given up his place in the crow's nest to the wind.

Behind him, twice as distant as the *Osprey*, the huge naval frigate flew its Union Jack with arrogant ease across the wind. A smaller man-of-war cruised in the *Command*'s wake.

"Six days as lonely as a hermit, and now we're to have a crush." Alex laughed, energy rushing through his blood.

"Savage," Lucas said quietly, the wind snatching away the word.

Alex turned to him. "Sir?"

"I think you should know, Serena—"

"Mention her name or speak another word about her aboard this ship and I'll cut your tongue out, boy," he growled.

The baronet's face turned to chalk.

"He'll do it too," Jin murmured to Aaron.

Alex chuckled. Jin was half the reason Redstone's reputation preceded him across a dozen seas. The former slave was a great deal more brutal and a great deal less honest than he himself had ever been or ever would be.

He turned his face to the bow and his quarry and waited.

He didn't have long. Four leagues distant, the *Osprey* sailed into a trough and her sails went flat. Alex cleared the space swiftly, sending off a warning shot. The *Osprey* fired back, grapeshot from her cannonades tearing through the *Cavalier*'s forward sails.

Alex set his stance at the helm, ignored everything but the brig in his sites, and set to doing what he did best.

For a tantalizing instant the image of Serena lying in his arms, her damp skin golden in the lamplight, her eyes filled with passion, passed through his mind like a carrot at the end of a race.

Second best.

The fight passed swiftly, cannon shot filling the clear sky with smoke. Despite her impressive guns, the smuggler was far too deep in the draft to outmaneuver the quick schooner. By the time the heavy *Command* arrived, the smaller warship following closely, Alex had hoisted his red flag with intention to board the brig.

"Her mizzenmast is shot by the board, sir," Jin said tentatively. "She won't go anywhere even if we skip off for a bit."

"Are you suggesting we turn tail and run, Jin?"

Alex's lieutenant cut a grin. "Never, sir."

"While the boys board this hulk, hail the *Command.* She's fixing to come within range."

Alex brought his ship board-to-board with the beleaguered smuggler. His sailors threw over pikes then planks and swarmed aboard, meeting no resistance from the merchantman's small crew.

A single shot came across the *Cavalier*'s bow, snapping a yardarm and taking a hand down beneath torn canvas. Sailors rushed to their crewmate's side.

"Mr. Redstone, amain!" The order to yield came from across the *Cavalier*'s larboard flank. Thirty yards distant, His Royal Majesty's man-of-war bobbed in the restive waves, her captain standing at the rail with several of his officers and a gentleman dressed to the nines.

Alex's lip curled. The Earl of Poole.

The smaller warship circled around the *Osprey*'s opposite side. Far out to the west, Lucas's empty barque floated nervously. Farther yet, to the north, another ship appeared on the horizon, sleek and light, flying a black bird of prey upon a yellow backing, the wind behind her. Ashford's ship.

Alex grinned.

"Not in this lifetime," he muttered, then raised his voice. "Ahoy there, Captain Halloway. I have a prize here I think you might find interesting. I daresay I wouldn't mind it a bit if you took her off my hands."

From so close a distance, Alex could see the commander's face wrinkle up and his eyes widen. Halloway leaned forward as though to get a closer look, then lifted the spyglass to his eye. He drew it down slowly.

"Lord *Savege*?"

Alex chuckled. He'd been acquainted with the weathered old mariner for years, a fine card player and a decent fellow.

"At your service, sir." Alex bowed. He should have revealed his identity years ago. This was the most fun he'd had upon the sea since the night Serena spent aboard his ship.

Poole snatched the trumpet from Halloway, his coppery hair glinting like metal in the midday sunlight.

"I always knew it was you, Savege," he spoke over the distance. "It couldn't have been anyone else."

"Lying dog," Aaron muttered.

Alex lifted his voice. "Good day, my lord. It is a pleasure to see you. I've got your cargo here ready to sink. If you would like to watch, be my guest." He added in a conversational tone, "Jin, get the boys off the *Osprey*, and her crew as well. Then fix Greek Fire targeted for her mainsail, but do not fire."

Jin frowned, but set to carrying out Alex's orders.

"Lord Savege," Halloway called, "I must insist that you stand down your guns and allow my lieutenants to board your vessel."

"I am afraid I cannot oblige, sir. But you are more than welcome to board this brig here. Her cargo— What's her cargo, Mattie?"

"She's full to the gunwales with powder, Cap'n," the

helmsman bellowed loud enough for the men aboard the *Command* to hear. "Muskets and pickaxes too."

"Pickaxes?" Alex screwed up his brow. "What do you plan to do with those in Bristol, Poole? Beat upon little old ladies?"

One of Halloway's officers spoke with his commander. Halloway's attention shifted north. The *Blackhawk* was closing, heading toward the small warship to cut her off from the other vessels.

"So you see, Captain," Alex shouted without the horn, "I recommend your swift examination of this smuggler."

"Savege," Lucas said at his shoulder. "You will also find a crate of pamphlets aboard, a call to arms against the government, purportedly written by Wilberforce. Forged, of course. They're meant to make anyone think the reformists are stirring up trouble and should be impeached."

"A crate of insurrectionist pamphlets, did you say, Sir Tracy?" Alex called across the water. "How enormously interesting."

Poole turned to Halloway, spoke quickly, and the naval commander paused. Then Halloway shook his head. Poole's shoulders caped, his bearing becoming more insistent. Halloway's first lieutenant moved closer to the pair, hand upon his pistol holder. Finally Poole backed off, leaving the naval officers to confer.

Alex watched, knowing Jin was counting his crewmen leaving the *Osprey*, making certain each one had returned, and probably counting the smugglers' sailors as well. A firepot lobbed at the brig's rigging would allow the *Cavalier* mere minutes to escape before the powder-loaded vessel blew into a thousand pieces.

Halloway again approached the rail.

"Remove your men from the smuggler, Lord Savege,

and my first lieutenant, Lord Poole, and I will board it and investigate."

Alex bowed, but his muscles tensed. Whatever Poole had said, Halloway's decision was far from customary. Rather, foolhardy under most circumstances. But Halloway was a wise, experienced seaman, and Alex had never in his pirating years fired upon a British frigate, only on private ships and foreign vessels. The naval captain must know that.

Within minutes the captain of the *Command*, his officer, and Poole were climbing onto the *Osprey*'s main deck. The *Blackhawk* had slowed its approach, holding the other naval vessel's attention. Alex went to the starboard rail.

"She is yours now, Captain Halloway," he said conversationally across the ten feet separating him from the *Osprey*'s rail. "As such, I ask permission to come aboard."

"Permission granted, my lord. Deposit your firearms upon your own deck first, if you will."

"Alex, don't."

"Don't worry, little brother," he said over his shoulder. "I'll be back."

"Then I am coming too."

"I would not recommend it. You've never been able to hold your temper with Poole. It would be a shame to lose it now."

"Damn you, Alex." Aaron limped toward the gangplank. He made it across without incident, Alex gritting his molars with every unsteady step his brother took. They set foot atop the smuggler and Alex gestured broadly.

"She is a lovely vessel, Poole. Why did you allow Lucas to purchase her, or are you a silent partner?"

"I don't know what you are talking about, Savege."

The man's blue eyes burned with rage and, Alex thought, fear. "You are a thief and will be punished for it. I have told Halloway this is your ship, showed him the pamphlets." He brandished a sheet of paper. "He is prepared to arrest you for treason."

"My ship? Treason? Why, Lambert, can't you come up with something better than that? By the by, you seem to be sweating profusely. Not accustomed to the weather, I suppose. Perhaps we should erect an awning for your comfort." Alex shook his head in sympathy.

"Lord Savege, Lord Poole's evidence against you, in addition to our coming upon you escorting this ship, is rather convincing," Halloway said grimly. "I must ask you to transfer this vessel's crew to my ship and the *Titan* so that I may commandeer it, and remain here to be taken into custody along with your men and the *Cavalier.*"

Hurried boot steps sounded upon the planking behind Alex.

"You're making a mistake, Captain," Lucas said, halting between the naval commander and Alex. "I am Tracy Lucas. I've been communicating with Lord Poole for some time regarding this shipment of arms to Bristol. I have documents aboard my ship—" He gestured to the merchantman hovering in the far distance. "—that prove my claims. Lord Savege merely intended to sink this vessel, to inhibit it from reaching its destination and the revolt that my mother, Lady Carlyle, and Lord Poole planned to occur there while blaming it upon Poole's political enemies."

Poole's face went white.

Halloway frowned. "The charge of treason is weighty, sir. If what you say proves untrue, Lord Poole can have you hanged."

"It will prove true."

Halloway took a considering breath, his barrel chest expanding slowly. Wind stirred the *Osprey*'s battered sails, the rigging black with powder dust, and planking and rails pocked with holes.

The naval commander turned to Poole.

"My lord, what do you say to these charges?"

"All lies," he scoffed.

"Like the lies you told my sister?" Aaron said in a steely voice.

"Good Lord, Savege," Poole drawled, "are you still testy about that after all these years?"

"A bit." Aaron's jaw was tight, his grip on his cane tighter yet.

"She was then and still remains a whore," Poole said, ice glinting in his sky blue eyes. "A perfect compliment to her criminal and crippled brothers." He laughed.

"Any of those are a good sight better than a treasonous bastard," Alex commented mildly.

"My sister," Aaron said, "is a great deal cleverer than you imagine, my lord, and she does not forgive easily. For the past eight years she has been watching you very carefully and collecting evidence of your untoward activities in government and shipping."

Alex turned to his brother, astonishment and pride for both of his siblings curving his mouth into a smile.

"She will shortly produce that evidence for the proper authorities," Aaron continued. "So you see, you chose to disappoint the wrong young lady, my lord."

"Lord Poole," Halloway said calmly, folding the insurrectionist pamphlet and tucking it into his waistcoat, "I am hereby placing you under arrest for the crime of treason against the Crown. Lieutenant, please see his lordship to the boat." He turned to Lucas. "Sir, by your own admission you are also complicit in these wrongdoings. Lord Savege," he looked at Alex, "I have no choice but to charge you with the crimes against property you have perpetrated. My crew will board your ship and—"

"There you're mistaken as well, sir." Lucas stepped between them. "You see, Savege is not Redstone. I am."

Alex smiled, beginning to see why Serena cared so much for this mama's boy.

"Is this true, my lord?" Halloway asked Alex.

"It is," the baronet insisted.

"Thank you, Lucas," Alex said, "but you are already in sufficient trouble without adding my misdemeanors to it."

"They aren't yours—"

A crack of cannon fire filled one of the *Cavalier*'s gunwales with smoke, the hissing whistle of shot flew above their heads, and the *Osprey*'s mainsail erupted in flame.

Alex cursed. Whichever one of his crew had done this, he'd hang from the thumbnails. Jin roared orders, and Halloway's officers scurried about the *Command*'s deck as the *Cavalier*'s sheets slid, the schooner preparing to pull away. Fire leapt along the brig's deck, running along the rigging and through the square sails one after another in rapid succession. Alex pivoted toward his brother.

"Aaron, go!" he shouted, then to Halloway, "There are at least six hundred pounds of loose powder in this hold. Get into that boat and get your ship out of here."

Halloway ran for the rail, his lieutenant at his heels. The nearby *Titan* swung its nose about, the wind that drove it away whipping flame across the smuggler's deck, curling around the mainmast and forward. Beyond, the *Blackhawk* altered its course in pursuit.

Aristocratic face drawn with fury, Poole yanked a pistol from his coat and cocked it.

"I should have done this eight years ago." He pointed it at Aaron.

"Oh, damn," Alex muttered, and stepped in front of the bullet.

Burning fire compressed his chest, a giant shattering fist of white heat. He staggered back, legs failing. He'd only the flash of a moment to glimpse Poole collapsing on the deck and his brother's grim face wreathed in pistol smoke, and to hope for heaven, before he hit the planking and all went black.

Chapter 24

Then, when I had made an end of this, I set out for home, and the immortals gave me a fair wind, and brought me swiftly to my dear native land.

—HOMER, *ODYSSEY*

Serena paced the drawing room of Savege Park, twisting a handkerchief between her fingers, untwisting and retwisting it until she made burn marks on her skin. Every few seconds her gaze darted out the terrace doors, beyond the gardens and lawn, to the sea.

"Serena, you are doing your nerves a disservice. This agitation will not bring them back any sooner."

Serena met Kitty's concerned regard and released a tight breath. She sank into a chair, clasping her hands in her lap to still their fidgeting.

"I beg your pardon, Kitty. You must be as worried as I."

Kitty's gray eyes, so much like Alex's, lit with sympathy.

"I am. But recall I have been worrying about them like this for years. I have become somewhat accustomed to waiting."

"Have you known since they began, when— Well . . ." She paused.

"Since that cur Lambert Poole made a mockery of my innocence? No, not then. But it wasn't long before I put two and two together." She smiled, her eyes sparkling with mischief. "My brothers think they are infinitely clever, but I have a few secrets even they do not know." She arched her slender brows.

Serena smiled. Then her stomach clenched and she stood and went to the doors again. Pressing her palm against the glass, she lined up her fingertips with the distant blue horizon.

"What if they do not return?" she said quietly. "What if Charity's heart is broken? Every day she wonders why he has been gone so long without any message or letter, and I cannot even tell her where he is. Oh, why didn't he tell her? This is insupportable. What sort of man leaves the woman he loves to go hunting down smugglers without a by your leave?"

"That would be both of my brothers, I daresay," Kitty murmured, not lifting her gaze from her embroidery frame.

Serena's knotted stomach flipped. She turned back to the window.

Days earlier, when she could no longer bear waiting alone at Glenhaven Hall, she had paid an unannounced call at the Park. Kitty had smiled at her in the same way when she mentioned Alex, and Serena knew that his sister understood her feelings. But they had not spoken of it aloud. The dowager's private revelation to her that she and her daughter secretly knew of Alex's other identity had sealed their silent understanding.

She chewed on her lip and lifted her gaze to the ocean.

Her heart halted.

In the glow of the sun hanging low over the water, a ship rested on the horizon, so far out it looked almost like a bird. She swallowed rapidly several times, tried to breathe, and failed at both.

"Kitty," she whispered, pressing her nose to the glass. "Kitty?" She could not manage more.

"Serena? Are you unwell?"

She shook her head, her hands shaking. If it wasn't the *Cavalier*, everyone would be so enormously disappointed. She mustn't raise Kitty's hopes, the dowager's, the servants', all waiting so anxiously.

Her fingers fumbled on the latch.

"Oh, dear," Kitty said upon a quaver, relief scoring her tone. "They are home, aren't they? Mama! They are home!" She leapt up, but Serena hardly noticed as she moved toward the door, and then she was running across the terrace and the lawn, toward the cliff dropping down to the beach below. All the while her gaze was pinned to the advancing ship. For a full sennight she chastised herself for not telling Alex the truth when she had the opportunity, for being too afraid to lose him that she made it happen herself.

But perhaps not forever. Please, not forever.

Breathless, Serena faced the ocean, squinting into the sunset. The ship had neared, its bow turned toward land. The *Cavalier*'s distinctive banner flew from the tip of the foremast, the sparkling saber declaring haughty confidence and sinister threat. It was the most beautiful thing she had ever seen. Her heart climbed into her throat, loosing the sob wedged there. She nearly fell to her knees in relief.

The ship drew closer, heading for the beach below, but she could not wait. She took the path she'd climbed days ago that seemed like an eternity, this time sliding down it, scuffing her hands and shoes and tearing her gown in at least a half-dozen places. She would greet Alex looking like a street urchin, but she didn't care.

Her need to see his face, to touch him and hear his voice, overwhelmed all else.

Her feet hit the pebbly sand running. The ship hovered beyond the shoal at anchor, and a boat had already taken to the water. Another boat followed.

Her legs and entire body flooded with cold. He was not in either boat. Mr. Seton, Mr. Savege, Billy, Mattie, others. But no Alex.

Numb with fear, she ran into the surf and to the first boat as Billy and another sailor leapt from it and dragged it onto the sand. Mr. Seton and Big Mattie bent, took up a blood-covered body from the boards, and Serena's heart shattered.

"Don't worry, miss," Billy called to her cheerily. "Cap'n's been shot, but he ain't kicked the bucket yet."

She choked on the swell of relief washing through her and gripped the side of the boat with shaking hands. Mr. Seton and Mattie lifted Alex, carried him to dry sand, and laid him down gingerly.

"We must get him to the house," Mr. Seton said. "Billy, run for Pomley and tell him we need the doctor."

Serena fell to her knees. Blood soaked every surface, on Alex's sleeve and brow and horrifyingly deep and dark on his shirtfront. She ran a palm along his cheek, pale beneath his tanned skin, and he opened his eyes.

"'Afternoon, my dear," he said, slurring his words, as though he were foxed. "Or— Is it still afternoon?"

"Yes. Yes." A hard sob rose in her throat. "Oh, Alex, what have you done?"

"Defeated the villain. As you requested." A twitch of his cheek seemed to indicate he wished to grin. Instead he winced and his eyes closed.

"The villain, my stepbrother, or the navy? Did Tracy come?" She looked up at Alex's lieutenant. "Did Sir Tracy arrive on time?"

"Nearly. He tried to take the blame for it all. He even claimed to be Redstone."

Her mouth dropped into an O. "He did?"

Mr. Seton nodded. "Alex wouldn't let him, of course. But the navy forgave our foolhardy friend here after he took a bullet meant for his brother. Now we really must get him to the house, ma'am. He has lost quite a bit of blood. We cauterized the wound, but he must see a doctor soon."

They lifted him again. Alex grunted, his brow tightening, but he did not open his eyes. Serena gripped his left hand, the only part of him not stained red.

"Alex, I must tell you something." Her voice trembled, her feet sinking into the sand as she ran alongside. "It is quite important. Are you awake?"

His eyes opened a crack, brow creasing deeper with each jarring step across the beach. "Mm. I typ—typically would not sleep with you present, but today it seems—"

"I love you." She didn't care that the men heard, or the whole world. She squeezed his fingers. "You must not die, Alexander Savage. I love you. Really very much. Very, very much."

Slowly, his lids lifted. His eyes shone rich and dark.

"I thought so." Then his mouth did turn up at one edge.

He slipped into unconsciousness.

The dowager invited Serena to spend the night at the Park. Mrs. Tubbs showed her to a lovely chamber appointed in gold and pale blue silk, with an exquisitely comfortable mattress on a four-poster bed with rich white satin draperies. It was a bedchamber fit for a princess in a fairy tale. Serena was supplied with dinner, tea, ratafia, and warm milk with honey—none of which she ate or drank. She lay atop the bed stiff as a board, unwilling to undress, afraid something might happen to Alex in the middle of the night. She had to be prepared.

At dawn his sister brought tea.

"He has not yet awoken," Kitty said soberly. "The physician came several hours ago. He inspected the wound and pronounced that he could do nothing. We must simply wait."

Serena withheld her tears until Kitty left, then cried into the lacy white linen-covered pillow until her lungs ached.

She went to breakfast but could eat nothing.

"I will bring some of my gowns to your bedchamber," Kitty offered, spots of gray beneath her eyes.

"We will send to Glenhaven Hall for Serena's belongings," the dowager said, setting down her coffee cup with a soft clatter, her hand quivering, "and for her stepsister."

Within the hour Charity arrived, embraced Serena for a full five minutes, and only then released her. Serena did not know what the dowager's message to Charity had been, but it mattered little.

Aaron appeared in the doorway, his smile wavering between sorrow and bliss. Charity went to him, and they removed to another chamber.

Serena waited. Charity eventually departed, tea came and went, and then dinner, conversation revolving around the events at sea. Aaron told them about her stepbrother's intervention and the Earl of Poole taken away in the naval frigate, his leg shattered. Serena ate little, said little, and slept not at all for the second night in a row.

Early the following morning a knock came at the

door. She turned from the window's view of the dawn-lit sea and dashed across the chamber.

Lady Savege stood in the corridor, her cheeks pale, eyes haggard. Serena's insides hollowed out to nothing.

"He is awake," the dowager said softly, moisture glimmering on the cusp of her eye.

Serena sagged, tears rising fast in her throat. She enclosed the dowager's shaking fingers in her own.

"Would you like to see him?"

"May I?"

"I don't believe he would have it any other way."

Serena walked through the corridors in a haze. A maid opened a door, and Lady Savege ushered her in, remaining on the threshold.

He seemed pale beneath the new tan of his skin, and weary, but his gaze followed her across the floor of the bedchamber as she approached. She halted at the side of his bed, sought his hand on the counterpane and laced her fingers into it. He returned the pressure, and her entire being flooded with utter peace.

"Although I would like to, I will not ask you to join me in here," he murmured, his gaze scanning her face.

"In where?" Her brows lifted, then slowly her eyes widened. She darted a glance at the large bed. "There?" she whispered.

His perfect mouth curved into a grin, tired but still teasing.

"If you accepted, you see, I fear I would not be able to stand by my promise to you at the present."

"Your promise?"

His drew her fingers to his lips and kissed them one at a time, then her palm in four places. He lifted his expressive gaze.

Serena's toes curled, heady relief warming her blood.

"Alex Savege, you are a thorough rogue."

"So they say." He smiled, his eyes closing. His grasp relaxed, and she drew her hand from his and left her pirate rogue to sleep.

By the time she returned home an hour later, Davina was gone. Without word or warning to her husband, she had departed in the middle of the night with a horse and every last one of Serena's, Charity's, and Diantha's jewels.

Serena met her father in his library. Face drawn, shoulders slumped, he took her hands and drew her into his embrace. She let him hold her until he released her.

"I beg your pardon, daughter. I have made a shambles of my life and yours."

"I suppose you have in some ways. But, Papa, why did you marry her? I never understood."

His brow wrinkled. "You were seventeen, becoming a woman. You needed a mother to see you properly introduced into society. And wed." He shook his head sorrowfully.

"Is that all?"

"She assured me of the necessity of it, and I believed her. She only wanted my lands, the proximity to the sea, I am afraid."

She squeezed his hands.

"Well, now we must turn that around and make a success of my sisters' lives. I daresay Charity will be able to bring out Diantha in a few years, and Lady Katherine and the dowager are lovely. They will help as well. Until then, you and I must be what they need in the lack of their mother. And brother." She squeezed harder.

News arrived the following day from London, via

Savage Park and the earl's solicitor. Sir Tracy Lucas, arrested for treason, had been brought before Lords and arraigned. Immediately Tracy turned over to Parliament documents, culled from several sources, proving the guilt of Lord Lambert Poole and connecting Poole's dealings to several commissioners on the Board of the Admiralty in a most embarrassing manner. With the additional testimony of Captain Halloway, commander of the HMS *Command*, which commended Sir Tracy for his noble behavior in the face of danger, the king pardoned the condemned and ordered him to repair to his estate for a probationary period of one year. The Earl of Poole, maimed and unable to leave his chair, appeared before the Old Bailey and had his sentence read: seizure of estates and assets, and exile.

Except for Mr. Savege's daily visits to Glenhaven Hall, made with her father and Diantha present, Serena did not hear word from the Park. Alex was recovering swiftly, his brother reported to the room at large. She ached to saddle her horse and ride the miles to him. But he knew her heart already. If he wanted her, he would let her know. Clearly, he did not want her as she had hoped.

Six unendurably long days after the *Cavalier* returned, she had news of the ship again.

"This one is lovely, Miss Charity," Mrs. Hatchet cooed, laying out another white ribbon on the shop counter for inspection. "Brides in the plate books are all wearing white ribbons this year. Though those lemon ones you've picked out are very fine as well." She smiled cheerfully. "That young Master Billy likes the yellows too. Says his mother favors canary. What a sweet lad. We'll be sorry to see him go now, and that fine Mr. Jinan as well."

Serena's head came up.

"Go? Is the *Cavalier* departing?"

Mrs. Hatchet's merry eyes shadowed.

"Dear me, Miss Carlyle, I thought you—I mean to say— Well, I must have mistaken it if you know otherwise, of course." The milliner gathered up the discarded ribbons and bustled to another area of the shop, her round cheeks like apples.

Charity's hand curved around Serena's elbow.

"Lady Savege is coming to tea today to discuss wedding plans," she said with a sweet smile. She had only cried briefly when she heard of her mother's unexplained defection. Since then she had not once mentioned Davina.

Serena made it through tea with hard-won calm, and the following three days of making arrangements for the wedding, during which Kitty came to Glenhaven Hall twice and said nothing about her eldest brother except that he was well. Serena's nerves frayed, her heart a welter of fresh confusion and growing despair.

The *Cavalier* was leaving again apparently, heading out on its summer cruise now that its master was exonerated by the Admiralty for bringing two treasonous lords to heel, and all was well and good. Serena ached inside, and for the first time in weeks she felt like a fool, not because she had told him of her love, but because she believed that would have made a difference to him.

The day of the wedding dawned bright and clear, midsummer flowers in full bloom across the gardens of Savege Park, spilling in pinks, yellows, purples, and whites from crystal vases and brass pots in the estate's chapel and the bouquet in Serena's hand. They filled the Park with sweet, heady scents. She moved along the aisle, rearranging blossoms, straightening the swaths of white and gold silk draping the pews, and trying to still the nervous trembling of her fingers.

She would see him today, and knowing he was leaving again, she would still love him. She suspected she would love him forever.

She made a final perusal of the simple adornments in the chancel, and turned to make her way back to Charity's readying chamber.

Just as on that day in the church in Glen Village, Alex stood in the chapel's narthex, leaning one shoulder against a stone pillar, watching her. He was dressed in impeccably white linen, black coat, and buff pantaloons, dark hair curling about his collar, gray eyes alight. And, just as on that day weeks ago, he looked like a fantasy.

Serena willed her knees not to fail as she moved toward him.

"Good day, ma'am." He bowed formally, but not deeply.

"Good day, my lord." She curtsied. She wanted to ask him about his injury, his journey, the pistol shot meant for his brother that he had taken instead, Lord Poole brought down by Aaron's hand, Tracy's courage, the *Cavalier*'s imminent departure. Everything. She looked into his soulful eyes and her tongue acted of its own accord.

"What did you say to your brother that day your mother invited us to luncheon, to encourage him to make a clean breast of it to Charity?"

The corner of his perfect mouth crept up.

"I told him that he should stop thinking with his— ah, extremities, and act according to his heart instead."

Serena released a slow breath.

"Astonishing advice coming from a rake."

"Reformed." His eyes glowed. Her heart did the

uncomfortable flip-flop she had become so accustomed to since meeting the Earl of Savege.

"Not still merely considering it?"

The vicar entered the chapel with a cluster of guests. Serena hid her warm cheeks behind her bouquet and went in search of her stepsister.

The wedding was beautiful, simple and tender. Charity spoke her vows in the strongest voice Serena had ever heard from her. Aaron's face radiated happiness. Serena's heart filled and overflowed, melting away the final remnants of old sorrows.

Across the aisle where he stood at Aaron's shoulder, Alex met her gaze and held it, his eyes sober. Then he smiled.

Chapter 25

Nor would anything have parted us, loving and joying in one another.

—HOMER, *ODYSSEY*

After making the appropriate toasts, Alex removed himself from the wedding celebration to his study, passing along the corridor by the rear entrance to the pantry. He could never walk in this part of the house now without imagining Serena partially unclothed in it. But as he planned upon that becoming the case with every alcove—and chamber, and stairway, and hidden closet—at Savege Park, it did not disturb him greatly.

Not *disturb*. But *arouse* was a different story, one he'd spent nine days of agonizing frustration waiting to make happen. Her words on the beach haunted him, as though he'd dreamt her speaking her love, like the steadiness of her grasp when she came to his bedchamber as he first awoke, the determined set of her jaw.

He could not wait any longer. Damn the gaping hole in his side, and damn doctors and mothers and brothers with too much time on their hands and too little faith in the human body to heal itself swiftly. He didn't care if his side burst open as he made love to Serena. At least he would die happily.

But he would rather live happily. With her.

Jin sat in a chair by a window, a slim volume of Virgil propped on his knee.

He stood. "How was the ceremony?"

"Didn't you attend?"

"Not my place."

"Not your place. Of course." Alex moved to his desk and slid open a drawer. "When will it be your place, my friend? When you are richer than a West Indian planter and own more ships than the entire Royal Navy?" He extended a folded sheaf of papers.

Jin's mouth curved upward. "Perhaps then, but I doubt it." He accepted the papers.

"They are all there, deed of purchase, license, draft of commission. Everything you need."

"I could have done this myself, Alex."

"You could have. But I wanted to, and it went quicker this way. A title is useful for some things. Now you can be upon your merry way and leave me in peace."

"Peace?" Jin lifted a skeptical brow. "She doesn't seem like the peaceful sort to me."

"She is a woman of many facets." Alex grinned.

"Of course." Jin regarded the papers in his grasp for a thoughtful moment then lifted his gaze. "I have been thinking about that story you told me, the one concerning Miss Carlyle's sister all those years ago."

"You have, hm?"

Jin nodded. "I have."

"What about it?"

"Well, I don't know, but . . ." He paused, his brow furrowing. "What did you say the girl's name was?"

"Viola."

"Viola. Not a common name." Alex's former quartermaster, now full owner of the swiftest, prettiest little schooner in the seven seas, narrowed his eyes, awareness and sharp intelligence winking in them. "Viola. Yes. I thought so."

"Jin?"

"Alex, thank you." He proffered his hand.

Alex grasped it tight. He took a deep breath. "Take good care of her, my friend."

"The very best." Jin slid his palm from Alex's and went to the door. He turned. "Congratulations. You deserve it." The panel clicked softly closed behind him.

Alex leaned back against the edge of his desk and drew in slow, measured breaths. His side ached and the skin around the wound itched terribly. But other than that physical discomfort of healing, nothing bothered him.

Nothing.

Jin was dead wrong. Serena had brought him the peace he'd looked for his entire life. He had never been truly brave until loving her forced him into it. Now, in the place where anger, guilt and regret had reigned for years, only life stirred, like the ocean each time a man took to it anew, wide and deep and full of astounding potential.

He ought to return to the wedding festivities. The guests from the neighboring counties would have arrived by now, the house filled with well-wishers. He should greet them, play the host, be the lord-of-the-manor that Serena had taunted him about, which was all he wanted to be now, in addition to her lover.

But instead he sat. The sun dipped over the ocean, casting the cerulean sky striated with strips of filmy, dove-colored clouds into shades of lavender, rose, and glowing ochre. A ship appeared from the north, moving languidly along the coast.

A knock sounded on the door.

"My lord." His housekeeper curtsied. "Your lady

mother requests that you join your guests upon the terrace."

He nodded. "Thank you, Mrs. Tubbs." His regard remained steady. "Thank you," he repeated.

She smiled, a look of satisfaction so purely unrepentant that he nearly laughed aloud.

"Yes, sir." She curtsied again and withdrew.

He stood then and made his way through the drawing room to the terrace, greeting guests as he went. Serena stood with Kitty near the newlyweds at the edge of the paving, her attention, like everyone's, focused on the *Cavalier* in the distance.

A crack of gunfire sounded and a puff of smoke appeared at the schooner's gunwale, then another, and more. Fountains of water spewed upward fifty yards toward the beach. Rocket flares catapulted into the sky, brightening the sunset with bursts of silver, red, and gold, then descending like graceful birds into the sea.

Aaron stood with his hand in his young bride's. He released her, and Alex moved down the terrace steps onto the lawn, his brother following. They walked in silence, halting just short of the cliff's edge.

"Jin has taken a privateer's commission," Alex said conversationally.

"The *Cavalier* working for the Crown?" Aaron shook his head, smiling. "Who would have imagined it?" He looked at Alex. "He is flying your colors."

"Our colors, little brother. A tribute, I suspect. He won't for long."

"Good."

"Good, indeed." Alex met his twin's gaze. He extended his hand. Aaron clasped it.

The final skyrocket petered into the drink with a fizzle, a drum sounded on the schooner's deck, and the square topsails unfurled on the mizzenmast. With elegant ease the *Cavalier* turned her bow west.

"Show is over," Aaron murmured.

"And you have your pretty wife to return to."

Aaron smiled, shrugged, and moved away to the house, easier upon his cane with each step. Alex looked back at the schooner, her canvas silhouetted by the sun's glow, a school of dolphin leaping in her shimmering wake. The most beautiful ship upon the ocean. No longer his. He took a deep breath and smiled wide.

A light footstep sounded behind him. He turned. Serena walked toward him gowned in blue the color of the sea within shallow shoals awaiting the tide, the wind whisking her honey hair about her face. Her lips parted, her gaze sought him, and heaven opened its bejeweled gates for him upon solid earth.

The voices of the guests moving back into the house faded as Serena reached Alex. His shoulders seemed so square and broad, his stance relaxed. The ship had nearly disappeared.

"That was a lovely display," she said. "Your guests enjoyed it."

"Mustn't disappoint the neighbors." He smiled and returned his gaze to the sea.

Her stomach clenched.

"That day in the gallery," she said, "you were trying to tell me that I could not have it both ways, weren't you? That I could not demand that you go off to fight Tracy and still expect—" She could not finish. Her heart was too full.

"You can have it any way you wish, Serena," he said quietly. "That is the beauty of life, I have recently discovered."

"Perhaps for you. What you said in the chapel today, teasing me, it—" She drew in a deep breath. "I cannot share you with other women, Alex."

He turned from the vast blue canvas to her.

"You needn't."

"I don't wish to share you with the sea either. I cannot be like Penelope, always waiting for Odysseus to come home. Or, at least I think that's what their names were. Anyway, after these past horrid weeks I have decided that my heart is not strong enough for that."

"Your heart, my dear, is strong enough for anything, I imagine."

She screwed up her courage. "So, I will go with you."

He did not immediately respond, a guarded look shadowing his eyes.

"Go with me where?" he finally asked.

"When you do your pirating. Upon the *Cavalier*."

"No, you will not."

She swallowed over the lump in her throat. "Why not?"

He stepped close and placed his fingertips beneath her chin.

"Serena, you needn't be Penelope because I am not Odysseus, unless at the very end of the story."

"The end?"

"I have sold the ship to Jinan."

"Are you purchasing a new ship, then?"

He dipped his head and regarded her with patient tenderness. "Yes, but something a bit smaller, I daresay. Suitable for two persons only."

Serena's heart squeezed, expanded, then spread its wings. "I meant what I said on the beach. Do you remember it?"

"How could I forget?"

Her throat was tight. "I only wish—I—"

The corner of his mouth tilted upward.

"Don't laugh at me," she whispered.

"I am not laughing at you. I am happy."

Her breath caught. "Happy?"

"Quite scandalously so." He took her hands. "What do you wish, my beauty?"

"Well, I have asked a great deal of you lately, which of course you have accomplished. Now I wish you would ask me for something."

"What something would that be?"

"I wish you would ask for my love." She had given it for so long to so many who had never requested it. Now she needed to hear it from him—from this man who already owned her heart.

His grasp on her fingers tightened. "I want your love, Serena." His voice sounded so deep. "I need your love."

"More than adventure and revenge?"

"I am finished with revenge, and I can imagine no greater adventure than spending every day and night of my life with you." His eyes were bright and full of promise.

She threw her arms around him and buried her face in his coat. His arms came around her, tight and wonderful, like he feared to let go of her and never would.

"Serena Carlyle," he murmured at her brow, "I adore you. Be my countess."

She nodded, tears of relief and joy surging behind her eyes. "Yes," she gulped, and gripped him tighter. "Yes, yes."

He pressed kisses into her hair and the wind swirled about them, dashing whitecaps on the surf below.

"Sing me a song," she said, muffled in shirt linen.

"Which song?" He stroked tresses back from her brow.

"Any song. I want to hear you sing. I want to feel it inside me again, like on that night."

"When I fell in love with you."

She lifted her head and met his soulful gaze. "You did? That night upon your ship?"

"How could you have doubted it?"

She shivered in awe, blissful pleasure streaming through her. She had doubted. Her heart had known, but the bulwark of loss and pain within had not allowed her to accept it. Now nothing could make her doubt again. He bent his head and kissed her, their mouths and devotion and souls meeting in a blaze of pure, perfect faith.

"Alex?" she breathed against his cheek when he finally released her lips.

"Mm, love?" He nuzzled her jaw then her throat, then the tender place beneath her ear.

"Why did you make me wait so many days to hear this?" Her palms flattened on his chest as though she would push him away, but she could not. Never again. "I have been going out of my mind not understanding your silence, imagining you planned to leave again."

"I knew that the moment I had you in my arms once more I would become . . ." His hands traveled over her deliciously. " . . . shall we say impatient?"

"Impatient?" She smiled and slid her palms along his shoulders, her fingers lacing through his hair as she pressed to his hard length. His impatience felt deliciously wicked and wonderful against her belly, stirring her in that heady, elemental way only he could satisfy. "What is wrong with that?"

"I imagined you would prefer me alive for the unforeseeable future."

Her brow creased.

"The wound required time to heal, my dear," he said with a slight smile.

"Oh . . . *Oh*." She pulled away, but he grabbed her

and drew her back into his tight embrace. Her fingers flitted to her mouth. "I cannot believe I didn't think of that. Although you might have at least sent a note."

He slid his hand around hers, turned her palm upward and placed his lips upon it.

"Do you think that would have sufficed?" He caressed her tender skin with the pad of his thumb. " 'Dearest Miss Carlyle, do not dare come near me, because if you do I may ravish you and subsequently perish.' Hm. Not a sufficient deterrent for my hungry lady love, I think."

Serena closed her eyes, shimmering all over with pleasure.

"I am serious," she said. "I have been thinking a wretched lot about myself lately."

"I daresay you are perfectly correct. Now you should allow me to think of you instead. And kiss you. And caress you. And undress you. And touch you . . . just here." He did so, just *there*.

"My lord," she gasped, leaning into his caress, "we are in plain view of everyone at the house."

"And you are in plain view of me, which invariably requires me to make love to you without delay. Although, of course, the dark suits the purpose just as well. As the sun has set, in fact, I don't see why we cannot commence now."

"But—"

"Try to stop me, Miss Carlyle."

"Not in a thousand years, Lord Savege." She sighed and sank into his embrace, the wind dancing about them in abandoned delight. Serena lifted her lips to his and whispered, "Lock the door."

Author's Note

I drew the chapter epigraphs in this story from two sources, sea chanteys—sailor songs—of the eighteenth and early nineteenth centuries, and the ancient Greek poem by Homer, *Odyssey*. In the poem, a great hero of the Trojan War endures years of hardships visited upon him by men and gods as he attempts to sail home to his faithful wife. Happily, he makes it back to her in the end, which is more than I can say for the sorry sailor lads featured in most sea chanteys. But so many of the chanteys are about women and love, I could not resist.

I offer heartfelt thanks to Stephanie W. McCullough for generously lending me her expertise in matters nautical. And to Esi Sogah and my editor, Lucia Macro, with whom I have the greatest pleasure of working, I give sincere gratitude.

Next month, don't miss these exciting new love stories only from Avon Books

Midnight's Wild Passion by Anna Campbell

Blinded by vengeance for the man who destroyed his sister, the Marquess of Ranelaw plans to repay his foe in kind by seducing the man's daughter. But when her companion, Miss Antonia Smith, steps in to thwart his plans, Antonia finds herself fighting off his relentless charm. And she's always had a weakness for rakes...

Ascension by Sable Grace

When Kyana, half Vampyre, half Lychen, is entrusted by the Order of Ancients to find a key that will seal Hell forever and save the mortals she despises, she has no choice but to accept. But when she's assigned an escort, Ryker, a demigod who stirred her heart long ago, she knows that giving into temptation could mean the undoing of them both.

A Tale of Two Lovers by Maya Rodale

Lord Simon Roxbury has a choice: wed or be penniless. Surely finding a suitable miss should be simple enough? But then gossip columnist Lady Julianna threatens his reputation and a public battle ensues, leaving both in tatters. To rescue her good name and his fortune, they unite in a marriage of convenience. Will it be too late to stop tongues wagging or will it be a love match after all?

When Tempting a Rogue by Kathryn Smith

Gentleman club proprietress Vienne La Rieux has her eye on a prize that would make her England's richest woman when a former lover, the charming Lord Kane, disrupts her plans. Neither is prepared for the passion still between them, but with an enemy lurking in the shadows, any attempt to mix business with pleasure could have tragic consequences.

At Avon Books, we know your passion for romance—once you finish one of our novels, you find yourself wanting more.

May we tempt you with . . .

- **Excerpts** from our upcoming releases.

- Entertaining **extras**, including authors' personal photo albums and book lists.

- Behind-the-scenes **scoop** on your favorite characters and series.

- **Sweepstakes** for the chance to win free books, romantic getaways, and other fun prizes.

- Writing **tips** from our authors and editors.

- **Blog** with our authors and find out why they love to write romance.

- **Exclusive content** that's not contained within the pages of our novels.

Join us at
www.avonbooks.com

AVON

An Imprint of HarperCollins*Publishers*
www.avonromance.com